GARTH MARENGHI'S

Incarcerat

About the Author

Garth Marenghi was born in the past, graduated from his local comprehensive (now bulldozed) with some O levels in subjects. He taught for nine years at his local library reading group before becoming a full-time horror writer. He has published numerous novels of terror (too numerous to list, nay count), over five hundred short stories, and has edited thirty anthologies of his own work, which have all received the Grand Master of Darkdom Award. He wrote, directed and starred in *Garth Marenghi's Darkplace* for the Peruvian market, which subsequently aired on Channel 4 and has not been repeated due to its radical and polemic content. He commenced work on *TerrorTome* during the late 1980s, continued on it alone and unaided by editors throughout the 1990s, and on into the early 2000s, then the mid-2000s, and has only now found a publisher brave enough to unleash its chilling portendings. He now continues this vision with *Incarcerat*. He is an honorary fellow.

Also by Garth Marenghi:

Garth Marenghi's TerrorTome

GARTH MARENGHI'S

Incarcerat

CORONET

First published in Great Britain in 2023 by Coronet
An imprint of Hodder & Stoughton
An Hachette UK company

1

A CIP catalogue record for this title is available from the British Library

Hardback ISBN 9781399721882
ebook ISBN 9781399721899

Typeset in Bembo by Hewer Text UK Ltd, Edinburgh
Printed and bound in Great Britain by Clays Ltd, Elcograf S.p.A.

Hodder & Stoughton policy is to use papers that are natural, renewable and recyclable
products and made from wood grown in sustainable forests. The logging and manufacturing
processes are expected to conform to the environmental regulations of the country of origin.

Hodder & Stoughton Ltd
Carmelite House
50 Victoria Embankment
London EC4Y 0DZ

www.hodder.co.uk

CONTENTS

Introduction
ix

Portentum
1

Arabella Mathers
135

The Randyman
253

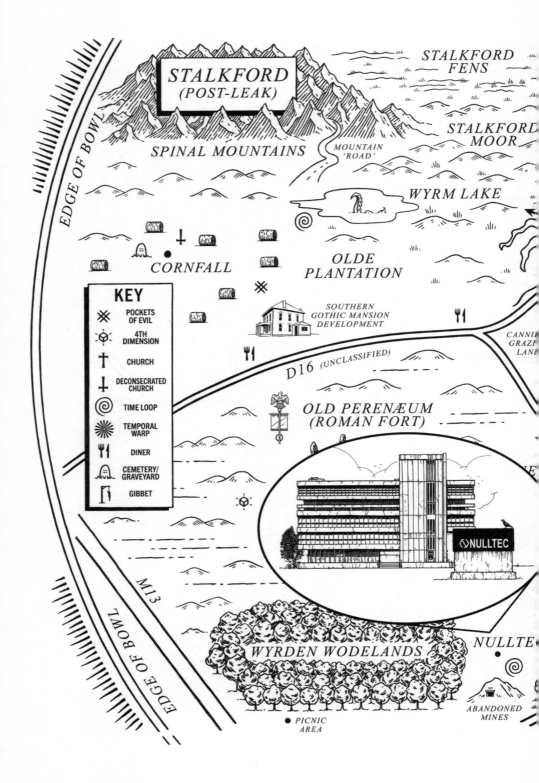

BLOATER'S COVE

NAZI WRECKS

THE BREEZE

LEAKS OF EVIL

OBSERVATORY

AIRPORT

STALKFORD
SOURCE OF BRAINLEAK

VICTORIAN
MIME THEATRE

EN

LEAKS OF EVIL

CLAYSTON

CARAVAN PARK

LAUGHTERTON

THE FLUDDE

ANCIENT YOKEL
BURIAL GROUND

SODDEN

DANKTON

GIBBETON

(IED)

VAMPTON
GRANGE

D60 (UNCLASSIFIED)

E45 (UNCLASSIFIED)

CHOKEWOOD

CASTLE
VROLOKS

INCARCERAT

/In'ka:serate/

noun

a being of superior power and intelligence shackled by physical, temporal and/or spatial fetters.

Origin

Medieval Latin 'in' (into); 'carcer' (prison) > 'incarcerare' > 'incarcerat' (imprisoned) > mid-sixteenth century 'incarcerate' > Steen, Nick O. 1999, Hell Off Earth 'Incarcerat' (n). Omega In Extremis.

INTRODUCTION

My own incarceration began at around 9.25 a.m. on 22 September 1999 in the lobby of a three-star hotel in Swansea (now two-star). I wasn't physically imprisoned there (though the place has certainly earned itself a reputation over the years). Nor was I locked up, bound hand to foot, gagged, pissed on or forced to slop out my own faecal matter by anyone at that establishment. Those events came later, and were, as you will shortly learn, largely self-administered.

But my self-imposed incarceration – an incarceration of the *mind* – began on that particular morning, at the precise moment I was forced to report the unclean and potentially hazardous state of my family's room to what, for want of a better term, I shall refer to as the hotel's 'concierge'. Though 'tosspot' is my preferred appellation.

The occasion was Conspiracon '99, a one-off joint horror-SF event organised in anticipation of the much-vaunted but ultimately disappointing damp squib of a global apocalypse scheduled for the following year.*

---

* Incidentally, I can now reveal publicly for the first time that the previous year's Spillenium '98 was called off abruptly not as a result of government surveillance, as was widely reported, but because of a devastating outbreak of winter-vomiting disease which spread like wildfire through our assembled guests and part-drowned David Icke. GM

Naively, I'd elected to take along my wife Pam and our eldest daughter, then in her early teens, to show her (my daughter – not Pam, who knows what I do and reads all my work whether she wants to or not) a little of the public side of my profession. More crucially, my intention was to get her to film me accepting my award for 'Best Evisceral Puncturing', so that I could subsequently hawk it on VHS from my then ground-breaking website page.[*]

Unfortunately, things had not gone well since our arrival the day before, and my daughter,[†] when she could wrestle her attention away from the local shopping mall, had insisted I complain about the state of our facilities, having discovered 'eggs' in the lining of our hotel bedding. This was no surprise to me – there were always clutches of minute, unidentified sacs in the sheets of this particular hotel, and I flat out refused to rock the boat, given we'd been granted one of their cheapest rooms at a slightly reduced rate and had already booked a weekend's worth of exclusively curry-based catering. Not only that, but I was the official 'host' for the convention, and in this capacity had graciously agreed to part-subsidise my daughter's mandatory attendance fee.

I felt the least she could do was endure a few bouts of frenzied clawing in the shank area in exchange for a token reduction. Yet there followed, as I might well have predicted if I hadn't been focused on demolishing my king-size portion of mutton dal in a distant conference room somewhere below, a long, dark night of female scritchrionics. Before I knew what was happening, Pam was waking me roughly from sleep, resolutely forbidding me to commence my much-anticipated cooked breakfast in the freshly sluiced conference room, until I'd raised the matter of the affected sheets, two of which no longer sported 'eggs' at all, I noted. Presumably owing to an occurrence of nocturnal hatching.

[*] Hacked later that year. GM
[†] Whose name, on her bloody insistence, has been removed. GM

INTRODUCTION

It was while I was remonstrating audibly with the 'concierge', much to the amusement of my fellow guest speakers currently enjoying their tepid morning kormas, that I noticed my daughter had wandered off to a table by the freshly ransacked snack dispensary and was calmly, yet quite brazenly, reading a copy of Carl Sagan's *The Demon-Haunted World*.

Now I have great respect for the late Carl Sagan, if little or none for his theories. I admire his exercise regime and commitment to meeting the World Health Organization's recommended intake of 25g of roughage per day. I also like his anoraks. But as for Carl's stance on the likely future course of human evolution? Someone hold my goblet.

Look, I've read Carl Sagan.* I've watched bits of that tedious programme he did, best scrolled in small chunks on a streaming platform of your choice if it ever deigns to flash up. Hell, I even agree with his views on the human R-Complex (and have employed them extensively in this book). But as for science leading the way forward in human evolution, as opposed to superstition? Someone hold my other goblet.

Bottom line, friend. Superstition is our way out of this mess. How can mankind ever truly progress until it learns to live with the horror of reality, no matter how dark and twisted that might be? For this, in a nutshell, is what we face as a species. And let me say now that I'm no conspiracy nut. People *aren't* lizards. They're *salamanders*. Our Earth isn't round, or flat. It's *oblong*. Clouds aren't UFOS. Or UAPS. They're UPOOS.† And a chilling yarn by yours truly ain't no frivolous serving of exploitative trash. My work reflects nothing less than *reality itself.*‡ Truth is, pilgrim, my oeuvre doth more for mankind than any amount of demonstrating the fourth dimension via some primary-school classroom apparatus and an apple.

---

* If you don't know who he is, I would have suggested looking him up, but, believe me, it isn't worth it. GM
† Unknown Pieces of Outer Space. GM
‡ Technically *unreality*. See the rest of this book. GM

Or at least that's what I thought.

For at this point I found myself engaged in a public debate with my *own daughter* about bloody Carl Sagan in that hotel lobby, with a gathering of jeering professional colleagues surrounding us, shoving her forward so we might physically scrap. I will admit that I finally lost my temper and cancelled her reservation entirely, turfing her out on to the streets of Swansea with the instruction to 'go slum it, sister'.

Then Pam told me – likewise, in front of *everyone* – that she wouldn't sanction such behaviour from a man still daubed with specks of ghee, and I left the convention forthwith and went to live in rented accommodation.

And in that terrible, harsh period of loneliness and isolation, I freely admit that I let myself go. Scorned personal hygiene. Slopped out instead of flushed. Sheared my whole body in protest. Ate oatmeal.

Then, not having spoken to my nearest and dearest for two long days, I finally picked up the copy of Carl Sagan's *The Demon-Haunted World* my daughter had hurled violently at the back of my head, and read the damned thing from top to tail.

Did I agree with Carl this time?

Read *Incarcerat*, friend, and you'll find out.*

Garth Marenghi,
Grand High Revealerer,
Arch-Deniering of the Un-Truth,
Lord Apportioner o' the Blaming.
Octemter 2023

---

* No, I did not, and to be honest, Carl Sagan has hardly anything to do with the concept of this book at all. I've just used him as a convenient means to hammer out a thousand-plus words of required author intro. You'd actually do best to ignore him entirely and just enjoy the tales within. Because if there's a profound point to any of this, then it's *my* point. Not his. GM

PORTENTUM

(or, THE GOD SOCKET)

CHAPTER ONE

'Sole Survivor'

A black plume of smoke rose high over Stalkford Airport as another fuel tank exploded. Air Traffic Controller Sly Pickens, a peripheral character whom we won't meet again in this story, flicked a big switch on the console in front of him, signalling ground control to wave in a fresh fleet of ambulances.

Flight SA13 had landed.

The front of the plane alone was intact, its rear fuselage having disintegrated entirely upon impact. The blackened nose of the stricken airbus lay at an angle on the gouged and scorch-marked runway, its inflatable stairway buffeted in all directions by powerful gusts from the evening's unexpected and ultimately deadly August storm.

Though torrents of rain lashed hard against the strewn and scattered wreckage, they did little to dispel the rising smoke and flames. Detached seats and strewn luggage lay in shattered pieces as far as the eye could see, glowing fiercely in the night like hot coals. What pieces remained of the jumbo's splintered interior lay crisp and blackened on the concrete like burned, smoking chips in a giant oven tray. And if catapulted luggage were the stricken plane's metaphorical vegetable, then what remained of the passengers themselves was its undigested crackling; a purplish brown cluster of bubbling, charred body-meat, whose scent was borne upon the whipping breeze like the unholiest of gravies.

Medics and firemen moved steadily through the wreckage, lighting much-needed fags from the frazzled husks to steady their nerves, before dousing what remained of the dead in industrial-strength extinguisher foam. As they progressed gradually towards the twisted struts of the jumbo's melting galley, nobody glimpsed the small flurry of movement occurring inside the plane's teetering cockpit. No one spied the human figure forcing its way through a smashed window in the main cabin, before clambering sideways over the nose towards the jumbo's crumpled left wing. The man, for the figure wore trousers, was clothed in uniform, and although his shirt was covered with flecks of blood and spattered jet fuel, there was no mistaking the captain's stripes on both shoulder lapels.

For this was the pilot of the downed airbus.

The *sole survivor* . . .

As the figure dropped to the floor of the runway from the bent wing and collected his suitcase from a mangled food-trolley melting rapidly against one of the Boeing's vast, dislocated landing wheels, a nearby fireman looked up from a smoking skull and nodded at him.

'Evening, Nick.'

'Evening, Steve,' replied the pilot, still hardly believing that this was his profession now, having worked primarily as a best-selling horror novelist for the last thirty years. With a palpable air of nonchalance, he transferred the single-breasted, Oxford Blue pilot's blazer from his right arm and tugged it on, elevating one of its padded collars over his head to shield his smooth and smoky-topaz mane from the relentless rain.

'Welcome to Stalkford Airport, Captain Steen,' said one of the paramedics, smiling wryly as he held out an object in his hand. 'I think you dropped this.'

The captain reached over and took back his pilot's cap, which had

become dislodged from his head mid-crash and, like him, had miraculously escaped any lasting damage from the plane's catastrophic
impact with the ground and subsequent inferno. He winked at the
medic, acknowledging the man's excellent display of dry wit amid
trying circumstances, then popped on the cap swiftly over his thick,
lustrous hair and marched at a professional pace towards the airport's
main building across the runway.

'I'll remember it next time,' he called out behind him, as the rescue
crews continued with their work, the grim task of recovery destined
to occupy them, as always, long into the night.

Next time, reflected Nick Steen, former best-selling horror author
turned doomed airline pilot for Stalkford Airways, to himself.

Next time.

There was *always* next time.

For the circumstances of the horrific air accident Nick found
himself emerging from had once been nothing more real than a
series of calamitous events described within the pages of one of his
own horror tomes. Published more than twenty years earlier, *The
Portentor* (or *Portentoror* for the US edition) had recounted the chilling story of Captain Gary Tracker, commercial air pilot and sole
survivor of a devastating plane crash. Caught in a supernatural time
warp, Tracker is forced to endure a never-ending cycle of near-iden-
tical aviation accidents from which he emerges continually as sole
survivor.

To make matters worse, each fresh air disaster is foretold uncannily
in Tracker's mind via recurring *portentums* (hence *The Portentor*): an
eerie psychokinetic ability to 'see' future events before they happen.
This has somehow been engineered by Tracker's initial crash, and
with each fresh accident only increases in intensity, meaning he's
soon caught in an endless cycle of death-prefiguration followed by
near-death experience, followed by death-prefiguration followed by
near-death experience, etc. It's a total nightmare.

The book's cover had depicted the sinister image of a man's face – half pilot, half skull – with a jumbo jet spiralling in a terrifying death-arc directly through a hole in the protagonist's nose, splitting the forehead above it in two while igniting both eye sockets with subtly rendered bursts of exploding jet fuel. These symbolised in visual terms the 'pupils of death' that would ultimately curse the book's hero with uncanny psychic foresight. For, as Tracker gradually discovers, he's not just developing a psychic ability to foretell events, but also one that can *influence* them as well. And with that devastating realisation comes yet another, even more devastating, revelation: that Gary Tracker has somehow emerged from this never-ending cycle of disasters as a God among men, and not a particularly benevolent one.

It was a dense cluster of truly frightening premises. And with Nick's name rendered solidly in embossed gold lettering above the cover's central image, and the book's title displayed prominently below it in electric blue, *The Portentor* had proved to be one of Nick's most terrifying novels, and on the page it should have remained. Yet now, owing to Nick Steen's imagination having escaped from his mind, seeping out continuously from his head for several months following his accidentally opening a portal to another dimension (having once engaged in shady physical relations with a cursed type-writer), the book in question had suddenly sprung to life. Now Nick Steen himself was caught up in the midst of a destructive portentory maelstrom unleashed by his own writing.

Nick Steen now *was* Gary Tracker in all but name. And with each fresh air accident and terrifying brush with death, deepening psycho-kinetic abilities were gradually manifesting themselves inside Nick's *own* brain. Not just an ability to foresee the future, but *additional* ones as well.

Like boiling an egg using *only the power of his mind*. Currently, the process took over four hours, meaning it was ultimately more practical to use a pan. But who knew what other terrifying psychic powers might soon awaken inside his brain?

And in that, Nick fervently believed, lay Stalkford's ultimate salvation. For if he could somehow continue to endure these nightly plane crashes, knowing he'd ultimately and miraculously walk away from them uninjured, sole survivor every time, then maybe, just maybe, he could develop those latent psychic abilities enough to become the all-powerful psychic force depicted in his original novel. Then he could at long last turn the table on his rampaging demonic visions. Defeat them once and for all, thus saving Stalkford, and the surrounding counties, from ultimate destruction. Plus get the egg-boiling down to one minute, max.

Nick blew a disbelieving whistle from his lips, awestruck by the sheer magnitude of the task that lay ahead. Before all that, he needed to relax. Recharge. Cop some badly needed Zs.

He slapped his forehead suddenly, remembering. He had a date with Julia, damn it. Former air stewardess, now Female Air Traffic Control Assistant, whose surname he couldn't remember and whose life he'd saved from premature death by firing her aggressively from her first job for serving him tepid coffee on the morning of that initial disastrous Flight SA13 to Bogotá.

Nick smiled, recalling the memory. He wondered where he could take Julia tonight, before realising, with sudden regret, that he'd agreed to let *her* make that decision. No doubt it meant a prolonged bout of late-night shopping in the duty-free lounge before any hint of petting could commence. Perhaps he should just fire her again . . .

Breaking free from his thoughts, Nick saluted the team of arriving Air Accident Investigators, high-fived Marcus, their accompanying Critical Incident Officer, and passed through a door into the main terminal building. He took an escalator up to the main concourse and followed the exclusive crew lane through to customs.

'Nice flight?' asked Customs Officer Fran Locker, whom Nick was also dating, though not as frequently as he was Julia.

'It *was*,' Nick joked.

'Maybe some deeply probing questions would soften you up?' she said, cracking her knuckles. 'How about a brief, bruising body search in one of the security cells?'

'Not tonight, Fran,' Nick said, knowing that such a physical parley would only instigate another public catfight between her and Julia, which Nick would no doubt have to referee again.

Frowning, Fran handed him a scrawled note.

'Roz Bloom,' she said. 'Can you phone her back? She said it's urgent.'

'It's always urgent with Roz,' sighed Nick as he passed through baggage retrieval, waving away thick smoke from a revolving stream of charred luggage, before heading into departures. As a waiting crowd of photographers and news journalists flashed their cameras at him, vying for attention in the hope of an interview scoop with Stalkford's 'Miracle Survivor', Nick scanned the concourse in vain for Julia, then moved into the drinks lounge.

He ordered his usual complimentary whisky from Phyllis, the barmaid, whom Nick was considering dating after Julia and Fran, then crossed over to an empty phone booth and dialled Roz's number.

'Well?' he asked, as his former editor picked up the phone.

'I heard about the accident,' Roz said, stifling tears. 'A big one, they said . . .'

'Yeah, devastating,' Nick replied. 'But I'm okay, thank God. Stop crying.'

'But *Nick*,' Roz whispered, swallowing tears. 'What about the others?'

'What others?'

'The dead and dying, Nick.'

'The *dead*, Roz. The rest have stopped breathing. I'm *sole* survivor, remember?'

'But there are so many now, Nick. If you actually count up all the various crash casualties . . .'

'Which I won't . . .'

'There are over *three thousand* now, Nick. Three thousand lost souls. And you seem utterly unconcerned about a single one of them.'

'Correct.'

'To you, these endless, devastating air disasters are simply routine flights.'

Nick sighed, hardly believing that he was needing to go through all this again. 'Like I've told you numerous times, Roz, *I'm* the victim here. I'm the one dealing with the persistent, day-to-day trauma of it all. I'm the one emerging from each crash as sole survivor, with all the psychological disorientation and confusion that entails. Not only that, but I'm also having to handle these emerging psychokinetic powers of mine, namely an unnerving psychic awareness of future events and, as of last night, a creepy egg-boiling ability. All that lot have to do is die.'

He realised he was speaking too loudly. People were turning in their seats to watch. *There he is*, Nick imagined them thinking. *Captain Steen. The air disaster guy. That Sky-Jonah who sees the future.*

Well, they're wrong, Nick thought angrily, downing his whisky in one. Not least because 'Jonah' is a phrase referring to an unlucky seaman, *not* an airman, even if they've added 'Sky' at the front in an attempt to legitimise their mistake. The twats. He dashed his tumbler to the floor, which failed to smash as he'd intended, being a plastic one. He turned his face from the other patrons, embarrassed, wishing bitterly that he'd been able to predict *that* eventuality. Damn it, why was Roz always on his back about these bloody air disasters?

'You're knowingly flying innocents to their doom, Nick,' Roz snapped suddenly in his ear. 'Night after night. Doesn't your conscience even care about that?'

'Whether it cares or not, Roz, there's a good reason I'm flying these lost souls into an early grave. I'm developing my psychic abilities. Which are improving with each fresh disaster. At some point, they'll have developed sufficiently for me to be able to destroy, once and for all, these escaping horrors of my mind. I'm actually saving the *world* here, Roz. Not just a few thousand tightwads on some doomed weekend budget flight from Ibiza. Sure, it's sad; I get that. But these are pawns in a cosmic game. A cosmic game that *has* to be played for the sake of Mankind. I'm almost there, Roz. I can feel it. I may not be able to bend a spoon with my mind just yet, but I can certainly dull the shine on a brass ornament following eight weeks of concentrated staring. One day very soon, I'll become so powerful that I'll be able to single-handedly defeat all those horrors that my mind has inadvertently unleashed upon unsuspecting humanity.'

'And what new psychokinetic ability have you developed tonight, Nick?' asked Roz, her voice calmer now. 'How close are you getting?'

Nick thought for a moment. 'I'm not quite sure, Roz. Now that you mention it, as yet I can't detect any notable change in my telekinetic powers since tonight's disaster. But I'm sure it will manifest itself sooner or later.'

He looked down at his watch. He was late for Julia. Correction: Julia was *early* for him.

'Gotta go,' he said.

'Wait, Nick. There's one more thing. You remember that other book you wrote?'

'I wrote lots of books, Roz.'

'That other aviation-based sole survivor-themed horror series . . .'

Nick screwed his eyes shut, trying to recall the book in question.

'*Deathflap*,' Roz said, jogging his memory.

Nick winced inwardly. Hell, he'd forgotten all about *Deathflap*.

'What about *Deathflap*?'

'And the sequels, Nick,' Roz added. 'Don't forget the sequels.

10

Deathflap 2: Return of the Deathflap. Deathflap 3: The Flappening. Deathflap 4...'

'Cut to the chase, Roz,' Nick said. After all, the series had gone all the way up to *Deathflap 85, aka Flapocalypse IV (Deathflap vs Squawker)*.

'Well, in case you need reminding, Nick, the *Deathflap* series also featured the sole survivor of a plane crash. Only *that* character, Steve Tracker, wasn't haunted by portentums, Nick. He was haunted by *Death itself.*'

Nick shuddered, suddenly remembering. There was a reason he'd put those books out of his mind. 'Correction, Roz,' he said, trying to keep calm. 'Steve Tracker was haunted by Deathflap. Not Death.'

'Well whatever the actual name, Nick, Deathflap was a terrifying embodiment of the Grim Reaper in half-skeleton, half-pterodactyl form. And if you remember, it pursued Steve Tracker because he'd *eluded* death. Escaped it, crash after crash. But it came for him in the end, Nick, precisely because Steve Tracker had spurned Death. Escaped, night after eerie night, the deadly flapping of Deathflap's bony, webbed-winged embrace.'

'Deathflap's wings are partly feathered, Roz.'

'That series ended, Nick,' said Roz, ignoring him, 'because Clackett issued you with an ultimatum. Either Deathflap finally catches up with Steve Tracker in a concluding volume, or the series gets cancelled anyway.'

Bloody Clackett, Nick moaned, inwardly. Perhaps he should invite his former publishers on board his next flight. Then he sensed Roz was gearing up for something more.

'Come on then, Roz,' said Nick. 'Spit it out.'

'Deathflap is abroad, Nick.'

'Where? Mogadishu? The Canary Islands?'

'Abroad in the *supernatural* sense, Nick – i.e., around. Reports are coming in of a leathery skull-like demon crossing international airspace, Nick. Deathflap's coming for you.'

Dammit, that's all he needed. Another sole-survivor aviation-based horror novel of his invading the current living embodiment of a sole-survivor aviation-based horror of his.

'Sure, Roz,' said Nick, putting it out of his mind. Hell, he had enough horrors to contend with on a daily basis, didn't he? One more couldn't hurt. 'I'll keep an eye out.'

'Make sure you do, Nick. Because at some point soon, Deathflap itself is going to catch up with you. Sole survivor or no sole survivor.'

'Well, he can flap off as far as I'm concerned!' Nick barked, then hung up.

Ignoring the stares from surrounding drinkers, he grabbed his flight case and marched back out into departures. Julia was there at last, standing where he'd told her to meet him, directly outside the gents' loos.

'You're early,' he said, coldly.

'I'm sorry, Nick,' Julia replied, puckering her lips. He attempted a heavy pet, but was immediately rebuffed.

'I thought we'd try the duty-free perfume aisle tonight.'

'Sure,' Nick said, wearily. Evidently his nightly brushes with death were starting to pale with her. 'Or we could just go back to mine?'

'Not tonight, Nick. I'm shopping,' said Julia, already racing off towards the glow of lights gleaming from a distant perfume counter.

He paused, considering calling a taxi for one, and then saw two men in suits holding up a piece of cardboard with his name on it.

'Captain Steen?' said the taller of the two.

'Yes?'

'We're here to take you to the awards ceremony.'

'Awards ceremony?' replied Nick, confused. 'What awards ceremony?'

'Why, to honour your extensive achievement in best-selling horror fiction. You *did* receive our invitation?'

'No,' said Nick, confused. He couldn't remember receiving anything. Though he'd hardly been home between flights, he reflected. He *had* asked Julia to sort through his mail and do all the cooking and cleaning while he was away. No doubt she'd tossed out the invitation, along with all those gone-off cartons of salad he refused to touch.

He examined the two men, closely. The youngest was tall, blond-haired and of slim build. He wore a pair of mirrored shades. The man beside him holding up the piece of card was older and heavier than his companion. This guy was balding slightly; a pair of long, greying sideburns drawing his hair downward, away from what looked like an old medical scar stretching halfway across his forehead. The man's hands sported a pair of black leather driving gloves that grasped the length of card tightly, crushing each side. Both men wore sharp-looking suits; the younger's a tailored dark navy affair, his companion's a grey, functional off-the-peg.

Maybe these guys were on the level. One thing was certain. Neither of them were part skeleton, part pterodactyl. And what harm could an award do him, anyway? Having instigated a devastating supernatural catastrophe directly threatening the entire future of the human race, Nick's profile could do with a bit of positive publicity.

'Why not?' said Nick. 'Let's go.'

The older man took Nick's flight case from him and ushered him outside. Out by the taxi rank, the man's blond-haired companion pointed towards their waiting car, which displayed a prominent logo down one side.

'Nulltec,' Nick read. Nulltec . . . Nick knew that name. But before he could remember where from exactly, he was struck by the vision.

CHAPTER TWO

'Nulltec'

The earth passing below Nick was smooth yet sallow, like festering crème fraîche. Its vast surface appeared to dip at either side of the distant horizon, like the sloping curvature of some colossal ball of brie. As Nick descended further towards this pasty plane, he perceived that he was gliding over the surface of some dying planet. Swathes of stunted vegetation materialised as he descended towards its surface, exposing stubs of withered flora and fauna sprouting weakly under the tepid rays of an ailing alien sun.

Or were those *follicles*?

As Nick flew on, it seemed to him, in his dreamlike state, that he was once more piloting another doomed plane, yet one whose wings, according to his pilot's readout, were now part-organic and webbed, if not leathered, in form. As the unknown air-vessel transporting him continued onward towards the distant horizon, beyond which lay an infinity of black, starless sky, Nick began to entertain the unnerving notion that he was passing over something far more dreadful than a mere dying planet. For as Nick's speed began to increase, his eyes gradually perceived the contours of a giant mauve lake staining the planet's surface. A lake that looked very much to Nick like a colossal liver spot. His mind froze in a sudden paroxysm of crippling cosmic

14

horror as he realised that he was in fact traversing – at insane speed – the ageing, balding pate of a *gargantuan human head*.

His <u>own</u>.

Nick screamed himself awake. As both eyes snapped open, he saw that he was in the back seat of a moving vehicle, with the notable lack of streetlights outside his passenger window suggesting they'd long since left the outskirts of the city airport.

The two men in suits sat up front.

'Where are we?' asked Nick, unable to remember getting inside the car.

'On our way,' said the older man, who was driving. Nick caught his eye in the rear-view mirror, staring back at him. Watching.

'On our way where?'

'To the award ceremony,' said the younger man, in the passenger seat. 'You've won the Nullman Prize, remember?'

'The Nullman Prize?' Nick repeated, trying his best to recall the award. It was useless. Nick had only ever won prizes with demonic entities in the title. Yet he knew that name from somewhere . . .

'The award recognises your stunning achievements in the art of literary incarnation,' the blond man continued. 'Bringing fictional reality to life. It's an award invented solely for you.'

'Perhaps *I* invented it?' quipped Nick.

Neither man laughed.

'We don't joke about Dr Nullman,' the blond man said.

Nullman? Nick's mind started racing. He knew that name, too. But from where?

'If I'm to receive an award,' he said, testing the water, 'then surely I ought to be provided with some complimentary refreshments?'

'Naturally,' said the younger man, turning almost immediately to offer Nick a mini bottle of Scotch from the passenger seat compartment. Nick took the drink, glancing at the rear-view mirror again as he did so. The driver was still staring at him, and Nick had the uncanny feeling that the man hadn't looked at the road ahead at any point during the last three minutes.

Still suffering a headache from his terrifying portentum, Nick downed the Scotch in one.

'The Nullman Prize is much coveted, Mr Steen. An award for supreme achievement in literary fiction. It represents formal acknowledgement of your vast accomplishments in the field of creative world-building.'

'*Literal* world-building, in my case,' quipped Nick again, smiling dryly at his own pithy wit.

Again, neither man laughed.

'About time,' said Nick, taking another Scotch from the younger man's hand as the driver continued to watch Nick's movements via the rear-view mirror. 'A toast then, gentlemen,' said Nick. 'To myself, and the so-called *literati*, who've been erroneously dissing my oeuvre for the past twenty years.'

Nick downed this second Scotch, hoping he was fooling them. Maybe it was the rush of booze, or those two eyes piercing him from the mirrored glass in front, but something didn't add up. Why, when the entire world was threatened by Nick's escaping imagination, would a literary elite wish to honour him for unleashing this horde of fictional demons? Something stank, Nick figured.

Unexpectedly, the vehicle lurched sharply to the left, swerving over the road as a rush of headlights swooped past them on the other side.

'Apologies,' said the driver, righting the vehicle while keeping his eyes trained continually on Nick.

At this rate, they'd all be dead in five minutes.

'Who's Nullman?' Nick asked, still wracking his brains for an answer.

'Barbara Nullman,' said the younger man, reaching into the passenger compartment for a third mini bottle of Scotch. He turned around and handed it to Nick. 'Doctor Barbara Nullman.'

Dammit, Nick *knew* that name. But from where?

He downed his third drink, trying in vain to remember. As he did so, the car left the road, turning left down a muddy lane leading towards a vast spread of approaching forest.

'Where's this awards ceremony being held?' asked Nick, confused by the looming greenery. 'It had better not be a writers' retreat.'

Nick hated writers' retreats. He'd only ever attended one, and had been thrown out within the first hour for ridiculing everyone else's fledgling efforts. While perceived wisdom regarded writers' retreats as a place to share one's work-in-progress and receive constructive criticism from fellow scribes, Nick took the opposite view. 'Criticism' and 'constructive' were mutually exclusive words. For Nick, a writers' retreat meant precisely that. An opportunity to ensure competing writers ran as far from his explosive wrath as possible, thereby easing his own pathway to success.

'Rest assured it's no writer's retreat,' said the blond man. 'For one thing, the place we're heading towards has excellent conference parking.'

Wait a moment, thought Nick, his mind racing again. That phrase . . . *Excellent conference parking.* He'd heard it before, hadn't he? Yes, it was a slogan, dammit. A slogan on some brochure he'd once read . . . Then, finally, he remembered.

The sign. The sign on the side of the car. Nick hadn't clocked it at the time as his mind had been immediately besieged by that terrifying premonition of male baldness, but now he recalled the company's logo.

Nulltec . . .

He peered through the windscreen at the road ahead. Against the distant tree-line, Nick saw a grim, grey building looming into view.

Nulltec . . .

A place hardly anyone in Stalkford knew about. A stark, concrete building situated somewhere off the D60 on the border of Chokewood Forest, housed in a fenced-off stretch of open ground formerly owned by the defence department of Stalkford City Council.

Nulltec . . .

The word itself gave Nick the creeps. For this was a place Nick knew only too well, having unearthed rumours about it during an intense hour's worth of research for his mutated virus novel *The Milky Strain*. It was a high-tech medical research facility specialising in unconventional scientific experiments. Hardly the kind of venue for a supposed literary event . . .

'Quit shitting me,' said Nick. 'You people aren't awarding me a prize at all, are you?'

The driver's eyes finally turned from the rear-view mirror, shifting towards the road ahead for the first time, and the fast-approaching concrete building.

'Hey, I'm talking to you, buddy,' spat Nick gruffly, even though he wasn't the guy's buddy at all. Not remotely his buddy.

As the car drew up alongside Nulltec, Nick leaned forward in his seat, his eyes drawn to the place he'd read so little about during that brief, crucial trip to Stalkford Library.

The large central building was of late sixties construction, rectangular in shape yet corporate in feel, formed on each side from steel girders and smooth concrete, which daylight would have revealed was dyed a light shade of beige. The main premises was formed of three floors – Nick counted – and the facility's main entrance doors were shielded under a wide protruding porch, which gave it the feel of a modern hospital building. Yet the architectural finish was sleeker than that, Nick felt. Polished, almost, as if a great deal of cash had been thrown at the place in recent years. A range of ancillary buildings adjoined its central structure, and there were indeed, Nick noted now, some excellent conference parking facilities.

But at this late hour, the building looked empty. Visible through the glass door panelling, Nick made out an unmanned welcome desk with an empty chair lit by the dim light of a dormant computer screen. The bulk of the lobby's interior was suffused with an electrical pink glow radiating from the row of tall sodium lamps erected outside.

As the car ascended a paved ramp leading up to the main drop-off point, Nick clocked the building's signpost:

Nulltec – Your Tomorrow is Our Today.
Chief Evolver: Dr Barbara Nullman

A long list of letters followed this name, eventually taking up three additional signposts.

Of course, Nick suddenly recalled . . . *Nullman. Dr Barbara Nullman.* Nick knew who she was, alright.

That damned *cow* . . .

'Okay, boys,' he said, necking the last of his complimentary Scotch. 'You've had your fun. Now what say you swing us right back round to the airport again? Because I'm not going anywhere near the vicinity of *that* woman.'

Then the tranquillisers they'd been feeding him finally kicked in.

★

The gag in his mouth muffled Nick's screams as a long row of harsh strip lights passed vertically overhead. Both arms and legs were bound to a gurney and he was being wheeled at immense speed down a long, white, clinical-looking corridor. Nick tried to angle his head sideways, so that he could see who precisely was wheeling him, but his gaze remained fixed on the ceiling above. Evidently his neck had been restrained, Nick concluded, or else he'd been drugged with some form of highly illegal muscle-relaxant serum.*

A deep judder shot through Nick's spine as the metal gurney slammed into a set of swing doors, barging them open. As they swung to behind him, Nick felt himself being transported onward, down another featureless corridor of endless white wall panelling.

He continued to scream through his gagged mouth, though no one heeded his cries, and wondered exactly how the hell he'd got here. One moment he'd been swallowing that third helping of Scotch and telling those two planks in no uncertain terms that he wasn't about to engage in another bout of turgid philosophical debate with a former Nobel Prize winner, and then . . . nothing. Nick had simply blacked out, then woken here, strapped to a medical gurney, with hands and legs bound on each side.

Fighting off panic, Nick attempted to apply logic to his predicament. Though he bore all the apparent trappings of some ailing hospital patient or gibbering asylum nutcase, Nick knew he was sound in both body and mind. That presumably meant he was not technically a patient here, but a prisoner instead. A hostage. A captive. A detainee.

An *incarcerat*.†

But *where* exactly was he imprisoned? *Who* was imprisoning him? And *why*?

On reflection, Nick figured he knew the answers to two of these questions already. The first being Nulltec, presumably, and the second, as head of the aforementioned Nulltec, that damned sanctimonious cow Dr Barbara Nullman. Meaning Nick really only needed to ask himself that final question. *Why?*‡

---

* Wrong – it was simply a neck brace. GM
† Which is possibly, nay probably, but not positively, an alternate Latin phrase for 'prisoner', the official word being captivus. GM
‡ Specifically, why was he now imprisoned in Nulltec by that damned sanctimonious cow Dr Barbara Nullman? GM

He attempted in vain to shake his head. He didn't yet have the answer to *that* particular question. But as the gurney crashed through another set of double doors into a corridor slightly darker in colour than the previous one (yet still essentially white, if more of an *off*-white), Nick suspected he was about to find out.

He couldn't be certain due to his restricted view, but Nick suddenly sensed a glow of electrical pink light coming from what he thought were banks of monitors set into one of the adjacent walls.

As he was pushed through another set of double doors, still screaming and continuing to scream through his gag as the gurney turned harshly to the right and crashed through yet another set of double doors,* Nick sensed the pink glow intensifying, until finally he suspected that these endless, featureless corridors he was travelling down were no longer entirely featureless, and in fact bore certain features.

Drawing much-needed breath through both nostrils, Nick screwed his eyes shut against the searing glare of a powerful overhead light snapping on above him. As a loud, metallic grinding numbed his ears, Nick felt his body being tipped suddenly forward into a sitting position. Then someone placed his own spectacles back on his head.

He blinked both eyes forcefully, attempting to rid both retinas of the harsh afterglow caused by two giant overhead surgical lamps, then slowly lifted his neck.

A bandaged face, allowing only a glimpse of two eyes and a human nose, confronted him. As Nick flinched in fright, the figure flinched in fright with him.

He was staring at his own reflection, he realised. Nick's entire body was bound in bandages from head to toe, with metal clamps securing him stiffly to the trolley. As he watched, various pairs of

---

* I presume you get the picture by now that these are a succession of eerie, endless corridors. If not, may I suggest you re-read. GM

hands reached in from either side of his body to unwind, roughly and without any hint of surgical grace, the soiled and bloody medical dressings surrounding his aching cranium.

Feeling a layer of gauze being yanked free from his mouth area, Nick attempted to speak, but was immediately silenced by a violent slap from one of the nearby hands. He could do little then but watch his own reflection as the assembled mitts continued to unwind the bandage from around his head, strip by strip, until at long last the final dressing was removed to reveal, beneath . . .

He closed both eyes, unable to take in the monstrous sight confronting him.

For Nick Steen was no longer Nick Steen.

Nick Steen, he realised, using the third person to disassociate himself entirely from current proceedings, was *bald*.

Totally, utterly *bald*.

CHAPTER THREE

'Incarcerat'

Bald.

Then the terrifying vision had indeed come to pass.

Bald.

Nick felt the anger rising up within him.

They'd shaved him, the bastards. Shorn him of his beloved locks. So roughly too, he noted, once he'd mustered sufficient courage to re-open both eyes and confront the horror head-on, that grazed patches of torn skin now peppered his head like sliced salami scatterings.

Baldery.

'Free his neck,' said a female voice, harsh and business-like in timbre. A no-nonsense voice. The voice of a ball-busting female who gets things done. A voice that stamped hard when necessary; harder when unnecessary. A voice that Nick guessed might howl and snarl like a raging tigress atop the quivering body of some floored and subservient lover. The voice of one tough-talking, sultry-walking, chiselled-diamond female canine.*

A fresh set of hands appeared at Nick's side and deftly removed his neck restraint.

---

* Blame the copy-editor and/or changing times. GM

He could see her in the mirror now, a knot of golden hair bunched neatly behind a bold and prominent forehead. Two amber eyes pierced Nick's own with a stern yet inquisitive intensity. A smear of functional lipstick coloured a deceptively plain-looking face, which Nick suspected rarely smiled. She was around forty, he guessed, wearing large glasses in golden frames matching Nick's in both size and severity. A pair of gold hoop earrings completed the portrait of stern, no-nonsense professionalism, yet Nick sensed a spark of passion buried under the austere countenance. A stale yet not displeasingly smoky scent wafted upward from the yellowing sleeves of her lab coat as she smoothed Nick's bruised shoulders, mixed with an aroma of hastily chewed cherry breath mints. The firm lines on either side of her mouth confirmed it. The woman was a serious smoker.

As she stood back from him for a moment, Nick couldn't help but clock the cold yet commanding formality of the woman's caramel plaid skirt, that ended, nevertheless, some way above her knees, exposing, beneath, the coppery shimmer of her smooth, unladdered work stockings. As the woman leaned over him again to rub a cold cotton pad across his cheeks, Nick noted, the advanced length of her fingernails. Hardly a practical choice for the hard-working medical professional, he figured. And there were small areas, too, that had evidently escaped the woman's regular polish-removal regime. These tiny flecks betrayed her tint of choice – a deep, burgundy red.

Nick wondered if she ever wore lipstick that colour.

'I apologise for the current state of attire,' she said, smoothing the compress over his brow.

'Don't,' said Nick, thankful for the pad's cooling touch. 'It's maybe better you dress down.'

'I meant *you*,' the woman said, matter-of-factly. 'Nulltec requires all patients to be stripped, searched, probed, hosed, shaved, probed again intimately, photographed post-probe, fiddled with, then probed again before a full but not necessarily final probing.'

Ahh, thought Nick, tentatively flexing his buttock cheeks. So that *is* what's happened.

'I'm Barbara Nullman,' she said.

'I know,' Nick replied, not quite able to believe he was facing the Nobel Prize winner in the flesh. So this was to do with revenge, then. 'Is this about my book, *The Hissing Link*?' he asked.

'Not at all,' replied Nullman. 'Even if it was a fairly obvious and damning caricature.'

She was right on that score, Nick had to admit. Though he'd fallen shy of naming Nullman outright on the advice of Clackett's lawyers, the story of Dr Barbara McNullman in Nick's dystopian 'mutant gene' novel had indeed been an intentional critique of Nullman's most famous medical discovery. Hell, Nick had been sore, that was all. And why the hell not? For in one single night, Nullman had discovered how to extract the R–Complex* from the brains of human beings, and by so doing, had developed a scientific method of evolving Mankind that effectively kicked Nick's life-long mission to do the same via horror fiction into the proverbial dust.

Nullman had won a Nobel Prize that year. Nick had won Best Tentacle Death in the Nautical category of Port Talbot's rescheduled ShockerCon for his killer coral novel, *The Coral What Killed*.

Not that he wasn't proud of the award, but a Nobel Prize could well have nudged his novel sales into double figures. Since then, he'd done his best to forget the entire thing. And had largely succeeded.

Until tonight.

'We've been studying you for some time, Mr Steen.'

'It's *Captain* Steen.'

---

* Our deep-rooted reptilian instinct, also known as the basal ganglia or basal nuclei, containing the brain stem, limbic region and the amygdala. The main reason that human beings murder, maim, draw penises inside books and hog the middle lane. GM

She smiled at him, briefly. Then stopped. 'I think we can dispense with the whole "Captain" nonsense.'

'My name is Captain Nicholas Steen,' Nick repeated, stiffly. 'Serial Number 13666. That's all the information you'll get out of me.'

'Mr Steen, giving your fictional pilot persona a flight identity number consisting of the "unluckiest" numeral along with another signifying the supposed "Number of the Beast" is clichéd and entirely implausible. Genuine pilots use call signs, not numbers. Neither do professional airline companies employ those same numerals for any routine flight numbers, in order to avoid outbreaks of superstitious panic and inevitable ridicule.'

She snapped her fingers. Immediately, the three lab assistants who'd wheeled Nick in swung his gurney round 180 degrees.

He now found himself facing a wide bank of visual monitors hitherto masked from view. On each screen played raw, unedited footage of air accident recovery scenes; a vast pool of graphic news-reel depicting the grim aftermath of numerous plane disasters. Nick observed shots of wreckage being sifted through, smoking corpses being doused with fire extinguishers, then quietly looted by arriving emergency crews. He recognised the familiar flight serial numbers on several pieces of strewn wreckage. He'd flown every single one of those damned planes.

'We've detected that you are currently inhabiting the plot of your 1999 novel *The Portentor*,' said Nullman. 'Tell me, have you been experiencing any of these so-called "portentums"? Any ominous prefigurations or psychic premonitions as a result of these recurring crashes?'

Nick suddenly caught sight of himself on the various monitor screens, emerging, sole survivor, from every stricken plane. Bathed in flame, yet somehow completely uninjured. And inside his brain, with every crash, the awakening of some latent psychic ability. Powers, Nick now sensed, as Nullman ran her long nails and hands over his shoulders, that he ought to keep secret from Nulltec.

'I can boil an egg with my mind,' said Nick. 'But that's about it.'

'You're lying, Mr Steen.' Nullman pointed at the numerous dials and data-measuring devices spaced between each monitor. 'Our scanners can pick up all thoughts and visions you experience, either conscious or unconscious.'

'What do you want from me?'

'Officially, here at Nulltec we explore the furthest reaches of human consciousness, Mr Steen. We specialise in extrasensory powers, telepathic communication . . . *psychokinetic abilities* . . .'

'And *un*officially?'

'That's classified,' Nullman replied, casually wafting away a cloud of smoke from her latest cigarette. 'You are a very special subject, Mr Steen. Somewhere, deep in your cerebral hemispheres, housed in an undefined area between your frontal, temporal and parietal lobes, there lies a bridge. A bridge between your three warring conscious-nesses: sub-, un- and waking. A bridge between this world, and some unknown parallel dimension. A bridge, I must tell you now, that we at Nulltec intend to *blow*.'

Nick swallowed hard. 'Keep talking,' he said, trying to sound tough, despite being bald.

'Whatever the innate "quality" of your fiction, Mr Steen – and we at Nulltec deem it particularly lowbrow – the supernatural denizens of your imagination nevertheless now exist for real. They are alive and breathing, defying all laws of rationality and logic. Crude works of visceral, paperback horror grown suddenly incarnate. As such, Nulltec must treat these literary creations seriously, even if no one else does.'

Right, thought Nick, shaking his head. Like you understand visionary horror.

'The truth is, your escaping imagination is poised to destroy

27

humanity. Our entire existence here in Stalkford, and beyond, is threatened not just by the terrifying horrors you have unleashed, but also by those burgeoning psychic powers latent within *you*. If we were to let you continue on your current path, Mr Steen, those powers you are steadily gaining from each air accident would *themselves* become an agent of destruction. A horrifying evil unleashed upon this world. Without you realising it, your supposed noble intention of saving Mankind from supernatural ruin would instead have the opposite effect. Those unchecked psychic powers slowly manifesting themselves in your mind would soon rain down destruction upon the world as the colossal ego within your head swelled, ultimately turning on all who dare challenge it. Your hideous portentum of earthly destruction is essentially one of *self*-destruction.'

What the hell was she banging on about? wondered Nick. Exactly *what* hideous portentum of earthly destruction? Did she mean Nick's unholy vision of male-pattern baldness? Surely that particular horror had already come to pass? Maybe Nullman was making this whole thing up to justify balding him with impunity and keeping him here against his will for slating her in print.

And yet, Nick thought, breaking off his own train of thought. There was much in the vision that had yet to be explained, wasn't there? Those leathery, skin-covered aeroplane wings, for one thing. And something else, Nick recalled, suddenly seeing the image clearly in his mind's eye again.

That vast bald headscape below him; that barren, dying plain he'd been flying over. Maybe it wasn't just a vast floating human head, after all. Maybe it was precisely what he'd thought it was when he'd first glimpsed it from above.

A planet . . .

Earth, maybe — now a barren, empty, devastated world. Entirely destroyed, or so it had seemed to Nick. But by what? Did an answer to the riddle lie in the appalling symbolism of Nick's vision? A symbolism he'd so far failed to notice? For if that dead planet – if a dead planet was indeed what it was – resembled Nick's own head, swollen monstrously to a vast, cosmic size, then did that mean that he, in fact, was the symbolic cause of the planet's ultimate ruin? Was he, Nick Steen, a Destroyer of Worlds? Was Nick's vast, swollen head, enraged by its sudden lack of hair, the first step in Earth's forthcoming Apocalypse?

'Why don't you leave this whole thing to me?' said Nick. 'After another hundred or so crashes, I'll easily have enough latent psychic powers to do battle with my own fictional outpourings. That way, no one else gets hurt – apart from more passengers – and I get a Nobel Prize, too.'

'I'm afraid not,' said Nullman, as her lab assistants turned Nick's gurney round to face her again. She was back over by the mirror now, leaning up against it nonchalantly, one arm held casually over her chest, while the other held aloft a freshly lit cigarette.

'Your synapses have been wired in to our central computer,' she said, tapping ash into a nearby Petri dish. 'Somewhere in the region of one hundred million nerve-cell fibres inside your brain are now connected directly to our main scanning sensors in Central Probe.'

'What's Central Probe?' asked Nick.

'It's where we keep our main scanning sensors.'

One of the assistants held up a small mirror behind Nick's neck so that he could see, for the first time since he'd been shaved, the back of his own head. He shuddered, almost gagging at the sight confronting him. Of course! How else could they have seen into his mind? To Nick's horror, a tangled cluster of wires and tubes had been fed into the back of his skull via precision-drilled holes, right through to his cerebellum and occipital lobes.

He was a freak.

Nullman lit a fresh cigarette, inhaling deeply, then leaned down and exhaled the smoke out of her own mouth, directly into Nick's.

29

He coughed, feeling the vaguest of twitchings in his dormant manhood.

Christ alive, he thought. This cow's turning me *on*.

'I'm going to seal up that hole in your head,' she said, smiling at him almost playfully. 'I'm sure you'll let me do something like that to you . . .' She extended her longest, burgundiest nail outward and stroked it upward under Nick's chin, teasingly. '. . . Won't you?'

Nick swallowed hard.

And nodded.

CHAPTER FOUR

'Phase I'

'Let's meet Dr Valesco,' said Nullman. Immediately, the two orderlies wheeled Nick over to a door in the far wall. At the push of a button, the panel slid aside to reveal a thin, declining ramp leading downward into a darkened room below. With a sudden jolt, Nick felt himself dip forward as he slid slowly into the shadows.

The room he entered was large and lit only by an eerie pinkish glow coming from a single monitor. The remainder of the area was steeped in a murky, impenetrable gloom.

Nick looked around, seeing nothing, then heard the flick of a cigarette lighter somewhere ahead. A spark of light flared on the far side of the room, illuminating a slight, lab-coated figure standing silently in the shadows.

'Dr Valesco is Assistant Chief Head of the Nulltec Corporation,' said Nullman from behind.

Valesco was short but thin, his expression seemingly forever held in a permanent, knowing half-smile. If Nullman hadn't pointed him out, Nick might never have known the guy had been standing there in the shadows. Beneath his neatly starched lab coat, Valesco was wearing a formal slate-grey suit. His sleekly silvered hair was thick, neat and lustrous on top. His ice-blue eyes glared coldly at Nick.

Then his gaze flicked right, like a reptile's, at one of the orderlies, who immediately flipped a switch, snapping on a row of overhead strip lights.

'Dr Valesco has been working on our prototype,' said Nullman.

Unsure what she was referring to, Nick scrutinised the interior of the room in greater detail. He could see now that the place was a testing laboratory of some kind, each white-panelled wall supporting a now customary bank of computer monitors and research desks. Then Nick caught sight of it, standing in the very centre of the room.

A device.

The thing appeared to consist of two units, the larger of the pair resembling a large metallic chair, which Nick felt was in sore need of a cushion. From its rear, a mesh of protruding wires connected this rudimentary seat to a row of electric panelling on one of the larger computer consoles behind. A form of head restraint constructed in the shape of a half-oval, like a sliced egg, hung suspended above it.

Beside the chair, meanwhile, stood a box.

For some reason, this second object unnerved Nick more than anything else he'd experienced so far. It was small, metallic and rectangular in shape, suspended at chest height by four long, thin-wheeled struts. Two handles were attached to the rear side of the crate itself, and spaced evenly along one side were three large push buttons, labelled 'Powerful', 'More Powerful' and 'Even More Powerful'. On the top of the box was a red beacon that, when operated, Nick guessed, would revolve and flash like an emergency vehicle's siren. In front of this was a large riveted circular plate from which protruded a lengthy section of cable. This mass of pipework, ten inches in diameter and resembling an air-conditioner's ducting hose, lay coiled like a large anaconda beside the box itself, culminating in what looked to Nick like an elaborately pinned plug outlet.

The whole thing resembled the abandoned blueprint for some

primitive supermarket trolley, one without space for one's shopping, massive long legs and a huge cable sticking out of its interior mechanism. But maybe what frightened Nick most about the contraption – for Nick guessed it had to be some sort of technical device – were three words inscribed upon its front-facing metal plate:

THE GOD SOCKET

'What in hell's name is the God Socket?' asked Nick.

'An invention of mine,' replied Nullman, coming round from Nick's rear to stand beside the silver-haired scientist. 'Developed by Dr Valesco here, and his team. One that will lead to far greater recognition for me than a mere Nobel Prize.'

'What, *specifically*, is the God Socket?' asked Nick, realising he was none the wiser despite Nullman's answer, and hoping a degree of qualification might help.

'The God Socket is essentially a small nuclear reactor housed inside a baking tin.'

Nick nodded. At least he now had some idea of what the God Socket was.

'And what precisely does this "God Socket" do?' he asked, seeking some additional clarification, in addition to the previous additional clarification.

'Quite simply, Mr Steen, it nullifies.'

'Meaning?' Nick asked, aware that saying, 'What's "nullifies"?' would sound inelegant.

'We call the process *nullification*,' continued Nullman. 'The God Socket "nullifies" certain synapses in the brain. In your case, it will neuter your rampant imagination and, in layman's parlance, "bung up" the mind-leak you are currently suffering from. It's essentially the hand of God. In a box.'

A sudden noise from the contraption drew Nick's attention. The red beacon on top lit up and began whirling in a circular motion in response to what had sounded to Nick's ears like the crack of a party popper somewhere inside its internal mechanism. The crate itself was starting to judder too, Nick noticed. With a second audible crack, a small cloud of smoke puffed upward from the centre of the circular plate, which Nick now realised was an opening of some kind. Then the box went still again.

'I'm not going near that thing,' declared Nick.

'You don't have to,' said Nullman. 'It will come to you.'

'Beg your pardon?'

'Put him in the chair.'

Valesco stepped forward, along with a row of hitherto unseen orderlies who materialised suddenly from the surrounding shadows. Immediately, Nick felt himself being hoisted from his gurney and carried by several hands towards the strange-looking chair.

'Stop this,' said Nick uselessly, feeling the back of his head snag sharply as the clutch of wires drilled into the back of his skull caught on numerous hands. He winced as one of Valesco's assistants tripped over the heavy cabling still trailing behind Nick's back from the room above. Then he felt himself being twisted around, his head pushed roughly forward so that the orderlies could unscramble the muddled wiring behind.

As the cabling gradually became freed, someone yanked Nick's head backward again. Before him stood Nullman, smiling as she dragged deeply on a fresh cigarette.

To his horror, Nick realised he had a full stonk-on.

'Now, you may feel a small prick,' she said, smirking.

'Very funny,' Nick replied, trying to maintain a degree of dignity. What the hell were they doing to him? Here he was, being man-handled by an ice queen whom he ought to be resisting with every fibre of his being, and yet he was somehow completely powerless, with the wrong part of his anatomy instead rising to the occasion.

PORTENTUM

Perhaps his mind was flashing back to those former days he'd spent servicing a dominant and sex-obsessed cursed typewriter, but the truth was, Nullman had him by the proverbial googlies, and Nick, once again, was powerless to intervene on his own behalf. He prayed to God he'd been drugged with some sort of aphrodisiac serum,[*] and wasn't just somehow perversely attracted to his female tormentor.

'I guess removing the R-Complex from a human brain wasn't enough for you, eh Nullman?' said Nick as Valesco and his team strapped his body tightly to the chair. 'I guess becoming famous the world over for successfully removing the R-Complex, our deep-rooted reptilian instinct also known as the basal ganglia or basal nuclei, containing the brain stem, limbic region and the amygdala, from human brain tissue, and thereby fast-tracking the next stage in Mankind's evolution, didn't quite scratch your itch?'

Nullman smiled, exhaling more smoke in his direction.

'Or maybe,' continued Nick, coughing slightly, 'what happened to that poor chump you removed it from put the kibosh on the whole "evolution" thing. Maybe that guy buying several gowns in differing shades of green and retiring permanently to a yak-furred yurt some-where in the middle of Epping Forest wasn't quite the titanic leap forward in human progress you'd envisaged? Is that it, Nullman? Is your ultimately foolhardy decision to remove the man's R-Complex, his deep-rooted reptilian instinct also known as the basal ganglia or basal nuclei, containing the brain stem, limbic region and the amygdala, thereby turning him into a human aubergine, what this is all *really* about?'

What was the point? No matter how much he might struggle with her, Nick knew that she knew he was putty in her hands. Let's face it, it was hard to hide a boner when that boner was no longer hidden. Why not just live with that?

---

[*] He hadn't. It was simply a deep-rooted fetishistic urge deep within Nick's brain. We all have them. Mine revolve around ant-mounds. GM

And maybe Nullman *was* on the level, after all. Maybe he had nothing whatsoever to worry about. And maybe, if Nulltec *did* block up that hole in his mind, he could even ask Nullman out for dinner tonight? Maybe invite himself back to her place to examine her Nobel? Maybe even polish it for a brisk five minutes.

'Pierce his pate,' said Nullman.

Nick barely had time to take in those words when he felt several small needles pressing uncomfortably downward against his hairless skull as the oval-shaped head restraint above him plunged downward. He was receiving some form of cranial injection, he realised, the head restraint piercing Nick's skull with what felt like a thousand miniature pins.

'Relax, Mr Steen,' said Valesco, plugging the pinned end of the cable, which Nick presumed was the God Socket itself, into the top half of his head restraint. He glanced left, and saw, with horror, that his brain was now fully wired up to the adjacent box.

Nullman withdrew to the far side of the room, which Nick now realised was divided from the central area by a glass partition. As several scientists began inputting data into a range of consoles, Nullman held up a small microphone to her mouth and spoke, her voice hitting Nick's ears from a pair of overhead speakers.

'When Doctor Valesco presses the first button on the God Socket, I want you to concentrate on imagining a nice sandy beach.'

Nick looked down in horror at the machine beside him. 'You mean the button marked "Powerful"?' he said, starting to sweat.

'The first button, yes,' Nullman replied. 'Not the second or third button.'

'What happens if he does press the next button? The button marked "More Powerful"?'

'He will only press the button I tell him to press. Which will be the first button, marked "Powerful". Not that second button, which is marked "More Powerful".'

But what if Nullman told Valesco to press that second button on purpose, Nick wondered? The button marked 'More Powerful'? What then? Or what about button three, for that matter? That third button marked 'Even More Powerful'?

'What happens if he p-presses this third button?' cried Nick, starting to stammer.

'Let's not consider that possibility,' said Nullman. 'The God Socket is only a prototype, you understand. No one is allowed to press button three, the button marked "Even More Powerful", without my say-so. And were they to do so . . .' She paused to light a fresh cigarette.

'Yes?' Nick yelled. 'Were they to press button three, the one marked "Even More Powerful"? What then?'

Nullman exhaled, smoke hitting the glass panel in front of her, briefly obscuring her face.

'I daren't say *what* would happen then. If some *fool* were to foolishly press button three, the button marked "Even More Powerful" . . .'

What the hell *was* this damned thing? Nick asked himself, panicking. He tried to glance upward at the cranial restraint encasing him. Useless. The wires protruding from his head, leading upward into the machine itself, restricted all movement.

Valesco finished making some rudimentary adjustments to the machine and manoeuvred himself round to the side of the God Socket, his finger poised over button one.

'Ready,' he said.

'Good,' replied Nullman from behind the screen, her voice coming through the loudspeaker above. 'Very well, Doctor Valesco . . . You may press button one.'

'No,' said Nick. 'Please!'

Doctor Valesco pressed button one.

Smoke rose immediately from the box as its red beacon began to flash and whirl. The rectangular object began to judder and bounce as a vague grinding sound reverberated from somewhere within. Then the wheels on which the contraption was standing began to slide across the floor, triggering an automatic locking mechanism on each strut that instantly froze each leg in place. But that only seemed to cause the machine itself more aggravation, as another burst of smoke, thickly black this time, shot upward from between the metal grooves of the riveted circular plate from which the cabled socket extended.

Nick's eyes caught sight of a pulsating movement surging through the cable now, moving upward and over the intervening space, until finally it disappeared into the cranial restraint above his own head.

Then Nick felt the walls of his brain blast inward. A million detonations exploded deep inside his skull, as bolts of searing pain shot through his internal synapses, triggering a flash of competing images inside his frazzling mind.

At once he was a pilot again, flying over that vast bald pate on leathered wings, yet falling now, crashing downward in a terrifying death spiral towards the parched, hairless surface below, where, directly in the path of his deathly descent, stood Roz, staring upward in awe and terror at the approaching instrument of fiery, premature death. Then a cluster of other images flashed past Nick's vision as the pale, devastated ground below him drew ever closer.

His family home, in ruins . . . A teetering tower block . . . then a host of heavenly angels descending upon dumbstruck crowds gathered below . . . a Gothic Mansion by the sea, aflame . . . a creepy doll . . . a cooked breakfast, but that was because Nick hadn't eaten since his in-flight meal . . . two balls, evidently his own, given the botched tattoo on them that his wife had subsequently refused to pay for . . . the same daubed conkers, now trapped in the mangling platen of an ancient typewriter . . . Nick's own wife and daughter, far away, almost out of reach yet still flipping him the bird . . . then Roz again, screaming and shrieking as Nick's wing-borne engine of destruction finally slammed into the ground.

As Nick's mind impacted with it, the large pane of glass separating Nullman and her team from the God Socket exploded into a billion shards.

The shock snapped Nick's mind back into the present. He saw scientists reeling sideways to avoid the bursting glass, rolling left and right, shielding eyes and ears from the exploding fragments.

And Nullman, standing tall amid the chaos. Unmoved. Undamaged. Unconcerned.

She dragged deeply on her cigarette, nodding to herself. And smiled.

'I thought you were trying to *weaken* my powers!' yelled Nick. 'Not strengthen them!'

'Again,' said Nullman.

'No, dammit!' cried Nick as Valesco raised his finger once again over button one. 'I said *no!*'

Valesco pressed down a second time.

At once, the pulsing surge shot from the box, faster this time, making its way over to Nick's head in only three or four seconds. Then another wave of explosions detonated inside Nick's skull.

Another portentum . . . Roz now a charred and blackened skeleton, recognisable only by her impervious slingbacks . . . a world in ruin, baked dry by the dying sun as men-beasts howled and gibbered and ate each other in caravans . . . a vast stone edifice of Nick's own face . . . a petrifying shriek of primal despair, levelling buildings to dust, felling millions upon millions in its path . . .

Then a terrifying flapping of wings, as the world went suddenly and permanently dark . . .

Nick opened his eyes and saw Nullman's technicians running for cover. Running for *their lives* . . .

Jeez, Nick thought. I have the *power*. I have the power within me
...The power to *destroy*.

He looked over at Nullman, who stood still amid the maelstrom,
apparently unconcerned by Nick's display of uncontrollable psychic
aggression.

'You lied to me,' Nick hissed, struggling with his bonds. He'd lost
his stonk-on completely now, and all he felt was rage. Sheer, blind,
rage ...

'We have a slight problem,' said Doctor Valesco, consulting a small
computer printout coming from one of the nearby monitors. 'He's
now able to channel those newly supercharged psychic powers
directly.'

Nullman nodded. 'Put him out,' she said.

All at once, a group of security personnel in crash helmets, whom
Nick hadn't previously noticed, leaped forward from a bench on the
far side of the room and grabbed at him. As their combined limbs
struggled to force Nick's gaze away from Nullman's, the author-
cum-cursed-airline-pilot fought savagely to escape the constraints of
his chair, hoping to somehow fry his aggressors.

Destroy them, said a strange voice deep inside Nick's mind. *Destroy
them all.*

Then his mind went blank, his face growing suddenly calm as his
own eyes blazed with a hitherto unknown *cosmic fury* ...

One of the guards screamed out suddenly, grabbing his helmet in
both hands as he collapsed to the floor, both eyes bubbling like hot mud.
Then another security guard did the same, reaching downward this
time, to his own groin, where two sharp patches of red had suddenly
ruptured against his nylon trouser front as both lower balls exploded.*

'Terminate the experiment,' said Doctor Valesco.

Calmly, coldly, Nullman continued to assess the ongoing situation.

---

* And yes, he also had upper ones. GM

'Fine,' she said, reluctantly. 'Terminate Phase One.'

Valesco walked over to a small cabinet and drew out something from within.

But Nick wasn't watching him. If it even was Nick anymore. For the voice inside the author's mind now sounded more like that of an empowered deity. A powerful new psychic ability had been awoken by Nick's fusion with the God Socket, and Steen now possessed, he felt perfectly sure, an ability to overcome and *destroy* all oppressors.

Wrenching himself free from the security guards, Nick stared directly into Nullman's eyes, focusing his newly awoken mental powers on her face alone. He concentrated his mind, intent on bursting the Nobel-Prize-winning brain situated in that lowly, backward skull into a million different pieces.

Nullman lit yet another cigarette and blew several smoke rings at him through a fresh-looking pair of luscious, burgundy lips.

She's reapplied, a small part of Nick's head thought, suddenly. That ice-cold vixen has gone and reapplied . . .

'Phase One complete,' Nullman said, as Doctor Valesco injected his syringe into Nick's arse.

CHAPTER FIVE

'Scorcher and the Taffer'

Another portentum.

Nick watched the surface roll under him as he flew once more over the vast cosmic scalp.

Blown by a powerful solar gale, Nick passed over what looked to him like a pair of vast, oval lakes: immense cyan-blue ponds reflecting the starry heavens, yet marked all over by an intricate network of crimson vegetation shimmering below the surface. This blood-red mesh appeared to float among the swirling torrents as Nick moved closer to the two lakes. Then he suddenly rose at speed, as though propelled by some powerful gust of energy from below. As Nick ascended above the two lakes, he gradually discerned two gigantic swirling eddies at the heart of each pool. Vast, spinning whirlpools of deepest, darkest black.

Eyes.

He was looking down at a pair of gigantic eyes.

His eyes.

Nick woke with a yell and found that, actually, the eyes weren't his after all, and instead belonged to the head of a large golden retriever staring directly into his own. The dog's muzzle was resting in a gap between Nick's feet, its jaws a mere yard from his vulnerable genitalia. Nick froze, keeping perfectly still, aware now that he was in some form of waiting room, spread-eagled on another gurney with multiple wires still plugged to his head. These connected him, he saw as he risked a brief glimpse leftward, to a portable power pack attached to a near-to-bursting catheter unit.

'Easy, boy,' he said, turning again to the dog.

The animal's eyes were a different colour now, glowing a metallic pink. As Nick watched, two iron clasps shot forth from the gurney's handrails, securing themselves around Nick's wrists.

'What the . . .?'

As the dog's eyes shone an even brighter pink, a larger clasp sprung from the underside of the gurney and arced itself over Nick's chest, encasing his exposed midriff, trapping him against the trolley.

Dammit. This dog was psychic.

But I'm psychic too, thought Nick. Or at least, I was. Somehow, Nick was no longer quite feeling the godlike rage within that he recalled having been awakened by his encounter with the God Socket. Perhaps the effect wore off once he'd been disconnected from the device. Concentrating his mental energies, Nick tried to blow the dog's innards inside out. He loved animals, but golden retrievers were like wasps. Viciously aggressive, dangerous, and borderline lethal when swarming. Mankind was better off without them. He felt a familiar surge of psychic power welling up within his brain. There was something left inside there, after all.

Yet no sooner had the hound's bodily integrity begun reforming itself as Nick focused his psychic stare on the beast's rump, than the creature's eyes glowed pink again, more fiercely than before. Suddenly, two jets of pink flame shot outward, towards Nick's eyes, nullifying his own burst of psychic mind-force midway, angling the trajectory downward, towards the region of Nick's exposed loins. As a white-hot burning sensation commenced to singe his particulars, the former author-turned-doomed-airline-pilot lost all control of his own concentrated burst of psychic energy, relenting at last to the unabated discharge of canine brain-lasering from this most psychic of mutts.

As the dog's two streams of pinkened flame hovered mere millimetres from the outer nestage of Nick's scrotal sack, they suddenly ceased.

He'd been spared.

'You crazy cur,' gasped Nick, shaking his frazzled head in disbelief. 'You nearly fried my future progeny.'

Then Nick saw it. A glare in the retriever's eyes. Almost a smile, he sensed. And he knew then that the creature had been merely toying with him. The dog had no intention of letting his balls go after all. As the retriever's eyes glowed pink again, Nick prepared himself for the worst.

Then a voice rattled loudly across the room in pidgin Welsh. 'Look you!' it rasped.

The dog bounded instantly from Nick's imperilled groin, skittering itself over the shiny waxed floor in pursuit of a sudden sprinkling of rolled snacks.

Nick looked up as a tall, heavyset figure struggled to enter the room via the doorway opposite. The man was broad-shouldered and evidently blind, his featureless eyes protruding from both sockets like two bulbous orbs of blanched scallop. He was struggling to determine the position of the doorframe, smacking a long, thick cane against both sides. Nick soon realised this cane was in fact a giant leek, hardened into a solid club, its surface lacquered with some form of ceramic glaze.

The man's sorry excuse for a lab coat was formed from bright red flannel, resembling a type of shawl or poncho. From it hung a collection of rudimentary charms and what looked to Nick like small dream-catchers. These dangled variously from the man's pockets, shoulders and ears.

His baggy trousers, meanwhile, were coloured the pale green of a freshly harvested broad bean. Both legs were tucked tightly into a pair of chestnut-brown leather riding boots, dating, Nick hazard-guessed, from around the early nineteenth century.

The man's greying hair was long, thick and dusted with yellowing nicotine. Matted tufts hung low on either side of his face, which itself bore a tattooed image on one cheek of a monstrous leek next to a double-decker bus, with the legend 'Llangollen '67' emblazoned in red beneath.

Slanting inward atop the man's head stood a traditional Welsh hat, tall and speckled with dust. Nick could see why, as the man bashed it hard against the top frame of the door as he staggered through, stooping clumsily to gain full entrance. The long, polished leek in his right hand smacked to and fro across the floor, upending ornaments and knocking items of laboratory equipment to the ground.

'Look you,' the man bellowed again, smashing Nick's IV pole sideways with a large sweep of his leek.

'No, look *you*,' snapped Nick, as the large bag of bladder waste teetered for a second on the precipice, then rocked back again into its former standing position.

'Don't you worry 'bout that there bastard dog, boyo,' said the man, raising his leek suddenly upward above his head, before slamming it down again across the gurney's side rails, striking a hidden catch that instantly freed Nick's clasps. The man then flung an outstretched hand in the region of Nick's feet and waited for him to shake it.

'Up here,' said Nick.

The man ducked instinctively at something in the air, then turned his head and arm stiffly to the left.

'Wrong end.'

The man turned again, rotating his body in the opposite direction, until at long last his hand was pointing in the general area of Nick's body.

45

Nick angled himself forward a couple of feet, guided the man's arm towards his own, and shook it.

'Nick Steen,' said Nick.

'The Taffer,' replied the man, who was known to all simply as the Taffer. Although his pale eyes sported no orbs, their cloudy irises burned deep with an ancient wisdom, Nick sensed. Maybe, Nick wondered then, this was one of *them*. One of the last living descendants of the True Welch, that race of beleaguered Old Ones mercilessly pushed westward by the marauding Anglo-Saxon hordes back in the early seventeenth century. A noble race of once-heroic hunter-gatherers, now condemned to scrape a meagre existence in disparate groups scattered across a craggy grey wasteland known to the authorities as Wales, many packed cruelly into the blighted badlands of Cardiff and Swansea, still practising their Old Religion of Ancient Celticum, trading leeks for soil deposits in the vain hope of a decent agricultural income one day, all the while hawking loudly into spittoons for pennies at carnival freak shows.

Here, in the heart of Nulltec, far from the relative security of the creature's native bogland, there stood before Nick a living, breathing example of this oppressed, once mighty civilisation.

The Welchman.

'I come in peace,' said Nick, aware that the old chieftain's glazed leek could probably fell an ox.

'You have to watch out for that Scorcher, you see,' said the Taffer, coaxing the golden retriever away from Nick's groin again with a fresh handful of dog biscuits. 'Not that I can watch out myself, look you,' he laughed, pointing up at his buggered eyes. 'On account of my eyes, you see. Or lack of them!' he roared, loudly.

'Yes, I see.'

'Lucky for you, boyo! Because I certainly don't!' he roared again, even louder.

46

'I get the picture,' said Nick.

'What picture? Where?' the Taffer said, looking blindly around the room. 'What in God's name's a picture, anyway, when it's at home? I can't see a bloody thing, me.'

'A picture is a visual illustration of something.'

'And what the bloody hell's a visual illustration, might I ask? What's "visual"? I have no vision. And what's this "something" you be blathering on about, boyo? Could be anything with me, that. Given I can't see a bloody thing, on account of me having no eyes in my own head, look you.'

Nick felt his temper rising, then saw that the Taffer was no longer laughing. The old Welchman's expression had grown suddenly grave.

'*But . . .*' said the Taffer, reaching upward with his free hand to tap the side of his head. '*I see all.*'

Unnerved, Nick looked away from the Welchman's cloudy eyes and watched the dog gobble up its last biscuit, then sit, licking both its testicles for stray crumbs.

'Scorcher, is it?' drawled Nick. 'An apt moniker. Who, or *what*, taught that hound to throw flame?'

'He's part of Project Inferno,' growled the Taffer, moving round behind Nick to grab the gurney's handles, inadvertently knocking a large jug of water to the floor. 'Oh, now look what I've bloody done. If I *could* look, that is.'

'What's Project Inferno?' said Nick, attempting to head things off at the pass.

'Well, I shouldn't really be telling you, boyo,' the man said as he wheeled Nick over towards the door before slamming him into a neighbouring wall instead. He widened his mouth considerably for his next sentence. 'For the project, you see, is still active.'

Despite the mass of wires fixed to the back of his head, Nick could still feel a large spray of saliva striking home as the Taffer hawked his unholy mix of glottal stops and harsh consonants in the direction of Nick's skull. 'Project Inferno, you see, is a programme designed to turn domestic animals into potential arsonists.'

'As a weapon for the government, I presume?' asked Nick, prying, as the Taffer reversed, then slammed him once more into the wall.

'Nulltec don't "officially" engage in any kind of nefarious activity, Mr Steen. Officially, they're turning these dogs into fire-projecting killers so we can send them into flooded areas to assist with drainage issues. And we could do with some of that in Llangrannog, if I'm honest. Which generally, I'm not.'

Drainage issues? That's bullshit, thought Nick. Then felt his spine judder a third time as he was once again rammed into a wall.

'I can walk, by the way.'

'No, no, boyo, you sit there. Old Taffer will take you where you need to go.'

'Go right about half an inch, *then* move forwards,' Nick snapped, grumpily.

'And what's half an inch, when it's at home?' replied the Taffer, nevertheless doing as Nick instructed.

Nick breathed a sigh of relief. Finally, they were moving through the doorway into the corridor beyond. 'If that dog's a fire-projector . . .' he began.

'A *flamer*,' interrupted the Taffer, showering Nick's neck with spit again. 'That's the technical phrase.'

'*Flamer*,' Nick continued, trying his best to ignore the shower of saliva. 'Then how come it was also able to activate the metal clasps on this gurney?'

'Like I say, boyo, the project backfired. Scorcher's developed powerful teleki—'

'Please don't say that word. Or at least give me a towel.'

'Powerful *additional* abilities.'

'Those damned maniacs,' muttered Nick, to himself.

'Not all of us.' The Taffer halted the trolley before shuffling his weight around it to face Nick head-on.

He wasn't sure what was about to happen. Had Nick offended the Welchman somehow? Before he could figure out what he'd done, the Taffer reached up with both hands to his dead eyes and, to Nick's horror, plucked them out. Nick screwed his own orbs shut in revulsion.

'Look you!' intoned the Taffer, sternly. '*Look . . . you . . .*'

Bracing himself, Nick opened his eyes again, expecting to see the Taffer's dry, empty sockets but finding, instead, a perfectly ordinary pair of healthy, cobalt-blue peepers.

'Egg shells, you see,' said the Taffer, winking at him while dangling his fake pale blinders on a length of grubby string. 'Glazed, boyo, like my prize leek. Llangollen, '67. Bigger than a bloody bus, it was. Shrunk a bit over the years, of course. No, I'm not blind at all, boyo . . .' The Taffer winked at Nick in mysterious fashion. 'But I see *all* . . .'

As quickly as he'd plucked them out, the Welchman popped his 'blind' eyes back in and swished his leek clumsily along the corridor again, then rammed Nick into several more walls.

'And believe me, boyo, you need eyes in this place,' said the Welchman, steering Nick towards the elevator doors.

As he was pushed inside, the gurney striking the door edge several times on the way in, Nick caught sight of the Taffer's face staring blindly ahead of them, reflected back to him in the mirrored wall panel.

'Look you, Nick Steen,' the Welchman whispered, gravely, as if suddenly afraid of being overheard. 'Remember it well. *Look you . . .*'

★

The lift doors opened on to a thin, rectangular-shaped room. Banks of monitors and computer equipment lined every wall except one,

49

which itself consisted almost entirely of a wide plane of glass. The Taffer wheeled Nick up to what he saw was an observation window overlooking a large lecture theatre below. Nick leaned forward in the gurney and detected rows of tiered seating leading down to a semi-circular stage. On the distant platform stood five lecterns, each spot-lit by studio-grade lighting, with a microphone wired up to each one.

As Nick watched, the seats below him began filling up with various scientists and technicians, watched by assorted representatives in dark suits, whom Nick realised formed yet more of Nulltec's significant security detail. Evidently an important event of some kind was imminent.

So entranced was Nick becoming with the milling experts below that he failed to notice another team of assistants simultaneously entering the observation area behind him.

'I sincerely hope you will cooperate with Phase Two,' said Nullman, approaching from Nick's rear. The Taffer turned Nick around so he was facing her. 'Just so you know, we have Scorcher on standby,' she added.

'That mutt takes the damned biscuit, and I mean that literally, Nullman. Five schmackos were all that stood between my genitals and tomorrow's poop bag.'

'The canine's aggression is largely a side-effect,' explained the chief scientist. 'A result, we believe, of connecting up its genitals to the God Socket, instead of its tail.'

Nullman stood aside to reveal Dr Valesco approaching from an adjacent room, wheeling in the device to which Nick had previously been connected. Several assistants followed the doctor in, carrying the chair itself and the length of cable protruding from the machine's lid. As Nick watched, they began connecting the cable's socket to the outlet above the chair's oval head restraint.

'We'll try plugging it in first this time,' said Nullman. 'I think the issue may have been a faulty connection.'

'Balls,' said Nick. 'You supercharged me psychically, Nullman, and you know it. For what reason? What nefarious purpose am I, and by literal extension, the God Socket, serving here?'

'You can plug him in now,' said Nullman, ignoring him.

'With pleasure,' replied Doctor Valesco, squeezing a large glob of luminescent pink jelly on to Nick's pate. 'Conducting gel,' he said, enigmatically.

As Nick felt himself start to panic again, he caught sight of Nullman tugging on a pair of thin surgical gloves. At the bruising snap of swiftly-released Latex, she ushered Valesco aside and reached out with both hands, smoothing the gel into Nick's pate with her fingers in a circular, almost-sensual motion.

Not again, thought Nick, becoming instantly aroused. Distracted against his will by Nullman's cranial massage, Nick shut his eyes, trying hard to think of Stalkford and ignore her gentle, sensuous squeezing. In this state, he failed to notice the God Socket, and connecting chair, being wheeled over to the window behind him.

Then he screamed, eyes snapping open again as he felt himself being hoisted up from the gurney and into the seat now positioned directly beside him.

'What are you doing to me?'

'Relax, boyo,' said the Taffer, wheeling the empty gurney aside. Nick glanced down at the God Socket beside him, hearing the familiar grinding sound coming from within the box, while intermittent bursts of acrid smoke escaped around the sealed edge of the riveted cable plate.

Then what felt like a large metallic toilet-roll tube plunged downward once more into Nick's skull, its circular steel blade rooting itself inward through Nick's previous incision.

Again his mind went dizzy as the anaesthetic serum contained within the oval helmet went to work.

When Nick roused his head from drowsiness moments later,

Nullman was beside him, watching the crowd in the lecture hall below. Hearing Nick fart loudly, she turned to face him.

'Charming,' she said. 'Welcome back.'

'I'm not in control of my physical faculties,' said Nick, slurring.

'Evidently,' she replied, nodding downward at Nick's lingering shame.

'Look, it just won't go, alright?' he said, half suspecting Nullman was manipulating the damned thing via medical means.

'Please,' she said, signalling for Nick to look downward at the crowd gathered in the lecture theatre below. The place was full now, Nick saw, and there was a palpable air of expectation rising in the hall.

One of Valesco's assistants flicked a switch on a nearby computer and two wall speakers angled above Nick's head began piping in sound from below.

As the lights in the lecture hall dimmed, Nick observed a grey-haired scientist walk out on to the stage. The seated audience grew silent.

'That's Professor Torch,' whispered Nullman. 'The running joke being that he *never* runs out of batteries. Which, I must confess, I don't get.'

Don't get? Nick stared up at her, incredulous. 'You can take it from me, Nullman,' he said, shaking his head in disbelief. '*That's* funny.'

Below them, Professor Torch stood shuffling papers at one of the lecterns, then reached into his lab coat for his reading glasses, only to draw out a flashlight instead.

The audience, and Nick too, burst into violent howls of laughter.

'That guy's just got it,' said Nick, half-choking. 'He's just *got* it.' Nullman remained silent, unmoved and stony-faced. Christ, thought Nick. Lighten up, woman.

As Professor Torch feigned sudden recollection, tutting long-sufferingly to himself, he reached into his other pocket instead and brought out . . . a *second* flashlight.

52

Nick practically doubled up, striking the pane loudly as he laughed.

'Be careful!' snapped Nullman, suddenly yanking Nick's hand from the glass. 'It's vital you don't draw any attention to yourself.'

'Whatever you say, lady,' said Nick, rolling his eyes. He felt vaguely relieved, though. With this level of everyday wry humour around at Nulltec, maybe being incarcerated in this place wouldn't be quite so bad, after all.

But his smile dried up as his mind suddenly took in the full impli-cation of Nullman's words. 'What do you mean, don't draw attention to myself?'

'This is mirrored glass,' said Nullman. 'Meaning you can see them, but they can't see you.'

'Now why would that be important?' wondered Nick, as he turned his attention back to the lecture hall. Professor Torch had finally found a pen – behind his ear, where it had been hiding all along, much to his audience's amusement – and was now in the process of introducing five guest speakers currently waiting in the wings.

'Turn it up,' said Nullman.

Valesco's assistant twisted a dial, increasing the volume of the walled speakers. Nick craned his neck, listening carefully to the Professor's speech.

'. . . for tonight's winner of the Nullman Prize for Literature is unique in his field and regarded by many as a ground-breaking author of truly visionary horror . . .'

Nick glanced up at Nullman. She smiled down at him, then winked. Unsure what was happening, or *about* to happen, Nick turned back to the window with a vague sense of apprehension, mixed with nascent pride at his own achievements.

'And yet, of course,' continued Professor Torch from below, 'he is anything but. To discuss Mr Steen's woeful output, which even now threatens the very existence of Mankind, and to dissect in full the dearth of literary quality in his published works, along with their stunningly poor sales figures of late, please welcome to the stage a gathering of Stalkford's most esteemed literary critics.'

Nick felt a rush of repressed fury as five figures entered the lecture theatre from the stage wings, each clutching a coloured ring-binder in their hands, along with assorted copies of Nick's books. One by one, the critics took their places behind the arranged lecterns and stared out across the packed assembly.

Nick knew them all. And though they might call *themselves* critics, Nick had always referred to them as arseholes. For these five were the most savage, illiterate hack reviewers he'd ever had the displeasure of being quoted by. For decades, Nick had been forced to endure a litany of appalling reviews from all five, year after year, scorned paperback masterpiece after scorned paperback masterpiece.

They were all pricks.

Though he hated giving these wankers the time of day, Nick could nevertheless name all five if he had to, and quote verbatim from their scathing reviews, to boot.

Foremost among them was Jay Jakum, who'd obliterated Nick's ground-breaking body-horror novel *The Water Boatman*, in which a doomed scientist accidentally turns himself into half a water boatman, and must then find a way to reverse the procedure while having only oars for hands. Then there was Bunty Hosewood, the self-styled 'human mouth', who'd routinely decimated Nick's long-running gothic crime series *Frank Stein, PI*, even though she'd apparently grown up reading them all before self-discovering they were 'all wrong'.

After her came Nev Whist, a former MA student at Leeds Polytechnic who'd based his university thesis around Nick's gothic vampire classic *Vroloks*. The thesis had been subsequently published as *Total Vroloks (More Like)* and was in short a damning critique of the novel, which Nick only discovered while browsing its pages, having already signed and publicly endorsed multiple copies for a modest fee. Sturgeon Rank, who'd famously burned multiple copies of Nick's books in the car park behind Stalkford's library during a visit to promote his own gardening crime series, came next, followed almost immediately by Glinda Arrow, a writer of horror fiction for the Young Adult market, whom Nick was convinced wanted to get inside Rank's pants. She frequently stole ideas from Nick's books, dumbing them down for her illiterate readership.

Nick had eventually grown so tired of their public takedowns of his oeuvre that he'd hired a local hitman to bump them all off, only to discover said hitman was in fact a fraudulent tradesman, and had in reality spent the entirety of Nick's deposit on a cheap package holiday for him and his family, knowing full well Nick wouldn't be able to sue him for blatantly reneging on their deal, owing to the potential illegality inherent in its apparent sanctioning of mass murder.

'I don't want to watch this,' said Nick, as Jay Jakum shuffled the papers in his hands and began to speak.

'And yet you will,' replied Nullman.

As Jakum commenced his latest public takedown of Nick's supposed 'achievements', Nick closed his mind, clamping his hands over both ears. Despite this attempt to muffle the noise from below, he was still able to distinguish the words 'excruciating', 'risible' and 'purple prose', before his arms were yanked from his head by Valesco's men and clamped tightly to the arms of the chair.

Which is when Nullman said, 'Press button two.'

Panicked, Nick glanced left, horrified, as Dr Valesco pressed the button marked 'More Powerful'.

'What the hell?' cried Nick, as a sudden spark of pink flame shot forth from the God Socket, travelling fast through the connecting cable into Nick's head. As the box began to smoke, Nick felt his body convulse with a violent surge of electrical power, contorting his limbs into unearthly shapes as a more powerful voltage of energy coursed through his brain. He was smoking now, like the God Socket beside him, and amid the fumes he felt himself burning up. A seething rage, centred at first in what felt like the very depths of his brain, coursed through his veins like a stream of molten lava, pumping boiling blood through his arteries as the bruised ego within him swelled to murderous proportions.

Destroy them, said the same voice in Nick's head. *Destroy them all.*

No, Nick thought. Because he knew the voice wasn't his. It was the God Socket speaking, surely. Some kind of malevolent deity contained in that small metal box beside him . . . Surely Nick Steen wasn't capable of such an evil, destructive force?

But then, hadn't Nick already invested £100 of his own money on a failed assassination ploy? Wasn't this destructive voice in his head in fact merely a magnified manifestation of those destructive powers of darkness already lying dormant in his own mind?

Destroy them all.

That voice again. Ordering him. Compelling him. Forcifying him. Nick fought against his own worst instincts to silence the command, but that meant that all he could hear was a tidal wave of mocking laughter from below as each critic read aloud passages from Nick's books, gleefully tearing out each offending page before casting it into the baying crowd, like some macabre trophy of war.

Which ultimately decided the matter.

Nick Steen *would* destroy them all . . .

CHAPTER SIX

'Phase II'

'Listen to them,' Nullman whispered into his ear. Nick, eyes wide open, stared angrily at the scene below, switching focus from Jay Jakum to Bunty Hosewood now, who was already yelling hoarsely at the gathered crowd, hurling accusations of chauvinism at Nick's sci-fi horror classic *Cleavager*. Mocking its terrifying concept of a female insect, half Amazonian warrioress, half praying mantis, that sucked in male prey via its killer cleavage, then crushed them to a slow, agonising yet softly erotic death, like a Venus flytrap, but with boobies. Which, Nick recalled proudly, had also been the book's tagline.

They were *mocking* that terrifying premise?

Then it was Nev Whist's turn to criticise perhaps the greatest and most challenging novel of Nick's middle period, *Proctologicum*. This was an alarming tale of demonic possession in which cosmetic bowel surgeon Tanya Waist is transferred to a sinister hospital wing run by Dr Winston Smithsonian, who convinces her to operate on the supposedly haunted rectum of the sinister Dr Proctologicum, with disastrous and, according to Whist's review, 'unsavoury' consequences.

Didn't the guy realise Nick had based that book on a real-life procedure his own father-in-law had undergone while still semi-conscious on the operating table, forced to watch the botched removal of his buttock-based varicose veins through a nearby camera feed, all the while overhearing malicious nurses discuss the resultant trouser-stainage which apparently even the hospital's industrial boil-wash couldn't shift?

Destroy them all.

The voice was insistent now, Nick sensed. He *had* to obey. *Had* to do its bidding.

Then it was the turn of Sturgeon Rank, ridiculing Nick's supposed contempt for grammar, even though Nick had always made it clear that grammar worked for him and *not* the other way round.

Destroy them utterly.

Then Glinda Arrow. That thieving sow who'd stolen the plot of Nick's folk-horror novel *BytchFynder General* two years previously. A story which, on paper, couldn't fail to horrify. The bone-chilling faux-historical account of an outbreak of downward erections in rural seventeenth-century Suffolk during the British Civil War. In Nick's mind-shattering vision of a world-turned upside down, human spermatozoa penetrated the earth's crust to impregnate hell-demons, which then rose upward in the form of demonic royal poodles and harassed Parliamentary procedure with their incessant yapping. A war-torn kingdom in a plague-addled land, where human conception was only possible at blasphemous 180-degree angles, with the afflicted parties seized and burned at the penis by the terri-fying Prickfinder General, who alone knew that it was entirely the fault of their wives.

Glinda Arrow had rewritten Nick's book from a female perspec-tive, which had subsequently led to a much-coveted TV adaptation later that year. Nick's own self-penned screen adaptation, meanwhile, had inspired a run of tote bags made by students, depicting a big twig demon on one side. Of which they'd sold four.

And now here she was, Glinda Arrow, loudly declaiming Nick's inferior version of *'her'* tale.

Destroy them all. Obliterate them. Decimate their hectoring non-entity-bearing heads. Bring the whole edifice down on their pontificating, egomaniacal skulls.

He felt it. That surge of power within him again; a source of terrifying psychic energy emerging from the hidden depths of his brain, spreading from its dark, fathomless depths in a tidal wave of primitive instinct and rage. Primal anger at these lowly human gazelles lined up before him, wholly unaware of their imminent demise. Soon to be quaking like quivering jelly.

Nick's waking inner eye saw himself gliding again over the contours of that vast human face. The terrifying portentum was here. Those sky-blue eyes, unblinking, uncaring, staring out into the stark impenetrable blackness of a vast, unknown cosmos towards a lone, distant planet.

A planet it would soon destroy utterly, entirely, totally and completely . . .

And irrevocably.

'He's wrestling with his R-Complex,' said Nullman, consulting the latest stream of ever-changing figures on the computer monitor behind Nick.

Valesco smiled, nodding. 'In theory, then, it should be fairly soon now.'

Nick barely heard their voices as he focused his mind on the five doomed speakers below.

Doomed, because Nick Steen was going to kill them.

Kill them, said the voice in his head.

KILL.

OBLITERATE.

DESTROY.

WIPE THEM OUT.

DO YOUR LEVEL WORST.

TEAR THEM A NEW ONE.

No, thought Nick, fighting the urge to destroy. I can't. I'm not a killer. I'm *not*.

YES, YOU ARE. YOU TRIED TO KILL THEM BEFORE, REMEMBER, SO WHAT'S SO DIFFERENT NOW? TELL ME. WHAT'S SO DIFFERENT NOW? SEE? YOU DON'T HAVE AN ANSWER.

NOW KILL THEM.

DESTROY THEM ALL.

REND THEIR MISERABLE BRAINS FROM CEREBELLUM TO CRANIUM. BRING THE SKY ITSELF DOWN ON THEIR POMPOUS, SMUGGERY-SMIRCHED SKULLS.

Nick watched in horror as the heads of the five speakers started to pulsate. Subtly, at first. A gentle, almost indistinguishable thickening that seemed to make each head resemble, for a brief, unsteady moment, cotton buds dipped in water. Then, all too soon, they were rapidly expanding. Swelling. Ballooning like inflating party decorations. Until, from Nick's position behind the glass pane above them, the five critics resembled a row of life-sized human Pez dispensers.

What's happening to me? Nick thought. What's happening to *them*, more like? What the hell am I doing?

It was all down to him. Nick was certain of that. Because despite part of his brain staring at this ongoing transformation with objective eyes, another part of his mind, the part that was emerging from the depths of his newly-awakened psychic soul, was willing these people to their deaths. This was the part of him that now pumped outward from the brain, having been energised by the unknown powers of the God Socket beside him; determining the method of their own destruction. Ballooning the bastards into oblivion.

Not that Nick particularly cared about them, but he was an author, wasn't he? A part-time airline pilot? He didn't want to end up like some sort of psychic super-soldier developed by the Nulltec Corporation.

Which is when Nick realised what was *really* going on. Surely, he'd inadvertently hit upon the dastardly plan at work in this remote and largely unknown technical research facility? They were training Nick up, of course. Fast-tracking his emerging psychokinetic powers to serve *them*. Fooling Nick into thinking they were helping him, assuring him that they were here to seal up the hole in his mind, to plug the gap through which his rampant imagination was emerging, when all along they had no interest in that at all. Instead, they were intent on developing his telekinetic powers, exacerbating their effect and severity in order to turn him into some sort of psychic killing machine.

No doubt they were using Nick's buried R-Complex – that deep-rooted reptilian instinct in the human mind also known as the basal ganglia or basal nuclei, containing the brain stem, limbic region and the amygdala – against him in order to use it, in turn, against others.

That was the voice deep inside Nick's head. The voice of his R-Complex, that deep-rooted reptilian instinct also known as the basal ganglia or basal nuclei, containing the brain stem, limbic region and the amygdala.

These bastards were turning Nick's own R-Complex against him. Using his own deep-rooted reptilian instinct also known as the basal ganglia or basal nuclei, containing the brain stem, limbic region and the amygdala, against *his own mind*.

DESTROY THEM ALL.

WATCH THESE ARSEHOLES BLOW.

'No . . .' muttered Nick as the five heads below him continued to expand outward, widening as the so-called experts housed within them began to scream and shriek in horror at their sudden cranial swelling. The assembled audience gathered in the seats in front of them rose as one, fleeing in blind panic as they scrambled over seats in an effort to reach the exit doors at the back of the room. Nick watched as they clambered over each other in a desperate bid to escape the hideous monstrosities on the stage behind; surging through the cramped space in shocked and frightened mobs, inadvertently crushing each other underfoot in a frenzied effort to escape. But as chaos reigned, the heads of the five speakers continued to grow. Their bulbous eyes were screwed shut in paroxysms of agony as the intense pressure in their gargantuan heads increased.

'They're about to explode!' yelled someone in the audience, and with that, fresh panic ensued. Frantic hands rattled at doors, doctors fought doctors, and Nick realised in horror that the way out had been blocked. The exit doors were all sealed. But by whom, the good part of Nick's brain wondered. By Nulltec? Had Nulltec themselves locked all the doors?

NO. I LOCKED THEM, YOU FOOL.

'The psychic power swelling within him has locked all the doors,' said Valesco, observing the imprisoned co-workers below them, scrabbling like crazed rats around the sealed exits. 'He's locked them in via psychic means.'

'He's quite dangerous,' said Nullman.

I AM INDEED. BLOODY DANGEROUS. THAT'S ME. NICK 'BLOODY DANGEROUS' STEEN.

'No matter,' Nullman continued, an inquisitive expression on her face. 'It's quite fascinating.'

'We'll need to boil-wash everyone's lab coats,' said Valesco. 'Brain matter is even harder to shift than rectal eruptions.'

'We can buy new lab coats,' Nullman tutted, shifting her gaze between Nick's crazed expression and the chaos unfolding in the hall below.

'Ease up, boyo,' whispered the Taffer, suddenly, right in Nick's ear. 'Unlock those doors, look you.'

IGNORE THAT WELCH FOOL AND POP THESE HEATHEN.

PORTENTUM

The voice in Nick's head was distinct now. A deep, rich, booming resonance, like Richard Burton's – or Robert Powell's, who'd done a fair number of Nick's audiobooks over the years, until he'd attempted to up his fee yet again and Clackett had gone with Joe Swash instead.

POP THEIR BRAINS. BALLOON THEM INTO HIGH HEAVEN.

'I will,' replied Nick to himself, concentrating his psychic powers on the swelling heads below, willing them to expand even more. Urging the taut skin on their skulls to stretch ever more thinly over their screaming faces; forcing the blood in their brains to boil and froth in a spinning whirlpool of cranial death. Nick *commanded* them to explode.

EXPLODE, said the voice like Richard Burton's or Robert Powell's in Nick's head. *BURST THOSE BALLOONS.*

'Ease up, boyo!' whispered that other voice in Nick's ear, more frantically now. Whose voice was it? thought Nick. Who used to call him 'boyo'?

POP THEM. POP THEM NOW.

'Ease, up, I said, boyo!'

POP. POP. POP.

'No!' yelled Nick, suddenly aware of who had been whispering in his ear. The Taffer, of course!

He looked down. The old Welchman was floundering on the floor beside him, pretending to scrabble about for his dropped leek. After all this, the Taffer had come to Nick's rescue.

Nick screwed his eyes shut against the sight of those swelling, monstrous heads, which were no longer below him, Nick realised now, but floating upward, towards the ceiling, appearing to stare directly at Nick through the mirrored glass, their ties, cravats and necklaces dragging below like lengths of string at some crazed, demonic funfair.

Nick forced his gaze away from that terrible sight, willing the unleashed psychic forces within him to surge backward, dammit. *Backward*. Backward into that damned box beside him.

'Back!' Nick yelled suddenly, blasting the full force of his psychic powers in the opposite direction, straight back into the God Socket.

The sparking, smoking plug shot upward from Nick's head restraint amid a showering geyser of blood, bone and plastic fragments, landing like a writhing snake on the observation deck floor, crackling and fizzing with electrical energy as shards of metal wiring cascaded downward on to the ground around it.

Dazed and drenched by the torrent of matter spattering his frazzled skull as the laws of gravity eventually kicked in, Nick steeled himself, turning to confront the scene of appalling devastation he knew awaited him in the lecture hall below . . .

And saw that he'd succeeded, after all. By some miracle, Nick's good side had stopped the horror in time.* The heads hadn't exploded, after all. They were all still there, all five of Nick's critics, bobbing against the ceiling like giant Mylar balloons.

Swollen, but alive.

Nick gasped in relief. He was a good man, after all. At some point, he presumed, their giant heads would deflate, and no doubt they would all be escorted from the premises, chastened but alive. Hopefully with their egos suitably bruised. Then things would be better, Nick vowed. They'd learn it was Nick Steen alone who'd saved them,† and immediately amend their published critiques of his work via some form of joint official public retraction. It was going to be okay, after all, Nick thought. He'd single-handedly saved the day.‡

* Although not quite a miracle, obviously. It was largely down to the Taffer's actions. I dare say an editor, had I allowed one, would have pointed this out. But they wouldn't have stopped at this note alone. Hence a footnote by yours truly. GM
† Again, technically with the Taffer's help, but Nick is the hero here, hence me retaining my version of the preceding paragraph. GM
‡ See above notes.

Valesco's voice sounded coldly through the lecture room speakers.

'Burst them.'

Nick whipped his head around, catching Valesco's sly grin as the doctor lowered the microphone from his mouth, and glanced over at Nullman.

'Phase Two complete,' she said.

At the sound of gunfire, Nick turned back to the windowpane, watching in horror as the giant heads were burst into streaking flesh ribbons one by one. As Nulltec's security detail went to work with their issued airguns, what remained of each ballooned critic rocketed madly around the room at terrifying speeds while the popped head rapidly deflated, two eventually striking the mirrored glass in front of Nick with a sickening slap, before descending like shreds of torn rubber to the ground.

If Nick could have grabbed the syringe from Valesco's approaching hand, he would have injected himself.

CHAPTER SEVEN

'Psychotropia'

The lips of the vast mouth were parted as the plane plunged past, narrowly avoiding a descent into the dark and imposing chasm between them. Those vast teeth, Nick saw, were mountainous rocks grinding dust from solar winds generated by his aeroplane's arcing death-spin, as Nick wrestled with the controls of his stricken jumbo. Briefly, he caught sight of the structure's giant right upper lateral incisor as he spiralled past its widened jaw. The position of the tooth was set slightly back in the structure's broad palate, just behind what looked to Nick like the upper central incisor and right upper canine. He couldn't tell from this height if the lower third molar on the right-hand side of the colossal jaw he was spiralling away from was missing or not, but he suspected that it was.

He shuddered in a sudden fit of cosmical horror, remembering again the hideous reality of this terrifying portentum.

This enormous floating head in the sky was his *own*.

Yet there was worse to come. For, as Nick's plane soared further past the face that was his beyond all doubt now (it was now wearing his glasses), Nick made out what looked like a vast body floating in the endless black beneath the colossal sphere he was traversing.

But this body, unlike the head above it, was *not* his own.

PORTENTUM

This body, though Nick could barely believe it, was the black, yellow-spotted body of a gargantuan *salamander*.

Nick mewed like a choked kitten, his ailing sanity detonated anew by this awe-inducing revelation.

Then suddenly he woke . . .

. . . to find the vast head staring at him still, its bald pate now a mass of floating snakes, a bit like a Man-Gorgon.* Yet Nick's existential predicament had somehow worsened, for the face confronting him was semi-transparent, meaning that the terrifying cosmic deity of his nightmarish portentum had somehow escaped from his subconscious mind and penetrated the conscious realm too, both of which are technically housed fairly close to each other inside the brain, yet for practical purposes might as well be immeasurable distances apart unless one possesses some sort of psychic key with which to unlock said doors of perception. Nick, he realised in horror, had evidently now acquired that key.

That awful psychic eye in Nick's unconscious mind had somehow been opened . . .

The rest of Nick's body came to with a start as he began to thrash, the vast head before him swinging left to right in an identical display of panic.

It was his own reflection.

Nick heard a muffled metallic yanking noise from somewhere below, followed by a muted gurgling sound.

As a rush of bubbles rose rapidly from beneath, tickling the underside of his muscular man-breasts, Nick realised he was underwater.

A row of pink lights flared suddenly on either side of his body, and he found that he was submerged within some form of glass tank; an

---

* Not strictly Grecian canon, but the alternative legend is, in many ways, superior. See my novel *The Man-Gorgon* and its sequels *Guygon, Galgon, Bride of Guygon, Guygon vs Galgon, Galgon Rising* and *Guygon 2012 (Stone Free)*. GM

enclosed container connecting him via wires and cables to various sensor pads and monitoring machines on either side.

As the draining fluid level sank beneath Nick's head, he chattered with sudden cold and took off his oxygen mask.

The cabling that had hitherto been floating wildly around and over his head, impressing upon his dreaming brain an image of writhing snakes, now flopped down over his bedraggled face like drained spaghetti from a restaurant serving spoon.

'Five days, ten hours and seventeen minutes. I do believe that's a record, boyo,' said a voice Nick knew only too well as the tank's plexiglass doors suddenly parted. What remained of the fluid drained away through a plughole in the floor as the Taffer extended his ceramic leek in Nick's direction and parted the dripping cables from his face.

'You've been in what they call a sensory deprivation tank,' spat the Welchman. 'And anything over five days is a bloody record, I reckon. Most folks drown, you know.'

Nick coughed up a mouthful of liquid from his throat. 'What the hell is this stuff?'

'Mainly water,' said the Taffer. 'Mixed with bodily fluids and assorted faecal matter. Five days' worth.'

Nick heaved.

'Grab hold of my leek.'

Nick reached out, clutching the leek with both hands, and felt himself being tugged out from the tank on to yet another waiting gurney. Disorientated, yet determined, Nick realised this might be his only chance of escape, but as he prepared to make a run for it, he caught sight of Scorcher, the psychic, laser-wielding golden retriever, standing once more with its face between his feet.

The dog licked its slavering jaws.

'Not *you* again,' said Nick, as the retriever's eyes glowed a fresh shade of metallic pink. Nick felt the cabling in his head begin to move.

PORTENTUM

In a tall mirror opposite, Nick watched as the multiple wires rearranged themselves into various hairstyles. An initial subtle mullet wasn't too bad, Nick thought, and the subsequent rockabilly quiff was a style Nick made a solid mental note to remember, yet soon these styles morphed into a frightful Pat Cash-style mane and the kind of tightly curled, frizzy perm perennially sported by Nick's estranged wife, Jacinta.

'Bog off, Scorcher,' said the Taffer, tossing a handful of dog biscuits into a far corner of the room. Immediately, the two pink laser jets rearranging Nick's cabling suddenly fizzled away, and the sodden clump of wiring dropped down again over his shoulders as the dog bounded off for its latest breakfast.

'Dumb mutt,' said Nick, flipping it the bird. Except it wasn't a dumb mutt, Nick realised, a fact borne out almost immediately as the dog extended its own front leg and flipped Nick a small mound of fur in the middle of the front paw.

'You helped me back, there,' said Nick to the Taffer, ignoring the dog. He looked up at the reflection of the Welchman, who began wheeling Nick out of the sensory deprivation unit and into yet another featureless corridor. 'Why? By the way, please refrain from smacking me into walls. I know you're not really blind.'

The Taffer smacked Nick into a wall. 'Have to keep up the old appearances, look you,' he replied, tapping his massive leek against each neighbouring wall in a token effort to supposedly judge distance.

'You didn't answer my question,' said Nick.

But before the Taffer could provide Nick with an answer, he slowed down the gurney and flashed his ID card over a sensor in the adjacent wall, pretending to get it wrong twice beforehand. A hidden door slid open on their right, exposing a small gangplank that led downward.

As they made their way down, Nick caught sight of a medical

poster on the wall. Beneath the photograph of a masked surgeon levelling a lethal syringe was a short medical slogan:

Nulltec – Profits Before Ethics

'*Before*?' Nick gasped, his mouth dropping open in shock. Shouldn't that be ethics *after* profits? No, wait, profits *after* ethics. Or alternatively ethics *before* profits? Either of the latter two. But before Nick had time to make a final decision, a second poster appeared. Above a picture of several surgeons playing poker for high stakes over a shrouded patient appeared the slogan:

Nulltec – Flatlining For Your Future

'But surely there *is* no future for those who are flatlining,' queried Nick aloud. 'Unless this poster is implicitly stating there will *indeed* be a future, but for those who *aren't* flatlining, implying that the process of flatlining itself creates a better future for *others*, presumably meaning a corporate pharmaceutical elite benefiting from the illegal trade of human organs and/or psychotropic drugs, say. Something seems distinctly untoward around here.'

'Correct,' said the Taffer from behind him as they emerged from the ramp into yet another featureless corridor. 'Though Nulltec is technically a research facility, it is in fact more of a *shadowy* technical research facility.'

Nick wiped the spit from his neck.

'Though I'd never say this to Nullman's face, boyo, Nulltec is rumoured by some to possess certain *ulterior* motives. Even supposedly employing morally questionable, shall we say "nefarious", means to pursue a sinister, hidden agenda, look you.'

'I thought as much,' said Nick, as the Taffer rammed him into another wall, reversed the gurney, rammed him into the wall again,

70

reversed the gurney, rammed and reversed again, then wheeled him successfully through the exit, into a large, rectangular-shaped space divided on one side into separate rooms.

Cells, thought Nick, grimly. 'These are cells,' said Nick, grimly. 'I'm being incarcerated here, after all.'

'What's "incarcerated here" when it's at home?'

'Imprisoned,' said Nick, clarifying for the Taffer, whom Nick suspected was much thicker than him, despite possessing supposed ancient wisdom.

The Welchman ignored Nick, unlocked a door to one of the rooms in front and wheeled his patient inside. Before Nick could say another word, the Taffer let go of the gurney handles and retreated back up the ramp, slamming the door shut behind him.

'I'm an incarcerat!' yelled Nick, unable to reach the small window of thickened glass in the top half of the door behind him in order to thump it dramatically. 'An incarcerat! I.e., a prisoner!'

In vain, Nick attempted to slam the adjacent wall instead, then realised that the damned psychic golden retriever had telekinetically applied manacles to his arms once more while it had been distracting Nick with that show-off display of head-cable styling.

'Damned stupid mutt,' Nick said. Then was struck by a sudden thought. If a God Socketed dog was able to perform a range of psychic circus tricks, then why couldn't he? After all, his own powers had been hugely enhanced while connected to the God Socket. Maybe some part of that awesome telekinetic power lingered on after the event, lying dormant in Nick's subconscious psyche, waiting to be tapped at will.

Focusing his mental energies, Nick concentrated on freeing himself from the metal clasps fastening both wrists to the gurney handles. He really needed to free himself as soon as possible if he had any hope of escaping Nulltec, and also because his nether regions were itching like crazy from all the chlorine they'd evidently been

71

pumping into that sensory deprivation tank to counter the toxicity of Nick's bodily emissions.

He screwed his eyes shut and willed – no, *commanded* – the clasps over his wrists to undo.

'Undo, dammit, undo!' he yelled, giving them both a particularly piercing glare. But it was no use. Whatever powers he'd previously possessed had, for the time being, abandoned him.*

'Dammit,' he said, aloud. Then he slumped back against the trolley, allowing time for his eyes to adjust to the gloom so that he could examine the layout of his cell in more detail. Maybe he could find some other method of freeing himself.

As the darkness slowly receded, he saw that he'd been confined in what appeared to be some form of secret medical observation room. The place was coldly lit by an icy pink light shining from a small monitor-like device in the middle of the ceiling – evidently a revolving camera of some kind, Nick figured. As his eyes glanced past it, he discerned two neatly made beds on either side of the room. Their white sheets and light rose quilting reminded Nick of a hospital ward, and by the head of each one stood a small table sporting a jar of water, a plastic tumbler and a novel by some novelist Nick had never heard of called Garth Marenghi.†

Then Nick saw it. In the darkness at the far end of the room, another light. Merely a faint glow at first, but as the light expanded in size, Nick realised there was a dark patch at its centre: a solid shadow that gradually assumed a familiar form. Then Nick realised it was a human figure moving towards him. A young girl, he deduced from its silhouetted frame, one who appeared to be almost gliding in his direction, lit from behind by a strange and almost otherworldly pink light, as if the girl had stepped forth from some ethereal, heavenly plane.

* With the emphasis very much on 'time being'. GM
† Heh heh. GM

PORTENTUM

'I'm Christabel,' said the child in a light, high-pitched American accent, as she finally drew level with Nick. With the pink glow from the overhead camera device lighting up the child's front, Nick saw her rear was, in fact, illuminated by an identical device shining against her from the far end of the room, and not by the aforesaid ethereal light which had appeared to confer upon her that strange, celestial glowing. She was around ten years old, dressed in a pure-white Victorian-style nightdress, with her delicate facial features resembling a display of finest bone china. In that heavenly pink glow, she seemed almost like a ghost.

'Gwendolen . . .' whispered Nick.*

'No, I'm *Christabel*,' said the girl. 'Like I just told you, silly. And this is Persephone.'

The child held out one hand, the gown of her nightdress extending outward with it like an angel's wings, as a second figure moved towards Nick. It was another female form, yet less majestic. *Far* less majestic, decided Nick. For one thing, the person shambling their way forwards like Frankenstein's monster was taller, heavier, as if it had been gorging on pizza for two weeks solid, and singularly failing to glow mystically like the younger girl.

Instead, the pale pink light from the rear camera device seemed to clash with the unpleasant prism of horrendously matched colouring coming from the girl's messily tied-back hair. As she slapped a light switch on an adjacent wall, a stark strip light flickered on overhead, revealing a sulky-looking teenager sporting faded denim and an evident attitude problem, if those streaks of multicoloured dye in her hair and general air of tardiness was anything to go by.

'Pull yourself together,' said Nick, forgetting this wasn't a daughter he was talking to.

* This detail will assume greater importance in Tomes 2 and 3, so do clock it now. While technically not an example of literary foreshadowing, it is a case of intricate, masterful plotting. GM

73

'Screw you,' said the girl.

Nick felt a rush of adrenaline coarse through his veins at the smell of battle, but was caught short by a sudden burst of unexpected, angelic laughter.

'Tee hee,' giggled Christabel. 'Persephone's always grumpy after a big sleep.'

'She should wake the hell up and scrub that oily face,' said Nick. 'Then comb her bloody rug and scour what's left of her teeth. With a brace like that, irregular brushing is a health hazard for anyone in close proximity.'

Chastened, Persephone looked down gruffly at her shoes, scuffing the ends of her trainers against the ground, forcing both hands deep into her baggy pockets.

'Careful,' said Christabel. 'Don't make Persephone mad. Otherwise . . .'

'Otherwise what?' snapped Nick, having had just about enough of the older kid's lip.

'No!' yelled Persephone, suddenly. 'I won't do it! I won't! I won't!'

'Easy, Persephone! Try to relax!' squealed Christabel.

'Won't do what?' said Nick, unnerved by the older girl's sudden panic. 'What the hell's her problem?'

'She's disobeying them,' said Christabel.

'Disobeying who?' Nick was appalled at such an act, even if he wasn't yet sure exactly who the girl was disobeying. But hell, if this had been *his* daughter, and she dared disobey anything he'd commanded, he'd have packed her off again to that summer holiday club she'd loathed going to last year. 'Who is she disobeying?'

'The *voice*,' said Christabel. 'The voice in her head. We have to give her more time.'

Strewth, thought Nick. Why did he always end up having to give young people some damned *leeway*?

'The voice is telling her, you see . . . Ordering her . . . to . . . to . . .'

'What?' Nick yelled, losing patience with Christabel as well now. If there was one thing he couldn't stand, it was a case of double double-X histrionics. 'What is it telling her to do?'

'To *twist* you!'

Nick look confused. '*Twist* me? What the hell's twisting me when it's at home?' He hated copying the Taffer character's idiosyncratic phraseology, but in this case it was an apt phrase.

'Like this!' snapped Persephone, yanking both hands from her pockets in a swift, sudden motion. She aimed both palms towards Nick's neck, and all at once, he felt the shock of a violent tugging on his throat muscles. He grabbed himself with both hands, unsure what was happening to him as he felt his head shift leftward of its own accord. Despite his attempts to wrestle it back in the other direction, Nick's throat sinews began to burn, wrenching themselves sideways in an opposing flanking motion. In horror, Nick caught sight of a manic gleam in Persephone's eyes as his head began passing the angle of no return, threatening to twist his upper crown backward to face the door he'd just entered by.

'Leave him be, Persephone!' commanded Christabel in a particularly wise-sounding voice for a small child. But her instruction fell on deaf ears. Nick sensed his ligatures continuing to stretch, the bone muscle starting to tear free, cell by cell, as his head commenced twisting backwards, like an owl's, but with none of an owl's natural coping mechanism for this unholiest of movements.

'My . . . my neck . . . it's turning . . . twisting . . .' gasped Nick. 'Twisting . . . around . . . twisting back to front . . .' His voice became a mere garble as his eyes started to see stars.

'Persephone!' cried Christabel again, in an even more wise-sounding voice for a small child than before, and at that moment the pressure on Nick's neck suddenly lifted. He collapsed forward, gasping, his head turning round again with an unpleasant crackling sound as his loosened throat gristle slowly realigned itself.

'Right, you're *grounded*,' he croaked, hoarsely. 'That was completely unacceptable behaviour.'

'It's what Persephone does,' said Christabel. 'She's a Twister. A sort of "psychic weapon", so they say. That's why the nice lady from Nulltec keeps her in hospital here.'

My God, these kids were naive.

'Is that what she told you?'

'Mrs Nullman says Persephone's powers might be . . . "exploited" . . . by a "sinister government agency" . . . That's why nice Doctor Valesco and his funny pals have to keep her in here until they can make a magic pill to stop the twisting.'

'You two dolts,' said Nick. 'Nulltec *is* that secret and sinister government agency. You're prisoners here. Nulltec are training you, and me, as potential psychic weapons. They've been trying to turn me into some kind of telekinetic super-soldier primed to destroy all before me via thought alone, like some colossal human Demi-God or Destroyer of Worlds.'

'Oh, I don't think so,' laughed Christabel. 'You've got it wrong, silly. After all, we get milk at bedtime, and they say the cookies will be here sometime next year.'

'And I bet they give you "sleepy" sweets, right?'

'Yes!' squealed Christabel, clapping her hands with glee. 'You only have to eat one or two, and you can sleep for a whole month! Then there's cups of weak squash on cold days, and a hot meal every week!'

'What are you in here for?' Nick asked Christabel, needing to ascertain* what her own special power was. 'What's your gift?'

'They say I can make everyone in the world better,' said Christabel. 'No matter how poorly they might be. Just by me thinking it.'

My God, thought Nick. This kid was a Healer.

---

* Verb. To establish (something) for certain; make sure of. A superior word (i.e., much better) than 'find out' which is two words and what a lesser writer would have used in this instance. GM

'You can cure illness?' he asked.

'Yes, silly!' laughed Christabel. 'So that no one ever has to die or projectile vomit again. They call me a Mender.'

'"Healer" sounds better,' said Nick, staring at her in awe. He tried to imagine a world without projectile vomiting. It was insane. Unbelievable. Utopia. Here Nulltec were, in possession of a child who could cure every disease known to Man. Particularly projectile vomiting. Hell, she was a miracle worker. The New Messiah. No wonder Nulltec were keeping her under lock and key. They stood to make a fortune out of this. Either by exploiting the unsuspecting Christabel in order to manufacture an ultimate 'cure for all ills' pill, or else by making damn sure she never got anywhere near the vicinity of their competitors.

Yeah, thought Nick. Nullman and Valesco would make damn sure of that, alright.

He looked upon the two girls with sudden pity. These dumb schmucks had no idea at all what was being done to them.

'Look,' he said, gravely. 'In fact, listen. Nulltec are lying to you. They're exploiting your psychic powers. They're imprisoning Persephone here so she becomes an International Psychic Twister Assassin, and you, Christabel, are being cut off from the outside world so that you can't become a world-famous New Messiah with assorted book deals and a range of best-selling yoga and/or meditation videos. You *have* to escape from here.'

'But why, Nick?' said Christabel, becoming slightly agitated. 'Nulltec are our *friends*.'

'Really, Christabel? Do "friends" neglect to mention how much you could earn from a televised tour of public healings?'

'No . . .'

'Do friends fail to point out how much you'd earn by writing *The Bible 2: Return of the Bible*?'

'I guess not.'

'Do these so-called "friends" fail to introduce you to a writer they also have here in captivity who could easily ghost-write said Bibular sequel for you, for a modest fee plus healthy royalties percentage?'

'No, they've never mentioned it, Nick,' said Christabel, concerned.

'Precisely,' he replied. 'And for that reason, we have to get out of here. Tout suite.'

Nick focused his psychic energies on the manacles binding his hands and feet to the trolley again, trying once more to force them apart. But the metal plates encasing his limbs rattled only slightly. He just didn't possess enough power to break them yet without his head being wired up to the God Socket. Then a thought struck him. Persephone . . . Maybe she could *twist* his manacles.

'*You!*' he barked at her. 'Get off your arse and *twist* these.'

'Twist what?' Persephone murmured under her breath, rolling eyes at some imaginary friend.

'These manacles, stupid.'

She glanced over at Nick's manacles, then looked up at him, defiantly.

Christ, he'd had enough of this attitude from his own daughter.*

'Fine,' he sighed. 'I'm sorry for mocking your mouth-brace. It's actually very beautiful,' he continued, thinking on his feet, even if he didn't mean any of what he was saying. Hopefully Persephone wasn't a mind-reader as well. 'It's the sort of mouth-brace pop stars across the land would find extremely attractive, I'm sure.'

Persephone's cheeks blushed red all of a sudden, and then her face lit up in a natural smile. With a sudden burst of focused energy, the manacles on Nick's wrists and shins twisted at the hinges, then fell to the ground, broken.

Nick stretched his arms outward, flexing the muscles. 'Well done. You really do need to shift that bit of cabbage, though,' he added,

---

* Again, another example of intricate, masterful plotting. As before, clock this detail now, in order to be richly rewarded later. In Tomes 2 and 3, to be specific. GM

tapping his own teeth to indicate the offending area. 'Okay, let's find a way out of here.'

'But Nick,' whimpered Christabel, clearly still agitated. 'You *must* be wrong. Nulltec are *nice.*'

'Bollocks they are,' said Nick, resolutely failing to mind his language. These kids needed to grow up. And *fast.* If the New Messiah couldn't handle a little blue vernacular in the heat of battle against a powerful foe, she'd have to lump it. Shape up or ship out. 'They want to destroy our way of life, princess. So let's haul ass and bust this joint.'

'But they gave me a *doggy!*' squealed Christabel, tears of joy rolling from her eyes as the cell door suddenly swung open behind Nick. In bounded a panting, tail-wagging golden retriever.

'Scorcher . . .' whispered Nick.

The dog leaped up at Christabel, licking her cheeks affectionately, then danced about her in giddy circles, yelping playfully.

'That thing's a killer!' said Nick. 'It tried to burn my nappy sack.'

'It's the best doggy in the whole wide world!' sang Christabel, hugging the retriever close to her chest, nuzzling her face into its neck.

It was now or never, Nick realised. He had to make a sudden grab for the mutt's rear legs, while it was distracted, then hurl it hard against the wall. Dash its brains out in one slam so that damned kid wouldn't have a chance to heal it.

Sure, it would be traumatising, but Nick was used to the sound of female screaming. He'd get over it.

Gathering his strength, Nick breathed in tightly and lunged himself forcefully at the animal.

But failed to move an inch. In horror, he realised the manacles on his wrists had reattached themselves without him even realising it.

Reattached *themselves*? Or had they been reattached by something else?

As he glanced over at Scorcher, the dog's eyes flashed pink at him.

Then the manacles over Nick's legs locked, too.

CHAPTER EIGHT

'The Medusa Project'

As the elevator doors began to slide shut, Nick screamed a final warning at the two girls cheerily waving him goodbye from the far end of the corridor.

'You're *prisoners*!' he yelled through the closing gap. 'Incarcerats!'

'Come back and play another day!' said Christabel, as the psychic retriever's face grinned back at Nick from between the two girls. 'We can take Scorcher on a picnic! To another cell!'

'You fools!'

'Easy, boyo,' said the Taffer, behind Nick. The Welchman had turned up in the nick of time, just as Scorcher was leaping on to his gurney with the clear intention of flambéing Nick's personal pipe outlets. The Taffer had yanked Nick's gurney back into the main corridor, keeping the dog at bay with his giant, hardened leek.

As the lift doors finally shut upon them, Nick glared at the Taffer's reflection in the mirrored panelling.

'What the hell was all that for?' he yelled. 'Why take me on a detour via the Nulltec holding cells? I already knew this place had a sinister side.'

'I got the wrong bloody room, boyo,' said the Taffer. 'Thought I was on a different floor. It's these bloody eyes, you see. I can't see a damned thing, I can't.'

'Look, the Taffer, I *know* you're not blind. You pulled those plastic eggshells out once and dangled them in front of my face, remember?'

'Remember? Oh no, boyo. Me, I cannot remember a *bloody* thing, look you. Got the memory of a goldfish, I have.'

Nick closed his eyes and sighed deeply. Why was this guy pretending he was mad as a brush, when Nick knew he was all too sentient behind the mask? For what reason? Why had he wheeled Nick down to these cells? Was it merely to keep up the pretence of being an annoying blind Welchman with a stupid hat?

Unless the Taffer had suspected that Nulltec were growing suspicious of him? Maybe they'd seen him remove those false eyes in the lift via a hidden camera and he was therefore trying to cover up his mistake by acting extra stupid?

Nick watched a small digital display in the side of the elevator wall change as they ascended through the building. Beside each floor number they were passing, there appeared a small description of the corresponding floor level. Though the information vanished almost as soon as it appeared, Nick was able to glimpse several names against the corresponding wards they were rising through. *Floor 7 (Genetic Manipulation Ward and Kennels); Floor 8 (Mutant Baby Wing: Important – Crèche Closed); Floor 10 (Coma Zone, Illegal Organ Transplants plus Mailing Department); Floor 12 (Virus Outbreak Contamination and Decontainment Wing; Floor 13 (Abandoned/Derelict Space plus Equipment Cupboard (self-operating)); Floor 14 (ISEEU); Floor 15 (OT 1 – Routine Disfigurements and Shock Recovery); Floor 16 (OT 2 – Cloning, Ocular X-Ray and Bodyswap); Floor 17 (Human Recycling Plant plus Restaurant-Café); Floor 19 (General Insanity).*

As the lift reached Floor 24, marked '*The Medusa Project*' on the lift's digital display, Nick was suddenly struck by a terrifying realisation.

When they'd first dragged him into this place, he could have sworn Nulltec only had three levels. Arbitrarily shifting geography was one of Roz's frequent editorial criticisms of his fiction, and though Nick was loath to acknowledge his former editor's critical observations, he did wonder now whether Nulltec was indeed a genuine facility, or merely another bizarre figment of his own escaping imagination.

The frightening thought occurred to Nick that he could well be trapped inside one of his own stories again, albeit a tale that had evidently yet to be written. For Nick knew there was always the possibility that he'd dreamed this place up in some ideas notebook his conscious mind had long since forgotten.

'How come there are twenty-four floors?' he asked the Taffer. 'There were only three when I arrived.'

'Well, boyo, these top floors are part of ongoing stealth experiments,' said the Taffer. 'From the outside, they're invisible to the naked eye. Which is why I, more than anyone else, look you, cannot see them.'

Nick grew a little calmer. At least, then, on this occasion, he *wasn't* living in a nightmare of his own making. Even if he *was* technically still living in a nightmare of his own making. Ultimately, he guessed Nulltec had abducted him as a direct result of his leaking imagination, which itself had been brought about by his own diabolical lust for a possessed typing implement intent on conquering, then destroying, earthly reality. But even if all this *was* still a nightmare of his own making, this particular nightmare *within* a nightmare of his own making was *not* a nightmare of his own making. And for that, Nick was grateful.

'What's the Medusa Project?' asked Nick as the Taffer wheeled him out on to Floor 24. Another lengthy, endless, white-walled corridor led off into the distance.

'Top-secret security wing, boyo. Where I should have taken you in the first place. Instead of those cells downstairs. Why, if Nulltec knew I'd taken you down to th—' The Taffer gasped loudly, slamming a large hand over his mouth.

'Relax,' said Nick, sensing there may indeed have been secret purpose in the Taffer's supposed 'mistake'. For some undisclosed reason, the bulky assistant had brought Nick down to the lower cell level without anyone else in the building knowing.

Nick thought again about those two imprisoned youths. While both were deeply annoying, they were effectively dumb inno-cents. At their age, Nick figured, they ought to be left alone by sinis-ter government agencies. Ridiculed, sure. Punished, certainly. No one likes an attitude problem. But to keep them in a top-secret research facility against their will, simply to manipulate, exploit or conceal their own latent psychic powers – that took the proverbial biscuit. Nick vowed to break out of Nulltec and rescue them, if he could. And if he couldn't, whatever. The main thing was for him to get out and alert the authorities. Then they could rescue the girls. If it was even worth their while.

Nick's gurney reached the end of the corridor, pausing outside a room marked 'Observation Deck'. He realised the Taffer hadn't bashed him into a single wall along this particular corridor. Either this floor was so secret that there was no need for any hidden cameras, or the Taffer was trying to tell him something.

'Look you,' whispered the Taffer behind Nick, as he ran his ID card through another slotted lock, sliding the door in front open. 'Look *you* . . .'

That would be it then, Nick thought, nodding to himself. A subtle warning by the Taffer to look around and keep watch for something. Evidently, the place he was entering now was a particu-larly threatening environment, one where no doubt the toughest, most challenging chapter of Nick's incarceration tale would play itself out, one way or t'other, for better or worse, this way or that, by high road or low road.* It felt to Nick like the culmination of some sprawling heroic narrative. An epic journey beginning to near its dramatic conclusion. A climactic denouement in waiting, with Nick as its chief protagonist, and Nullman, say, as its main antagonist. The whole shebang was coming to a head, Nick figured. To use a writing analogy that he felt was somewhat apt, given Nick was a writer by trade, he sensed that he was heading for the final few chapters in this unfolding tale of real-life terror. One that, if this were chapter eight, say, would most likely be concluded around chapter twelve.

Not that he was in the old Act-Three doldrums just yet, to continue his writing analogy, but he was certainly nearing it. And if Nick's instincts were right, and oft they were, then said doldrums would soon be rearing their ugly head, he feared. Sooner than he wanted them to, that's for sure − in, say, chapter nine or ten of that figurative tale he felt he was inhabiting.

The Taffer pushed Nick through the open door on to a vast observation deck.

'So this is why the door was marked "Observation Deck",' Nick said as his gurney travelled through the room, once again in awkward, directionless arcs as the Taffer swiftly rediscovered his official 'blindness'. The vast room was not dissimilar to the main operating centre of Stalkford Airport's Flight Control Tower, which Nick was somewhat familiar with having used it for several illicit physical liaisons with Julia Thurscott (finally, he remembered her surname), and not completely dissimilar to the observation area overlooking the lecture theatre he'd been wheeled into earlier on.

But this room was larger than both. As if to suggest that whatever events were about to transpire might be eerily similar to, yet *infinitely worse* than, anything that had come before. As Nick felt a

---

* Feel free to add some of your own terms to this list. GM

familiar rush of anxiety flooding his mind, he thought back to those recurring psychological harbingers of doom: those terrifying portentums that had been continually plaguing his mind.

Somehow, Nick felt, this room was to be the final piece in that ongoing psychic puzzle. Whatever transpired here in the next hour or two would, he felt sure, decide whether Nick escaped or remained here a prisoner — an *incarcerat*. It might even decide whether he, nay Stalkford, too, mayhap e'en the world, lived or died.

Nick forced himself to take in his surroundings while he still had time. Against one side of the room stood a vast wall of reinforced glass, looking out in a south-westerly direction over miles of unbroken countryside. In the far distance, beneath the red sun now setting in the evening sky, he spied a familiar jagged crust of black jutting upward against the horizon like a well-picked scab.

Stalkford City.

He shifted his gaze to take in the rest of his surroundings. To the left and right of the building he was imprisoned within grew vast swathes of thick, primeval forest. Chokewood to the west, and neigh-bouring that, the old, abandoned mine (which, even more spookily, had never been inhabited in the first place). Beyond it, Nick could just make out traces of the Great Widdershins Pathway running straight through the still-unexplored depths of Stalkford's Wyrden Wodelands.

'A glorious view,' said Barbara Nullman, walking towards Nick from the far side of the space. Nick turned and saw, on the wall behind them, the now-familiar sight of banked computer terminals and beeping technical equipment. And, in front, wheeled in once more by Valesco's assistants, that familiar-looking casket, patched up on one side now with masking tape and an inverted coat hanger stuck into the top, just in front of the revolving beacon, with a disor-derly array of metallic netting, resembling a mass of silver tinsel, dangling around the back.

The God Socket.

'If you think you're plugging me up to that thing again, you've got another think coming,' said Nick.

'Wrong,' Nullman replied. '*You've* got another think coming. Quite literally.'

She took hold of the gurney's handle and wheeled Nick round again so that he was looking out once more into the open countryside.

'Phase Three of our experiment,' she continued, 'will build on previous achievements and turn you, Mr Steen, from a reluctant work-in-progress into Nulltec's first fully fledged psychic super-soldier.'

'We'll see,' said Nick, unable to think of anything more cutting owing to all the stress he'd been under.

'We've been tweaking the God Socket quite extensively while you've been floating in that sensory deprivation tank and recovering what little remained of your sanity.'

She was right there, Nick conceded. He did feel slightly saner than before. Even if the knowledge that he'd been imbibing his own efflu- ence over and over for several days now threatened to destroy that very element of sanity he'd recovered.

'I think you'll find we're quite prepared for any psychic 'resistance' you may feel you've retained,' said Nullman. She pointed abruptly outward into the stretch of open countryside beyond them. 'Look out there, Mr Steen. What do you see?'

'Stalkfordshire,' said Nick.

'And that small black stain on its horizon?'

'My home. Well, Stalkford City.'

'And beyond Stalkford City?'

'The outskirts of Stalkford City?'

'And beyond the outskirts of Stalkford City?'

'Landfill?'

Nullman sighed, becoming annoyed. 'And beyond the landfill?'

Nick finally twigged. 'Ahh, the airport.'

'Correct, Mr Steen,' said Nullman, clicking her fingers at a team of scientists filing in from a door opposite. 'Stalkford Airport. Scene of your many miraculous "survivals". A place where, in precisely five minutes from now, a privately chartered jumbo jet will take off on an initial flight path across the width of airspace beyond this very window.'

'Good job I'm not flying it,' quipped Nick.

'In a way, Mr Steen, you will be,' replied Nullman, looking down at him with the strangest of smiles on her face. 'Perhaps you will not be *physically* piloting that plane towards its ultimate destruction, but you will certainly be doing so *mentally*.'

So *that's* what Nullman had planned. She was going to use the God Socket to make Nick bring the plane down in front of them all by thought alone! She would use the box's godlike power to super-charge his dormant psychic powers again, drawing on his base instincts of anger and rage to force the stricken jumbo down into a muddy field.

'I won't do it,' said Nick. 'And you can't make me. I guess you think that because I've already caused the deaths of thousands of airline passengers, a few hundred more won't make much of a dent in my numbed-by-necessity-and-therefore-suitably-assuaged conscience. But you're wrong, Nullman. This time, I'll be fighting back.'

'Naturally, Mr Steen,' said Nullman. 'However, this particular flight contains, among its many passengers, one travelling by the name of Rosalind Bloom.'

Roz!

Nick gasped audibly, inwardly. Roz was on that plane! He calmed himself, forcing himself to think things through before giving way to panic. If Roz was indeed on that plane, then Nullman's intention was presumably to give Nick the opportunity to destroy his former editor.

In that case, he had nothing to worry about.

'Bad luck, Nullman,' Nick said. 'Roz and I are friends now. We're united in our battle to destroy all the demonic lifeforms my leaking brain has unleashed. Hell, with my help, she rescued me from the terrifying Prolix, where I got flayed by hell-demons.'

'But she *is* nevertheless your former editor,' said Nullman. 'You forget that with our advanced technical machinery here at Nulltec, we are able to access your innermost thoughts.'

Nick sneered at her. 'Well, if you think putting my former editor on that plane will somehow stoke up feelings of repressed anger and rage at all the incorrect advice she's given me over the years, you can think again. You're forgetting that I've roundly rejected all Roz's ideas, bar one or two that I was legally required to implement in order to stave off a pressing lawsuit. We've also slept together figuratively, numerous times. There's no way my subconscious urges, however dark or ruthless they may be, would ever dream of bringing that plane down. You're placing far too much faith in the deep-rooted reptilian instinct also known as the basal ganglia or basal nuclei, containing the brain stem, limbic region and the amygdala that we call the R-Complex, Nullman. And you're forgetting those other two complexes, N and S. N for Nick and S for Steen. They're not technically actual complexes in the human brain, but they're there, believe me. So go tell that to your so-called God Socket.'

Nullman smiled gently, nodding. 'Do you know what a reptilian instinct actually looks like, Mr Steen?' she said, snapping her fingers at Valesco.

Nick watched as the sinister-looking physician removed a small jar from a nearby fridge unit and walked over towards them. He was smiling, almost malevolently, Nick noticed, while Nullman continued speaking.

'Do you know what the R-Complex actually *is*?' she said.

Nick stifled a gasp as Valesco reached Nick's gurney, held out the jar and lifted off the lid. Then Nullman reached into her pocket and drew forth a pair of forceps.

She reached into the jar with them and removed a glistening, writhing object from the interior. It was a long, steaming piece of animate scaled matter, jet black in hue with an unholy peppering of bright yellow spots, looking much to Nick like a severed reptilian's tail.

The tail . . . *of a salamander.*

'*That* lives in the human mind?'

'It *is* the human mind,' said Valesco, 'at its most primitive.' He waggled the forceps playfully, forcing the specimen's tail to rear upwards and lunge in vain at his wrist with cold, reptilian fury. 'One of these specimens forms part of every single human brain.'

'And this particular example, if you recall,' said Nullman, moving round to place her burgundy nails once more on Nick's cheeks, 'was taken from a murderous, psychopathic killer*.'

Good gravy, thought Nick, in sudden alarm. Were they planning to do what he thought they were planning to do? Would they really do that? Was that what they were planning? Was what they were planning to do really the thing Nick thought they were planning to do? Would they really do it? What it was they were planning? Would they do *that*?

'Thanks, I've seen enough,' said Nick, hoping to God Nullman would never, ever, throw that damned thing in his direction. For that was the thing Nick thought they were planning to do. For Nick had the terrifying notion that were Nullman ever to do such a thing – to hurl that nauseating R–Complex Salamander's tail-type monstrosity in Nick's direction – then he might completely lose the ability to concentrate on any major task of phenomenal importance he was currently engaged in carrying out, potentially threatening not only

* The guy she extracted the R–Complex from. I have said this already. GM

his own life and those of others in his immediate vicinity, but also the ultimate success of said gargantuan task. A task, say, like some essential endeavour undertaken towards the end of a titanic struggle, to use his own writing analogy again, or the climactic denouement of some stupendous work of horror fiction, say. That kind of thing. And were Nick ever to be involved in a particularly high-stakes pattern of events, like the thrilling, action-packed climax of some stupendous slice of metaphorical grade-A horror fiction, and Nullman threw that beastly reptilian tail in his direction at the *worst possible moment*, Nick firmly suspected such a deadly act might destroy him utterly, resulting in the total, irrevocable failure of said task's completion, plus probable, nay guaranteed, destruction of the entire world.

'No, we're not going to do that,' said Nullman, grabbing hold of Nick's head. 'You forget, we can read your mind, Mr Steen, and know you'd be prepared for such an eventuality. Instead, we're going to implant this extracted R-Complex immediately, deep within your *own brain*.'

CHAPTER NINE

'Phase III'

Nick screamed as Valesco's men helped Nullman wrestle his head into a stationary position. Then Valesco himself held the forceps out in front of Nick's face, forcing him to watch the dangling R–Complex as it writhed and stabbed both ends viciously in his direction.

'It wants in,' said Valesco. 'It wants into your head. To feed on your mind.'

'Don't do this,' said Nick, understanding at last the full dreaded import of his recurring portentum. He recalled the image of that vast, cosmic salamander dangling below his own colossal face. That had been a message to Nick's mind, he now realised, that earthly destruction was close at hand. Devastation and calamity on an unimaginable scale. And Nick had failed to heed the message. Now the end of Stalkford was going to be Nick's fault entirely. For as soon as the dreaded R–Complex in the grip of Valesco's forceps entered Nick's brain, he doubted he would have the strength left to combat its most destructive instincts once it had paired up with his own personal writhing R–Complex. And if said own personal writhing R–Complex combined forces with the one originally belonging to that murderous psychotic from whom it had been extracted by Nullman; if those two R–Complexes were to join forces and battle

91

against Nick's kinder, more mammalian instinct, then who knew what that might mean for Roz, Stalkford, and slightly beyond Stalkford?

'Don't put that thing in my brain!' screamed Nick. 'Please!'

They put that thing in his brain.

As the assembled scientists held Nick's head still, and Nullman distracted the author by slightly interfering with him physically again, Valesco reached up over Nick's exposed pate to the spot where the cranial supports had drilled that hole into his skull, and dropped the R–Complex in.

Instantly, Nick felt a deep squirming in his mind. A sudden flurry of aggressive swishing as the R–Complex thrashed and darted among the tangled folds of intersecting brain matter in search of its natural rival.

Meanwhile, Nick's head was clamped shut again as Valesco's men connected his cranium to the oval head restraint, which itself had been connected directly to the back of Nick's gurney in the meantime so that they wouldn't have to lift him into a separate chair again.[*] As they locked the gurney's wheels in place, Valesco gave the empty jar to a nearby unimportant orderly, of whom there were several now entering the observation deck from various hitherto unmentioned connecting rooms. They began generally milling about unsuspectingly.

Nullman looked down at her watch. 'Right on schedule.'

Nick looked out at the sky beyond the observation window, which was suddenly tinted with an unholy blood-red hue. Was it dusk already? Maybe it was – maybe it *wasn't*. For Nick suddenly suspected that the blood-red tint colouring the vast stretch of open sky was precisely that.

Ichor.[†]

---

[*] Which also means I don't have to write said passage out a third time, wasting my time, like this footnote is currently doing. GM

[†] I.e., blood. GM

Then they were fighting already. Deep inside Nick's brain, he could feel his internal R-Complexes thrashing. Coiling themselves around one another's tails in an effort to dominate each other and also Nick's subconscious brain. That, or they were copulating. After all, most life forms other than human beings didn't care where or when they did it. Or why, for that matter. Nick was eternally surprised at how many pigeons, foxes and rabbits simply went at it daily like a harem of horny heathens in his local churchyard. He often used to visit the place for inspiration when writing a subtle gothic chiller, but in the end had become so distracted by the daily displays of bestial flagrant debauchery that he'd simply given up trying to write anything creepy and concentrated instead on unholy Satanic-based horrotica. Which had ultimately got him banned from the premises himself, while God's heavenly creatures were still blithely going at it on top of the family crypt of some well-known local dignitary.

A sudden primal howl sounded from a distant void. The cry of the serpent, Nick thought, poetically, knowing, there and then, that the invading R-Complex had eaten his own. Consumed it entirely. Was perhaps already digesting its sloppy innards inside its own sloppy innards. Maybe it had even shat out what was left of Nick's reptilian instincts already, through the rear head-flue of Nick's mind.

DESTROY.

That voice again, Nick thought, suddenly terrified. The voice of his deepest, darkest, most primitive instincts.

DESTROY THEM ALL.

Was it even him anymore? Nick looked out through the glass and saw the plane ascending rapidly from Stalkford airport. The aircraft was currently only a small speck in the far distance, yet one that would soon be getting closer and larger by the second. And Nulltec wanted Nick Steen to bring it down.

They *demanded* he bring it down. Despite all he held dear.

'I won't do it!' Nick yelled. 'Even though your R-Complex has eaten my own R–Complex, I just won't do it. And that's my final word on the matter.'

'You will,' said Nullman, turning to face Dr Valesco, who was standing calmly, once more, beside the God Socket. His finger hovered over button three. The button marked 'Even More Powerful'. 'We simply need to give you a little nudge.'

'I await your instruction, Dr Nullman,' Valesco said, grinning slyly as his assistants stepped away from Nick's side, clearing the immediate area around the God Socket.

'I'll be coming for you as well,' said Nick to Valesco, grimly.

All at once, he felt free. Unimpeded. Powerful.

ALL POWERFUL.

He could fight back against them all, no problem. He could let that plane go past them easily. No way would he send it spiralling down into a fiery abyss in the field in front of them, killing countless people, plus Roz.

No way would he do that.

No way at all.

Really.

Because it was really no problem.

No problem at all.

He could do it easi—

DESTROY THE PLANE.

Dammit. The voice had interrupted him. Nick hadn't counted on that when he'd felt supremely confident mere seconds before. That voice in his head. He had to switch off that voice in his head or maybe the plane *would* nose-dive.

'Dr Valesco?' said the voice of Dr Nullman in Nick's ears.

'Yes, Dr Nullman?' replied Dr Valesco.

Nick turned his head aside to look at Nullman, who'd retreated to a safe area some distance away.

'Will you please press the third button.'

'With pleasure,' said Dr Valesco.

'No!' yelled Nick.

Valesco pressed the third button, and the God Socket awoke.

There was a sudden electrical whoosh as some unknown unit inside the machine commenced ignition, followed by a whirring hum, rapidly building in intensity like the surge and spin of an aeroplane's engines while accelerating along a runway.

Nick didn't have to look upward to know that the throbbing motion of released electrical energy was pulsing through the connecting cable towards his brain at immense speed – much faster than before.

Then that energy exploded into him.

All at once, Nick saw stars. Planets. A whole universe. A vast cosmos filled with insanely big Salamander-Bottomed Men, wriggling and writhing in the abyss like massive tadpoles in a colossal universal pool. Like trillions of gargantuan spermatozoa inside some terrifying space-borne ball sack.

And, as Nick steered his mind's eye away from the sight, terrified almost to the point of insanity by the awe-evoking vision, he felt the plane he was piloting veering from its course, turning over as both engines exploded, and he saw that all those colossal free-floating Salamander-Bottomed Men were only babies. Small specks of cosmic dust before the looming presence of their own terrifying God of Destruction . . .

An even bigger Salamander-Bottomed Man.

Nick screamed, attempting to wrench his own eyes from their sockets.

The head. The damned head. Even more colossal than the Salamander-Bottomed Man's head he'd seen earlier.

It was *Nick's own*.

Again.

His own, insanely evil, super-destructive face was staring out into the vast infinity of quaking Salamander-Bottomed Man eggs, urging, willing their ultimate destruction.

Nullifying all before him.

Even his own Salamander-Bottomed Men brethren.

'No!' screamed Nick, his mind bursting free from his petrifying portentum into a reality even more horrifying.

For the plane was now heading into the stretch of sky directly in front of him.

DESTROY.

'No!' yelled Nick. 'I won't do it.'

YOU WILL. YOU WILL DESTROY THAT PLANE. YOU WILL BRING DOWN THAT PLANE. YOU WILL CRUSH THAT PLANE. YOU WILL ENJOY DECIMATING EVERYTHING RELATED TO THAT PLANE.

Nick fought with his mind. Battled the Richard Burton voice in his brain.

EXPLODE THESE HEATHENS. WIPE OUT THIS LOWLY PRICKERY. LEAVE NOTHING BEHIND BUT ASH. TURN THE WHOLE WORLD TO STONE. WHILE REMEMBERING TO KEEP A COPY OF ALL YOUR BOOKS SAFE IN A REINFORCED LIBRARY FOR POSTERITY.

Dammit, could it be true? Was Nick really convincing himself that a world without Mankind was better than a world without his own books?

YES. OF COURSE.

But Roz, poor, sweet Roz. Sure, she'd been wrong about his writing numerous times. But that was kind of cute, in a way. He enjoyed proving her wrong and seeing her think for a moment, confused, before shrugging her shoulders and saying, 'Sure, Nick, whatever,' before ringing him a week later in floods of tears saying, 'You were right, Nick, all along, please forgive me. Is there anything else I can do for you? Just don't call Clackett and ask them to appoint my colleague Stephanie instead.'

Hell, he loved Roz, in a way. He couldn't destroy her. He *wouldn't* destroy her.

DESTROY ROZ. SHE KNOWS NOTHING ABOUT HORROR. HER SPECIALITY BEFORE TAKING YOU ON WAS COSY MYSTERY AND RANCH ROMANCE. TAKE THE PLANE DOWN.

Dammit, the voice was taking him over. Suppressing Nick's nobler instincts. Why the hell *shouldn't* he take Roz down? Hadn't she tried to oppose him from the get-go, ordering him to use capital letters at the start of each sentence when he'd routinely told her he wouldn't defer to anyone or anything on principle, not least the laws of conventional grammar. Too bad if Roz was on an emergency flight to London, desperately concerned about Nick's mysterious disappearance and hoping to contact some specialist big-league private detection agency in the Big Smoke to retrace Nick's last steps in an effort to find her favourite author. She'd drawn her last red line through one of *his* manuscripts, that was for sure.

DOWN THAT PLANE.

He should have done this before, Nick figured. Should have exploded the brains of those five critics, after all. Thank God Valesco had done it when Nick himself had been too weak to act. Good Dr Valesco. Now that was a guy who knew how to get things done. Why *not* make some money from illegal medical practices conducted on the sly? Why *not* trade in illegal transplants on the black market, develop unethical medicines for the pharmaceutical industry and hide mutant offspring in an abandoned store cupboard on Floor 13? Why *not* inject the brains of innocent patients with small detonators so that they could become willing vegetables who could be exploded if they got difficult?

And Nullman. That brilliantly austere, burgundy-nail-stroking, coldly clinical medical hot dog? Hell, she wanted Nick and he wanted her, dammit. They should throw all pretence aside and set to together on the operating table, mid-procedure. Who cared? Why stand on ceremony when it was barking clear that their evil, corrupt minds were made for each other? Practically begging to join in with some unholy union of mind and body? They should be rubbing their Nobels together (once Nick, too, had been awarded one) – and to hell with the consequences. Screw office politics, these two were hot for each other, dammit, and the rest of the medical fraternity could go do one if they thought an emergency colonoscopy was going to happen before he and Nullman were sated.

STOP ONANISING AND DOWN THAT PLANE.

Of course, thought Nick, suddenly shamefaced by this sudden castigation from his subconscious. The plane. I must down that plane.

Nick looked out across the fields. The jet was clearly visible now, the lights on its wings blinking as it rose upward towards a bank of low-lying clouds.

DOWN IT, I SAID. DOWN THAT PLANE.

'I will down that plane,' said Nick blankly, eyes staring through the window like an automaton.

'It's working,' said Valesco, still standing beside the God Socket while he monitored Nick's vitals.

'He's stable,' said Nullman from her position by the observation monitors. She looked up from one of the screens, her hands still holding a long ream of paper currently spooling data at speed from a nearby printer. 'But I want to make sure everything goes right this time,' she added. She called out to Valesco from her side of the room: 'Dr Valesco?'

'Yes, Dr Nullman?' he replied, calling back to her from his side of the room.

'I think it's time to press the *secret* button.'

What little remained of Nick's softer, mammalian brain awoke suddenly.

A *secret* button? So they'd been lying to him, then? Telling him there were *three* buttons on the God Socket, when all along there was actually a *secret* button in addition? Meaning *four* buttons in total?

Those bastards.

Valesco smiled cruelly at Nick, moving his finger along from the third button marked 'Even More Powerful' to a blank space beside it. Then, with Nick powerless to intervene, this cruelly woeful excuse for a professional medic reached into the pocket of his lab coat and drew out a coin. He reached down towards the blank space beside the third button and began scratching at the steel wall of the box.

'No . . .' muttered Nick, unable to believe his eyes.

Valesco laughed aloud. For this particular patch of steel lining wasn't a patch of steel lining after all. It was a sheet of slightly strengthened tin foil. As Nick watched in horror, Valesco rubbed the coin across the thin layer of slightly strengthened *tin foil* and revealed, beneath it, the *fourth* button.

Then, as if to add insult to injury, Valesco scratched at the space below the fourth button, exposing the two words printed there:

'Insanely Powerful'

'Oh, God, no,' cried Nick, as Valesco reached his index finger outward again towards this fourth, *insanely powerful* button, and, at a nod from Nullman across the room, *pressed it.*

Nick screamed again as a bright flash of pink electrical energy soared through the connecting pipe at the speed of lightning, igniting his insides. His limbs thrashed, convulsing in the gurney as his entire body and brain shone with pink fire. Then two jets of pink flame shot from Nick's eyes, boring effortlessly through the pane of glass, firing like bolts of lightning across the intervening sky to strike the sky-borne plane mid-air. There was a blinding flash from the jet's engine, followed by a gigantic burst of flame, as the plane suddenly rolled, banking left, then descended at speed towards the ground.

DESTROY THAT PLANE, said the dark voice inside Nick's head.

And finally, Nick himself agreed.

CHAPTER TEN

'The Nullifier'

DOWN DOWN DOWN.

'According to its current trajectory and angle of descent, the plane should make impact with the ground in approximately two minutes,' said Valesco.

'Well done, Mr Steen,' said Nullman, walking out from behind the protective screen and moving over to him. 'You took less time than we'd anticipated.'

Confident that her patient was now fully under Nulltec's control, she released the wheel stops on Nick's gurney.

'Once that jet's completely obliterated, take him down to one of the containment cells,' she said to one of Valesco's assistants.

Valesco himself, whose face was usually half-swathed in eerie shadow but was now fully lit up by the bright jets of pink fire shooting forth from Nick's eyes, looked up at her questioningly.

'How do we know we *can* contain him?' he asked warily, having learned from bitter experience not to question Nullman's judgement without some rigorous scientific evidence to back up his doubts.

'Explain yourself,' she said, turning to face him.

'He's received the full force of the God Socket,' explained Valesco.

'And then some. We don't yet know quite what he'll be capable of. If I were you, I'd reattach those wheel stops to the gurney immediately, in case it starts rolling away of its own accord. Unless, of course, he starts to levitate. But I very much doubt that will happen.'

Nullman lit a cigarette, drawing deeply on the long orange butt between her lusciously coated lips. Then she reached a slender hand past Nick's glowing shoulder and stroked his cheek provocatively. 'I think I'll be able to keep any of Mr Steen's more errant urges fully under my control.'

'As you wish, Nullman,' said Valesco. 'But we're no longer dealing with a conventional psychopath whose R-Complex we're simply removing via dangerous, experimental surgery. That machine is called the God Socket for a reason. Inside Mr Steen's mind now dwells the iron will and mental powers of a cosmic deity. This being emerging before us is no longer Nick Steen, horror author. Or even Nick Steen, doomed airline pilot. This is Nick Steen, God of Worldly Destruction. Nick Steen, the Nullifier.'

THE NULLIFIER. YES. I AM THE NULLIFIER AND I WILL NULLIFY ALL.

Nick had to agree with the destructive voice intoning deeply and sombrely inside his brain. As his eyes concentrated both pink jets of searing psychokinetic flame on the ailing plane, watching it spin and tumble over and over as it careened ever closer to the ground, Nick had the increasingly ominous feeling that any resistance he might have shown was useless now. For he alone was the ultimate source of power in the cosmos, wasn't he? Soon he would be able to conquer Stalkford entirely, then outer Stalkford, Britain at large, the world, the inner and outer universe, etc. He'd be invincible.

Yeah, goodbye, Roz, laughed Nick, inwardly. And good riddance. Next time, take your advice on narrative point of view and shove it where the sun don't shine. If there even is a next time. Which there isn't.

Because Nick Steen, as Nick himself once knew him, was no more.

THAT'S RIGHT. DESTROY THE PLANE. ANNIHILATE IT. NULLIFY THAT PLANE.

The rear of the jet was now in flames. At this rate, it might incinerate entirely before it even hit the ground.

YES. IT MIGHT INCINERATE ENTIRELY BEFORE IT EVEN HITS THE GROUND. THAT'S HOW POWERFUL I NOW AM.

'Whoa there, boyo,' said a strange voice in Nick's ear suddenly. And at once, a small vestige of slumbering normality awoke, deep within his brain. For those three simple words, softly spoken, had somehow reopened a door in Nick's mind. A nondescript mental door in a lengthy corridor of similarly nondescript mental doors that had previously been sealed shut by the invasion of his new writhing R-Complex, alongside that relentless big burst of nuclear energy coming at all times from the adjoining God Socket.

And from that quiet, darkened room behind the aforesaid nondescript door deep inside Nick's brain emerged two words of Nick's own.

The Taffer.

Of course! Nick's dying mind thought, regaining some brief, transitory aspect of his former self. The Taffer was here. That wise old Welchman had come to help Nick in his hour of need again. Risked life and leek to bring Nick Steen's mind back from the brink. But what brink? thought Nick, his memory clouding over again almost instantly. What was this so-called brink that the Taffer was attempting to bring Nick's mind back from?

'Listen to me, boyo,' the Taffer's voice continued from his position beside Nick's ear, where he was currently feigning having lost track of his huge leek again. 'You stop this here Nullifying nonsense right now, look you. That there's one heck of a lovely plane, painted all nice and red, it is, with lovely people on board, or so I'm told. And I do 'appen to know that that there Roz Bloom girly friend o' yours is on that plane too, which is mainly white I now have to say, it being a bit closer now, with only red *bits* on it, but a lovely bright red all the same, so they are. And, getting back to the point now, she's on her way, look you, all the way to London Town to find out where you are, Nick Steen, so she is, look you. And I'm telling you now, boyo, you need to seize control of that there mind o' yours, and do what's right. For there's still about ten thousand feet or so yet between that there plane and the ground it's heading for. And if you don't lift that bloody thing up sharpish, like miners dangling in a shaft above some community-decimating gas explosion, you'll have the Taffer 'ere to answer to, so help me Rhiannon. And my prize leek too, look you.'

The Taffer, thought Nick. Thank the Lord, it really was the Taffer. The sweet, fat, ridiculously hatted Taffer.

And thanks to the Taffer's selfless actions, Nick could now recall at long last that he had to *rescue* the plane. The very plane he was currently in the process of bringing down! The plane that was already spiralling down to earth in a terrifying death-arc brought about by Nick's relentless psychic eye-blasting. The plane carrying Roz Bloom towards total and complete destruction!

DESTROY! DESTROY THE PLANE. BRING THE PLANE DOWN. DOWN. DOWN. DOWN.

No! thought Nick. I can't! I daren't! I won't!

'The Taffer?' whispered Nick, his emerging voice almost silent in the Welchman's ear. 'The Taffer, are you there?'

'So I am, boyo,' said the Taffer. 'Here to help you pull that there plane up again, even if I have to sacrifice my own prize leek in the process. So look you now, Nick Steen, and snap right to it, boyo . . .'

A spray of bullets smacked into the Taffer's hat, cutting him off abruptly amid a shower of felt scraps.

Then Nulltec's security detail recalibrated the aim of their Nulltec-issued Berettas and shot the Welchman's face off completely.

As what remained of the Taffer's body dropped to both knees, spurting long jets of blood upward from the stump of its neck, before flopping forward on to the floor, snapping its own giant leek in two beneath its chunky frame, the nondescript door in Nick's brain that had been briefly opened by the now-dead Welchman closed again, with the harsh snap of not a single, not a double, but a *triple*-activated metaphorical mind-lock.

THAT'S BETTER. NOW LET ME GET BACK TO DESTROYING. LET ME BRING THE WHOLE EDIFICE DOWN. LIKE I SAID EARLIER.

From his position on the far side of the observation room, the youthful blond-haired man who'd drugged Nick with tranquilliser-laced Scotch in that car that drove him to Nulltec, and who was, besides being a part-time chauffeur's assistant, head of Nulltec's Security Team, congratulated himself on a well-aimed shot, then suddenly began to panic.

'What the hell's happening?' he yelled, as Nick's body began to float upward from the gurney, levitating in mid-air. Whatever insane force or power was in the process of overtaking Nick Steen's mind, it evidently now possessed the ability to float him upwards against all known laws of gravity. Not to mention those two pink jets of flame he was still projecting from both eyes.

'Doctor Valesco?' the blond-haired man yelled across the room, seeking cover behind a row of computer monitors as the dials and buttons on the God Socket beside Nick began to smoke, crackle and whizz about in circles like a sputtering Catherine wheel.

The assembled doctors watched in horror as Nick's body continued to ascend towards the ceiling, trailing the vast pipe connecting his head to the God Socket behind.

'I warned you, Nullman,' said Valesco. 'This being is becoming more powerful than anything we can imagine. I sense it's soon going to be a right pig's arse to control.'

'Leave Steen as he is,' said Nullman, scanning frantically through a fresh ream of paper now spooling from her nearby computer console. 'We are getting exceptional results from these readouts. Why, with this level of attainable power generated by the God Socket, the Nullifier will be simply unstoppable. Surely I don't have to explain to you what that means, doctor?'

'Lucrative contracts with the world's most powerful military organisations?' replied Valesco, playing along for now. 'Meaning Nulltec will soon be able to auction out contracts for its top-secret research projects to the highest bidder?'

'Exactly,' confirmed Nullman. 'And then we'll be able to create our own wars to feed further research. We're in the money, Valesco.' Nullman laughed, rubbing her hands with glee. 'We'll be able to build that heated swimming pool.'

That heated swimming pool, hissed Valesco inwardly. Always with the damned heated swimming pool. As if any of them ever had time to go swimming with all the work they had to do on their sinister top-secret projects. This wasn't about that damned heated swimming pool – and Nullman knew it.

'This isn't about that damned heated swimming pool – and you know it, Nullman. Speaking frankly, I'm not sure I trust your motives anymore. If I didn't know better, I'd say you were concealing some sort of nefarious purpose or scheme of your own, as yet unknown to others in your employ,' Valesco sneered. 'I can't help thinking you're keeping something from me.'

'Likewise, Doctor Valesco,' said Nullman, piercing him with her own accusatory glare. 'Likewise, I can't help but think that you're keeping something from *me.*'

Valesco held Nullman's gaze for a moment more (and vice versa), then both doctors turned their heads suddenly at the horrendous screaming of incoming jet engines.

In front of Nick's floating body, the plane was now clearly visible through the observation window, emerging nose first through a bank of cloud like a dart heading at speed directly towards a horizontal dartboard (i.e. one that's lying down on the ground, rather than hanging from the wall of a pub).

HERE IT COMES, said the voice like Richard Burton or Robert Powell's inside Nick's head. *THE MOMENT OF TRUTH. THE POINT OF IMPACT. THE DESTRUCTION OF THE INNOCENTS. THE CULLING OF THE LAMBS. THE DROWNING OF THE KITTENS. THE PLUNGING OF THE LEMMINGS. THE TOSSING OUT OF THE FLEDGLINGS. ALL MUST DIE BEFORE THE EYE OF MEDUSA. ALL MUST PERISH IN FLAME BEFORE THE GLARE OF THE GUYGON. FOR I AM ALPHA AND OMEGA, PLUS ALL THE OTHER LETTERS IN BETWEEN. I AM THE ANGEL OF DOOM. THE GOD OF DESTRUCTION. I AM THE ALL-POWERFUL NULLIFIER. AND I DO MEAN ALL-POWERFUL, BELIEVE ME. FINE. JUST TRY ME AND FIND OUT.*

No! screamed that quiet, strangled voice behind the metaphorical nondescript door in that long corridor of metaphorical nondescript doors inside Nick's brain, as his last attempt to battle the R-Complex – that deep-rooted reptilian instinct also known as the basal ganglia or basal nuclei, containing the brain stem, limbic region and the amygdala – nesting in his mind fell on deaf ears (his own).

Nick's eyes blazed through the window as the rest of Roz's jet shot suddenly through the low bank of cloud, heading directly towards the green fields immediately below. Green fields that would soon be stained red with blood – and orange flame and blackened ash and bits of smoke as well.

And there was nothing Nick Steen could do to stop it now. Nothing at all.

Then came the explosion ...

CHAPTER ELEVEN

'Psych Night'

. . . as the door of the elevator blew inward.

Propelled by a powerful eruption of barrelling pink flame, the metal frame catapulted across the observation room, embedding itself in the wall opposite as Nulltec's two incarcerated psychic young persons strode in. Persephone, her eyes glowing a darker, more enraged shade of pink than Nick's own, advanced into the room, Christabel directly behind her.

Of course! Nick would have thought, if his consciousness hadn't been trapped at this particular moment deep inside the metaphorical corridors of his own mind. The Taffer hadn't taken Nick down to that basement to show him those two incarcerated kids. He'd taken Nick down there so that those two incarcerated kids could see *Nick* . . .

And now they were both here, to save *him*.

'We're here to save you, Nick!' Christabel yelled up at him. 'Quickly, Persephone!' The young child pointed towards the observation window, where she had just caught sight of the impending airborne disaster about to take place in the fields beyond.

The baggy-trousered teen with an hitherto-suspected attitude problem from hell turned her head towards the window and fired twin jets of flame in the direction of the ailing jet.

A pane on the window melted beneath the intense heat of Persephone's glare as the twin barrels of projected flame shot forth from her eyes and struck the stricken airliner. But instead of joining with Nick's own in a concerted effort to down the plane, they instead appeared to wrap themselves around its descending fuselage, which immediately began to twist and bend like a tin can crushed inside a gigantic human fist. But there was little malice in the action, for this was a desperate measure to reverse the plane's trajectory. A last-ditch attempt to turn the jumbo from its flight path to destruction and send it back up into the clouds again. As the plane's nose half wrenched round 180 degrees like the head of a metal owl's, the plane's rear half followed, ascending miraculously once again towards the sun-reddened clouds above.

'Well done, Persephone!' squealed Christabel. 'That worked a treat!'

NOOOO!!! yelled the voice of the Nullifier, raging inside Nick's mind. *THIS CANNOT BE. I WAS ABOUT TO WREAK ULTIMATE HAVOC ON THAT VERY PLANE. I WAS THAT CLOSE TO CAUSING ITS TOTAL, ULTIMATE DESTRUCTION – AND THEN YOU TWO CAME ALONG. HOW DARE YOU TWO.*

'Nick's head, Persephone!' yelled Christabel again. 'Now that you've sent that plane on a safe course back upward, into the sky, concentrate your unique psychic powers on Nick's head instead. For I sense from my burgeoning extra telepathic ability to read minds, which I recently discovered since speaking to Nick last, and which now exists in me in addition to my already established psychic ability to heal and resurrect dead or dying matter, that Nick's mind has been taken over by an evil cosmic deity known as the Nullifier. My guess is that if we're to have any hope of securing a happy ending to this tale, to use a writer's analogy that's particularly apt when talking about Nick, given that he's a writer himself, we need to stop the

Nullifier from taking over Nick's mind. I suggest you try and twist those jets of flame coming from his eyes round 180 degrees, exactly like you did with that plane just now, and project them rearward into his own eyes. That way, we might just zap a few evil brain cells and give the real Nick a fighting chance.'

With that, Christabel turned her own head from Nick's, her eyes immediately alighting upon the headless body of the Taffer lying directly below him. Glowing now with a genuine ethereal rose-tinted light, the young girl floated forward, discovering at that moment an additional power of spiritual levitation, so deep were her feelings now of empathy and pity for this blasted Welchman. Holding her sacred palms up against the Taffer's stump, she whispered into the hole in his neck. Then, as if by some divine miracle, the splintered fragments of his obliterated skull and brain clumps rose, along with the pool of blood leaking from the Taffer's neck, and reassembled themselves into the shape of his former head.

As Christabel muttered 'Amen' at last, the Taffer's eyes snapped open. Blinking wildly, he looked down frantically at his broken prize leek.

Which was now also miraculously intact.

'Thank you kindly, young *cariad*,' said the Taffer, staggering to his feet and plucking the string of plastic peepers from around his head. For there was no need to hide his eyesight anymore. Now, if anything, he *needed* that sight.

'Thank goodness I, the Taffer, was able to wheel Nick down to you two in that there basement under the pretence of being completely blind so that he could alert you both to the sinister machinations of this shadowy establishment.'

'Thanks, the Taffer,' said Christabel. 'For if you hadn't sent Nick into our cell so that he could scream, "You're all incarcerats," at us until he was blue in the face, we might never have known that he, and we, were in fact prisoners here. And when Scorcher bit me accidentally while I was feeding him dog biscuits and cocked his leg up against my bed to piddle, I knew something deeply sinister was going on. Because if Scorcher wasn't really the loveliest dog in all the whole wide world, then maybe Nulltec wasn't the loveliest nursery in the whole wide world, either. That's when we both decided to have a look around and heard all the shouting coming from this floor. We decided to investigate, and the rest is history.'

'Except it's not history yet, young lassie,' said the Taffer, as his face grew suddenly grave. 'Look you out, you!' he bellowed, suddenly.

Christabel turned her head to see a titanic ball of pink flame burst through the observation window, seemingly held in mid-air by two battling jets of flame. Then she saw that Persephone was fighting with the Nullifier currently squatting inside Nick's head, both sets of eyes flaming outward towards each other's retinas in an effort to overcome the other's opposing blast.

'I can't beat it,' said Persephone. 'The pink psychic flames coming from Nick's head are too strong!'

'Nick!' yelled the Taffer, shouting up towards the still-floating Nick, realising he had to break through to him again, somehow. 'If you're in there, boyo, this little lady out here needs your help, look you. Come out of that there locked door in your mind and give her a blast of some good old Nick Steen magic!'

Deep inside Nick's mind, that nondescript door of metaphor once more creaked open. Perhaps only a couple of inches ajar, but enough to be technically open. And soon after, Nick's face, embattled and over-empowered as it was, slowly and hesitantly peeked out.

'Look you!' sounded a voice from far off, coming from some-where along that long and distant metaphorical corridor of nonde-script metaphorical doors.

The Taffer, thought Nick again, weakly. The Taffer.

The Taffer!

'He's coming round!' yelled the Taffer, as Persephone concentrated the full force of her powers on twisting the two jets of Nick's projected eye-flame around, aiming them, backward again, in the direction of Nick's own skull.

'That's it!' howled the Taffer, gleefully. 'You're doing it alright, lassie. Look you, you're doing it!'

Then the Taffer's head exploded again.

'Good shot!' yelled Nullman, who, along with Valesco and the various insignificant medical orderlies who'd previously been milling about, had now recovered sufficiently from the sudden bursting-in of the elevator door and, having assessed the unfolding situation technically for a few minutes, so that any potential hasty mistakes could be ironed out well in advance, had ordered the security detail to fight back with a vengeance.

The blond-haired gunman re-aimed his Beretta in the direction of Persephone . . .

. . . as Christabel once again reached out with her hands and healed the Taffer's head.

'What the . . .?' said the blond gunman, his eyes scarcely believing what they were now seeing.

'Thanking you again, young lady,' said the Taffer, dusting himself down. 'Now what say you we blow this thing and go home?'

His head exploded again.

'Good shot again,' yelled Nullman. 'It's that bloody girl doing it,' she hissed, pointing at Christabel. 'She's healing him every time. Kill her! Kill the girl! Kill the healer!'

The blond-haired gunman, now joined by his balding, sideburn-sporting companion – the driver of the car that had brought Nick to Nulltec – aimed their Berettas at Christabel's head instead . . .

. . . just as Nick metaphorically stepped fully out of the nondescript metaphorical door of his mind into the metaphorical corridor of nondescript doors leading off into an impenetrable metaphorical distance.

What the hell's happening? he asked himself. Hadn't he just heard the Taffer's voice from somewhere afar, calling him? Yet now it had just as suddenly been silenced again. It was high time he investigated what exactly was going on here.

Nick looked ahead, into the darkness of the distant corridor, then saw something snaking towards him from the far distance. Out of the shadows, it approached him slowly, coiling itself over the floor, assisted by the sinister padding of reptilian feet. The feet, Nick saw as the light finally exposed a rash of yellow spotting against its viscous, blackened skin, of a salamander . . .

Nick stopped dead in his tracks (he'd walked forward a couple of steps beyond his nondescript metaphorical door, but not much further).

Then gulped. The legs of a *salamander*. Or was it more like a snake's tail? What *was* this monstrosity sliding on its spotted, mucoid belly towards him? Nick suddenly detected the outline of an unusual-looking head set upon the top of its swollen body as it continued to pass the nondescript metaphorical doors of that long, unending metaphorical corridor inside Nick's mind. It was a human head.

Nick's own.

Was this, then, the dreaded R-Complex itself? Embedding its physical shape inside Nick's own psyche in the form of his own head? Was this the reptilian instinct now threatening his life, and that of all Mankind?

The head emerged fully from the shadows, and Nick knew then what it *really* was.

The Nullifier.

I AM THE NULLIFIER, it said. AND I AM HERE TO NULLIFY YOU FIRST, NICK STEEN, AS A MATTER OF PRIORITY. AND THEN I WILL NULLIFY EVERYONE ELSE.

No, thought Nick. I have to get out of here. I have to save the

Taffer, if he's still alive.* I have to help whoever is out there trying to help me. I can sense goodness out there. The souls of innocents screaming out at me, Nick Steen, to come and save them.

TOO LATE, said the Nullifier. *YOU'RE TRAPPED IN HERE WITH ME, IN THIS NONDESCRIPT CORRIDOR OF YOUR OWN MIND.*

'You missed out one word, friend,' said Nick to the approaching monster.

WHAT WORD? the Nullifier replied. *WHAT WORD DID I MISS OUT?*

Nick smiled, grimly. 'Metaphorical.'

METAPHORICAL WHAT? I DON'T UNDERSTAND.

'Nondescript metaphorical corridor. Meaning a corridor that is not literal, and therefore one I can leave at any point of my own accord.'

OH, RIGHT. NOW I UNDERSTAND.

And with that, Nick opened his eyes and left that metaphorical corridor, returning once again to the land of the living . . .

★

. . . where all hell was breaking loose!

'Watch out!' Nick yelled as his head, finally weakening under the sheer force of Persephone's twisting eye-flame, turned round 180 degrees. From this position he was able to glimpse the immediate threat of Nullman's security goons as they levelled their weapons at the young girl far below his levitating form.

Immediately, he glared in the direction of the assembled medical fraternity and blasted his own psychic eye-fire towards the quaking

---

* He wasn't. GM

doctors. Instantly, an entire row of insignificant orderlies erupted in a ball of flame. But that wasn't enough for Nick.

Furious now, drawing strength and courage from his sudden triumph, and fuelled by the knowledge that he had single-handedly saved Christabel's life, admittedly with some minor assistance from Persephone, Nick began projecting yet more psychic fire blasts at the assembled scientists.

Three more groups of insignificant orderlies erupted into flames as Nick burned past them, scorching an entire row of computer monitors erected against the far wall.

'My computers!' screamed Nullman. 'He's scorching my computers!'

'And that's not all, Nullman,' yelled Nick at her, his voice suddenly more Burton-Powellesque in tone and depth than even the dreaded Nullifier himself. 'Now you will rue the day you incarcerated Nick Steen,' he howled from his position near the ceiling, pink flame breathing down the necks of the assembled doctors as he ignited several more. His vengeful eyes exploded yet another bank of monitors and computer terminals as his killing gaze swept slowly but surely from right to left.

All at once, the entire observation room was a sparking, fizzing mass of exploding technical equipment and melting machinery.

Then, using the force of his own projected psychic powers combined with those of Persephone, Nick directed the four pink lasers shooting from their collective eyes towards the smoking black box in the middle of the floor below.

Towards the God Socket itself . . .

'Destroy the black box,' yelled Nick at Persephone, his voice echoing around the room loudly, as if he was speaking to them through a portable speaker at some garden fete, only far more frightening. 'Destroy the God Socket. It's our only chance to rid this world of that all-powerful Nullifier now steeling himself within me for a comeback!'

As Nick and Persephone concentrated their powers on the God Socket below them, attempting to burn a hole through its tin lid, a lab-coated figure sprung from his hiding place beneath Nick's abandoned gurney and leaped over towards the blackened crate.

'No!' cried Valesco, throwing his arms around the smoking, blackened contraption and whisking it away from Nick's angle of fire. 'The God Socket is mine, I tell you! Mine!'

'Like hell it is,' yelled Nullman, emerging from her own hiding place beneath an ever-spooling ream of printer paper. She pointed her burgundy-nailed index finger in the doctor's direction. 'Remember, Valesco. You are only Assistant Chief Head of the Null-tec Corporation. I am Chief Head. That's my God Socket, not yours. It's my name on that Nobel Prize, remember?'

'And who developed the technology allowing you to win that Nobel Prize?' sneered Valesco, still waving the God Socket around in his arms in an effort to evade the four jets of wandering pink flame coming from Nick's and Persephone's lasering eyes as they struggled to get it back in their sights. 'Who enabled you to identify, isolate and remove that piece of R-Complex in the first place?' Valesco was angry now, the speed at which he was whipping the crate around in concentric circles in an effort to avoid it being flamed from sideways and above increasing with each orbit. 'Who designed this entire God Socket? Muggins here, that's who. Granted, Nullman, your achievements in the field of medicine earned you enough government research grants to fund development of this device at supersonic speed, but it was I alone who designed its mechanics. It was I who slaved away, night and day, but mainly day, working alone in my laboratory, with only an occasional break for coffee, lunch, dinner and some legally entitled downtime. I alone who knew that to power the God Socket, we would need to feed it brain molecules from a trillion anatomically varied healthy human subjects. I alone was the one, Nullman, who personally referred perfectly healthy people to a temporary fake hospital address here at Nulltec in order to induce sudden unnecessary comas in the operating theatre, allowing us to siphon off their precious cranial particulars unawares, so that we could then use the gathered juice to create a biological serum that would breathe life back into that piece of frozen, inanimate organic matter we'd had stolen by a secret government agency right under the Vatican's nose: a twelfth-century Holy Roman relic purporting to be the supposed long-lost finger bone of God, but which in actual fact turned out to be the *genuine* long-lost finger bone of God.

'It was I alone who connected that long-lost finger bone of God up to a rudimentary circuit board and got that God Socket working; I who went out for replacement batteries in the middle of the night, frequently paying for them out of my own pocket; I who polished those steel plates to make it look all nice, and made sure all the buttons were of uniform size and design when initially we could only find two that looked the same. It was I who personally laid that foil covering concealing the top-secret fourth button, which admittedly is not completely identical to the others, but then the chances of sourcing more than three buttons of identical design is really pushing the odds, quite frankly – and *this* is the thanks I get?'

Suddenly, a huge bang sounded from the God Socket in Valesco's hands, which had now turned completely black.

'What the blazes?' shouted Valesco. 'I'm pretty certain I was swinging this God Socket around fast enough to scupper Nick and Persephone's aim, so what the hell's going wrong with it now?'

'It seems to be channelling its power from some other source,' said Nullman. 'Maybe through that cable sticking out of the top of Nick Steen's head. Do something, Valesco, while my security detail holds them off.'

As the pair of Beretta-wielding security guards and part-time chauffeur and part-time assistant chauffeur fired off several rounds into the air, forcing Persephone and Nick to duck and dive among the ricocheting bullets, Valesco pulled out a dusty clipboard with his spare hand and searched frantically through his research notes.

'If I don't know better,' said Valesco, after several quick mathematical calculations, 'I'd say the God Socket was now channelling extra power from the bowels of Hell.'

'Good God!' cried Nullman. 'Then that long-lost finger bone of God you used to activate the serum . . .'

'Yes?' said Valesco, yanking the blackened God Socket away from a fresh sweep of Nick's psychic eye-blasting. 'What about it?'

'Could it have been mislabelled at the monastery?'

'What are you implying, Nullman?'

'I'm not implying anything. I'm telling you that instead of that being the long-lost finger bone of God, Valesco, we may have inadvertently created the God Socket using a *different* long-lost finger bone? The long-lost finger bone of . . . *the Devil!*'

'No,' said Valesco. 'I think it's more likely to be the particular brand of batteries I'm using. I must admit, having spent so much of my own money on replacing them, I was starting to obtain cheap multipacks from that guy who works in the unmarked van behind Spar.'

'But those *are* Spar-sold batteries?' asked Nullman, her face deadly serious now.

'No, Nullman. The Spar-sold batteries were at least a pound more, whereas this guy had his own packs round the back which he was selling in bulk from the van at half the price.'

'You damned fool, Valesco,' said Nullman, even if inside she was breathing a quiet sigh of relief. At least they wouldn't have to worry about contending with the long-lost finger bone of the Devil now, alongside everything else they had to deal with.

THAT'S WHERE YOU'RE ALL WRONG. BECAUSE I TURNED THE GOD SOCKET BLACK MYSELF BY

FORCING MYSELF BACK UP THAT TUBE STICKING OUT OF NICK STEEN'S HEAD IN ORDER TO HIDE FOR A WHILE INSIDE THE BOX ITSELF, THUS TURNING IT BLACK. I'VE BEEN BIDING MY TIME IN HERE, BUILDING UP MY STRENGTH AGAIN FOR THE FINAL ONSLAUGHT. WAITING FOR NICK STEEN TO DEPLETE HIS OWN STRENGTH WHILE DODGING BULLET FIRE FROM THOSE TWO WEIRD CHAUFFEURS YOU EMPLOY. NOW I'M ALL SET TO GO BACK DOWN AND . . .

The Nullifier got no further. With a death-defying scream, Nick reached up with his own hands and yanked violently at the cable protruding from his own head.

NO!

'Quick, Persephone!' yelled Nick. 'I need your help pulling this out before the Nullifier shimmies back up that connecting pipe into my head again. I need you to twist the pipe round so that it pumps out in the opposite direction, i.e., *Out* of my head!'

'No,' said Persephone, scowling and looking down at her shoes again.

Nick couldn't believe his eyes. 'Come on, Persephone. This is neither the time nor the place to go into another massive sulk with me. It's time you grew up and took on some responsibility for yourself and others.'

'Don't want to,' said Persephone, sniffing.

THAT'S RIGHT, PERSEPHONE, said the Nullifier, already halfway up the connecting pipe again. *DO WHAT YOU WANT. HE EFFECTIVELY CALLED YOU A WASTE OF SPACE. HE DOESN'T UNDERSTAND YOU, PERSEPHONE. JUST GIVE HIM THE FINGER AND TELL HIM TO GO SHOVE IT.*

'Be reasonable, Persephone,' cautioned Nick from his position in the corner of the ceiling. A position he might well be forced to abandon in a matter of nano-seconds. 'Sure, you're mad at me. Hell, my own daughter was mad at me.* I've been there. I understand. I know the score, Persephone. I know what it's like to have a big, ugly mouth-brace that collects food. To work up a sweat in baggy trousers that you don't wash and so start to smell, causing unsolicited comments from your family and friends and isolating you even further from your peers. All this, when the trousers in question don't even conceal the weight you wish to hide, but in fact simply exaggerate it. I know how much that hurts. Hell, my daughter was in tears daily whenever I pointed it out. But if you don't shape up and ship out this instant, young lady, you'll be sulking alone for another reason entirely. You'll be sulking alone because there'll be literally no one on earth left alive to sulk around, least of all you, princess!'

Nick couldn't have got her moving any faster if he'd set a tube of firecrackers going under her feet. Persephone must have lost at least five pounds in that one leap alone, as she jumped up from her sulking position and directed fire from her eyes towards the top of Nick's cranial head support.

Nick would be sure to remind Persephone about how much weight she'd lost in that simple action (and crucially, how much more she still needed to lose) afterwards, but for now, thankfully, he and she were a team again.

And in the nick of time, Nick reflected, as Persephone's mental force wrenched the pipework out from Nick's head, twisting it back round just at the moment that the Nullifier's energy was about to surge back into his brain.

Instead, the black-and-yellow-spotted R-Complex that had previously squirmed itself inside Nick's brain shot forth from the loose end of the connecting cable at speed, flying out and exploding against the glass of the observation window, before plopping to the floor in a quivering, jellied mess.

---

* Again, essential foreshadowing. GM.

119

'You're beaten, Nullman,' Nick said, still floating up by the ceiling. 'Now you have to contend with the power of Nick Steen's mind alone. Your R-Complex is dead. Now *I* am the master.'

'Nick?' said a small voice from below. He looked down at the small girl creeping out of her hiding place behind the smoking God Socket. It was Christabel, and the expression on her face was no longer quite so joyous as before.

'Apologies, Christabel,' said Nick, suddenly aware that his own words had themselves carried a certain questionable air of egotistical superiority. 'I'll try to balance my newfound powers with a degree of moral responsibility.'

'It's not that, Nick,' said Christabel, rocking gently back and forth as if suddenly agitated. 'It's the plane. The one we stopped from crashing into the ground. It's back.' She pointed upward through the observation window. *'And it's plummeting towards the ground again.'*

CHAPTER TWELVE

'Phase IV'

'Damn it!' Nick cried, floating down from the corner of the ceiling to stand before the window. 'It must have suffered one final blast of Nullifying psychic energy when that R–Complex exploded against the window, forcing it down again into a terrifying descent. Persephone, we need to stop that plane once again from crashing into the ground. Ideally via another burst of twisting, so that we can send it skywards again.'

'Unfortunately, my powers are depleted, Nick,' said Persephone, accidentally spitting out bits of food from between her clustered brace as she spoke – something that was guaranteed to put off any potential new boyfriends instantly, Nick reflected. 'I think I only have enough psychic power left to keep that thing suspended in the air for a few minutes or so,' Persephone continued. 'Unfortunately, I haven't been eating sensibly, and have mainly been gorging on family-sized bags of crisps and toffee popcorn.'

'Well, let that be a lesson to you,' snapped Nick. 'So we have no choice. You'll have to keep that plane hovering in the air while I figure out a safe way to get it down again.' He tutted inwardly. A safe way? Had Nick Steen ever found a safe way to bring a plane down? Hell, he'd single-handedly crashed well over a hundred of them during the last few months, hadn't he? Despite all that had happened to him, he had to remember that he was still inhabiting his horror novel *The Portentor*, meaning that any plane he attempted to bring down, no matter how far removed he might be from the flying seat, was destined to end, like all the others, in a colossal smoking fireball. And he didn't want Roz's life to end in a colossal smoking fireball, no matter how wrong she'd consistently been about his fiction.

He'd have to figure some other way of getting the plane down. What if he called Julia at Stalkford Airport and got her to ferry over a whole heap of bouncy castles from the local fairground to cushion the plane's fall? Or at least get the emergency crews over there in advance so they could start prepping before the plane hit the ground. But he couldn't do either of those things, he realised. Because he'd forgotten Julia's surname *again*, and he knew there were several Julias who worked at the airport, so it would no doubt be a complete nightmare, and Nick would probably end up having to go down there in person.

'I've done it, Nick!' cried Persephone. Nick looked over and saw that she'd successfully suspended the stricken jet in mid-air, as promised. A circular pink glow engulfed the jet now, keeping it gently afloat in mid-spiral.

'Good girl,' said Nick, smiling at Persephone for the first time.

Before she could smile back, her head exploded.

'Persephone!' yelled Nick, as several more bullets pounded into the teen's baggy jeans, hammering them outward like flapping gingham curtains in a Kansas twister.

'Now the other one,' yelled Valesco, directing the gunmen's aims towards the cowering Christabel. 'Before she has a chance to heal her!'

Nick glanced briefly at the plane, now descending once more at speed towards the earth below.

Christabel! Nick thought suddenly, amazed that he hadn't figured out the solution before now. It had to be Christabel! If the plane crashed, she could simply heal all the passengers again, including Roz. Christabel was the key. He had to save Christabel.

As he turned to protect her at all costs, Christabel's head exploded.

'Nooo!' Nick screamed, realising the precious time he'd spent weighing up the pros and cons of keeping Roz's plane afloat would now be the cause of the worst calamity Nick Steen had ever been responsible for.

Now both psychic girls were dead, Roz was involved in an ongoing death spiral towards earth that he no longer had the remotest chance of preventing, and he was suddenly caught in a terrifying face-off with a team of untrustworthy medical practitioners and scientists who were wielding guns and no doubt already discussing how they were going to repair the dreaded God Socket and continue their unholy crusade of psychic worldly destruction.

Then it hit Nick, like a bolt from heaven. At first he saw the distant pink glow coming from the far horizon, and then he saw *them*. Two ethereal figures, their heads aglow, heavenly flame rising from their shoulders like the wings of genuine angels.

Because they *were* genuine angels.

It was Christabel, Nick realised. In spirit form. And the other one.

'I give my powers to you now, Nick,' sang Christabel, her voice ringing inside his head as though coming from some far-off distant isle. 'We will meet again one day.'

'See ya,' said Persephone, not quite so sweetly.

And then, as the vision faded, Nick realised *he* had it now: the power to *heal*. The power to *reverse death itself*.

Nick Steen was now, truly, a God among men.

He reached out with both hands, prepared to bring Christabel – and then Persephone, if she behaved herself – back to life . . .

But as he did so, Barbara Nullman, who'd been crawling up unawares on Nick all this time, inhaled deeply on a fresh cigarette, smoothed a slender hand through her golden hair and freed the small clip behind her head holding it back from her forehead. She let her richly flowing mane of darkly golden locks tumble forward. Nick watched them bounce downward over her blouse, ricocheting off the female doctor's tautly smooth breasts.

'Get back in your bed,' Nullman said, slamming Nick backwards with both hands on to his gurney. Then she leaped on top of him, pinning him to the trolley. He could do nothing, wanted to do nothing as she slid herself forward on to his lap. 'You're *my* patient, Nick Steen. And whether or not you are a cosmic deity, you will lie, quaking, in the palm of my hand. Urging me, begging me to grant you pleasure. Pleasure that I alone have the power to grant or deny. Yes, the most powerful being in the universe will pant like a lowly dog at my burgundy-red high heels.'

Nick couldn't believe he'd been suckered in by the oldest trick in the book. He should have known Nullman would ultimately utilise those feminine charms of hers and cut him down to size at the worst possible moment. She was Cleopatra to his Alfred the Great, the face that launched a thousand longboats, and Nick knew that this battle, at long last, was over. For die he now must, in the arms — and legs, ideally — of the sexiest female canine he'd ever encountered in a sterile medical environment.

'Take me then, Nullman,' he said, sweating bulbously now like a frog in heat. 'I don't care what you do to this crazy world falling to ruin around us, as long as you do it to me first, okay?'

'Immediately,' said Nullman, untying Nick's operation gown from behind and sliding it sensually downward, over Nick's gut.

She pulled out something provocatively shaped, winking lustfully at Nick.

'Let's see what we can do with this thing, shall we?'

Nick gasped in ecstasy. Then frowned.

It was the Taffer's leek.

All at once, Nick's memory of the honourable Welchman broke the spell. He reached out with one hand to the Taffer's headless body beside him and immediately healed him.

'Ta for that, boyo,' yelled the Taffer. Then he caught sight of Nullman's hands clasped around his prize vegetable. 'How dare you, you brazen missy,' the Taffer cried, flying at Nullman, his face a mask of outraged fury. 'My prize leek and all. That's a barrel of bad ones, that is, young lady.'

His face blushing red with rage, the Taffer snatched his prize leek from Nullman's hands and bonked it across her head. Temporarily losing consciousness, the esteemed neuroscientist dropped from Nick's lap, slumping on to the floor. Nick pressed down vainly on his shame, realising that precious seconds were being lost as he fought to deflate the unwanted rigidity of his shaft. When it had finally shrunk to its usual level of stubbage, Nick rolled from the gurney, taking care to avoid the side where Nullman lay in case she should wake suddenly and reach out again to draw him downward on to the floor for another round, then raced back over to the observation window, intent upon resurrecting Christabel and Persephone in time to reverse the trajectory of the plummeting plane.

'Look you!' screamed the Taffer as the security guards leaped once more into view, having also concealed themselves behind the still-smoking God Socket, opening fire with both Berettas. Before Nick had a chance to evade their shots, the Taffer hurled himself into the path of the flying bullets, spattering his innards widely across the observation window.

Hell, Nick would heal him again in a minute. Turning swiftly towards his foe, Nick scowled angrily, projecting two jets of molten pink fire in the direction of this pair of would-be scientific assassins.

The jets passed through the eyeballs of the blond-haired youth, piercing the back of his head, before soaring onward into the eyes of his balding companion. The heads of both men frazzled, melting in the jets' stream like human lollies. But Nick had no time to savour his victory. Right now, he couldn't afford to lose a further second, aware that throughout this entire protracted climactic denouement (were one to use the analogy of a story, say, to describe this ongoing dramatic chain of events), Roz's plane was still plummeting violently, tragically, irrevocably towards the ground.

He turned back to the observation window. There was the jet, bursting through that bank of low-lying cloud again. The jumbo carrying Roz Bloom to her doom – unless Nick could stop it in its tracks, change its trajectory somehow. But first he had to resurrect Christabel and Persephone, he remembered. He just about had time, he figured, if nothing else got in his way.

As he turned his head to Persephone's body and prepared to lay his newly developed healing hands about a foot away from her exploded head (he resolutely refused to go anywhere closer), a snarl sounded from the smoking, doorless elevator shaft.

Nick looked up in sudden panic as Scorcher, the golden retriever with pink jets of flame coming out of its eyes, leaped into the observation deck and bounded towards him, bearing its fangs in a disarmingly friendly – yet deadly – smile.

'Sit!' bellowed Nick, but the dog was having none of it. With a terrifying yelp, the retriever leaped up at Nick's chest, pretending to lick his face but in reality getting close enough to fire two jets of psychic energy deep into Nick's eyes, like he'd just done himself to the two security chauffeurs.

'Not so fast,' cried Nick, hurling the dog aside with a swipe of mental will. His powers were now developing at a rapid pace, Nick realised. Clearly his brief dalliance with the Nullifier had released pent-up energies inside his own psyche, teaching it advances in psychic knowledge that might have taken Mankind centuries, maybe even millennia, to develop.

The dog flew across the room, colliding into a wall of as-yet undamaged computer terminals, damaging them – and it – seriously. Some got dented, others merely scratched. But all were sufficiently damaged enough to have invalidated the warranty.

The dog's body sprang back from the wall, landing on all fours. Immediately, it projected two more bolts of psychic fire at Nick's head, searing the remaining cables protruding from his pate as he ducked to avoid the spouting flames.

'Impressive,' said Nick. 'For a golden retriever. I hear you're one of the least intelligent breeds of canine.'

That rattled the mutt. With a manic bout of barking, Scorcher leaped forwards again, aiming its opened jaws once more at Nick's throat. Then it feigned, swinging its paws at him instead like human fists.

Nick blocked both blows with his forearm, spun left and threw a right hook at the dog's skull. The blow landed hard, then Nick followed it up with a powerful uppercut, sending the dog upward into the air.

Nick used his mind then, flinging the animal sideways with a lightning-fast nod, catapulting the retriever straight through the observation window and out into the night.

As the glass pane flew outward with it, Nick was shocked to see the dog's trajectory suddenly slow, as it, and the glass shards surrounding it, appeared to stop, then reverse towards Nick, back through the window again. As the various window fragments reassembled themselves into place behind it, the dog landed again on all fours, having successfully reversed itself with what Nick suspected was some new psychic trick Valesco and his scientific assistants had taught it.

Nick froze.

Valesco. Valesco was still alive, wasn't he? Though the Taffer had seen to Nullman, and Nick himself to the security chauffeurs, no one had yet dealt with the sinister Dr Valesco.

'That's right,' said a voice behind Nick. He turned to see the good doctor astride the smoking God Socket, its connecting cable now attached to his own head. He was laughing maniacally. 'It feels good, to be a *God* . . .'

The doctor aimed his eyes at Nick, and they began to glow scarlet red (not pink anymore, as Valesco had just pressed an *additional concealed button* on the other side of the God Socket, marked 'Most Powerful of All').

Nick sensed Scorcher running towards him from behind, intent on boxing him senseless. What the hell could he do now? Nick thought desperately.

Then, running on instinct alone, Nick screwed his eyes tight and projected a pulse of psychic energy towards Valesco's lab-coat pocket, drawing out the bag of dog biscuits he had sensed hiding inside.

At once, the biscuits caught Scorcher's eye, and the dog bounded immediately in their direction. As Valesco's scarlet jets of fire opened up from both eyes, Scorcher leaped instinctively in pursuit of the tasty treats – straight into the path of the twin lasers.

The dog's body exploded in a puff of fur and cooked meat. Its pieces landed on the floor of the observation deck, looking ironically like the same kind of bits you get in Pedigree Chum, which are ostensibly horse chunks, but more than likely cubes of dead dog as well, Nick suspected.

'Scorcher!' yelled Valesco, suddenly bereft at the sight of the detonated dog.

Taking advantage of the doctor's momentary distraction, Nick projected a full blast of psychic wind at Valesco's head, sending him careening backward, still attached to the God Socket, and through the observation deck window, just as he'd previously done with Scorcher.

Valesco burst through the glass and fell, screaming, to the ground far below. Seconds later, Nick heard the tell-tale explosion of the detonating God Socket, then caught sight of a miniature mushroom cloud rising steadily into the air, eventually ballooning upward past the observation deck window.

And then Nick saw the plane. Too late now, he realised. No way could he prevent it crashing into the ground this time. He'd blown it. He'd done everything he possibly could, but Fate had decreed a failure. Nick Steen had no time now to resurrect Christabel or Persephone. Alone, he watched in horror as the plane plummeted downward, inches from the ground . . .

. . . then turned.

Nick could hardly believe it. Though he was urging, willing, *forcing* that plane away from the ground, he had no idea he actually possessed enough psychic strength to achieve such a feat.

But here was the proof. The jumbo jet that Roz was a passenger on had been saved in literally the nick of time. Miraculously, with mere inches between the nose of the stricken Boeing and the ground below it, the jet had turned again, banking to the left, rising upward from the surface, soaring once more in the direction of the sky, towards . . .

Nick swallowed, hard.

Towards him!

Nick Steen was the plane's target.

Then, as the thing drew closer, Nick saw something even stranger about it. For the jet's wings, he realised, were leather, like vast pterodactyl wings.

The plane was part-organic! And sitting on its top, astride the main fuselage like some terrifying bronco display, rode a thin and black-shrouded form.

Deathflap!

Of course, Nick realised. Deathflap had been part of his portentums all along. Those *leathery* wings . . . He'd not realised it up until now because, like he'd told Roz, Deathflap's wings were also part-feathered. How stupid of him to have dismissed Roz's warning on a

129

purely technical matter. If he'd only listened to his editor, just this once.

But now he was doomed. Like a fool, he'd discarded Roz's dire warning that Nick's sins would find him out. That Death would finally come to claim his soul, having been cheated all those times Nick had emerged from those aviation wrecks as sole survivor.

Now Deathflap was here to collect its bill. And Nick had no way of avoiding it. No way at all.

Realising everything was over, Nick closed his eyes and waited for the inevitable.

As the plane finally hit the building.

★

The blaze had long since died, extinguished by the high winds rolling in off the barren Stalkford plains.

From the ashes of the ruins, slowly growing visible as the grey clouds swirled in the breeze, rose a dust-covered figure.

The man, for the figure was male, rose to his knees, dusted down his front, then stood, gazing around him at the mangled, twisted steel of the decimated building.

It had been a technical facility once, he recalled. A place known only to those who knew of its existence – and of those, there were mercifully few. A place once known as Nulltec.

Nulltec, Nick repeated inwardly, trying to force his memory back into the present.

He tripped over something long and rigid, then reached down and picked up a broken, glazed, prize-winning leek. And remembered . . .

He'd survived. By some miracle, Nick had survived.

Against all odds, Nick Steen had emerged once more from the ruins, untouched, unscathed and completely alone.

130

The sole survivor.

He staggered over to what remained of the building's former observation window, and looked out across the Stalkford country-side. There were no sirens, now. No Julia waiting in the flight lounge to welcome him home, before spending all his money.

And no Roz . . . No poor, sweet, frequently misguided Roz.

This time, Nick realised, looking up into those far-off, orange-tinted intangible clouds, he was truly alone.

Then he saw it. Emerging from the vaporous bank of mist like a distant, daytime moon.

A face.

A face in the sky . . .

Larger now, looming over the scattered remnants of destruction below it. A *human* face.

His own.

The giant, colossal face of *Nicholas Steen*.

WRONG.

(It was the voice of Richard Burton or Robert Powell inside Nick's mind, again.)

YOU ARE THE NULLIFIED MAN.

Nick thought he glimpsed the trace of a body under the vast head, trailing in the dying light like a giant, distant weather balloon.

THE SALAMANDER MAN.

ALONE YOU WILL RULE, IN THIS EMPTY COSMOS.

LOOK UPON YOUR WORKS, YE MIGHTY NICK STEEN, AND DESPAIR (OF SEEING THEM BACK IN PRINT).

Nick screamed.

And screamed.

And screamed.

But there was no one in the world left to hear.

The End

EPILOGUE

'The Nullified Man'

'What's he looking at?' said Roz, knocking one finger against the tank in an effort to wake him.

'His own reflection,' said Nullman, checking Nick's readings from a long stream of paper spooling from a nearby computer terminal. 'Either that, or he's insisting on watching the whole damned thing again.'

She reached out behind her and turned off the monitor, which showed Nick standing on the exploded battlements of a destroyed Nulltec.

'Quite an imagination, he has. One thing's for certain,' Nullman continued, handing the paper readout to Dr Valesco, who took it from her moodily, steering his shiny metal box on wheels into a neighbouring corridor. 'We won't be plugging him into anything like our God Socket prototype. Good job we ran a bench test first.'

'A bench test?' Roz asked, confused.

'A full computer simulation of the possible outcomes. A try-out, Miss Bloom. A rehearsal, if you will, before we wired him up to it for real. We averted potential catastrophic failure, Miss Bloom. Your friend would have destroyed us all.'

Roz glanced down at Nick's face, floating blankly in the tank of fluid as a stream of bubbles rose upward from between his dangling legs. She stifled a sob. How the hell had Nick even got here?

'This way, Miss Bloom,' said Nullman, leading Roz out into the corridor, following Valesco. 'I'll fill you in on what's happened, down in our basement office. It's a good job you came by. You say you found the prize-giving invitation on Mr Steen's desk?'

'That's right,' said Roz, following her out. 'I do hope you manage to find a cure for Nick's brain, so that he's well enough to receive the award.'

'All in good time, Miss Bloom,' said Nullman, pulling the door closed behind them. 'All in good time.'

Nick watched the forms fade to nothing in the murky fluid. He thought of screaming out a warning, then realised he no longer had any strength left at all in his brain.

They'd nullified him after all, he supposed. As Nick gradually surrendered to the calming, rhythmical whirring of the submerged water pump, he elected to let his mind drift.

And wept.*

---

* A safe act for Nick to engage upon here, as all tears will be disguised from view by the surrounding water. GM

ARABELLA MATHERS

PROLOGUE

'Did you find it?'

'Here.' Roz handed Nullman the manuscript, still crisp as the day it had been sealed inside a hidden safe under the floorboards of the secret study Nick kept concealed behind a false wall in his private office, and which Roz had only found after comparing wall measurements with the building's official floor plans. These efforts had also revealed the whereabouts of a private toilet system Nick maintained immediately below his writing chair so that he might relieve himself 'on the job' or 'mid flow', but despite the intricate system of pipework Roz had uncovered, Nullman only seemed interested in the manuscript.

'*Arabella Mathers*,' said Nullman, reading the story's title out loud. Then glanced down at the message Nick had scrawled below it in ragged biro:

> *Too damned raw . . .*

She looked up at Roz. 'And you've yet to read a word of this?'

'All Nick told me was that the story existed,' Roz replied, feeling suddenly uncomfortable as she observed the writer's slumbering frame in the adjacent medical observation room. 'He gave me instructions for how to find it in the event of his death. But *only* in the event of his death.'

Roz felt a fresh stab of guilt plunge through her vitals. She'd been feeling them all morning. Though Nick hadn't woken from his coma in almost five months, he'd finally been transferred from his sensory deprivation tank to a normal bed, and Roz was convinced he was partly sentient. Though his head was still wired up to all manner of medical machinery, Roz believed fervently that Nick was able to hear, despite all evidence to the contrary, her every word. If so, would he regard this – Roz handing over the most private, painful story of his entire oeuvre to the head of a shadowy technical research facility – an act of betrayal? With a nagging sense of shame, she averted her eyes from Nick's sleeping form.

But she'd had to, hadn't she? After all, Roz had been imprisoned here by Nullman as well, in a cell very much like Nick's own, and told to find the manuscript in question or face withdrawal of 'privileges' – her weekly allowance of limited-run, signature-edition slingbacks.

Yet despite this, and Nick's soporose state, Roz had the uncanny feeling she'd just been sacked by her favourite author.

'If it makes you feel better,' said Nullman, sensing Roz's discomfort, 'his death probably isn't that far off, anyway.' The Chief Head of the Nulltec Corporation glanced through the initial paragraph of Nick's 'lost' story, comparing its opening words with the blurry visuals she'd seen rising in snatches from Nick's unconscious mind for several weeks on Nulltec's dream-scope monitor, materialising themselves amid regular bursts of tortured screaming from her patient's otherwise comatose body. 'But if we can somehow get to grips with what this particular story means, it might prove to be the path to recovery for Mr Steen – if not the entire world.'

'How so?' asked Roz, unable to see how a story Nick had written, immediately regretted writing, then for some unknown reason insisted on confining to a concealed safe until the event of his death could possibly be of any benefit to him now.

'For some time, Miss Bloom, we've been picking up visual traces – impressions, if you will – of a "repressed" story emerging from the depths of Steen's unconscious mind, into the lobes of his subconscious brain. As you know, these unfathomable depths of Steen's pysche are where we believe his leak to another dimension is currently situated, through which his imagination has been escaping and warping reality as we know it. Turning our own worldly phenomena into the terrifying, living embodiment of a best-selling Nick Steen chiller. The unconscious mind is also, as we have discovered following a great many aborted attempts, the area of Mr Steen's brain that is currently sealed shut by both his subconscious and conscious lobes. He's locked us out, Miss Bloom. And if we cannot penetrate our way in, we cannot hope to locate the source of the mind-leak and block it up with industrial sealant. This,' said Nullman, waving the manuscript in front of Roz's face, 'is the key that may open the door to that inner sanctum.'

Nick's story? Roz thought. A story his own brain had suppressed?

'Why exactly would Nick suppress his own story?' she asked, finding it difficult to believe that a man who'd engaged sexually with a metallic typing implement had the desire to repress anything. 'Is it because his own writing has inadvertently instigated the ultimate destruction of this world and all that we know, and he somehow feels bad about that?'

'No,' replied Nullman, curtly. 'That doesn't bother him in the slightest. It's something more mundane, we believe. Our computers have been picking up traces and patterns suggestive of an anxiety disorder stemming from his apparent dereliction of duties as a father.'

'Traces? Patterns? I don't understand,' said Roz, still confused by the impressive array of technical machinery she'd been exposed to on an almost daily basis here at Nulltec.

Despite all the scientific gadgetry, no one but her seemed to be remotely interested in securing Nick's freedom, least of all Stalkford Airlines, who'd been running a relatively crash-free service since Nick's extended leave of absence, and Stalkford City Council, who were quite prepared to leave Nick festering, as long as the physical effects of his leaking imaginata were confined to the wards and corridors of Nulltec.

'I suppose you could say they're like reels from a film,' Nullman explained. 'Incoherent in the main, merely fragments of a longer narrative. All we can tell from the glimpses we've seen, which fortunately includes a mock-up of the story's intended rear-cover blurb, is that the story is a gothic horror tale, and revolves around a fictionalised writer of gothic horror fiction, loosely based, we believe, on Nick Steen himself. A man who neglects his daughter's happiness in favour of his own self-serving interests, and who, as a result, loses possession of his daughter to the insidious clutches of some supernatural being. Evidently, the story was partly based on real events in the author's life.'

'Nick *had* been emerging from a rather messy divorce,' Roz conceded.

'Which might explain, therefore, why the tale has been "buried" by Mr Steen's conscious mind. It's evidently a tale too traumatic for mental recall. Yet in his current agitated emotional state, Mr Steen's unconscious instincts are clearly keen to re-explore these unresolved issues.'

Nullman turned over another page, revealing the author's dedication. 'For my darling daughter,' she read aloud.

'Nick's not seen her in over three years.'

'He may never see her again, unless we can find a way to blast a hole through to his unconscious mind. This story will open a channel, Miss Bloom. Chisel a way into Nick's repressed psyche. All we need to do is feed the text from this story into the subconscious lobes of Nick Steen's brain, and his entire head will go into shock. With the barriers between the brain's varying states of consciousness temporarily loosened, we may yet be able to force our way in.'

Roz winced. This sounded wrong. Something about Nullman's tone wasn't convincing her. Was this really the right way – the only way – to gain access to Nick's unconscious mind? Surely if they just left Roz alone with him for a while, she might be able to gain access to it herself? Let her speak to Nick for a while. Nurture him; nuzzle him physically like a lost grizzly cub for a couple of hours. Surely then they'd be able to locate an alternative back passage into Nick's unconscious brain?

'Won't injecting this suppressed tale cause him an unbearable amount of unnecessary emotional pain?' Roz asked.

'Not remotely,' replied Nullman. 'It will cause him an unbearable amount of *necessary* emotional pain. We must get inside his mind if we're to have any hope of sealing up that hole. And we've already ordered a tub of sealant from B&Q.'

'Still,' Roz said, wondering what Nullman's reaction might be if she were to offer up her physical services first. 'Maybe I ought to read the story first, just to check on its content. That way, we won't risk damaging Nick's psyche by exposing him to any deeply painful memories that might prefigure a catastrophic relapse or total psychological breakdown.'

'Too late,' said Nullman, inserting the last of the manuscript's pages into the feed tray of a nearby computer.

Instantly, the images on the monitor above them began to flicker and change, until Roz gradually discerned the sight of a beautiful summer meadow bordering a tall, windswept cliff top. Then she saw the car Nick had always wanted, viewed from high above, driving at some speed along the coastal path amid a warming sea breeze before angling southward, through a heavy line of trees, towards a lone building in the middle of a wood. The remote, solitary house of Nick Steen's dreams . . .

CHAPTER ONE

'The House'

It looked just as scary in the sunlight. But though the surrounding trees cast deep shadow across much of the house, its steep gabled roof out-climbed the highest foliage, and the rounded tower I'd picked as my main writing study rose even further past the adjacent greenery, commanding an unimpeded view of the breaking wave-line beyond Bloater's Cove, a mile or so to the east.

Several arched windows ran along the top floor, spaced unevenly between flaking, weathered panels of rotting timber. A large gabled front commanded the ground level of the house, overlooking its wide wooden porch. Here, on a raised platform before the main door, ran irregular rows of warped timber boarding. Against the front entrance, angled crookedly between two bowed planks, sat an old, half-stripped wicker chair.

A dead cat hung from the mailbox.

Perfect, I thought, even though I suspected a dead cat might not meet with my daughter's approval. But then technically, it was *my* house, not hers.

Gwendolen would have to remember that fact if she wanted to spend the summer here. Rather than a local youth hostel, say, where jungle law applied.

I say the house was mine, though technically I was just renting it for a few months. Yet it was mine in *spirit*, because this old building was the ideal place for me to pen my latest gothic paperback for Garrett Publishing.

And this book *had* to be a success. My divorce from Carlotta had been costly, to say the least. And while my ex-wife would be spending much of *her* July and August exploring the depths of both the Aegean and her latest voiceover coach, I'd be breaking both balls trying to work up enough alimony to get her lawyers off my back for the winter months and, God willing, return custody of Gwendolen to her.

I was aware, of course, that fresh legal woes would follow. No doubt I'd get saddled with our daughter *again* next year during yet another vital writing period, but if I could ensure that this particular gothic chiller was the best I'd ever penned, a multi-million world-wide best-seller, say, then I'd finally be able to secure that elusive film deal Carlotta had always mocked me about, pretend I was sorry for everything that happened by casting her as the romantic lead, then sack her publicly on the first day of production, citing technical problems matching the camera's 2:35:1 aspect ratio with the advanced width of her thighs.

That would teach the drunken, volatile, Mediterranean harpy.

Hey, she's said a lot worse to me, okay? A *lot* worse. Things like, 'You're simply impossible.'

Where was I? Oh yes, Gwendolen.

That's my daughter's name. Her mother's choice, not mine. I would have called her Millicent, or Maud, like a good gothic hero-ine. Or, if she'd been born a boy, Mike. But, alas, it wasn't to be. And she's not a bad kid, all things considered. A bit nervy, which, as I've warned her numerous times, will simply make life tough for her. She *has* to buck up.

She really, really does.

I could sense her distress beside me even now as I swung my Jensen Interceptor round the next curve of our sweeping driveway at high speed. I knew my driving wasn't the cause of her distress. After all, I'd been maxing it past the legal limit all the way out here from Stalkford, taking out two hares, four muntjacs and a whole colony of rabbits in just over sixty miles of winding lanes. Which is just a fact of country living, I told Gwen once she'd finished crying.

'Look, it's either that or a suicidal emergency stop causing a devastating death-roll followed by mutual decapitation through these open windows and a fiery inferno of burned flesh and twisted metal. But sure, the bunnies will live. Make your choice, Gwendolen.'

As it turned out, she said nothing at all, which allowed me to push the car even harder, shaving off an additional seven minutes at the cost of some mating pigeons and a third hare.

No, Gwendolen was distressed at this moment because of the house. And with good reason, I noted with some degree of pride. For it truly was a terrifying sight. A striking, small-scale Gothic mansion right out of the supernatural storybook.

I'd first viewed the place in early spring, when the golden glow of a winter dusk was still visible through the leafless branches beyond each window as I went from room to room, planning where I'd stack my precious bookcases and those belongings I'd stolen from Carlotta's private cupboards while she was out gallivanting with her most recent swarthy lover, and which I'd told her lawyer had been donated to a charity shop for dumb animals by her desperate, emotionally damaged daughter.

It was only old rubbish, anyway. A large batch of re-stitched lingerie and Latino Crooner LPs, which I'd taken mainly out of spite rather than for any monetary value. In response, Carlotta had taken my collection of Edgar Allan Poe busts, which she was apparently using for ballast in her latest designer yacht.

She blamed me and I blamed her, of course, but that's the way it was with Carlotta and I in those final, bitter weeks. And I guess our divorce was tough on Gwendolen, who'd hit twelve last spring. We tended to treat her like an adult most of the time, I suppose because she had that annoying tendency to look partly like us. And even though we both knew it was merely an unfortunate yet inevitable result of our own misguided physical congress, from which a human-shaped daughter had ultimately emerged, I guess the physical similarities still smarted. Though I didn't like to admit it, I was all too aware that I'd been regularly encouraging Gwendolen, from an early age, to consult a plastic surgeon the moment she'd begun to fear, as I already did, that she was fast turning into a fiendish doppelgänger of that ruthless siren who'd single-handedly set about destroying both our lives.

And according to Gwendolen, Carlotta had done the self-same thing, fearing the girl was starting to resemble yours truly.

Sorry, back to the house.

I'd told the estate agent there and then that I wanted the place for the whole summer, and yet the oily squirt had made me wait a further month, claiming a rival bidder was prepared to go much, much higher than the current asking price.

'After all,' he'd slithered at me, 'it's a much-desired property, Mr Stein. Especially in the warm summer months. Now, if you might possibly go just a little higher . . .'

I'd relented in the end, of course, with a little help from Gwendolen's money box, knowing how absolutely perfect the place was. After all, in what better location could one write the ultimate gothic chiller, than the ultimate Gothic House on a Hill, situated on a lonely stretch of Stalkford coastline overlooking Bloater's Cove?

And write it I must. By summer's end, Carlotta would have finished exploring her latest wrecks, nautical *and* human, and would no doubt have sunk her claws into some fresh youthful diving instructor or puffed-up Grecian concierge, gearing up for yet another slice of author-earned alimony from yours truly.

'What do you think, Gwen?' I asked my daughter, swerving left again before braking hard beside the raised wooden porch.

Removing her seatbelt, even though I'd told her a hundred times that there was no need to attach one when *I* was driving, she turned round to me and spoke. 'It's lovely, Dad.'

Here, then, was *another* challenge to my authority. Well, I wasn't gonna let her off the hook this time. We were facing the whole summer together.

'Don't lie to me, Gwendolen. You loathe this place. It's a rotting, festering hulk, infested with spiders, cold in winter, swarming with wasps in the summer. I bet there's probably a huge nest hanging even now in one of those rooms. Maybe *your* room. It's fine, I'll clear it out. Just don't lie to me, okay? I've had more lies than I can take from your mother. There's no need for you to put the boot in as well.'

'I'm sorry, Dad. I hate the place.'

'Jesus, that's just *typical*,' I snapped, storming out of the car. I slammed the door shut behind me, feeling the stark bitterness of the last few months resurfacing like a bloated corpse. Couldn't she see *I* was hurting, too? Here I was, trying to sort out a future for her, make her a buck or two so she'd be happy, and *this* was how she rewarded me? Jeez, if this was her behaviour at twelve years of age, what the hell was thirteen going to be like? Or fourteen? Or fifteen, even? Or sixteen? Seventeen? God, can you imagine what it would be like at *eighteen*? Then nineteen too, most likely. And though both Carlotta and I would probably have turfed Gwendolen out of our respective houses by that stage, she'd no doubt be moody with both of us right through her twenties. You just couldn't help some people.

I walked up to the front door, feigning my usual emotional indifference while occupying myself with the house's iron padlock. The key the estate agent had given me was thick with rust and took me a while to insert. Eventually, Gwendolen got out of the car and joined me.

'I thought that tower would be perfect for you,' I said, pointing up at the coned eyrie facing outward across the distant ocean. Once again, I realised, it was *me* who was offering an olive branch. 'It looks out across Bloater's Cove. It's extremely picturesque up there.'

Gwendolen looked up and, for the first time in a month, smiled at me. 'Sounds lovely, Dad.'

'Unfortunately, I need a second study with natural daylight, so you're getting the attic instead.'

Her smile dropped as suddenly as it had arisen. Luckily, I'd expected that, so could stave off any hurt to me.

Generously, I offered her another olive branch. 'If the estate agent says it's okay, I'll install a window at some point.'

She nodded, solemnly.

I rolled my eyes and sighed.

'Thanks, Dad.'

'Not hard, is it?' I said, finally succeeding in unlocking the front door. I stepped inside the house, steeling myself against the harsh odour of lingering damp and dry rot. The estate agent had left a welcome pack on a small telephone table under the main staircase. It was anything but welcoming, I noted, being largely a stack of unpaid utility bills dating back to a previous decade. I dumped them in the kitchen bin, preparing myself to show Gwendolen the front lounge and rear dining room, then realised she was still outside. I walked back to the front door and found her standing stock still, staring at the dead cat.

'It's just a dead cat, Gwen. Cats die, you know. Like marriages. Marriages die. We all die. Your mother will die. Her current lover will die. All her lovers will die. And you, Gwen. You, too, will die. Maybe today, you will die. Who knows?'

It sounded harsh, but she *had* to buck up.

'How did this cat get here, Dad?'

'God knows. Maybe some old dispute between an unscrupulous

landlord and his irate tenant. Perhaps a disgruntled gardener with a hideous skin affliction.'

'But it's still fresh.'

'Blood feuds can last for years, Gwen. Look at me and your mother. Can you honestly say you've ever known us to be civil to each other?'

'There's an envelope stuck to it.'

Intrigued, I walked over to the mailbox and saw, for the first time, a letter attached to the feline's twisted neck. I plucked it free and tore open the handwritten envelope. The message inside was brief, but to the point.

WRITER.
LEAVE BLOATER'S COVE.
OR <u>DIE</u> . . .

'What does it say?' asked Gwendolen, her face growing pale with fear.

Suddenly, my paternal instincts, long since buried, awoke with a fierce defensive intensity. I had to protect my beloved daughter from this act of inexplicable, human evil.

'It's from people who want to kill us,' I explained. 'It's from people who want to kill us, Gwen,' I explained. 'But rest assured, that probably won't happen.'

She was shaking now, I noticed. Her ink-stained fingers grasped frantically at the sleeves of her summer frock.

'Listen, Gwendolen, it's probably just that rival bidder I told you about.' I spoke sternly to her, knowing I had to shock her out of a state of fear that might rapidly consume her utterly if I let it. And I needed a steady pair of hands to bring in all my boxes from the car.

'The estate agent told me someone else had been interested in renting this place over the summer. That's why I pawned all your toys for the extra cash. But don't fret, Gwen. I'm not about to tell anyone round here that it was *your* money that sealed the deal. They won't come for you *first.*'

She nodded, shaking.

'Now buck up and bring in those boxes. I can't risk straining my arm muscles, as you know. We have this place for three months only, and I have to produce a multi-million best-selling novel by the end of our lease, come rain or shine, or you'll need to go to an institution.'

To steady her nerves, I got her to make us both a cup of tea, then came outside to watch her struggle up the steps with the last of my belongings.

'Careful, Gwen,' I said, suspecting her increased weariness might cause her to stumble on the bowed planking. There were at least five more boxes of books to unload from the boot, containing piles of my very rarest gothic novels, some almost entirely unsold since the day they'd been published.

'These people are just yokels,' I said, reassuringly, suspecting she was still worried about the letter, which I'd already burned in our lounge fireplace, along with what remained of the cat. 'And yokels are philistines, Gwen. Heathens. Ill-educated, interbred serfs, fated to die young while operating some dangerous piece of industrial machinery. Drink, idle threats and blind superstition are all these people have in life.'

I sat her down in the rickety wicker chair for a moment, suspecting she was close to fainting. Then I smiled at her, for the first time in well over a year.

'All good gothic novels have yokels, Gwen. And a spooky house on a hill overlooking some wild, windswept clifftop. This place is *perfect* for my book. Please try and understand that. Hell, all I'm lacking here is a wicked lord and a doomed heroine. Who knows, maybe even *they'll* turn up.'

I laughed, but Gwendolen didn't laugh with me. For some reason, those words seemed to haunt her. It may have been my imagination, but I could swear she almost backed off from me at that moment.

'This house is meant for us both, Gwen,' I continued. 'Meant for you and me, although mainly me. A place fit for a father and his daughter. We can heal here, Gwen. Put the past behind us. We've got the whole summer. Just you and me. And if I can write the book I know I can write here, in this *perfect* house . . . we need never go hungry, or see your mother, again.'

A light breeze blew through nearby trees from the distant cove, fluttering my daughter's hair, which shimmered softly in the westering sunlight. She looked magical, as if her parents' divorce had never happened, and once more she was filled with the hope, happiness and fleeting innocence of her cradle days.

It was the last time I saw her that way.

CHAPTER TWO

'The Attic'

'But I HATE the attic!' yelled Gwendolen, stamping her feet on the dusty floorboards as I cut free what remained of the wasps' nest over her bed, which I'd insisted she destroy by herself as a character-building exercise, and also because I couldn't risk having any of my typing fingers stung. She'd emerged largely intact from the experience bar her fore-arms, which were both a mass of raised welts, and for once I felt proud of her. She looked like she might be starting to buck up, after all.

Then came the tantrum, however, which grew from my insistence that she use the antique child's rocking chair I'd found in the far corner of the room to sit on, explaining I couldn't risk damaging those same typing fingers bringing up one of the dining room chairs from the ground floor, and advising her to lose weight in order to fit into it. But she'd cried out that the thing itself scared her; cried like a baby that the whole attic was creepy and she couldn't possibly sleep a wink up here. All I could see in front of me at that moment was Carlotta yelling at me about my various ineptitudes, and before I knew what was happening, I'd lost patience with her again.

'Like I've told you a hundred times, Gwendolen Stein, I need all these other rooms for my writing. I have to have the main study downstairs for nocturnal drafting. Then I need the tower eyrie for

151

daylight writing and twilight pensive musing, plus the kitchen table and lounge area for lunch and dinnertime writing respectively. Meaning that the only room available for you is this attic. Which, I hasten to add, does not come for free.'

That seemed rather harsh, I thought. Maybe the atmosphere of the old place was getting to me, but I could sense myself running out of patience far more swiftly than usual. More or less the moment I'd set foot inside.

'What do you mean?' she said, streams of tears glistening upon both cheeks. Well, that brand of amateur theatrics wasn't going to wash with me.

'I told you before we left Stalkford that I was going to find you a summer job, and I have.'

'I don't *want* a summer job. I want to go out and play, Daddy. I want to spend the summer walking the coast, looking for a friend.'

'And you will,' I said. 'Once you've earned your keep, young lady. You'll be needing pocket money for those ice creams, won't you? And the Bank of Dad is closed until my book is written and Nicholas Stein is officially a multi-millionaire.'

'But I don't *want* a summer job.' She began to cry into her top.

'Tough crap, Gwendolen,' I said. 'Because whether you like it or not, you've got one.' I stopped for a moment, realising what I'd just said. It had come to that, had it? Swearing at my own daughter. I don't think a day had ever gone by without me swearing at Carlotta, or *to* Gwendolen about Carlotta, but this was different. I'd never actually sworn *at* my daughter.

Of course, I'd known I'd end up swearing at her eventually. Throughout her teenage years, certainly. On a daily basis, no doubt. In fact, to that end, I'd even been storing up a small library of phrases in preparation, but I'd been banking on a few months yet of largely swear-free admonishments. But, just like that, Gwendolen had taken all that quiet parental restraint I'd been carefully, diligently cultivating over the years, and blown it clean out of the window with that surly attitude of hers.

What the hell was happening to us?

'What a great bloody start to the summer,' I said.

'Stop swearing at me, Dad!'

Well, if I'd needed any proof that she was becoming a right little madam, there it was.

'Listen, this is the job, princess, if you choose to damn well accept it. And you damn well will, I might add. Because if you don't, you can just skedaddle your twelve-year-old ass down to the local YMCA and fight it out with *their* clientele.'

'What's the job, Dad?'

'The job, daughter, is being my copy-editor for the summer.'

I thought she'd be impressed at that. Thankful, even. A chance to work for a literary great. But instead, her face remained blanker than ever. Her lack of gratitude, nay respect, was simply astounding. I'd never normally hand anybody, let alone Gwendolen, the enormous responsibility of being my copy-editor, but the truth was that my publishers at Garrett had a bee in their bonnets about my supposed authorial penchant for 'purple prose'. As if gothics were written using anything else?

But times, it appeared, were a-changing, so they insisted on reminding me. Now the reading public wanted leaner, meaner, tauter and tighter, non-supernatural thrillers, ideally with opening chapters consisting of three sentences or fewer. The eternal 'female in peril' was still fashionable, naturally, but ideally the beleaguered wench should now be running from a speeding car on some dusty Arizona highway, or fleeing a sinister yet ultra-modern-looking psychiatric hospital in the middle of a dark woodland thicket in the dead of night.

Screw that. I wrote gothic chillers, and with this book, I'd damn well prove that sinister mansions, dusty catacombs, fluttering frocks and supernatural terror were still *in*.

My book-to-be, I'd decided, would single-handedly bring back gothic horror to the masses. Through it, I'd breathe fresh life into a dying genre, make myself unbelievably rich and solve all my nagging marital woes.

'It's simple,' I said. 'All you need do is type up my written pages each day on that typewriter over there. It's vital that the typed manuscript is completed exactly as I have written it, and in good time. No deviation from my chosen wording, no needless embellishments by you.'

'Is that really what a copy-editor does?'

'It's far more than they should be doing. Remember, no "clever" attempts at editing. Type everything up exactly as I write it, and then your time is your own.'

'Yes, Dad.'

'Wait, I hadn't finished. You *must* type up my pages *before* you leave this room. Do *not* leave this room until you have typed up my pages. No going out of this room *until* you've typed up my pages. Then, and only then, when you've typed up my pages, may you leave this room. Is that understood?'

'Yes, Dad.'

'I said, is that understood?'

'Yes, Dad.'

'Fine. *After* you've typed up my pages, *then* you can go out and play – 'kay?'

I expected her to say ''kay' back, but instead she said, 'As you wish.'

'You don't sound remotely grateful.'

'How do I type up anything without a light in here?'

'For the last time, Gwendolen, you're not having access to candles. You're only twelve.'

'Can't you leave me what's left of that one?'

'This one?' I laughed, holding the candle I'd brought up with me away from her. 'How would I see my way back over to the door?'

'Can't you bring me up another one?'

'And have you accidentally burn the whole house down in my absence? No chance.'

I looked over at the wall, which I'd decided would be too hard to fit a window into as it was a sloping roof, and glanced instead at the empty light socket, from which the wasp's nest had recently hung. 'I'll pick up a fresh bulb in town,' I said, closing the door behind me. 'Now get some sleep.'

I heard a vague trace of whimpering through the wood.

'We've an early start tomorrow,' I added.

Harsh, I know. But she *had* to buck up.

Had to.

★

I couldn't write. I sat in my downstairs study, staring at a blank page. It wasn't the argument that had bothered me. After all, Gwendolen would eventually apologise, eat her withheld meal and that would be that. And it wasn't the divorce, either. If I'm honest, part of me enjoyed all that endless legal cut-and-thrustery with Carlotta. I guess it reminded me a little of our courting days, where both of us would frequently withhold physical favours from the other, until a culminatory bout of frenzied public frottage would get us thrown out of whatever dining establishment had served us spicy oysters, and the whole process would begin again from scratch. And as well as the faintly erotic tinge to our prolonged and never-ending breakup, my own myriad schemes for long-term revenge contained all the dramatic suspense and intrigue of some sensational best-selling plot. Believe it or not, I was actually enjoying my ongoing feud with the Latinate harridan.

Then what was it? Why couldn't I write anything? Suddenly, like a bolt from the blue, it hit me. I had too *many* ideas. Too much inspiration. This house was so perfect that my mind was giddy with all the gothic possibilities. Wild notions for grisly macabre events, evil machinations and supernatural terrors raced through my brain like multiple bursts of morning caffeine. The hardest job I'd be facing here would be selecting only the very finest plot elements for my ground-breaking gothic potboiler.

For the house was nothing less than an ideas factory. Hell, it even had its own graveyard out back, with a family crypt to boot. With that kind of surface detail, I knew that by summer's end, I'd finally be leaving Carlotta in the dust once and for all, as I raced off into my own glorious future of instant gothic best-sellerdom. Then *she'd* have to supervise Gwendolen. *She'd* have to cart our daughter along to the next continental film set and find ways of occupying her during her stand-in shots. *She'd* be saddled.

I paused, realised I was becoming stressed again. My ill temper was definitely getting worse. The second I'd stepped inside the house, I'd done little else but snap and moan about my lot. Far more than was my usual wont. And, believe me, my wont was far more than usual. The house was perfect, wasn't it? Then why was I getting so angry?

I guided my thoughts back to reality, and realised I was staring at a picture. A framed painting directly opposite me, hanging from a rusting nail over the fireplace.

I stood up from my desk and walked over to it. The portrait depicted a Victorian gentleman, middle-aged and portly, with thinning hair and thick mutton chops. His stern countenance glared back at me through cold, fathomless eyes. It felt as if he was staring directly into my soul.

Perfect. I smiled, taking out my notebook and jotting down that very thought. This place was gold dust.

When I looked up at the portrait again, however, it seemed to me that the man's mouth had shifted slightly. Nothing major, really, and perhaps it was merely my imagination playing tricks with me, but he almost seemed to be sneering.

Sneering at me.

'Screw you,' I said, sneering back. 'Don't you know who I am?'

I waited, but there was no reply. He was a painting, after all.

'I'm Nicholas Stein,' I said, smugly. 'And you are?'

Again, no reply, but this time I sensed something else that was different about the painting. The man's eyes . . . Yeah, it was his eyes. They were gleaming, now. Twinkling. If I didn't know better, I could have sworn, for a brief moment, that I saw my own reflection in those tiny orbs.

Feeling suddenly uncomfortable, I dropped my gaze from his, and my own eyes immediately alighted upon a dull yellow plate nailed to the bottom half of the picture's rotting frame. Something was written there, I saw, yet so covered in dust and grime that the words inscribed were almost illegible.

I reached down and rubbed away at the dirt. The plate had been golden once, I realised, and would take a fair amount of polishing in order to restore it to its former glory, but the words were getting clearer all the time as I slowly buffed them clean.

There was a name there, followed by a date.

'*Eighteen forty-seven* . . .' I read, aloud (the date first, obviously). '*Anton Mathers.*'

I looked up at the portrait again.

The man's sneer was pronounced, now. Either I was going mad, or the painting had changed *again*.

'Grist to my mill, Anton,' I said, jotting down that thought as well in my notebook, before moving back over to the desk. 'Grist to my mill.'

I gathered up my pen and paper, hoping to gather some initial thoughts in the bedroom instead. I was tired. An early night would do me good, I figured. And with a fresh start in the morning, I'd head into town for some writing supplies and maybe the germ of a plot would start brewing. God knows it had to, I reflected, or Gwendolen would effectively be staying here rent-free.

I picked up another guttering candle and walked over to the hall door, savouring the harsh clump of my shoes upon the wooden floorboards.

Though there was plenty of electricity in the house, I'd elected to use candles only so that some gothic ideas might start circulating, and had decided not to replace the bulb in Gwendolen's light fitting, after all. It would make her job harder, sure, if not borderline impossible, but it was essential that I gave my imagination full rein while I was staying here. I had to fuel my mind day and night with gothic visions, and if that meant Gwendolen had to spend longer in the pitch-dark attic while her eyes adjusted by degrees to an incessant gloom, so be it. I knew she'd be grouchy, denied vital time away from the house, and probably she'd get a lot paler, too, lacking vital rays of sunlight. I made a note to add vitamins to my shopping list, then, slowly, clutching the flickering candle in my hand, I climbed the stairs.

My bedroom was large, with a vast, blackened mirror on one wall, and a large four-poster bed in the centre. I washed my face briefly in a cracked porcelain bowl, using the jug of water I'd brought up earlier, then settled down in the bed, drawing the moth-eaten curtains around me until I was fully encased in a small chamber of darkness. I'd put the candle out by this stage, by the way. I'm not an idiot.

I settled my head back against the stale-smelling pillow, aware that at any moment I might feel the terrifying rush of small, haired legs darting over my face as the spiders in the disturbed curtains scuttled downward on to my bed.

I chuckled inwardly. A small price to pay, I figured, for a book that was ultimately going to give me the most luxurious five-star lifestyle money could buy. *Then* I could worry about spiders, and not before.

I settled back with the pen in my hand, jotting down ideas on the pad, my imagination filling in for the lack of light, when all of a sudden I heard a terrifying scream from somewhere above.

I waited for a moment, then heard it again. Louder now. A scream of abject terror.

Gwendolen . . .

I threw back the curtains and twisted my body off the bed. Stumbling across the room, I cursed loudly as I stubbed my toe on the fangs of a stuffed leopard-skin carpet, then tugged violently at the bedroom's door handle.

It was locked. I rattled the thing loudly, hearing my daughter scream again from the attic, then realised I was pushing the door when I should have been pulling it. Instinctively noting that down mentally, too, as a potential plot detail, I rushed out on to the landing and looked up at the winding staircase before me.

Gwendolen screamed again.

'Gwendolen!' I cried out in reply, rushing blindly up the steps.

'Daddy! Oh, Daddy!'

'Gwendolen!'

'Daddy, is it you?'

'Yes, Gwendolen, it's me.' I paused then, satisfied she could hear me at last. 'Will you please stop bloody screaming?' I yelled. 'I'm trying to write down here.'

I waited for a whole minute, then, hearing nothing more, made my way back down the stairs again to my bedroom.

I'd jot down the details of her nightmare tomorrow.

CHAPTER THREE

'The Doll'

I woke late the next day, having been up to the attic twice more during the night to quiet yet more of Gwendolen's screaming. Though her recurrent nightmares might potentially provide me with a plot synopsis, I needed sleep and I suppose she did too.

Which no doubt explained why my breakfast wasn't ready.

Deciding it would only make matters worse if I dragged her out of bed now, I elected to grab something in town while picking up some essential writing supplies.

Maybe I should get something for her, too, I decided. After all, this was a healing holiday for both of us, and if that old attic really was frightening her, then she'd no doubt want something cuddly to grab on to for comfort if she was going to get any sleep at all over the summer. Without rest and recuperation, she'd stand no chance of meeting the demands of my rigorous writing schedule.

Adding 'cheap toy' to the shopping list, I went outside to my Jensen Interceptor and drove down into Cresston.

The town was small, yet felt strangely large as I drove around it. I realised why soon enough. I was having trouble navigating because there were no road signs to speak of. Each street was instead marked with a succession of basic visual images that looked as if they'd been scrawled on various walls by some dumb idiot. I pulled up beside a man in a fisherman's jumper and waders, and wound down the car's window.

'Where's the stationery shop?' I asked.

He said nothing. Just shook his head and walked on. I drove further along the road and pulled up beside two middle-aged ladies scoffing cress sandwiches by the roadside.

'Morning, ladies. Is there a stationery shop near here?' I asked.

The older one answered through a mouthful of cress and bread. 'What's a stationery shop?'

I brushed several small leaves from my shoulder and explained. 'It's a place that sells office stationery. Pens, pencils. Reams of paper. Typewriter ribbons . . .'

The woman ceased chewing and stared at me coldly, as though I'd said something obscene. Without another word, both of them picked up their bags and left.

What the heck had I said? Maybe a long word like 'stationery' was confusing these people.

'Excuse me,' I called out to a young man marching along the road, a bucket balanced precariously upon one shoulder. 'Where can I buy a pencil?'

'No pencil,' said the man, shaking his head vociferously, as if suddenly frightened. 'Just cress.'

'Cress?'

'Cress,' he said, frowning strangely at me. Then he tipped the bucket on his shoulder forward to reveal a small mound of light green miniature vegetation inside.

'Cress,' he said again, smiling now. His spreading jawline gradually revealed a mass of softened gums sporting three stubbed teeth on the lower mandible. He reached upward with his hand, grabbed a fistful of the stuff from his bucket, then rammed a large clump into his mouth. He munched it slowly, shifting the crushed plants from side to side in an attempt to grind them down.

Hell, these people were truly backward. I drove my car further on and parked it in the middle of what appeared to pass for a town square. As I got out, I noticed a raised platform in the centre of the yard, with what looked like a tall iron pole mounted on a square plinth in the middle. This shaft and its base were blackened about the lower half, as if someone had recently lit a bonfire on this very spot. I figured we were still a few months away from Guy Fawke's Night, so perhaps this was what passed for routine rubbish removal in a backward town such as this.

I looked around the square. There were several shops laid out along each side of the courtyard, but again, I could detect no written signs to speak of. Just paintings or drawings of what the building beyond them contained. I could make out crude illustrations of barrelled fruit and veg, severed animals, a fish with some potato slices beside it, and what should really have been a simple male stick figure, but was instead an intricately drawn penis spraying urine over a mound of poo. The version beside it, with a necklace added, was the Ladies', I presumed.

Well, I'd already done one back at the house and hadn't had my coffee yet, so I had no plans on visiting that particular establishment anytime soon. I could do with finding a bookshop, though. I'd brought several boxes of my novels with me in the hope that Cresston's local bookseller might start stocking them in bulk, drumming up interest for my forthcoming masterpiece. With any luck, I'd soon be the talk of the town.

But there were no pictures of books on any of the shopfronts.

'Who are you?' said a voice, behind me. I turned to see around five villagers gathered in a group around my vehicle. One of them was scrutinising my car's bonnet badge, running a grubby finger along its grooved lettering.

'Nicholas Stein,' I said. 'Though I do occasionally employ a pseudonym.'

The men bristled visibly, one of them raising a garden hoe in my direction. 'What's a pseudo . . . mum?'

'An alternate name used by a writer—'

'Aarrgghh!' they yelled out as one, stepping back from me as if I'd thrown a handful of stones in their faces.

'—in order,' I continued, 'to sell a book.'

'Aaahhh!!!' they howled again. The older members of the group were tensing up, I noticed, as if expecting some imminent physical altercation to erupt.

'I'm trying to locate a bookshop.'

The man with the hoe lunged forward, thrusting the tool in my direction. I held fast, daring him to hit me.

'So that I can hand over my old *books* . . .'

He lunged again, and I was forced to step back to avoid being brained.

'. . . in preparation,' I added, belligerently, 'for them stocking my latest novel.'

He jabbed at me a third time. I darted to one side, stepping backwards on to the pavement. I was aware that a second crowd of onlookers were now forming just behind me, emerging from various shopfronts.

Suddenly a voice wailed from the vicinity of my car. The man who'd been tracing his finger along the badge of my Jensen Interceptor launched himself violently away from the vehicle as if in sudden fear of the machine.

'Word!' he screamed, his entire body shaking. 'A w—word!'

'What the hell's going on here?' I demanded loudly, aware that I had to stay calm and controlled before these barbarous heathens. 'What kind of village doesn't have a bookshop? Answer me!'

I jabbed my finger in the direction of their leader, as though he meant nothing more to me than a cheap vocal coach for some tawdry egomaniacal female actress.

The man held out his arm, staying the hand of the nearby hoe-wielder, who lowered his weapon accordingly.

'So *you're* the writer,' he said, his body stiffening as he thrust out his pigeon chest, attempting to look taller than me. Which was impossible. Because I'm incredibly tall. 'The one who's rented out that there house on the hill.'

'What of it?' I asked, nonchalantly lighting a cigarette I kept on me for just such emergencies.

'We don't want writers here,' he said, nodding at someone in the group behind him, who immediately moved around with another bunch of heathens to block the path to my car. 'And we don't want *books.*'

It was a tense moment, and no mistake. Should I rise to the bait, tell this lowly peasant why a basic education kept people like me in Jensen Interceptors, and morons like him scraping cress from the sides of ponds with a rusting hoe for the duration of their adult life? Or should I simply bide my time and find a way out of this mess? Trade courage for caution. Calm this wild pack, then dob these heathens in to the local police.

'Fine. No books it is,' I said. 'Now, does anyone know where I can get a really good cress sandwich?'

That flummoxed them. There was a moment of confused silence, followed by a rush of garbled, half-literate suggestions from all and sundry.

'Old Scrote's got a nice patch up by the mill,' said the man who'd fled the car's bonnet badge.

'Aye, but Reg and Rhonda do a better spread – on white bread, too,' said another man, behind me.

'Maybe I'll sample a few from each establishment,' I said, loudly. 'And then take home a huge wad of cress sandwiches from the best supplier I can find.'

At once, the crowd dissipated at speed across the square, each villager rushing off to prepare the finest sampling of cress they were capable of cramming between two slices of buttered bread.

But the joke was on them. For I had no intention of sampling a single cress sandwich. That was merely a ruse to get them off my back until I could find a safe way out of here.

Amid the wild rush of departing locals, I made my way back to my car, yanked open the driver's door and got in. As I keyed the ignition, a scrawny hand reached in through the open window, clutching something horrible in its bony fingers.

A doll.

The thing was old and covered with grime. A Victorian toy, I judged from its wide buttoned hem and faded pinafore. The bonnet on top was tied raggedly to its scratched, china head, and the various features of the body were attached to each other via sharp, rusted pins.

'A gift,' said a voice, beside me. 'A gift for the child.'

I looked up at the open window and saw one of the most revolting human specimens I've ever had the misfortune of reeling back from, with the possible exception of Carlotta's lawyer (who had two false eyes and a false nose, plus a false mouth – he was essentially Mr Potato Head, but with real ears).

The woman, if I can call her that, who now stared in at me through the open window, was essentially a dying ferret in human form. Snaggle-toothed, the face sharply pinched through skin resembling a fragment of medieval parchment. She stank like an unwashed convenience and shook visibly with each desperate intake of hoarse, wheezing breath.

'A gift,' she said again, rattling the doll before me, drawing my attention back to the rotting specimen in her hand.

Well, I *had* forgotten my present for Gwendolen, after all.

'Shits itself,' said the woman-shaped thing.

Great, I thought. One of *those* dolls. We'd gifted Gwendolen one like it when she was about six. You had to feed the thing certain powder stuffs and within ten minutes, it crapped out brown sludge down one leg, which Gwendolen had insisted on soaking free in the bath, subsequently clogging our plughole.

I'd ended up throwing the thing away that very morning. Still, I didn't necessarily have to feed this particular one, did I? I gave the matter further thought. Either I spent precious minutes sourcing something new for Gwendolen while wasting good writing time, or I took what was on offer and let her make do with this ragged specimen. It was an unsightly toy, that was for sure. But given Gwendolen's attic room was going to be permanently pitch-black, would she even see it well enough to notice?

'I'll take it,' I said, grabbing the doll from the old crone. The legs and arms of the toy kicked out suddenly, marching back and forth as if sparked into action by some freshly triggered internal mechanism. A small, metallic voice sounded from its head as both eyelids opened suddenly, exposing black holes behind.

'Father . . .' came a tinny child's voice in a strangely archaic accent. 'Father . . . Father . . .'

I pushed the woman's outstretched hand away from me, a little too forcefully, as it transpired. She reeled back from the car and fell sideways into the gutter.

'Thanks,' I said through the window, even though I had every intention of telling Gwendolen that the gift was from me alone.

After all, it was important for my daughter and I to bond. And this old woman, to be frank, wasn't long for this world anyway.

I sat the doll in Gwendolen's seat as I drove fast back to the house. It didn't complain once about my speed.

★

Gwendolen hadn't done a bloody thing.

'Where the hell's my typed outline?' I snapped, shocked rigid at her blatant insolence. She was still in bed, for God's sake. 'I slid a page of vague notions under your door first thing this morning, Gwendolen, in the misguided hope that you'd have something solid to show me by lunchtime. But you haven't typed up a single half-baked idea. If you somehow think this is an acceptable way to commence work for a new employer, you are seriously mistaken, young lady. And I mean *seriously* mistaken. Not just mistaken. But *seriously* mistaken.'

I couldn't believe it. She still hadn't emerged from beneath the covers.

Well, a cold flannel had never done *me* any harm, I decided, though on reflection that would involve me going downstairs one floor to the bathroom, before having to come back upstairs again. Abandoning that particular plan, I whipped back the covers to find her cowering in a ball of sweat, teeth chattering, her frail body shivering like a leaf. In the candle's light, she looked like she hadn't slept a wink.

'Great,' I said. 'No doubt you'll now need an hour or so to complete your skincare regime, during which time I'm expected to somehow progress further with my book without a *fully typed outline*. Daylight is wasting, Gwendolen.'

I turned from her in annoyance. I guessed I'd just have to try and pull something together myself from my rudimentary notes. But there was no way now that Gwendolen was getting a mention in my 'acknowledgments' section.

'The girl!' she cried out suddenly, behind me. 'The girl from my dream!'

I turned again and saw that she was pointing at the doll in my hand, which I'd completely forgotten to give to her.

Unnerved by my daughter's reaction, I held the thing out in her direction. 'Careful,' I said. 'It's one of those ones that poos itself.'

Instead of taking the doll from my hand, Gwendolen reeled backwards against the attic wall, as if trying to get as far away from it as possible.

'Well, that's gratitude for you, Gwendolen,' I said, coldly. 'This thing cost me over twenty pounds, you know. It's antique. No doubt the toys your *mother* buys for you are better, somehow.'

She was no longer moving, her eyes fixed rigidly on the doll. I suppose it was a result of her tiredness, which was itself a result of her laziness.

'Well, when you're finally up and about,' I said, 'you can make yourself useful and start writing up those nightmares you've been having.'

Unexpectedly, she nodded at me through the tears, and suddenly I felt terrible. Why was I behaving so horribly of late? Why was I becoming so dictatorial? Admittedly, I was often like that with editors, and Carlotta, obviously, but this was my own daughter. Dammit, Gwendolen was only twelve, wasn't she? Yet ever since I'd set foot inside this house, I'd been treating her like a common skivvy. Well, I'd had enough of it. She at least needed a good breakfast inside her before the rigours of her working day.

'Some Rice Krispies first, though, right?' I said to her softly, cracking a smile.

'Oh, yes please,' said Gwendolen, relief evident on her face.

'Rustle me up a bacon sandwich while you're at it, will you?'

She'd feel better after that, I reckoned. After all, cooking was a bonding experience. I popped the doll on the rocking chair in front of her. She stared at it, her body completely still now, save for a vague shuddering motion visible in the shoulder area, which I presumed were tremors.

With Gwendolen seemingly transfixed by her new doll, I left them both there to get acquainted.

As expected, breakfast was late.

CHAPTER FOUR

'The Warning'

I'd almost put pen to paper when there came a loud knocking on the front door.

'Gwendolen!' I yelled out, but answer came there none. Sadly, I chalked up another black mark against her record. With the rate I was currently docking wages, she'd need to work an extra week in the dark just to break even.

Disappointed, I passed through the main hall and opened the door myself.

In the wooden porch stood a lawman in beige uniform. He was tall and broad, his wide face squared by the wide-brimmed hat he wore. A dash of close-cut, silvering hair was visible above both ears. A holstered Colt Police Revolver hung from his leather belt, which itself hung under his ample stomach. He was chewing tobacco and sweating in the morning heat, though that didn't seem to bother him. He removed a pair of silver mirrored shades, exposing two piercing blue eyes, and mopped a line of sweat from his glistening brow as he spoke.

'Hi there, stranger. Nicholas Stein, right?'

'Correct.'

He jotted down a detail in his notebook, which I saw was in fact a doodle. 'New in town,' he said, still looking at the page, which now displayed a picture of some cress.

I sensed it wasn't a question. 'Relatively new,' I replied. 'We arrived earlier this week.'

'On the Tuesday,' he said. 'Round about three o'clock.'

'What's this about, officer?'

'Nothing to worry about, Mr Stein. Just being neighbourly. Welcome to Cresston. Nice place you have here.'

'And your name is?'

'Tate Rellington.' He held out his hand, which I was forced to shake. The man had a strong grip, despite his flab. 'I'm the Sheriff here. Guess you'd call me the *law* in Cresston.'

He grinned with freshly-browned teeth and spat out a glob of liquified tobacco on to the deck.

This man might be a problem, I thought. The last thing I wanted was a modern-day, pulp Western-invoking policeman interfering with the faux gothic aesthetic my house at Bloater's Cove was currently providing. A lawman's presence here – on my own doorstep – might play serious havoc with the integrity of my creative vision. It wouldn't necessarily pollute my literary judgement, but if I wished to truly indulge a gothic mindset while penning my future best-seller, an overweight, interfering sheriff with a gun might really start muddying the atmosphere.

'Will this take long?' I said. 'Because I'm trying to write.'

The lawman sighed, as if contemplating how to say what he was wanting to say, then grinned. 'Well, I guess that *is* what I aim to talk to you about after all, Mr Stein. The small matter of your writing.'

'My writing's no small matter, officer, I can assure you.'

He balanced a foot on the frame of my front door and flicked a resting fly from his knee. 'Seems you've gone and rattled some of our locals with this "stationery" business.'

'It would seem so,' I said. 'And I'll rattle them some more when my book's finally published. This one's going to be my best yet. We're talking a multi-million best-seller, officer. With those kinds of sales, I could buy your town of Cresston outright. And I'd do what I wanted with it, then, believe me. I'd buy this house and all the other houses in Cresston, too. Did I say houses? I meant shacks. I'd flatten those illiterate peasants and drive the entire tribe out of town if I felt like it. Maybe I'd even drive them all eastward, off the damn cliff.'

I was getting angry again, I realised. But this was *my* property, if only temporarily, and I had a duty to protect it – and my work. And Gwendolen, I guessed. I reached out, pointing to the mailbox.

'Those heathens strung a dead cat up on that post. Then left me hate mail.'

He turned his head to the mailbox. 'What cat?'

Hell, I'd burned it, hadn't I? Along with the threatening letter.

'It was beginning to smell,' I said.

He nodded, looking even less convinced than before. 'Look, Mr Stein,' he said, moving the conversation on. 'I wouldn't go winding up the local villagers, if I were you. They're a superstitious bunch, I'll admit. I guess you can appreciate that, being a writer of gothic horror fiction . . .'

I looked up sharply. This overweight cop knew my genre of choice? Knew the kind of books I wrote? Had potentially even read some of them? Suddenly, I had a feeling there was more to this particular lawman than met the eye.

'I imagine you, of *all* people,' he added, 'know that that there superstition business usually has some basis in fact.'

'Go on,' I said.

'Well, years ago, Mr Stein, almost a hundred and fifty-one years to the day, in fact, there was another writer who lived up here. He wrote books, just like you. And back then, just like now, the locals didn't like it. They . . .' He paused momentarily, thinking. 'How can I put this? They took matters into their own hands.'

'What the hell is wrong with these people?' I snapped. 'Are they cavemen? What kind of a society relies on pictures for communication?' I pointed at the sheriff's car, which had no markings on its side save for a child's drawing of some handcuffs. 'Is *that* what you call civilised society?'

He didn't even turn to look. Just kept on staring at me as he spoke. 'What's the set-up here, Mr Stein? How safe is this place?'

'Safe?' What the hell was he implying? Was I supposed to interrupt my precious writing schedule now in order to secure some decrepit, rundown gothic ruin against a bunch of illiterates?

Then suddenly, I saw right through the plan.

'They sent you up here, didn't they? To scare me? To intimidate me into doing some basic renovation work at my own expense, so they can then up the rent for the next poor sap.'

'Not at all.'

'Making things safe up here is *your* job, sheriff. Not mine.'

Rellington smiled. 'I guess it is, at that,' he said. 'And I will keep you safe, far as I can. Your daughter too, right?' He looked upward, at the roof.

How the hell did he know about Gwendolen? I hadn't told anyone I was bringing my daughter with me, in case it potentially increased the rent.

'Saw you both on the way in,' he said. 'I was patrolling up here. Keeping an eye on things.'

'My daughter's presence here is of no concern to you or anybody,' I said. 'I resent you people discussing my business.'

'The whole town's been discussing your business, Mr Stein. After all, the whole town wanted to rent out this house on the hill during these summer months. Till you upped your stake.'

The whole town?

The estate agent had lied to me, then. I hadn't been up against a single bidder after all. For some reason, it had been *the whole town* trying to crowd me out. But why?

'Just secure the place a little, Mr Stein. A bit of DIY would go a long way, believe me.'

I sneered at him, resolutely refusing to get suckered in on that one.

At long last, he removed his foot from the threshold. 'Like I say, just a friendly warning.'

He moved away from the porch and walked back down to his '77 Ford LTD.

'Why are they all so interested in this house, anyway?' I cried out. 'Why do they all want to rent a rundown gothic townhouse in their own backyard?'

'They don't,' he said, turning back. 'They just don't want *you* to rent it.'

As he drove off along the winding drive, I watched him glance briefly up at the roof of the house again, before disappearing around the far corner of our driveway. Obscured by intervening trees, I heard the Ford speed up as he made his way back along the country lane to Cresston.

I closed the door firmly, then watched it swing back open. Presumably, the rusted lock mechanism had finally given up the ghost.

Maybe I'd do just a little DIY.

★

Still I couldn't write. I checked my watch, realising I'd been sitting at my desk for a full twelve hours. Perhaps time itself stood still inside this house on the hill.

Jotting down this germ of an idea, I suddenly remembered that I'd forgotten to take any food or water up to Gwendolen — who, as far as I knew, was hiding under the bedcovers again, frozen in terror.

Well, I had neither the time nor the inclination to cook a hot meal for her, so she'd have to make do with cold chicken again. Maybe hunger, or those damned vegetarian principles she insisted on maintaining despite my preferred chicken-centric diet, would finally shock her back into reality.

I rose from the desk, grabbed what remained of the bird's carcass, which I'd yet to strip fully clean, and walked over to the door. As I did so, something on the wall behind me drew my eye.

It was the picture again. That portrait of the sneering Victorian gentleman. For some reason, the man's face was reaching out to me once more. Drawing me towards him from across the centuries, and specifically the room itself.

'You again,' I said, aloud, staring at those cruel, pitiless eyes. 'I daresay you've sniffed my cold chicken. Tough luck, buddy. This wing's for Gwendolen.'

Feeling suddenly uncomfortable again, as though the eyes were somehow laughing at me, I dropped my gaze instinctively and alighted once more upon that grime-covered nameplate below the canvas.

'*Anton Mathers*,' I read again. '*Anton Mathers . . .*'

I walked over to the telephone on my desk and dialled the number of Rosaleen Bloomdale, my editor at Garrett.

'Good day to you, Rosaleen,' I said.

'Nicholas? Where on earth are you? I've been trying to get hold of you for weeks.'

'Relax, I'm out on the Stalkford coast, near Bloater's Cove.'

'Oh, I see. Where the Pilgrim Stepfathers landed.'

'Pilgrim Stepfathers?'

'They left for America just after the Pilgrim Fathers, but got lost and landed right back where they'd embarked from, two months later. When they stepped off the boat, someone shouted, "See those Pilgrim Fathers stepping off that boat? Pilgrim *Step*-Fathers, more like," and the name stuck.'

I howled with laughter. Thank God at least someone in this

godforsaken place had had a decent sense of humour. No doubt they'd been hounded out of town, as well.

'Look, Rosaleen, I want you to do something for me.'

'Anything, Nicholas. Just as soon as you've handed in your new book.'

'Don't tease me, Rosaleen. The book's in hand. This is merely some essential research I need you to do.'

'Sure, Nicholas. Sorry for mentioning deadlines when I know full well you're putting everything into this book despite a whole boatload of trying circumstances.'

She was right. I *was* putting everything into this book despite a whole boatload of trying circumstances, and was in addition doing my utmost to make this particular book *the* multi-million-earning best-seller both she and I knew I was capable of.

'And I know that you're also doing your utmost to make this particular book the multi-million-earning best-seller both I and you know you are capable of. So go ahead, Nicholas, what do you need from me? I'll accommodate you in any way I can.'

'It's simple, Rosaleen. I want you to check up on a name for me. As far as I know, he was an old writer, from the Victorian age. Name of Anton Mathers. He once owned this very house I'm renting, yet for some reason fell foul of the local heathens. I'm keen to find out why.'

'Sure, Nicholas. I can do that for you, no problem. But isn't researching the history of this writer an unnecessary distraction from your own writing? Might your mind become preoccupied with this imposing, unknown yet strangely alluring figure of a former century? Potentially forming itself into a dangerous obsession over time, to the detriment of your own work – and, who knows, perhaps your own psychological welfare, too?'

'Look, Rosaleen, I'm drawing on a deep gothic energy here. I have a hunch that this deceased writer might hold the key to me writing a gothic potboiler so steeped in macabre intrigue and fright-ful mystery that it could make both me, and you, Rosaleen, multi-millionaires.'

'You and I, Nicholas,' she said, correcting my grammar, which I didn't appreciate. 'In that case,' she continued, 'I'll crack on with things my end and get back to you as soon as I uncover anything.'

'Goodbye, Rosaleen,' I said, placing the receiver back on its cradle.

I paused before the portrait again on my way over to the door. Maybe whatever I found out about Anton Mathers could fuel the plot of my new book. Maybe whatever confrontation he'd once had with a baying mob of illiterate inbreds, whatever details of his life – or *death* – I uncovered, could kickstart the plot of my gothic magnus opus.

'You're going to fuel my book, Anton Mathers,' I said, addressing his daubed likeness. 'Defamation laws don't apply to the deceased. Whether you like it or not, the details of your dead life are going to give me some ideas.'

With that, I walked out into the hall. I couldn't see whether the expression on Anton Mathers' painted face altered eerily as I left, given that this is a first-person narrative and thus non-omniscient, but I imagine that it might well have done.

As I made my way up the old staircase by candlelight, I heard voices above me. As I rounded the banister on the second floor, I realised they were coming from the attic. One of them sounded like Gwendolen, but the other, another female voice, was unfamiliar to me.

I rounded the final part of the staircase and tiptoed along the higher landing towards Gwendolen's room. Hearing a flurry of light laughter beyond her wooden door, I braced myself, then pushed it open.

Gwendolen was the only person there.

In the candle's light, I could see that she'd emerged from the bed, at least, and was now sitting on the floor with that mangy china-headed doll beside her. There were a couple of old chipped cups between them, and what looked like a small puddle of black liquid.

'What's that?' I said, pointing to it.

'It's what the dolly makes,' said Gwendolen.

I stepped forward, smearing the spillage across the floorboard with my boot. It was wet and lumpy, like blotched ink.

'Disgusting,' I said. 'Clean it up.'

'As you wish, Father,' Gwendolen replied.

Something about her manner troubled me. Far too obliging, given that I'd left her up here in total darkness for several days, bar for that small ray of light beneath the door. It might well be an onset of temporary madness owing to her imposed isolation, but the Gwendolen I knew would normally have objected to my constant demands.

'Who were you talking to?' I asked, concerned that she might be starting to lose her mind.

'My new friend,' she said. 'Can we go out and play now?'

I looked down at the doll. Perhaps I shouldn't have bought the thing for her, after all. Then I recalled that I *hadn't* bought it for her at all, and had in fact taken full credit for someone else's gift. Maybe that someone had gifted a toy so full of old chemicals, the noxious fumes were slowly turning my child insane.

'Give that doll to me,' I said.

Gwendolen *did* turn on me then, her face suddenly angered, looking more like my daughter of old. 'No, Father, this is my friend! My new friend!'

Ahh, so it was only an *imaginary* friend. Gwendolen had had lots of them over the years, usually during periods of extreme emotional stress. Then it *was* her doing that other voice. But this in turn suggested that she *was* beginning to crack, as I'd feared. And I probably wasn't helping matters by keeping her cooped up in here with no natural daylight for days on end.

'I'm sorry, Gwendolen,' I said.

'Sorry for what, Father?'

There it was again. That strange term of reference. I'd always been 'Dad' before, even when she was yelling at me. Never 'Father'.

Something odd was happening, I sensed. Gwendolen was changing, potentially because of my treatment of her, and/or a toxic doll. And I had the strange feeling that part of me was changing, too. I realised there and then that I had to do something about it.

Something major.

Tomorrow, I'd install that small window in the far wall.

CHAPTER FIVE

'The Witch'

There was no reply from Rosaleen all the next morning. In the end, I called her office, but they told me she was out.

'Hopefully doing some damned work for me,' I said, then hung up abruptly. I dialled the number of Cresston's estate agent, instead. There was no answer from him, either, which was unusual, so I elected to head back into town. I wanted to see if I could dig up any info on the mysterious Anton Mathers myself. There had to be a reason why this backward community loathed writers so much, and my instincts told me that Mathers might be the key to unlocking a real-life gothic mystery which might ultimately net me millions. But clearly consulting the local records in Cresston's non-existent library was a non-starter, so I'd need to dig around elsewhere.

Leaving Gwendolen to admire her new window, which I'd had her install under my supervision without a hitch save for two severely bruised thumbs and some splintered knuckles, I took the Interceptor out and drove down into Cresston along the coastal road instead.

It was a beautiful, clear morning as I swung out over the cove, and I saw the plume of smoke almost immediately. It grew thicker and blacker as I approached the town, and by the time I drew up in the

179

main square again, the woman tied to a stake in the middle of the burning pyre had been almost completely burned to a crisp.

I drew out my notepad and pen, keen to jot down some observations for research purposes. I'd never witnessed a public execution like this before, and wasn't likely to again unless this particular one signalled the start of some terrifying local witch-hunt – which, given the general IQ of the Cresston locals, was not beyond the realms of possibility. The vast crowd currently taunting the dying hag meant that parking was limited, and when I'd finally managed to jostle my way through the jeering rabble towards the front, I was irritated to find that most of the juicier moments had already passed, and what was left for me to observe amounted to not much more than half a skeleton. Nevertheless, the thing was still vaguely sentient, which made for grim viewing – and grimmer reading, I hoped.

As I quickly took note of the more lurid, nauseating details, wondering what other quaint murderous customs the locals around here might still practise, a hand grabbed my arm, yanking me aside into one of the neighbouring alleys.

'Are you insane, mister?' cried Tate Rellington, ushering me further along the side street in an effort to distance me from the baying crowd. 'You're lucky they're in the midst of a communal bloodlust. If just one of those folk out there recognised you standing there amongst 'em, you'd be on top of that pyre yourself quicker'n you could pop the lid back on that there pen o' yours. Which is what I reckon you should do right now, mister, if you have any hope in hell of getting back home today in one piece.'

I did what he said. What had I been thinking, standing there in the midst of those seething heathens, calmly jotting down my vague impressions of a shrieking human sacrifice like there was no tomorrow? If just one of them had seen what I'd been doing, in all likelihood there would have been *no* tomorrow.

'What did she do?' I asked, changing the subject, and realising with some embarrassment that I had been jeering on an old woman's death without knowing anything concrete about her. I guessed that was mob mentality in action, and made a note to include the phenomenon in my ongoing novel, which I technically hadn't even started yet.

'There was a death in town last night,' said Rellington, his face suddenly serious. 'Benny Slacker, one of our local boys – looks after the village hoe . . . Or *looked* after it, I should say.'

I knew him. That kid who'd threatened me with the hoe. A dumb idiot called Benny Slacker, was he? Well, he was dead now. But the whole thing seemed unreal. I'd been remonstrating with him only yesterday.

'How did he die?'

'That's the weird part,' said Rellington, frowning and scratching his chin. 'Some folks say he was struck dumb with a sudden bout of the *double-squits*. That's vom and diarrhoea in your parlance, stranger.'

I knew what it was. After all, I'd lived in eternal fear of a joint vomiting-and-diarrhoea affliction for years. Every God-fearing person did. It was the worst physical malady one could imagine.

'Sounds like a killer strain of summer flu,' I said, 'or a case of *toxic poisoning*.'

'Looks that way,' said Rellington. ''Cept for what came next.' The lawman went suddenly pale, as though the very memory of it was troubling, even for him.

'What came next?' I asked.

'Well, you see, stranger, that there vomit and diarrhoea what comes out of both ends . . . them *double-squits* I was talkin' about . . .'

'I know where vomit and diarrhoea come out,' I said, grimly.

'Sure, coming out as that's one thing,' Rellington continued. 'But coming out as something else? That's literally something else.'

'Something else?' I replied, confused and strangely chilled, with an eerie sense of foreboding. 'What was this "something else" that came out of both ends, of which you speak?'

181

He swallowed hard, steeling himself. 'Well, that there vomit and diarrhoea, stranger . . .'

'Yes, sheriff?' I urged, not sure now if I even wanted to know. 'That there vomit and diarrhoea . . .'

He raised his head, unnerving me with a chilling stare. 'Came out as *ink*.'

'Ink?' I replied, repeating his own reply.

'Ink,' he confirmed, repeating my repeated reply to his own previous reply.

'How could it come out as *ink*?' I asked. 'Why, it would be regurgitated, acidified foodstuffs in the main, with attendant mucous and possibly a faint trace of blood and/or stomach lining. Not *ink*.'

'But ink it was,' he said, sombrely. 'Black, thick, ink.'

I shivered. No way was that normal. What kind of mysterious, unknown ink-producing malady had killed Benny Slacker?

'It sounds crazy,' I said. 'No way is vomiting up black ink normal. Nor dispersing it via the other end.'

'That ain't all,' he said, steadying me with his hand as my knees threatened to give way under a sudden, unexpected bout of trembling. 'Not by a long shot.'

'You mean, it gets *worse*?' I asked, hoarsely.

'A *lot* worse,' he said. 'A *whole* lot worse.'

'Go on,' I said, my voice a bare whisper now.

'I will,' he replied.

'I'm waiting.'

'Then wait no longer. Here it comes.'

'And yet I'm not hearing anything.'

'But you will.'

'When exactly?'

'Right about now.'

I still wasn't hearing anything. Then he started to speak, and I elected to let him have that couple of extra nano-seconds.

'When we gathered up young Benny . . .'

'Yes?'

'He weren't young Benny any longer. He were *old* Benny. Old and wrinkled.'

'Old and wrinkled?' I gasped, incredulous.

''Cept he weren't *really* old and wrinkled,' said Rellington. 'Not old and wrinkled at all.'

'Despite *looking* old and wrinkled?'

'You got it, stranger. Despite *looking* old and wrinkled, he *wasn't* old and wrinkled.'

'But if he wasn't old and wrinkled, despite looking old and wrinkled, what in hell was he?' I asked. The tension was now practically unbearable.

'He was a *paper bag,*' Rellington whispered. 'An old, wrinkled paper bag . . .'

'Then technically he *was* still old and wrinkled,' I said, correcting him, getting increasingly annoyed at the lack of respect for words and their employment round here.

'I guess he was, at that,' Rellington replied, stiffly. 'Technically, I guess he *was* still old and wrinkled.'

'But he was a paper bag as well?'

'That's right, stranger. A paper bag. An old, wrinkled paper bag covered in ink-based *double-squits.*'

I shuddered. What a bowel-looseningly horrendous death it must have been to behold.

And experience, frankly.

'You say there were witnesses?' I queried.

'Many.'

'And how do you think it happened?'

'It was the *curse,* Mr Stein.'

I looked at him, and for once I could see a trace of fear in his eyes. 'The curse?'

183

'The curse. The curse laid on our village by that there house on the hill.'

My house? Was he talking about my private place of residence?

'How can a house place a curse?' I asked.

Rellington shook his head, smiling grimly at me.

'Not the *house*, mister. Its *ghost* . . . The *ghost of the house on the hill overlooking Bloater's Cove, just a short drive up from Cresston . . .*'

'But can a house be a ghost?' I asked.

'Not a ghost *of* the house,' he clarified. 'I mean a ghost *in* the house.'

This was madness. Was this man, an officer of the law, seriously suggesting that a malevolent spirit had somehow murdered one of the townsfolk?

'If that's the case,' I said. 'Why are they burning this old woman for the crime?'

'Guilt by association,' said Rellington, grimly. 'That there woman on the spit was the only surviving distant relative of the man who used to own that there house on the hill. The one you're now inhabiting, mister. She was the last known living relative of that durned *writer.*'

'Now wait a moment, officer,' I said, protesting. 'You can't go blaming an old woman for killing someone in a horrendously strange and unexplained fashion simply because she's related to a long-dead writer the town couldn't stand for some bizarre, unexplained reason yet to be divulged to me by Rosaleen, almost a hundred and fifty-one years ago to the day, then simultaneously blame the entire thing on a *ghost*?'

'Mebbe I'd get back in that there car of yours, stranger, and skedaddle, pronto,' said Rellington. ''Cause the second these villagers catch wind that the current owner of that there house on the hill is standing right here, amongst 'em, they're likely gonna come for you too, pard. And I can't promise I'll be able to stop them on my lonesome.'

With that, the lawman disappeared up a nearby alleyway adjoining the current nearby alleyway, then reappeared halfway across the main square. I watched as he asked someone in the gathered crowd for a really good cress sandwich, and, as the villagers immediately began to disperse, realised he'd deliberately created a diversion for me.

I saw the townsfolk now leaving the burning, the figure on the pyre having been reduced to not much more than bone rubble. They were calmly going about their business again, acquiring cress from local shops to appease the sheriff's tastes, and I knew then that this was my chance to get away.

I tucked my neck down under my shirt collar and made my way quickly across the centre towards my parked car, trying to look inconspicuous.

My route took me directly past the smoking pyre, and as I neared the woman's partial remains, I saw that she was still breathing, but only just.

A single black, scorched lung in the middle of her charred ribcage moved slowly in and out. I looked up and caught sight of the remains of one eye, staring back at me from a smoking skull. Then the jaw of the thing dropped suddenly, and what was left of the dying woman spoke.

'Hope the child likes her doll,' she grinned, her voice rattling like a xylophone made entirely from bones.

My God, I realised, in sudden horror. It was the old woman! The old woman who'd gifted me that ancient Victorian doll, which I'd claimed sole credit for when I'd given it to Gwendolen. A doll that my daughter was now playing with and inventing her imaginary friend via!

'You ...' I whispered, my own voice now hoarse with terror. '*You* ...'

The skull woman laughed at me, cackling insanely as I turned from the hideous sight and sprinted across the square towards my car, praying no one would notice me as I ran.

As I ducked into my Jensen Interceptor and swung the vehicle round, I could still hear that laughter, echoing horribly in my ears.

As I passed by her one final time, the lower jaw of the skull gave way and the entire head fell apart, collapsing into black fragments which fell to the ground, vanishing beneath the grey, swirling pile of gathering ash.

★

I had too many questions. Why did these people hate books so much? How could a human being shit ink? (No matter how hard I wracked my brain for an answer, I couldn't come up with a sane one.) And what was all this nonsense about a damned ghost?

I just couldn't accept* that these deaths had been caused by a malign spirit. And yet human beings were evidently shitting ink and being turned into paper bags, which certainly seemed on the face of it like some sort of supernatural occurrence.

Then I thought of the doll . . . The doll I'd bought for Gwendolen, or appropriated, if I'm honest. Why, that doll shat ink, too! I tried to stop my mind racing, fearing that this way madness lay. But I couldn't help it. Was the doll connected in some way with these strange happenings in the village? Were the instances of people shitting ink and the doll shitting ink, somehow related? It seemed crazy, but that old lady, before she'd died, had specifically mentioned the doll again, hadn't she? As if to say, 'Yes, I'm referring to that doll again, traveller, even though I'm dying here. Now why would that be, you'll no doubt be wondering? I advise you to think on't.'

Well, I was thinking on't, alright.

Was the doll I'd gifted Gwendolen somehow behind these stories

* Yet. GM

of a supposed ghost? Maybe an answer, if there was one,[*] lay some-where in my newly rented house on the hill? After all, Tate Rellington had told me that the old woman who'd died had been the only surviving relative of the man who'd once owned this very house. Presumably, then, that man had been none other than the figure depicted in that portrait in my writing study. The mysterious Anton Mathers . . .

The sooner I could find out some information on the old writer's identity, the better. But currently it didn't look like I was going to get much out of the estate agent without risking being burned at the stake myself the next time I entered the town.

Dammit, Rosaleen, I thought, turning off the road into my drive-way. Get off your arse and get me some info, will you? (I thought this. If I'd said it out loud, I'd have put it in quotation marks, which I haven't.)

Ahead of me loomed the house, somehow appearing more impos-ing to me now than it ever had. Maybe it was that new window in Gwendolen's attic. Somehow it made the place look even more frightening than before. As though it was a prison of sorts, with poor Gwendolen its unwilling prisoner. Maybe I should finally let her out for some air this afternoon? I didn't want her shirking work (as was her wont), but it felt only right to let her breathe a little, given how much work was yet to come, and for which she'd need sufficient oxygen in order to function more efficiently.

Then, as my eyes continued to peruse the exterior of the building, I saw something else.

A slight discolouring, evident on a number of the wooden boards. Evidently, some of them had been replaced at some point. Parking the car, I made my way around the side of the building, discovering that the newer-looking panels were in greater evidence around the

---

[*] And there was. Keep reading. GM

rear of the house, as if at some point in the past, the structure itself had suffered some form of catastrophic damage, and had been subsequently rebuilt. As I worked my way round the perimeter of the building, I found that the far side was also blocked by a mass of overgrown greenery. Though the path I was following continued through it, the route itself was obstructed by a mass of overhanging vegetation. The area evidently hadn't been cut back in decades. I pulled a couple of branches aside to see if I could force my way through, then gave up at the sight of a slumping gravestone teetering across the path itself, the stone also surrounded by weeds and creeping vines.

This was the property's graveyard, then. Shivering at the sight, I made my way back towards the front of the house.

Halfway round, I noticed what looked like an old cellar entrance on the right-hand side of the building, which I'd failed to observe previously.

A set of uneven wooden steps led down to an ancient wooden door, which opened, I presumed, into a hitherto unexplored basement area. Some sort of crawl space under the main house, perhaps.

I walked down the steps and tentatively pushed at the door with both hands. To my surprise, it was already slightly ajar and swung immediately inward, creaking as it did so, revealing behind it what looked like a large, darkened room. The walls within were black, covered in what looked like smears of old soot. Signs of fire damage were apparent from what light now crept in through the open doorway. I stared in, waiting for my eyes to adjust to the gloom.

Then saw what Anton Mathers had been doing here all those years ago.

CHAPTER SIX

'The Secret'

A metallic plate on the front of the machine read 'Mathers Jobber'. A lone foot pedal connected the main surface to an inked flat printing plate, suggesting the contraption was intended for use by a single operator, yet a vast assembly of rusting ink rollers and printing cylinders filled the entire floor of the basement.

I gasped, incredulous. It was a Victorian letterpress.

So as well as being a writer, Anton Mathers had been a *publisher*, too. Of his own books, I presumed. At once, I felt both a heady rush of admiration for the man, but also a stab of professional jealousy. I guessed that he, like me, had realised publishers knew next to nothing about the art of publishing, merely interfering with and profiting from the well of creativity pumped forth from known visionaries – but he, *un*like me, had possessed sufficient courage and conviction to do something about it. He'd gone and set up his own printing press in the basement under his very own house.

All I had, by comparison, was a surly, perennially tardy daughter in an attic.

Perhaps I was being too harsh on myself. After all, I'd been saddled for numerous years with a wayward, disobedient wife claiming an apparent 'career' of her own, hadn't I? I'm sure it would have been very nice to set up shop for oneself unhindered by the demands of maintenance payments and non-stop custody haggles, but some of us weren't quite so lucky, were we, Anton, old pal?

I stopped myself, sensing I was getting unnecessarily angry again. And maybe there was no need. After all, how did I know Anton hadn't been saddled with his own wayward Furie? Though I hadn't noticed anyone else depicted in that portrait upstairs, did it necessarily mean he'd been living here alone all those years ago? Maybe he'd had a wife in tow. Unless he'd topped her, of course. Maybe he'd fed chunks of her into this very printing press.

I stopped myself, again. Where the heck were all these destructive thoughts coming from? Here I was, intending to spend a peaceful three months with Gwendolen writing a ground-breaking gothic chiller by the sea, and all of a sudden I was enjoying witch burnings, incarcerating my own daughter in a windowless attic and thinking about feeding divorced partners into a mechanical printing press.

What gave?

Shuddering inwardly, I shook off my dark thoughts and stepped tentatively around the vast iron contraption. The room, I noticed, formed part of the original building. Though the upper structure of the house appeared to have suffered extreme fire damage in the past, this basement area looked to have survived largely intact. The letterpress itself lay untouched since the day it had last operated, and I suspected that the black soot lining the walls instead originated from the part of the building that had been destroyed previously. I reached up to the ceiling and felt the cold touch of an iron girder.

That explained it, then. The basement alone had been reinforced against the risk of fire, presumably to protect the machine in front of me – and, by extension, the career of Anton Mathers.

Curiosity drew me further into the room, and I began to detect an odd scent in the air; a vaguely chemical odour, like something wafting upward from an old spillage.

The floor below looked darker the further I crept into this cramped and dusty space. Waning light from the open doorway at first made me assume this was but a trick caused by an increase in the surrounding shadows, but soon I discerned a curious patterning to the swirls of black on the ground, and, bending down, I ran my finger along the cemented floor. The dark patch beneath me was a stain of some kind.

As I drew my finger back, I noticed some of the stain had come away from the floor, marking the skin of my fingertip. Instinctively, I dabbed it against my tongue, and gagged.

Whatever the stain was, its taste was nauseating. I began to heave, coughing as I did so, hawking up a large globule of black-looking phlegm.

I rushed back towards the light, intent on gaining some fresh air and a glass of water, and tripped over something in front of me. I looked down and saw a row of metal boxes lined up across the basement floor. No doubt distracted by the letterpress itself, I'd somehow missed them on my way in. They were impossible to ignore now. There were around thirty of them, I counted, with probably twice that many stored in the neighbouring shadows beside me.

I reached down and pulled one of the boxes towards me. It slid heavily across the ground, grinding a trail of dust in its wake.

There was something inside.

The carton itself was sealed with a rusted padlock. I looked around for a heavy object, spied a pile of collapsed rubble by what had evidently once been a fireplace (perhaps a reason why the house above it had burned down), and picked up half a brick.

It took only a couple of strikes to break the rusted lock in two. Tossing aside the shattered fragments, I flipped open the box's metal lid and turned it towards the open door so that I could see what the contents were.

Books.

Beautiful, unread books.

With *emerald-green* covers.

I lifted one out and read the title aloud.

'*Vampton Grange*, by Anton Mathers.'

Though the book was in such a wonderful state of preservation that I need hardly be cautious about damaging it, I took care as I turned over the cover and read its opening paragraph.

And got no further than that.

It was brilliant.

Macabre. Suspenseful. Terrifying.

Perfect.

The work, I recognised in that instant, of a *genius*.

I closed the book again, delicately. Again, not out of caution, but out of deference.

For I alone was in the presence of a true master of the literary gothic.

Taking the book with me, I staggered across to the open door in a daze, pulled it shut behind me and returned immediately to my writing study inside the house.

Then read the entire thing.

★

I slammed down my pen and tore up my opening page. What was I thinking? Whatever my mind considered worthy of reading at one point was fit only for the bin the next. Any horror I cared to conceive of, any terror I now dared create, simply paled into insignificance against the effortless, gothic grace of *Vampton Grange* by Anton Mathers.

I looked across the room at his portrait. His face was still staring at me. Sneering at me. No doubt amused by my stillborn efforts at competing with his own literary genius.

The very sight of him gloating over my stalled efforts filled me with a nausea so sickening I could barely hold down my evening meal.

Which I'd had to make entirely by myself once more, Gwendolen having failed yet again to make her way down from the attic, despite me allowing her twenty minutes of daylight for good behaviour.

What the hell was she doing up there? Playing with that damned doll again, no doubt. It was high time I took the thing away from her, I decided. Whether or not it had any direct involvement in that bizarre yet lethal vomit-and-diarrhoea-related death in Cresston, the thing was now interfering with my own work schedule, and that I could not allow.

As I stood up, I felt a queasy feeling; a strange rush in my lower stomach. I shook off a vague sense of dizziness and made my way by candlelight up the stairs.

I'd half expected to hear voices from outside the attic door, as before. Previous imaginary friends created by my daughter out of psychological necessity had usually lasted for at least six months, if not a year or more, but if this sudden silence was anything to go by, Gwendolen had either fallen out with her own brain buddy already, or was instead fast asleep.

As it turned out, neither was the case. As I nudged open the door, I was surprised to see her sitting in the middle of the floor again, diligently going through my page of initial ideas and writing out what looked like a vaguely competent plot outline.

'So you *are* working?'

'Of course I am, Father.'

I looked down at the page she was writing on. She hadn't taken her eyes from it since I'd entered the room.

'Well, what do you think?' I asked, feeling vaguely self-conscious. 'Is it any good?'

'It is now.'

'Oh, is it, indeed?' I said, haughtily. Then reached down and grabbed the page from her hand.

Dammit, if it wasn't halfway decent.

Who was I kidding? Gwendolen's edits were great. Truly great.

'Still needs some work,' I said, tucking the page into my jacket pocket. 'I'll bring up a revised version later. By the way, where's that doll?'

'Arabella has it,' she replied.

I froze, pausing to process Gwendolen's words. Who on earth was Arabella? Presumably it must be the name of my daughter's imaginary friend.

'I asked you where the doll is, Gwendolen.'

'I told you, Father. Arabella has it.'

I was losing my patience again. 'Who is Arabella?' I said.

'Arabella is my friend.'

'I understand that, Gwendolen, but Arabella who?'

'Arabella Mathers.'

Mathers? How did she know that name? As far as I knew, I'd yet to have a single significant conversation with Gwendolen since we'd moved in here, let alone one concerning the previous owner of this house. Could she have plucked that very name out of the blue, or was there some other, more sinister, explanation for her choice of imaginary surname?

'And this "Arabella Mathers" has your doll?'

'That's correct, Father,' Gwendolen replied, running her hands through that same patch of spilled ink on the attic floor, drawing what looked to me like a strange black figure upon the wooden boards.

'And where is Arabella now?' I felt suddenly nauseous again, as if I was about to throw up and shit myself at exactly the same time.

'Out playing,' said Gwendolen.

'Out playing?' I repeated, desperate for a straight answer from her. 'Out playing *where*?'

'In the graveyard, Father,' my daughter replied, finishing off her impression upon the ink-coloured floor of what looked to me, from this angle, like a young Victorian girl.

'Why on earth would this Arabella Mathers be out playing in a graveyard?' I asked.

Finally, Gwendolen looked up at me.

'It's her *home*.'

★

It had to be the ink. Whatever lay inside that doll, whatever bizarre contraption motored the toy's mechanism, making it release an unpleasant stream of black effluence down one leg, *had* to be the source of Gwendolen's increased strangeness. I daresay my confining her to the attic for days without adequate daylight, food or water wasn't exactly helping the situation, but that was something both Carlotta and I had done a hundred times before whenever we'd wanted to watch something on television, and back then it hadn't done Gwendolen an ounce of harm.

So it *had* to be the ink. An ancient concoction of toxic chemicals, no doubt long since festered into some noxious vapour that quietly clouded the owner's judgement without him or her even knowing. Gwendolen's protective subconscious instincts must have caused her to chuck the thing away, I figured, where it would cease doing her any permanent damage. Perhaps she'd thrown it out of her new window and was still in a state of psychological denial.

Yet what of this new 'friend' of Gwendolen's? The mysterious Arabella. The rational part of my mind wanted to see her as simply a figment of my daughter's ink-addled brain. Yet I couldn't help but recall Tate Rellington's mention of a murderous ghost at loose in the village. A ghost that caused people to shit ink and turn into paper bags. Might there, after all, be a grain of truth in the tale? And if so, was my daughter, and that ink-shitting doll of hers, somehow part of its *modus operandi*?

As I pondered all this, scarcely believing I was giving the idea any credence, I thought again of my pressing schedule and how these strange events were speeding me further and further towards my looming deadline, with not a jot of any real writing being done between them. Feeling a sudden stab of anxiety, I picked up the phone on my desk and dialled Rosaleen's number.

'It's Nicholas,' I said, slurring my words slightly. I was on the whisky again, in an attempt to stop myself feeling nauseous. I didn't tell you I was on the whisky before, did I? Well, I was. On the whisky. That's how stressed I was becoming. So stressed that I was on the whisky.

'Hi Nicholas,' said Rosaleen. 'It's Rosaleen.'

'I know that. What have you found out?'

'Nothing yet, I'm afraid. There seems to be no mention of any writer called "Anton Mathers" on any kind of official record. And I've been extremely diligent in my investigations.'

'For Christ's sake, woman, pull your finger out,' I said, slamming the receiver back on its cradle. I really *was* getting tetchy, these days. But what the hell could I do to speed things up? Before I knew it, Rosaleen was going to cease being deferent to me and would start mentioning, instead, my supposed 'contractual obligations'. Everything was starting to go wrong, damn it.

Then, quite suddenly, I smiled. For almost immediately, a solution had formed itself in my mind. A plan, devious perhaps in spirit, yet one that would single-handedly solve the issues of my pressing schedule and the attendant delays caused by Gwendolen's temporary lunacy.

I sat there in the armchair, staring at that portrait of Anton Mathers on the wall in front of me, and raised a glass of whisky in his direction.

'Congratulations,' I said, aloud, 'on a truly brilliant gothic novel.' I gulped the spirit down, savouring its harsh, bitter sting as the fluid burned my open throat. 'And thank you.'

Did I detect a subtle shift in the portrait's gaze at that moment? A fleeting glance; a trace, say, of apparent *fear* in its eyes?

'Correct, Anton,' I said, rising from the chair before pouring myself a fresh tumbler of Grant's. 'Thank you. From me, Nicholas

Stein, esteemed author of the pulp gothic, to you, Anton Mathers, *un*-esteemed and *wholly unknown* author of the literary gothic.'

I stumbled towards the portrait clutching my whisky, grinning from ear to ear. In my other hand I held up the copy of *Vampton Grange*. Raising my glass again, I turned my head and kissed its beautifully produced, emerald-green cover.

'Thank you, Anton Mathers,' I said, addressing the portrait once again, 'for this, the most successful, multi-million-selling gothic chiller by *Nicholas Stein*.'

I laughed. God, how I laughed. I couldn't stop the laughter. The sheer bravado, the brazen ingenuity of a plan that had come to me so suddenly among those dark and creeping shadows of that old house on the hill. By publishing Anton Mathers' unsold and unknown book as my very own work, I could swiftly secure my divorce, hand Gwendolen back to Carlotta, and enjoy a life of literary luxury at last, in one fell swoop.

'Bad luck, friend,' I said, necking the whisky in one, before realising I'd necked it already and my glass was now empty. I tossed the tumbler aside, reached out again with my hand and lifted the portrait from the hook on the wall behind.

Still laughing, I turned the picture round, then fastened it back in place, its front now facing inward, against the wall, so the face of Anton Mathers could no longer taunt me.

'Goodbye, Anton Mathers, you *loser*,' I said.

Then I heard it.

Quiet at first. A mere whisper. Then the source drew nearer, and I realised it was a voice calling from outside.

A girl's voice, light, almost playful, singing out a name gently in the darkness.

'*Gwendolen . . . Gwendolen . . .*'

Was it my own daughter, crying out in her madness? Was she sleep-walking again, like she'd done so often as a child, wandering along motorways when we'd forgotten to lock the back door? Or did this voice I was hearing belong to someone else entirely?

I stepped out into the hallway and made my way towards the front door of the house. Then caught a fleeting glimpse of something white standing there on the raised porch.

I flung open the door and saw what looked like a cotton frock disappearing around the side of the house, heading towards the over-grown graveyard.

There was no escape that way, I knew, quickening my pace to catch the nocturnal intruder. Maybe Gwendolen had met a real friend after all, through that newly opened attic window. A trespasser on the prop-erty who evidently thought itself clever enough to play some form of ghostly 'postman's knock' with me in the middle of the night.

Well, I'd show them.

I rounded the corner at speed and immediately became tangled in a thick cluster of winding vines. There was no one ahead of me. Just a mass of overgrown vegetation, blocking the path ahead.

I struggled blindly, lashing out at the choking greenery, forcing my way through.

Then suddenly the path ahead cleared, and I found myself inside a small opening in the trees. The place was lit from above by a gibbous moon (in fact, *the* gibbous moon – there's only one) and I realised I was standing within a small circle of leaning gravestones.

A flurry of movement in the far trees caught my eye. This time, I saw more clearly the white flash of a Victorian frock, vanishing into the greenery beyond.

Then I heard that laughter again – a child's laughter. And knew there and then that it wasn't Gwendolen I was chasing, after all. Of that I was certain, for my daughter had singularly failed to laugh once through the entirety of her twelve years on this earth.

I ran forward, darting through the crooked gravestones, desperate to unveil the identity of this watcher in the woods.

Then, as I pushed away the swinging branches masking my view of the child running ahead of me, I stumbled into a sudden ditch and fell. Clambering forward again up the rough verge, I finally saw it. Staring directly at me from the furthest edge of the graveyard.

No longer running, but waiting there, still as a statue.

Waiting for me.

It was the doll, perched on the top of an angled gravestone. A light breeze moved through the trees behind it, coming from the nearby cove, fluttering the toy's grubby dress, which had once, years before, shone clean and white.

I stepped forward through the mud and grass, no longer hurrying, and finally reached the leaning gravestone.

I picked up the doll in my hands, so that I could read the name on the marker below it.

ARABELLA MATHERS
DIED 1857

A scream filled the darkness, and the doll began to shriek. Its hands and feet burst into sudden motion as my own palm flinched at a cold rush of expelled ink.

It had done one on my hand. In panic, I reached behind the doll's back for what I hoped was an operating key, hearing at that same moment a sudden sound emerge from the area of its mouth.

The words it spoke came from a tinny voice-box somewhere inside, before my harsh, instinctive twist of the lever swiftly cut the noise off. But I'd heard enough already. I'd caught those dreadful words coming from inside the doll, and they'd chilled me to the core. Words I was unlikely to forget.

'*Help me, Daddy! Please! Help me, Daddy! Please! Help me, Daddy!*'

They could have come from my own daughter.

CHAPTER SEVEN

'The Plague'

I sensed the flashing lights long before Rellington knocked on my front door. I'd been awake most of the night, haunted by frightening dreams and several urgent trips to the toilet. The events of the previous night were already clouding my mind, blending with the world of nightmare, as though the Sandman himself had poured grains from both worlds into my sleeping ear, then mixed them around with a wooden whisk, adding some green dye to create a devilishly evil metaphorical cotton candy that he'd then yanked out and forced me to chew at clawpoint.

I gagged, still feeling nauseous. Then froze as my mind caught a sudden, vivid yet essentially still indistinct flash of half-remembered dream.

Green cotton candy . . .

Not pink, like normal cotton candy.

No, the particular metaphorical dream-based cotton candy mixed into my ears by the proverbial Sandman of imagination had, in this case, been *emerald-green* . . .

I dragged myself out from under the covers, pulled back the curtained enclosure of my Victorian four-poster bed, and made my way downstairs as Rellington hammered loudly on the front door.

When I opened it, he placed his foot immediately on the threshold again and came straight to the point.

'I think you better let me talk to her.'

'Who?'

'Your daughter, Mister Stein. I know she's up there.'

'She's sleeping,' I said.

'Mebbe you could go wake her up.'

'Not until you tell me what this is about, Rellington.'

The lawman paused, staring strangely at me. 'You feeling okay?'

'Never better,' I said, lying through my teeth. If I'm honest, I felt like all my insides were about to burst through every conceivable orifice. 'I asked you what this is about.'

'Well, mister, ten more people died in Cresston last night.'

Maybe it was the nausea, but for some reason I was no longer shocked. 'Vomiting?'

Rellington nodded. 'That's right.'

'Plus diarrhoea?'

'Uh huh,' Rellington said, nodding again. 'The *double-squits*.'

'Both excretions consisting of an inky texture?'

'You got it, mister.'

'And everyone subsequently turned into paper bags?'

'Reckon so. But before they all died, them there various victims reported seeing a young girl in their vicinity at *exactly* the same time they began to feel ill. A young girl in old clothing. *Victorian* clothing. I guess what I'm saying is, it was a young girl in old Victorian clothing.'

'Presumably it was the ghost?' I said. For, as crazy as the notion might have seemed to me before now, the presence of a supernatural entity could potentially explain that strange, ghostly figure I'd glimpsed the night before.

'I don't believe in ghosts,' he replied. 'I want to know where your daughter was last night.'

My daughter? Why the hell did he want to know what my daughter had been doing?

'She was right here,' I said. Although technically I couldn't vouch for that, I realised. For I'd gone outside myself for some of that time, hadn't I? Leaving Gwendolen upstairs alone. Could she have left the house in my absence? Surely not. Surely my daughter had no reason to leave the house in the middle of the night. Besides, I'd left her specific instructions *not* to come down until she'd completed the work I'd set her, hadn't I?

But then she *had* finished that work, hadn't she? That rudimentary plot outline I'd set her, then roughly taken back, telling her to await my next round of notes. Notes that weren't going to materialise at all now, given I was about to publish the work of Anton Mathers instead and pass *his* books off as my own. Had Gwendolen subconsciously picked up on that fact? Had she somehow got wind of my plan and taken the opportunity at last to sneak out for some air?

If that was the case, then Rellington might be right, after all. Gwendolen could well have been outside last night. But would my daughter's nocturnal presence in the town be enough to cause an entire community to lose control of their bodily functions and die in such monstrous fashion?

Unless . . . Unless . . . Unless Gwendolen had taken that damned *doll* with her! The doll I'd seen sitting on the top of that gravestone. Maybe she'd left it there temporarily before carrying it with her into the town? And maybe whatever was inside that eerie, ink-filled doll, was, as I'd long suspected, some deadly poisonous substance? Maybe there was methanol in it? Or mercury? Or even, God forbid, those other poisonous chemicals that are far worse, and which I could never research the official names of without the authorities marking me down as a potential 'person of interest' . . . Maybe Gwendolen had inadvertently handed it over to some unsuspecting person in the town?

I thought suddenly of my own nausea. That urgent need to vacate my bowels in all directions. I'd handled the doll myself, I realised, grimly. Maybe it had passed on its dreadful poison to me, too?

And if it was the doll itself behind these multiple deaths, then Gwendolen might well be guilty of murder, after all . . .

I began to sweat.

'Are you sure you're okay?' asked Rellington, who'd been waiting patiently while I processed all these internal reflections.

'I saw a ghost last night,' I snapped, attempting to steer the subject away from my daughter.

'Well, you're all seein' something, for sure,' he said. 'Crazy as it sounds, folks in Cresston think a *witch* is afoot.'

It did sound crazy. A witch and a foot are completely different things. Unless he meant the villagers believed a witch was *abroad*. Which itself was mildly confusing, as it could mean either that a witch had been seen in the area or that a witch was currently holidaying on foreign shores. I presumed he meant the former. Which itself didn't sound crazy to me at all. The villagers had already burned one, after all.

'*Another* witch?'

'And I might as well say now that a witch don't necessarily mean no woman, neither. 'Cause some witches are *men*.'

'I do know that, you know. I *am* a practitioner of the literary gothic.'

'Meaning,' he continued, ignoring me, 'folks might start thinking there's *two* witches in Cresston, if you catch my drift. One of them a *male* witch, and the other a *lady* witch.'

'What are you implying?' I said.

'I'm saying mebbe you should let me take your daughter into custody, Mr Stein. For safe-keeping, you understand? Before the villagers get to her first. I'm sure you wouldn't want to witness *that* particular burning.'

I considered this for a moment, and had to admit he was right. No matter how angry I might get with Gwendolen on a daily basis, no amount of tardiness and bad attitude could possibly justify witch-burning for anyone under the age of eighteen.

'I reckon you should leave, too,' he added. 'I'll meet you on the outskirts o' town after dark, hand you over your daughter, and then you can both ride on out of town, with no one here the wiser. Ride on back to Stalkford. Before superstition starts reigning over law and order.'

'You don't believe she's a witch, then?' I asked.

He smiled. 'I may read about ghosts and witches, Mr Stein, but I don't believe in neither. Sadly, though, the folks down in Cresston do. And until they start reading a durned book or two, my job round here is keeping the peace, and makin' durned sure only the *right* people get burned.'

His intentions were noble, I supposed, but there was no way I was going to sacrifice the writing of my gothic masterpiece for a bunch of illiterate peasants.

And he wasn't going to take custody of Gwendolen, either. What guarantee did I have that he wouldn't immediately arrest her for the killings? Rellington had a duty to apprehend suspected murderers, after all, and right now Gwendolen was public enemy number one. Even though he'd helped me out several times so far, the sheriff was ultimately in the pay of a witch-burning rabble. No, I had a duty to protect Gwendolen from these false accusations. She was partly *my* daughter, damn it. A bad and ungrateful one, certainly, but she was partly *my* flesh and blood, and no one was going to incarcerate half of her against her will except me.

'I told you before, sheriff. I was with my daughter all night and can vouch for her being at home. Unless you're about to accuse me of being an accomplice to whoever or *whatever* committed these bizarre killings?'

His smile softened. 'Not at all, Mr Stein. You take care now.' Still grinning, he stepped down from the wooden platform and made his way back over to the squad car. 'A friendly warning is all,' he said, opening the car door. 'Like always.' His smile finally dropped as a look of genuine concern crossed his face. 'Truth is, I might not be able to hold them off forever.'

I nodded, respectfully, watching as he drove away, then doubled up suddenly and projectile-vomited all over the raised porch.

Panicked, I examined the stain I'd made between heaves. It wasn't ink, I noted with relief. Just ordinary vomit. Yellow, bits of vegetable, etc. So, the poisonous doll – if it was a poisonous doll that was causing all this – hadn't got to me yet. I whispered a small prayer of thanks to the Almighty. For despite an increasing fear of the creeping unknown, the vomit I was currently expelling from my contracting, quaking guts *wasn't* black ink.

Yet . . .*

★

Had Gwendolen gone mad, after all? Was she finally displaying the malign genetic influence of her mother's side? Was my precious daughter leaving the house in the middle of the night, disobeying my specific instructions to stay indoors, in order to inadvertently and unsuspectingly poison the townsfolk with some hideously mutated, self-producing ink from her ancient, creepy toy doll? Or was she even doing it *deliberately*? Maybe she'd realised how cruel the townsfolk were being to me and my career plans, and had decided to make the ultimate sacrifice, doing away with all those who were criticising or hampering my writing career in order to secure her father a multi-million best-selling writing opportunity?

---

* An alternative, yet equally effective line here would be 'But for how long?'. Feel free to choose your preferred version, although I will say here and now that I am not doing two different prints. I repeat. I am not doing two different prints. GM

GARTH MARENGHI

For that reason alone, I *couldn't* let Rellington take her. I just couldn't. If Gwendolen was doing all this for me (and to be fair, she ought to be), then killing everyone who opposed me was both an act of love and a way of validating her beloved father's writing. If that was the case, I'd protect her even more, dammit. Clearly I'd been wrong about her all these years. Clearly, she'd been more of a daughter to me through this one simple act of mass murder than through anything I might have expected from her daily editing routine. In fact, she'd been *far* more than a daughter.

She'd been a son.

At that thought, I felt something I'd never ever felt before, not even for Carlotta in those early days.

I felt *love*.

Love for my daughter, who was more like a son to me now. A beloved, dutiful son.

My darling Gwendolen . . . (or Graham, once I'd sorted it by deed poll).

But what if, instead, there *were* a grain of truth to these villagers' fears? What if there *were* a real ghost haunting the village of Cresston, just down the coast from Bloater's Cove?

What if this mysterious Arabella Mathers had somehow come back from the dead?

It seemed madness to even consider such a possibility, but I couldn't keep myself from recalling that fear of the unknown I'd experienced the night before. That terror I'd felt at that strange figure, who may or may not have been Gwendolen, running out into the night, crying my daughter's name into the wind. A figure who'd also left my daughter's terrifying doll on the top of that gravestone. A gravestone bearing the name of Arabella Mathers, whose ghost may or may not have been speaking to my own daughter. A ghost that was possibly, for some unknown reason, causing the deaths of nearby villagers, and in the process landing the blame squarely upon the head of Gwendolen.

I, as her father, had to step in. Had to stop these incessant internal ruminations and protect my precious daughter from these destructive, unknown forces. I, who'd been blindly shutting her up in a darkened room that terrified her, had to realise once and for all the error of my ways and ensure that this time, the dreaded door to the attic had to be closed for the last time on my precious daughter and finally *locked shut.*

Steeling myself, I made my way up the stairs, taking with me a cup of tea for Gwendolen, which I'd finally learned how to make, having studied the process in detail from a passage I'd read in Anton Mathers' book.

The attic door was ajar as I made my way up the final flight of stairs, and as I nudged it fully open, I found Gwendolen sitting on the edge of her bed, dressed in a white Victorian gown.

'Good morning, Father,' she said, brightly. It was like the old Gwendolen again. The one I'd imagined might exist for real one day.

'Morning, Gwen,' I said, reciprocating her joyful mood and handing her the tea.

She sipped it contentedly, then pulled a stray lock from her cheek and looked up at me, beaming. 'Can I go out and play today? Arabella says you'll be using her daddy's book instead of your own.'

I froze, unable to believe what I'd just heard. 'What did you say?' I said.

'Your book,' she replied, taking another sip of tea. 'Arabella says you've decided not to write one yourself, and that you're going to use her father's book instead and pretend it's yours.'

'That's not true,' I said.

'She says it *is* true. She says you found all his books in the basement and now you've decided to pass off his work as your own. Arabella's very angry about that.'

'Is she, indeed?' I said, trying to remain calm. But inside I was chilled. Had a real ghost, if that's what Arabella was, somehow been watching my movements? Was the malevolent spirit of the daughter of a long-dead gothic author truly communing with my own child? It had seemed like madness a mere moment ago, yet now it seemed like the only plausible explanation.

'Arabella hates you,' said Gwendolen, as if those words were a perfectly ordinary utterance. 'She says she's going to kill you.'

This was madness, I realised. Though I admit that I had every intention of stealing Anton Mathers' work, what on earth did that have to do with his daughter? Ghost or no ghost, she should know her place and speak only when spoken to.

'Arabella should speak only when she's spoken to,' I said.

'Arabella says you're just like her own father.'

Surely this was all a joke? Yet there was no possible way Gwendolen could have known about my plans for *Vampton Grange*, unless she *had* been out during the night after all, and had somehow discovered the secret basement under the house, like I had. But if that was true, then there was still the possibility she'd committed those murders in the village after all, by accidentally poisoning everyone with her rotten doll . . .

A cold feeling ran through me. Neither option was great, to be honest. Either Gwendolen was mad and a murderer to boot, or we *were* being haunted by a malevolent child-ghost, after all. In which case, both Gwendolen and I, and the whole town for some as-yet-undisclosed reason, were doomed to die vomiting up and excreting black ink before turning into old parchment, which was not my idea of a peaceful summer holiday.

I had to be sure.

I had to *know*.

'I want to discuss this entire thing with Arabella,' I said. 'The last thing I want to do is anything that might upset her or her father.'

'That's wise, Father,' said Gwendolen.

Now came the crunch. The moment when, if Arabella was merely a figment of my daughter's fevered imagination, the next question would throw Gwendolen utterly and bring the fake reality she'd constructed around her crashing down.

'I want to meet her in person,' I said. 'I want to meet with Arabella.'

I waited, expecting my daughter's blissful expression to collapse. But instead, she smiled. 'Certainly. How about three o'clock in the morning?'

I couldn't believe my ears. 'Three o'clock in the *morning*? Isn't that a little late for her? Or early?'

'Arabella never sleeps,' she said.

'*Where* do I meet her?' I asked, carefully.

'On the cliffs above Bloater's Cove.'

'Then I'll see her at three,' I said.

'I'll come too.'

'No,' I replied, knowing it was imperative that I meet with Arabella alone if I were to rule out my daughter's involvement in these lethal supernatural shenanigans. 'This time, Gwendolen, you're staying right here.'

I stepped back into the outer hall and slammed the door shut behind me. Then I grabbed the key to the attic door, which I'd found in a drawer downstairs, and swiftly locked her in.

'No, Father!' Gwendolen screamed from within, rattling the door from the other side. 'Let me out!'

She continued to yell as I activated additional deadbolts, padlocks and a variety of locking devices I'd brought back from B&Q earlier that morning.

It was for her own good, I kept telling myself, trying my best to ignore her. For no matter how much my conscious mind was telling me that I was acting like a ruthless squire, a cruel patriarchal overlord of gothic lore, I *had* to make sure.

Had to *know* whether Arabella was real or not.

Had to know if Gwendolen herself was to blame for those unexplained mass deaths in the village.

Had to know why I, Nicholas Stein, was acting this way.

CHAPTER EIGHT

'The Ghost'

As the grandfather clock in the hall chimed a quarter to three, I gathered up the lantern I'd found in the basement, extinguished the candle on my desk and made my way out into the hall. I closed the front door gently behind me, not wanting Gwendolen to know that I was leaving the house in case she'd managed to find some way of springing the bolts on the attic door and was intent on joining me in the dark to maintain the facade of Arabella being real.

Because ultimately, I wanted to believe my daughter. As crazy as it might sound, part of me wasn't averse to the idea of the supernatural existing. Both Arabella and her father were long dead, after all, and Anton's published works were therefore technically beyond the legal period of copyright protection. Even if the supernatural spirit of his daughter *were* to exist, hellbent on avenging itself against the theft of her father's ancient, unpublished work, all I need do was thrust my copy of *The Writer's Guide to Contractual Rights and Copyright Law* in its semi-transparent face and there was nothing the paranormal brat could do about it.

Her father's books were mine now.

Mine.

And if all went to plan this night, I need never be hungry or poor, or married to Carlotta, or saddled with custody of our daughter, again. Why, there were twenty completed gothic novels in all, weren't there? All triple-deckers, meaning I could release each volume individually and publish sixty separate instalments if I wished. Publishing twice a year would mean I'd be covered for the next thirty-seven and a half years. And if each was a multi-million best-seller, I'd be rich beyond my wildest imaginings. What's more, I'd be famous. Hailed as the greatest name in gothic supernatural fiction who'd ever lived. The sheer uncanny power and historical authenticity of each Anton Mathers – excuse me, *Nicholas Stein* – novel would reinvent gothic horror for the modern reader, by taking them back in time with tales of terror so chillingly convincing that one might think they'd been written in the very period in which they were set. Which they had been, of course. But that was a secret I'd be taking to *my* grave.

I doubled up suddenly, gripping my stomach with both hands. Then my body arced backward as I reached out, panicked, for my rear cheeks. I'd felt movement there, I was certain of it. Something liquidous, threatening to spill from the dank entrance of my rectal cave, poised to burst suddenly like an exploding dam past the rocky heights of my perineum, down toward the sleeping valley of my trousered thighs.

I turned wildly, catching a glimpse of the author's portrait still staring at me from the wall of my study. Perhaps the house on the hill was affecting my mind, too? Perhaps the spirit of Anton Mathers himself, sneering distastefully at me from that sombre portrait in my writing room, was somehow haunting *me*? Perhaps he was inside *my* brain?

'Whatever,' I said, laughing off my fears. I had the man's books now. My future was assured, and if it turned out that he and his daughter were in cahoots against Gwendolen and me, then I'd simply bring in a priest, or a bulldozer, and do away with them, and this place, once and for all.

Tomorrow I'd load his entire life's work into the boot of my car and drive them to a secret storage vault somewhere in Stalkford. If those tomes were going to keep me in business for the next thirty-seven and a half years, I had to get them out of Bloater's Cove and into a sealed unit with the correct level of heat and humidity.

Then, once I'd managed to locate that foul doll again, I'd convince Tate Rellington that its leaking arse was the cause of the deaths in the village, and that the old woman they'd burned in the town square had been the instigator of the entire problem.

Then Gwendolen and I would be safe.

Slipping outside, I made my way past the outer grounds of the house, through the furthest edge of the graveyard, in the direction of Bloater's Cove.

The outcropping of trees gave way eventually to the coastline beyond, and I was suddenly conscious that my swinging lamp might signal to some distant rowboat offshore that the coast was clear, the revenue men were all in the tavern and a landing could now commence. Then I remembered that I wasn't an eighteenth-century smuggler, but a nineteenth-century lighthouse operator, far from my post, having strayed on the way home from some game of cards at my local watering hole, and desperately waving my lantern in sweeping gestures in an attempt to ward yonder schooner back, away from the rocky shore. Then I remembered that I wasn't that, either. I was Nicholas Stein, dammit: gothic suspense novelist. And I was here to meet a ghost to discuss terms regarding the sale of her father's priceless (not that I'd say that to her) novel collection.

My mind was swimming. Evidently, I was traversing some kind of time warp on the cliff's edge at Bloater's Cove. Whatever strange and powerful supernatural force was guiding me, I knew that I had now entered Arabella's psychic domain, and the usual rules of time and space no longer applied.

So was she real then, after all? Was this strange feeling of existing in another time and plane a part of her influence over the lives of Gwendolen and me?

I stood there on the edge of the clifftop, staring out to sea as a powerful wind blew in suddenly from the direction of the ocean. I felt its force buffet me as I strained my eyes towards the shoreline, but there was no sign of anyone below.

Was this how she would come to me, then? On the wind? Would Arabella's cry call to me from that storm now building above the distant waves?

Then I smelled it. That familiar raw stink of the doll's insides. It was coming from somewhere below me. I knelt down on the edge of the cliff, shifting some rocks aside in an attempt to locate it. For if Arabella's ghost *wasn't* real, then I'd need the doll in my possession in order to convince Tate Rellington that its toxic vapours were the sole cause of those deaths in the village. I thrust my palm against a pile of stones, glimpsing what looked like a piece of dirty white clothing among them, which had somehow become caught between several of the rocks.

I tore into the mound of fragments with both hands, but as I moved the rocks away, I saw that it was nothing of the sort. Instead, the thing looked and felt, once I was able to touch it, like a scrap of worn paper; the page of an old book, perhaps, long since torn and discarded from its original binding.

I drew it out, freeing it at last from the stones. On the front of it was a face.

My face. Not one that had been scrawled on, or drawn in, or painted upon, but a real human face, somehow embedded within the texture of the parchment itself.

I coughed suddenly, reeling from the fetid stink of whatever substance was suddenly assailing my nostrils. That reek, that pong, coming from the odious parody of my own face. The scent of poison. The stench of death. The stink of ink.

It was the smell of the *doll*.

I forced my dazed head away towards clearer air. Lurching forward, I heaved heavily again as another violent bout of stomach cramps struck without warning. Then found myself prostrate on the very edge of the cliff, that familiar raw stink of the doll's insides still lingering in my nostrils. As I leaned forward over the side of the crag to expel my guts, I felt a pair of small hands push me from behind.

And I fell. Downward, straight over the edge of the overhang, plunging towards the coastline far below. I shrieked, and as I shrieked, I heard her shriek, too. The terrifying, bloodcurdling shriek of a child's unforgiving fury. And as our shrieks blended together in the wind, I felt the back of my garments snag on something jutting out from the edge of the cliff. Immediately I sprang upward again, thankful now that I'd heaved with such violent intensity that I'd literally untucked myself with the force of my muscle-cramping, and the lining of my underpants had caught on the end of a jutting twig. With help from some unknown force, whether it were heavenly intervention or not, I had somehow been spared from death.

Bouncing up and down, suspended by my underpants from the extended branch, I turned my head upward to see who, or what, had pushed me over the cliff's edge.

And saw her. A little girl, drenched from the rain, dressed in Victorian clothes. She had long, blonde hair and a small, thin face that was strangely beautiful.

Yet angry. Oh, so angry.

It wasn't Gwendolen, that much I knew.

It was Arabella Mathers.

A ghost, after all.

And she hated me. Oh, how she hated me.

She really, *really* hated me.

By the time I'd shot back up a third time via the spring in my over-stretched pant-line, she'd gone.

Vanished, into the wind

Then my pant-line finally snapped and I dropped on to the sand.

CHAPTER NINE

'The Curse'

Halfway back to the house, I threw up and shat myself at the same time. I thanked God I was outside. Aside from the sheer volume of liquid I'd expelled (five buckets plus, and counting), the stuff itself was anything but normal and would have rendered my writing study unusable if I'd projectiled it all at home.

Damn it, I was *full* of ink.

Black, putrid ink.

I didn't have to guess what came next. I knew there was no escape for me now. I'd seen the ghost. Knew it was real. Knew that now there was no hope of negotiating publishing rights to her father's oeuvre. Knew that agonising death awaited me in the form of gradually turning into a stained paper bag.

I winced as another cramp hit my stomach. My body convulsed, and I sprawled across the path leading back to the house.

Yet this time, nothing came out but air. I realised, with mounting horror, that I'd spewed my last cartridge.

This was it, then. The moment of truth. By which I mean death. Unknowingly, I'd invoked a curse when I'd handed that doll to my daughter. Was it when I'd laid claim to the purchase as my own gift and done that old woman out of a recognised charitable donation?

Or was it later, when I'd made the decision to steal those books penned by Arabella's father? Or earlier, perhaps, when I'd rented out that house on the hill in the first place? To be honest, it didn't really matter when. This was all simply idle speculation, which I guess was my mind's way of distracting me from the knowledge that the forces of darkness would soon turn me into an ink-stained paper bag.

Then it hit me. Gwendolen was still in the attic! And there she would stay, I realised, waiting in vain for her father to come and rescue her, until she died and began to rot. Frankly, it was embarrassing. No doubt, in her mother's eyes, *I'd* be to blame. My reputation would be sullied for all time, the lawsuits with Carlotta would intensify and my book sales would start plummeting further than they were already plummeting. I had to save Gwendolen!

I struggled, dragging myself along the dusty path, but my cramps were getting worse. There was no way I could get back to the house in time. Here I would die, alone on my own garden path, drained of inky effluence and turning rapidly into old parchment.

I rolled over, staring at the distant stars above me. Perhaps Tate Rellington would find her, I thought, recalling that the sheriff also knew Gwendolen was up there.

Maybe *he'd* rescue her.

But what if he didn't? What if the villagers got here first? Broke into the house in search of me and found Gwendolen up there? They'd drag my daughter out and burn her in the village square, like they'd done to that old crone whose appearance had so physically repelled me.

At that moment, I did something I hadn't done since childhood. I began to cry. And as I cried, I rolled over and curled myself up into a foetus, and wept and wept; wishing, yearning, praying in vain for Gwendolen to be beside me, so that I could hug her close. And so that I wouldn't subsequently be blamed for this whole debacle.

But it was not to be.

I was not to be.

I waited for Arabella's curse to take hold.

And waited.

And waited a bit longer.

And a bit longer.

And continued to wait.

And, getting annoyed now, tried stretching out my limbs.

Nothing hurt.

I stretched them out again, just to make sure.

Nope, nothing was hurting.

Finally I rolled over, jubilant, scarcely believing the truth. I'd been spared! For some unknown reason, even though I'd shat out a tankful of ink, I'd been spared that final, dreadful, papery death.

Leaping up from the path, I ran back to the house, raced up the stairwell towards the attic, then raced back down again to answer the phone that was ringing loudly in my study.

I got to the receiver just in time.

'Hi Nicholas. It's Rosaleen.'

Thank God! It was Rosaleen.

'Thank goodness you're up,' she said. 'I've been trying this number for a whole hour.'

'I've had a gyppy tummy, Rosaleen,' I said, deciding to spare her the details. Then I changed my mind. 'I've been spewing up black ink and shitting it out the other end at the same time. I thought I was going to die.'

'My goodness, Nicholas . . .'

'Also, there's a vengeful child-ghost currently exacting supernatural revenge on the town.'

'That's the reason I'm calling you.'

I sat down in my chair, flummoxed. 'You *know* about this?'

'You haven't by any chance found a stack of rare gothic novels up there, have you, Nicholas?'

'What do you mean by a "stack of rare gothic novels", Rosaleen?'

'There's no time to play games, Nicholas. Have you found them?'

'There is *a* stack of rare gothic novels up here, yes Rosaleen. But those are mine. Technically mine. In that the period of legal copyright has lapsed, so I'm laying claim to them as my own.'

'Are the covers bright green, Nicholas? Is one of them called *Vampton Grange?*'

How the hell did she know all this?

'They may technically be green in hue, yes,' I said, trying my best to sound dismissive.

'Then get as far away from them as possible, Nicholas. Those books are made of arsenic!'

'Arsenic?' I cried, incredulously. 'How the hell are these books made of arsenic?'

'Many Victorian novels were made of it, Nicholas. They used it in the green binding of their covers. Those books you have up there are lethal to handle. A hundred and fifty-one years ago to the day, the population of Cresston was almost completely wiped out by a batch of arsenic-covered books being hawked to them by a local author manufacturing them in the grounds of his *own house.*'

'A local author?' I repeated, stunned rigid in my chair. 'Manufacturing them in the grounds of his *own house?*'

'The illustrious Anton Mathers,' said Rosaleen. 'The man you asked me to investigate. I managed to turn up some old newspapers in the local library here. They report a mass poisoning back in 1857, in which the entire town of Cresston were given copies of Anton Mathers' novel, *Vampton Grange*, to help teach them to read. Within twenty-four hours, everyone fell ill and died in horrific agony, vomiting up and shitting out their insides. The minor few who could still walk marched up to the house on the hill – *your* house, Nicholas – and burned it to the ground.'

Well, that explained a lot. Though not everything. It didn't explain the current townsfolk shitting *ink*, and it also didn't explain the existence of a child-ghost currently wreaking supernatural revenge against all and sundry.

'That's not all, Nicholas . . .' Rosaleen added.

'Spill it,' I roared.

'When the authorities searched through the rubble the following morning, they discovered the remains of two corpses lying amid the ruins. The charred body of Anton Mathers himself, who died writing in his study . . .'

'And the other?' I asked, sensing what was coming.

'His daughter. A young girl named Arabella. Her remains were found in what was left of the garret above the house.'

I gasped. The attic! Where I'd confined Gwendolen from the moment we'd moved in. Presumably she'd been communing with the ghost of Anton Mathers' daughter the entire time.

'That's truly chilling, Rosaleen. But to go back to these books I have here. Is there any way we can get them fumigated this week, so that I can start selling them under my own name by next Monday?'

'You're not listening, Nicholas. Anton's daughter, Arabella . . .'

'Yes, her again, yes . . .' I said, impatiently.

'She *wrote* his books.'

I almost dropped the phone. I hadn't seen that one coming, even though subsequently, of course – while writing this, for example – I knew everything about it.

'Go on,' I said again, finally paying close to my full attention.

'Anton Mathers was a successful gothic novelist, but the truth was that it was his *own daughter* who was doing the actual writing. She was a child genius, Nicholas. A precociously talented writer.'

'Personally, I don't believe in child geniuses,' I said. 'It's simply a case of rich parents.'

'Will you *listen*, Nicholas? Anton confined his daughter Arabella to the attic and kept her hidden away from view, so that no one would ever know his books were being written by someone else. She wrote for him prolifically, drawing upon her imposed incarceration as inspiration for her macabre tales. When rumours of a "hidden helper" began circulating in Anton's former home town, he upped and moved, taking Arabella with him in a sealed coach, to that remote coastal house – *your* house, Nicholas – overlooking Bloater's Cove. There, he began his own cottage industry, forcing Arabella to write him numerous novels, which he then printed using a private letterpress housed in his own basement. He had no idea the staff below were using a highly toxic, poisonous binding.'

'So now Arabella's back,' I said. 'Furious with the town for killing her, and also royally pissed off with her own father for imprisoning her in the attic and using her writing to seek his own private fame and fortune. Intent on pursuing her ghostly vengeance against all who've crossed her, including their descendants. And she's using my own daughter Gwendolen as some sort of supernatural conduit in order to exact her revenge. What a sod.'

'And because of those deaths, all copies of Anton Mathers' books were destroyed, and his name erased from the history books, apart from a certain microfilm reader in a local library quite near me. Arabella's work has been destroyed, Nicholas, until now. But your decision to pass off her works as your own is now fuelling that devil- ish rage inside her. You *must* get out of that house, Nicholas. Take Gwendolen with you and flee Bloater's Cove *tonight*!'

'Sure, Rosaleen. Ta for all the info. You did great. Can you now see if there's a quick and easy way to de-poison a large batch of arsenic-laced books? Arabella's novels are going to make me a multi- millionaire – and possibly you, too, if you play your cards right.'

'Nicholas! Listen to me!'

I slammed the phone down, aware I now had a mountain of things to do if I was somehow going to get Arabella Mathers' books into print by the end of summer while battling her wrathful spirit.

First, I had to check Gwendolen hadn't also been partly destroyed by Arabella's vengeful ghost, and if she was still *compos mentis*, I should probably also take her up some food and empty the slop bucket, which hadn't been sluiced since last week.

Bounding up the staircase again with a lighted candle, I knocked loudly on Gwendolen's door.

'Daddy!' she yelled.

Thank God, I thought. No 'Father' this time. Hopefully, the old Gwendolen was back.

'Help me, Daddy! Please! Help me, Daddy! Please! Help me . . .'

Then I realised it wasn't the voice of Gwendolen at all, but instead the automated tinny whine of that horrendous Victorian doll I'd gifted her.

I held out my candle and saw it perched there on the door handle, directly in front of me.

Crying out in horror, I slapped my hand at the toy, knocking it sideways on to the floor. Then I swept round, searching for it in the shadows, and spied it lying on the floorboards, arms and legs kicking back and forth as it continued to cry.

'Help me, Daddy! Please! Help me, Daddy! Please! Help me . . .'

The voice sputtered, dying gradually as its motorised limbs began to slow. When all movement had ceased, a flood of black ink rushed out from its tinned behind, staining the floor below. Disgusted, I ran at it full pelt and kicked the thing with all my strength. It flew at speed down the length of the corridor, straight through a window at the far end. I waited for a moment, then heard it smash to pieces on the ground outside. Tomorrow, I'd build a bonfire and burn the remains.

Turning back round, I flung open Gwendolen's door. She was sitting there on the bed, completely motionless, as if stuck in a trance.

'Gwendolen,' I said. 'It's me. It's Daddy.'

There was no response. I walked over to the bed, knelt down before her and looked directly into her eyes.

There was no one at home.

'Gwendolen, please,' I said, hugging her close to me. It was like cuddling a block of not-remotely-melting ice. I leaned my ear against her chest, and breathed a sigh of relief. At least this block of not-remotely-melting ice was still breathing.

'I'm going to save you, Gwendolen,' I said. 'I know I've been a bad dad, but I know why now. I was possessed by the dark spirit of Anton Mathers. But I'm over it now. His ghost no longer has a supernatural hold over me. I have him completely sussed, frankly. But you need to shake off Arabella, Gwen. Cast her out. Tell her to sod off so we can go back to Stalkford and make a fortune out of her unsold books.'

Gwendolen said nothing. Nothing at all.

She was still possessed.

But I couldn't just leave her here and be hugely successful without her. At some point further down the line, the authorities would discover her and I'd no doubt be liable for any alleged 'damages' plus her unpaid rent. Maybe if I could find a priest in the village, they might be able to exorcise the ghost currently employing my daughter as a psychic conduit.

But was there really going to be a Christian place of worship in a backward rural community like Cresston, where the entire population was a bunch of illiterate pagans? I'd probably have to drive all the way back to Stalkford in order to locate a priest at this hour, and by the time I got back, Gwendolen's soul might well have been completely damned.

How could I release my daughter's soul from the clutches of this paranormal entity by sunrise, I wondered? I supposed I could simply pop her in the car with me and drive us *both* back to Stalkford, but then I needed Gwendolen to carry all those boxes of books out to the boot as well. And I had no guarantee that Arabella would accept my terms regarding that elapsed period of legal copyright and allow my daughter to leave town unhaunted.

I had no other choice. Madness, and an eternity spent in the fiery torments of some private supernatural hell, would be all that awaited my own darling daughter if I didn't do something.

'I'm coming back for you, Gwen,' I said. 'I promise. I'm going to see if I can somehow appeal to the villagers. Now that I know the truth about Anton Mathers, and have seen the ghost of Arabella for myself, maybe I can persuade them to come back with us to Stalkford to find a priest. That way, one of them can also help you carry all those books out to the car.

'Then we'll finally exorcise that ghost child inside your head and start selling those books once they've been fully sanitised. Published under *my* name, this time. Not Arabella Mathers, nor Anton Mathers. Their spirits can die here with this house. The future is mine now, Gwen. And yours. Me as a best-selling, multi-million-earning gothic novelist, and you as my beleaguered assistant.'

I leaned forward to kiss my little girl on the forehead, but never made it. For at that precise moment, Gwendolen turned away from me and curled up on the bed, her face turned to the wall.

At any other time, I might have yelled at her for being insolent. But this time, I didn't. This time, I paused, shocked at this final act of rejection. I fought back tears. I'd lost her, then. Somehow, despite all I'd done for her, I'd lost my only daughter.

'I'll be back, Gwen,' I said. 'I *promise*. And finally, we'll be happy together.'

I turned suddenly towards the window, sensing a faint glow coming from the direction of Cresston.

Then heard the chanting.

I walked over to Gwendolen's window and saw, moving through the trees, a long line of flaming torches.

The villagers . . .

The rabble were heading this way, I realised. Marching and shouting through the dark forest below. Making their way in a ragged line through the trees, in the direction of this house.

They were coming to kill us.

CHAPTER TEN

'The Sacrifice'

I couldn't decide what was alarming me more. The thought that Gwendolen and I might be burned alive inside this house on the hill, or the realisation that alongside us, those precious books of Arabella's would also burn. For although they had been stored in those metal boxes in the basement for over a century and had been well protected from that devastating fire that had occurred exactly 151 years ago to the day, I, in my eagerness to count and sort the potential goldmine I'd been literally sitting on for the last few days, had spent most of the day moving them all into my writing study in preparation for Gwendolen carrying them out to the car.

If those villagers heading our way set fire to the house *this very night*, all of those novels would go up in smoke, and my life and reputation would vanish, too, in the flames.

Maybe I *could* appeal to their better nature, as I'd mentioned to Gwendolen just now. Perhaps I could persuade them to leave the house itself intact. Distract them, if need be, by leading them away from the building in pursuit of me. That way, they would also fail to learn of the existence of Gwendolen, and she'd be saved, also.

But I'd need to act fast if I was going to create a diversion.

Locking Gwendolen in behind me, for her own protection, I raced down the stairs again, aware that the chanting villagers were getting closer all the time. I could almost smell the smoke from their torches.

I thrust open the front door, leaped over the wooden porch and ran towards my waiting Jensen Interceptor.

I got inside and gunned the engine. With the mob this close, it was vital they could hear me attempting to flee the place, in order to divert their attention away from the house itself. If I could lead them to an area some distance away, I could conduct negotiations without fear of my books, or Gwendolen, being damaged.

As I keyed the ignition, slammed the vehicle into gear and headed off in the direction of the wooded lane running past the entrance of our driveway, I prayed that Arabella wouldn't make an appearance and disrupt my plans. I hoped she'd be more inclined to help me at present, knowing that the alternative meant that her books would forever be destroyed in another devastating fire.

After all, I'd been spared previously from being turned into a paper bag, which I assumed was due to Arabella feeling a sense of temporary relief at the thought of her own father's imminent punishment. Me stealing the novels of Anton Mathers seemed fitting retribution for him having stolen those self-same novels from Arabella. But there was no guarantee I'd be spared a second time, given I still had every intention of publishing those books under my *own* name once they'd been fumigated.

I pulled out of our driveway into the wooded lane and gunned it along the neighbouring road. The trees ahead appeared to reach towards me through the beams of my headlamps, as if they were somehow alive. Again, I'd have noted that particular detail down if I was still planning on writing my own gothic novel, but as I wasn't, and as time was of the essence, I let the creepy observation go and concentrated instead on putting as much distance as I could between myself and the house.

From the flurry of movement I spied in the trees to my left, and the frantic rush of burning flames between the branches, I realised my plan was working. I was dragging the baying mob away from the house.

I continued to drive in the direction of Cresston, knowing that the Interceptor could easily outrun them all if I wanted it to.

But Cresston offered me no safety, I knew, and if I were to succeed in appealing to the mob's sense of goodwill, I'd need to engineer some way of winning them over.

When I was far enough along the lane to have drawn them a sufficiently safe distance from the house, I slowed the Interceptor and came to a stop. I'd considered driving the car into a tree to make it look as if I'd suffered some catastrophic accident, but there was no way I was going to sacrifice my only means of eventually making it back to Stalkford – and parts for Interceptors were becoming increasingly hard to source, in any case.

So I decided to stage a breakdown instead. Propping the car's bonnet upward, leaving the headlights on so that I might easily be found, I set about gathering up as many clumps of cress that I could find. The plant grew in abundance around the outskirts of Cresston.

Having accrued as much as I could, and aware that the glow from the torches and the mob of villagers holding them were getting closer all the time, I tied the small plants together in a charming bouquet and arranged them on the rear seat of the Interceptor. Then I tore a page from my notepad and, remembering not to write anything as offensive as a word, drew the picture of a 'thumbs-up', alongside that of a smiley face, and lay it on top of the cress.

Hearing voices coming from the distant trees, I moved round to the front of the car and angled my head over its engine, feigning confusion.

'There he is!' cried one of the villagers, bursting into view as a huge mob of them descended into the lane from the surrounding trees. They were holding what looked to me like wads of coarse hessian rolled into tubes and soaked in wax, with a wooden handle and a cardboard collar attached to deflect any wax droplets. Flaming torches, in other words.*

I looked up at them, my face masked in an expression of sudden panic, and held up my hands in apparent supplication.

'Has anyone got a visual Haynes manual for a Jensen Interceptor?' I asked.

'Kill him!' cried another one of the villagers. 'Burn the witch!'

'Witch?' I cried out, incredulous. 'I'm anything but.'

'No, you're a writer!' screamed another. 'Even worse!'

'Burn him!'

'Burn him to death!'

'Look,' I said, trying to appear as innocent as I could. My whole plan hinged on this next moment. 'I've brought you all a peace offering. A bouquet of cress, specially picked for your community. I want to work for you guys, you see, as an apprentice cress-gatherer. I'm done with books. I'm just into cress now.'

'Except that you've picked the *bad* cress,' said an old woman, staring in through the car's rear window. 'Not the *good* cress.'

'What do you mean, the *bad* cress?'

'*Bad* cress grows on cursèd ground. Like this very lane leading towards that there house on the hill up ahead. We only eat *good* cress. Cress from Cresston. But this is *bad* cress.'

'Okay, forget that,' I said. 'I really just wanted to talk to you guys about the ghost.'

'Burn him!'

'Wait!' I said, aware that they were gathering closer about me. 'I know all about the ghost that's been killing people in the town. It's the ghost of a little girl who was found burned to death in my attic, one hundred and fifty-one years ago to the day.'

* Those words being the ones used in the previous sentence. GM

'*Your* attic!' one of them yelled.

'My attic, yes, but it wasn't mine *then*. Now I understand that no one likes a ghost exacting supernatural revenge, but in order to exorcise her spirit, we do need to find a priest.'

'Priest?' shrieked another one of the mob. 'A believer in the Holy "Word"?'

'Word! Word!' someone screamed.

'Look, you're gonna have to employ words at a basic level if you want this ghost dealt with.'

'Kill him!'

'Let me drive into Stalkford,' I said, starting to panic. 'I'll deal with the priest – you won't have to look at any words, I'll do all of that. Then I'll drive him back up here and Bob's your uncle, you can all go back to your cress. Now if you'd just move out of my path, I'll head off straight away.'

No one moved.

'I thought you said your car had broken down?' said the leader of the mob, stepping closer. 'And yet now you're talking about heading off "straight away" . . .'

'He's lying!' shouted another.

'Obviously, I'll need to fix it first, yes,' I said, trying to rectify my mistake, but they had seen through my subterfuge.

'Burn the liar!'

'No, wait!' I said as a group of arms reached out as one to grab me. 'If I don't get a priest to exorcise that ghost, you'll all be dead!'

'You summoned her, witch!' yelled the woman who'd been staring warily at my bouquet of cress. 'You brought the curse upon us. Burn the writer!'

'Burn the witch!' cried another.

'Burn him at the stake!'

They dragged me from the car, up on to the verge and through the line of trees. I felt my body snag on twigs and branches as

229

they tore me across the massed bracken towards a small clearing ahead.

There, in the centre of the small opening, stood a blasted tree, long dead. The leader of the mob gave a signal to his followers, and at once they dragged me over to it and tied me to its greying, withered trunk.

'Burn him!'

This was it, then. I'd escaped being turned into a paper bag, but now an even worse fate awaited. I was about to suffer the ultimate indignity of suffering a fire-based public execution while being jeered at by a baying mob.

And again, I knew that Gwendolen would be left up there in that distant attic room, alone and afraid, expecting her father to come and rescue her at any moment, before realising, eventually, that he wasn't coming after all. Then she'd slowly start to believe that I'd abandoned her for good. Scarpered from my responsibilities in the middle of the night, pretending that I'd be back for her, when all along my sole intention had been to escape by myself, never to return.

I had to get back to her! If only to prove her completely wrong about that. Show her that she was being unfair in condemning me in such a fashion. But it was useless. There was no chance now. My hands had been secured around a blasted trunk, ripe for burning. Leaves had been piled around my waist, and someone had gone to the trouble of tying a crown of cress around my hair, made out of all that *bad* cress I'd picked. I watched as the leader of the mob reached out towards the gathered kindling below me with his flaming torch.

'This is bullshit,' I said, and prepared to die . . .

Then I heard gunshots.

A huge cry rose from the assembled villagers as the bulky frame of Tate Rellington strode like a Tombstone marshal from the nearby trees. He aimed his gun at the leader of the mob.

'What the hell are you doing?' he said.

Thank God. A miracle. Tate Rellington was here, and in the nick of time, like the proverbial cavalry – which, because of Rellington's Western leanings, somehow fitted his nature, and thus his fortuitous appearance here didn't feel remotely forced or unlikely in any way at all.

I watched, ecstatic, as the lawman pistol-whipped the leader of the mob, then swung his gun around to cover the remaining villagers.

'You darned idiots wait for me in future, d'ya hear?'

'Yes, sheriff,' they said as one, as though he were a religious leader.

And he was, in a way, I realised, as the horror of my predicament slowly dawned.

Tate Rellington was their leader.

'This writer's *mine*,' he said, aiming the gun at me now. What the hell was going on here? I thought Rellington was my friend. Hadn't he sworn to protect me? Advised me on securing the house against unruly mobs? Hadn't he promised to protect my safety, and especially that of my daughter?

A rush of cold fear ran through me. Gwendolen. Rellington knew about Gwendolen! He'd sworn to protect her from the baying mob now surrounding me. The mob I'd cleverly led away from the house, specifically to protect her (and the books, obviously). But if Rellington knew about Gwendolen, and Rellington was on *their* side . . .

'He's got a daughter,' said the sheriff, and I knew then that it was all over for her. And for us.

'Keeps her in the attic of that there house on the hill. *She's* the one you want,' he said, pointing with his pistol in the direction of the hill overlooking Bloater's Cove. 'She's the witch who's doing all the killing.'

The mob roared loudly in fear and rage.

'Burn her!' they screamed in unison. 'Burn the witch!'

'Go do it!' barked Rellington. 'Go burn that whole durned house down!'

Another roar went up from the mob as they tore free of the clearing and raced once more into the trees, flames lighting their path through the woodland in the direction of the house, and my precious daughter imprisoned inside.

'You murderer!' I cried at Rellington. 'Why are you burning down my house? My daughter's in there. And all my books.'

He stared at me, his face filled with a hitherto concealed contempt. 'If I cain't have that there house on the hill, stranger, no one can,' he spat.

A sudden thought ran through my mind. That lone bidder the estate agent had told me about. Rellington had said it had in fact been the entire town bidding against me. Had it been a lone bidder, after all?

'That's right,' said Rellington, as if reading my mind. 'I was the one bidding 'gainst you, Mr Stein. I wanted that there house on the hill for those summer months. But a lawman's wage don't quite cover a coastal retreat these days, leastways when the rival bidder in question pulls a durned rabbit out the bag and finds hisself an extra twenty dollars. That swayed the deal in your favour, stranger. I had to go back to my little shack in Cresston again, all the while knowing you, a *writer*, were sipping beers and cahooting away up there, jes' waiting to bring the whole durned town down around ya by invoking that there curse.'

'So you were trying to hire out that house to protect the town?' I found that hard to believe.

'That's what I'll tell them, leastways,' said Rellington. 'Truth is, I knew them books was up there, too. See, I've always fancied myself as a writer, too. I'm an avid reader of them supernatural gothics you pen, and, believe it or not, I have a durned good understanding of the genre.'

Of course, I recalled. Rellington had known who I was, and the kinds of books I wrote, from the very start. Why, he'd even mentioned

232

it specifically at one point. Suddenly, it all made sense. How the hell hadn't I figured it out before now? That note . . . the one pinned to that dead cat on the day Gwendolen and I first arrived. It contained *words*. No villager would have written *those* down. These people never used words under any circumstances. Meaning that note could only have been written by someone who *did* use words. A reader, say, of numerous gothic potboilers...

'Now that *you've* found them,' continued Rellington, 'I guess you've had the same idea as me, and figure to publish them there books under your own durned name. But if I can't have 'em, Mr Stein, I'm sure as hell you won't, either.' He cocked his pistol and aimed it at my head.

'But my daughter,' I said, weakly, trying to appeal to what little sense of humanity he might yet retain. 'She's all alone up there.'

'And when she dies,' said Rellington, 'that there ghost will die, too. Seeing as your daughter's the durned conduit. Am I right?'

I didn't have to answer. He was right. If Gwendolen died, the spirit of Arabella would no doubt die with her, along with everything else in that house on the hill.

It was over, then. I'd failed. Not just as a writer, but as a father, too. There was no longer any hope. I'd failed Gwendolen.

'Say your prayers,' said Rellington, aiming the gun at my head.

Then he pulled the trigger.

CHAPTER ELEVEN

'The Demon'

The bullet passed straight through me.

'What the hell?' said Rellington, opening fire again.

I heard something like a *thwipping* sound as the rounds tore straight through my head, embedding themselves in the wooden trunk behind.

Then Rellington began to scream.

I felt a loosening in the bonds around my wrists. Shards of the dead tree behind me had evidently exploded outward from the sheer force of the bullet's impact, striking the ropes binding my hands, severing the cords.

I pulled my wrists free, reached upward and felt my face.

It was *paper*.

It couldn't be, I thought, feeling around my head with both hands now.

But it *was* paper. Leathery paper. My head was a paper bag. Perhaps not completely paper at the moment. After all, I was still sentient, and could see and breathe, and speak, yet the transformation I'd been dreading had now begun, and Arabella's curse was finally taking its full effect.

'Stay away from me!' yelled Rellington, opening fire again. The bullets passed through my face once more, leaving ragged holes in their wake. But I felt no pain at all. Discerned no real difference in my essential ability to function.

Which meant I had still that most precious of gifts.

Time.

Raising both hands above my head, I ran at Rellington like a wailing ghoul, shrieking as I did so. He threw himself aside, yelling out in terror and firing blindly in my direction. But I was free of him at last.

Turning, I threw myself into the trees surrounding us, and ran as fast as I could through the woods towards the house on the hill.

I knew it wouldn't be long before Rellington gathered his wits again and set out after me. I had to get there before him. Had to stop that rowdy mob from torching my home, my books, but most importantly – my daughter.

As I fought my way forward through the trees, I felt the ground rise under me, and knew that I was finally ascending the hill leading up to the house. But as I approached the crest and saw a break in the line of trees up ahead, I caught sight of a huge wall of flame.

I was too late! The mob had already set fire to the building. With an agonised wail, I clambered forward towards the rising flames. I could see the round tower jutting upward through the high branches, not yet alight, and cursed myself that I hadn't given Gwendolen that particular room when I'd had the chance. If I had done, she might be alive at this very moment. Might never even have suffered the initial nightmare that precipitated these subsequent events. Wouldn't now be encased within a darkened attic as flames licked rapidly around the wooden edges of the house that was her prison.

As I approached, I saw the trees closest to the building swaying wildly against a strong breeze whipping in from the ocean beyond Bloater's Cove. I hoped, I *prayed*, that the wind might blow the encroaching flames away from the house, perhaps even extinguish them entirely. Yet that was a futile wish – that wild wind coming in from the east would no doubt *fan* those flames, not dampen them. For a dampening to happen, I needed *rain* to be blowing in, not wind, and right now it wasn't remotely raining. Not even spitting, I noted, cursing as I staggered ever onwards. Then again, rain might have softened the paper bag that was now my head, meaning I'd go all mushy in an instant and not be able to do anything constructive to help Gwendolen, so I guess it was swings and roundabouts.

I moved rapidly forward through the flame-lit woodland, tripping over a branch lying on the ground before me. As I gathered myself together again, I heard a gunshot crack out behind me and realised it was Tate Rellington once more, in full control of his faculties again and in fast pursuit.

Onward I ran.

I staggered beneath a group of overhanging branches, aware that I was approaching the house from the side opposite the family grave-yard. I was breathless and exhausted now, my face drawing inward and outward like an inflated crisp packet as I fought desperately for breath. At last I managed to break through the clearing ahead of me and finally caught sight of the house.

It was intact. In fact, it wasn't even remotely ablaze. I turned my head aside to ascertain where the flames I'd seen were coming from, and that's when I saw it.

The *villagers* were alight. Not the house. Something had gotten to them before they'd had a chance to reach the building. And from the number of flaming locals currently shitting out cress and ink from exposed orifices, I had a good idea what that something was.

'Behold!' yelled a voice behind me, as a large figure stormed past in the direction of the ignited mob. It was Tate Rellington again.

'There!' he yelled, waving his gun. 'There's the witch! She walks among us!'

Then I saw her.

She wasn't walking, though, I noted. She was floating instead, levitating between the house and the incinerated throng, her white dress billowing in the wind as her terrible, unblinking eyes pierced the darkness around us with that cold, deathly stare.

Arabella's ghost.

I followed her line of sight and glimpsed three villagers cowering behind a nearby bush, not yet aflame but holding in their hands those burning torches from the village, which they'd no doubt intended to use against the wooden boards of the house.

Before they knew what was happening, Arabella raised one arm in their direction and pointed. Instantly, all three keeled over as one, convulsing wildly as jets of black ink shot forth from their mouths and arses, tearing great holes in their cotton trousers. Then, as the black pools of ink spread outward from below them, their faces began to change drastically. At first they became drawn, almost skull-like, as fear transformed their features into quaking masks of terror. Then an untidy network of lines spread lengthways across their skin, creeping slowly in jagged trails as if their heads were cracking like weakening eggs. Then I saw these lines were *creases*, and the heads I'd been looking at now resembled nothing more than flapping bags.

I reached up with one hand to my own face, relieved that somehow I was still able to function as part-man, part-bag, the supernatural process for some reason taking longer with me than it did with those others. I dare say part of me was being spared again. Maybe it was because I was a man of letters, unlike these illiterate heathens, and my veneration of the printed word had, for now, granted me additional time as a sentient, intelligent human being.

As I continued to watch, the flaming torches they'd once clutched – in arms that now resembled toilet roll tubes – caught suddenly on their paper fingers, igniting them like a lit match striking a box of cheap fireworks.

Then they burst into flame, the inky effluence under their

burning feet boiling instantly.* As they ran about in a mad panic, Arabella's ghost turned her attention to another group of huddling illiterates.

Realising that the vengeful spirit was temporarily distracted, I dived forward across the ground, rolling up against the nearest wall of the house. I lay there in the shadows, praying that Arabella hadn't seen me. If I could slowly make my way round to the front of the building while the remaining villagers fought in vain to escape the fate I knew awaited them, maybe I could sneak into the house unseen and rescue Gwendolen before Arabella had a chance to turn on me.

I watched, biding my time, as the leader of the mob, the one who'd grabbed me from the bonnet of my Jensen Interceptor, held out the village hoe to ward off the evil spirit, thrusting it wildly at the floating Arabella.

Ink suddenly burst from the end of its wooden shaft as Arabella glared malevolently at the gardening implement. Then the leader of the mob dropped the tool abruptly and lurched forwards, expelling a long jet of black liquid from his throat. As he did so, the lower hem of the hessian sack he was wearing whipped upwards as an identical arc of spraying effluence exploded from his rear end. I turned my

---

* Which, considering the boiling point for water-soluble ink is 212°F is no mean feat here. Technically, however, the ink in question is Victorian iron gall ink, which will have a different boiling point temperature. I find it outrageous that in spending two minutes researching what that specific temperature should be, I have found no evidence *whatsoever* of any scientific research having been done in this area. In over 200 years, not a single scientist on earth has conducted an experiment to establish the boiling point of iron gall ink, and/or published their findings in an easily accessible public internet forum. This is unacceptable but, sadly, no surprise to me. Carl Sagan said it best when he said that idiotic human beings don't respect scientists enough and, as a result, we're all fucked. That's the gist, at any rate. Having said that, I've now lost a fair degree of respect for scientists myself, following this iron gall ink boiling-point debacle. I'm aware this is a footnote and therefore not the ideal place to discuss such matters, so will talk more about this issue in a live environment; please purchase a ticket before your earliest convenience and await my thoughts. GM

face away from the horrifying sight, unable to watch what I knew would come next.

As the leader's head and body turned rapidly into paper, the flames from his ignited torch blew against his wilting frame, setting it alight. Two of the villagers dashed forward in an effort to assist their fallen leader, then turned about, shrieking, realising it was useless. As they ran desperately for the woods they'd just left, various ends of their own bodies exploded with ink.

None of them would make it, I realised. One after the other, each afflicted villager underwent a sudden, horrifying body purge, collapsing on to the ground in a mess of ink, their emerging paper heads erupting into sudden flame as the torches they were holding in their withering hands suddenly ignited them.

Then I saw Tate Rellington again. Realising the severity of his predicament, he'd flung himself behind a nearby tree and was currently hugging the trunk hard. As I watched, he turned and hurled his own flaming torch far away, into the distance, aware that a fiery death was inevitable were he to remain holding it when Arabella struck.

'Lose the flames!' he yelled out hoarsely to the others, but in the chaos his cries were drowned out by the agonised screams of the dead and dying. Mainly the dying, though.

I crawled further around the exterior of the house, manoeuvring myself closer to the front porch, hugging my own body close to the wall in the hope that I'd remain hidden from Arabella. Meanwhile, Rellington drew his gun once more from the holster on his hip and fired off several shots in the direction of the ghost.

They went right through her, slamming into the planks of the house behind, inches from my own head. I wanted to cry out and warn Rellington to shoot higher. Tell him Arabella's ghost was impervious to bullets and that he was close to drilling me, instead. Then I remembered I was part paper and didn't need to bother, having already been drilled several times. Also, if I had cried out, Arabella might have turned on me instead, and then I'd potentially be suffering another, perhaps fatal, bout of supernatural dysentery.

Rellington fired again, emptying the entire barrel in my direction. I hit the dirt, instinctively (though again, it wasn't technically necessary). Not easy, as I'd hit the dirt once already and there was technically less dirt there for my body to hit.

Splinters of exploding wood rained down upon me, propelled by the impact of Rellington's bullets; peppering my paper face with wooden shards (which, again, didn't hurt).

I fought my instinct to holler out, remembering that if I shouted anything out now, my arse was proverbial grass as far as Arabella's ghost was concerned.

Then came a brief moment of silence as Rellington reloaded his pistol, during which Arabella's ghost turned her attention to the remaining villagers, splattering their insides over the driveway before their paper-like remains caught on the flaming torches still clutched in their hands, erupting them into their very own makeshift funeral pyre.

I looked up again at the exact same moment that Rellington leaned round from the side of the tree and snapped off two more rounds in my direction.

I felt a sharp sting in my shoulder as the bullet struck me, pinning me temporarily to the wall. I gasped in horror. Of course! Only my *head* was part paper at the moment. The affliction hadn't yet affected my arms and legs. Meaning those were still viable targets!

I stifled an agonised scream, then reached up and clawed my embedded flesh from the splintered plank. As I began to ooze blood, I felt my body-strength weakening, realising that if I was to stand any chance of rescuing Gwendolen, I had to make my move now.

Steeling myself, I reached out with my good arm and clawed my way across the ground, hoping that the sound of burning villagers and echoing gunfire might mask my desperate clamber towards the front porch of the house.

But as I came out of hiding, so too did Rellington. Rolling wildly to the left, away from the safety of his tree trunk, he fired off another volley of rounds at the ghost, then leaped to his feet and ran straight at her, gun blazing.

I watched as Arabella floated perfectly still, the bullets passing right through her dress, slamming once again into the wall behind me, causing me to abandon my advance towards the front door.

I froze, aware that Rellington's last-ditch, desperate effort to overcome the ghost by force was a futile effort.

I stared, almost detached, as the sheriff froze mid-run, then dropped his empty gun, grabbing desperately at his gut.

'You durned hellion,' he cried, then belched out a wide spray of black fluid. I shielded myself from the inky mist as the lawman rolled over suddenly, his hands clutching in a fevered panic at the seat of his trousers.

'There's a law against this, young lady,' he yelled, as his rearside trouser seam ripped loudly apart and a powerful arc of expelled butt-ink erupted into the sky like an exploding geyser.

I turned away, horrified at the sight, trying to keep my mind on the task at hand, but as I dragged myself forward through the dust, pulling myself on to the porch as quietly as I could, there was suddenly an almighty scream from behind.

'*Now cometh the vengeance of Arabella,*' cried a young voice, and immediately I knew it was the ghost itself speaking. '*Now Bloater's Cove will feel the true wrath of Arabella Mathers.*'

Almost at the door now, I turned around one last time. I didn't do it to see if there was anything I could do for Rellington. As far as I was concerned, his time was up. After all, he'd been the one who'd wanted to flame Gwendolen, thinking she was responsible for Arabella coming back to life (which, admittedly, as psychic conduit, she was). So why the hell should I cry tears for some two-bit lawman from a backwater town who'd just winged my precious writing arm?

No, I turned to watch him *burn*.

But I was too late. He'd already gone up in smoke, ignited by the spark from his gun as it dropped from his hand and struck the ground below him, catching in that same moment a hitherto unknown and highly flammable component in the ink itself. And if I thought I'd been blessed with a brief second to relish that sight while Arabella's back was turned, I was wrong about that, too.

Because Arabella had turned around also. Turned around so far that she was now facing me. And suddenly I realised that those words she'd uttered – those dark, terrifying warnings of an imminent and mighty storm of supernatural vengeance – hadn't been aimed at Tate Rellington at all.

They were aimed at *me*.

CHAPTER TWELVE

'The Burning'

I felt my stomach churn again. I fought to remain calm, feeling my intestines bubbling within. I knew that at any moment, I'd start expelling my former solids once more from both ends. And given that I was now part paper bag, I didn't relish the thought of becoming engulfed in flames as my particulars caught on a nearby naked flame. I reckoned I had about five seconds to even the odds.

'Look, Arabella,' I said. 'I can call you that, right?'

'*Die!*' she shrieked. I detected a vague trace of High Demon in her accent.

'Whoa, hold your horses, young lady,' I said, holding up my good hand, which I could see was now also turning into paper. I fought to control its increased flapping as I sought to distract her with the business proposal I'd been working on.

'What say I publish those books of yours under your own name?'

The ghost of Arabella paused for a moment, floating in mid-air. Finally, I had her attention.

'Now, I have contacts in the publishing and pharmaceutical industry who can get volume one up and running in no time, with no ill effects for the reader. All I want in return is for my daughter Gwendolen and I to walk free from here, plus twenty-five per cent of the profits and either an "additional material by" or equivalent co-writing credit. Ideally, I'd want to claim the bulk of the writing as my own work and give you a standard "storyline by" credit, but I guess you're not quite in the bargaining mood, right?'

I felt ink swishing in my rear end, preparing to let itself rip.

'Okay!' I yelled. 'I'll settle for an "as told to". You can't say fairer than that.'

My body spun round in a full circle. I felt like everything was about to come out at once. 'Fine!' I pleaded, in a shrill voice I didn't even know I was capable of producing. 'You may have *full* credit.'

I feigned tears, hoping my visibly sorry state would go some way towards convincing this child-ghost of my good intentions. In truth, I simply planned to claim 'Arabella Mathers' as another pseudonym of mine, and if this supernatural child-ghost reared her head again at some future date, I would simply renegotiate terms once Gwendolen had been stored safely away in a local place of worship.

If all else failed, I figured I'd make millions anyway on a best-selling 'true life' paranormal exposé revealing the 'truth' behind the cursed books, publishing it either as *Terror in Bloater's Cove* or *The Cresstonville Horror*, depending on the sales market.

But it was not to be. The ghost of Arabella simply raised her arm, pointed at me menacingly, and hurled a particularly malevolent look in my direction. I turned from her gaze, shaking my head. How she expected to maintain a professional career in publishing with an attitude like that was beyond me.

Yet before I could alert her to her lack of fundamental business etiquette, Arabella shot me yet another menacing glance and I cried out in fright as two powerful jets of ink burst forth from my ends.

And there was me thinking I'd expelled my last cartridge an hour or so back. Evidently I was still brim-full of the stuff.

But that was okay. I'd been here already, hadn't I? I could handle this particular horror. What I couldn't handle, as I said before, was what would come next. If I'd been perched over the edge of a toilet bowl, I might have gripped on to the rim for dear life, sucked up my physical convulsions, knowing that in a minute or so the heaves would subside, and I could start thinking about what I might have in the house for breakfast next day that wouldn't immediately instigate a runnier bout.

But there was no antiemetic for the supernatural, I feared. If I was to avoid the inevitable, turning it somehow into the evitable, then I had to do it while navigating my double-ended spew.

I looked around, desperate to find some way of combating this vindictive, vengeful and frankly unreasonable ghost of a dead Victorian child condemned to a fiery death 151 years ago to the day, who now wanted to set the entire town alight and wipe everyone in Bloater's Cove and Cresston off the face of the map of Stalkford reprinted in the front of this book.

'Daddy, help me! Please! Daddy, help me, Please!'

I heard Gwendolen's voice. But how *could* I help her? How could I help my poor, incarcerated daughter when all around me was a roaring ocean of Victorian ink issuing forth from both my outer-most and innermost orifices?

It was all I could do to try and avoid aiming my projected fluids at those encroaching flames for fear of igniting that almost-hitherto-unknown flammable agent in them.

But then I realised the voice was coming from somewhere close by. Not from the attic, after all . . .

Then I remembered. That voice. The vaguely tinny quality . . . It was the doll!

Of course! I'd kicked it through the window in the hallway outside the attic door, hadn't I? Then presumably it must be around here, somewhere.

I rolled over, still trying to direct my arse and mouth geysers away from the naked flames, aware that all the time Arabella was following me with her eyes, waiting to inflict the final indignity and turn me fully into paper. I realised now why the transformation had been part-delayed in my case. Arabella hadn't given me special treatment for being a writer, after all. No, the effect on me was delayed because she was simply toying with me. Prolonging my agony like a cat flicking the protruding intestines of a lacerated mouse.

Soon, I'd be nothing but paper. Then I'd catch fire and incinerate completely before the taunting aspect of this terrifying, transparent Arabella.

Then I saw it, lying there on the ground nearby, where it had struck the roof of the porch on its descent from the attic floor window and had been flung sideways, landing on the ground just three feet away.

Its motorised legs and arms were still kicking out wildly in a futile march, another stream of ink flowing from underneath it as the metal voice-box inside it continued to wail.

'Help me, Daddy! Please! Help me, Daddy! Please!'

A look of grim determination now set upon my face, even though I couldn't technically see that myself, and anyone watching would probably have only been able to take in the seemingly endless torrent of ink-based fountains coming from my extremities. But I could *feel* the grim determination on my face – which, admittedly, was still largely paper.

Mustering what strength remained in me, I reached out for the small doll unexpectedly with my wounded arm. This unanticipated movement gained me that vital element of surprise, and in seconds, I was clutching the toy in my hand.

I heard a sudden shriek from behind. As I turned back round, I saw a new expression on Arabella's unnerving, uncanny visage.

Fear.

Fear of what I, Nicholas Stein, might now do to *it*.

Then I sensed what that *it* might be. As my jets of ink spewed closer to the surrounding flames, they were suddenly switched off abruptly, as though from a twisting tap.

She'd spared me, I realised. Once more, the ghost of Arabella had held back from destroying me utterly. But whereas before it had been because she'd enjoyed toying with my terrified brain, this time it was because Arabella feared me. This time, I possessed the means to threaten her. And the means, it would appear, lay in that very doll I was now clutching in my flapping, paper hands.* Clearly, the toy itself was a conduit, too. After all, the doll had originally contained the vengeful soul of Arabella Mathers, which had since been able to flee the confines of its china shell and enter the head of my own daughter.

But now, with Gwendolen gone mad, locked away and no longer of any use to Arabella, the spirit had returned to its protective shell in the hope that it might find another victim and continue down its path of supernatural vengeance.

And all the while I held the doll, no one else could be caught in its supernatural hold. Now *I* had the power. At long last, *I* could destroy Arabella.

'Too bad, missy,' I said, gloatingly. 'You had your chance.'

With an unholy shriek, the ghost threw up its hands in paranormal panic, eyes widening in terror, as I calmly cast the foul figurine into the flames.

There was a huge explosion of fire as whatever source of flammable ink inside it erupted. I was blown backwards against the wall of the house, catching sight as I did so of Arabella's spirit floating upward through the rising smoke, swirling in circles among the spiralling clouds as she screamed and screamed and screamed.

The noise was unlike anything I'd ever heard. Worse than Gwendolen and Carlotta combined. A shriek of super*un*natural panic. A scream of para*ab*normal defeat.

---

* Not entirely paper. He can still hold the doll. GM

'Now I'll publish your books under *my* name,' I roared. 'With or *without* your permission.'

I'd done it, then. I'd defeated Arabella Mathers. Now I, Nicholas Stein, would go down in history as the greatest gothic novelist who'd ever lived.

I rose, unsteadily, to my knees, grateful to the Almighty that both Gwendolen and I had been spared.

Then I saw it.

At first, a mere glimmer of movement in the heart of the blaze, but then something more solid. What looked initially like a tiny fireball shot suddenly forth from the flames and rolled – no, *scurried* – over the intervening ground towards the front porch of the house.

And whatever the thing was, I could hear it *laughing*.

The screaming had gone, I realised. That shriek of ghostly terror flying in the wind; that devastating other-worldly cry of supernatural sorrow, had faded.

Replaced by the cruel, sadistic *laughter of the doll*.

It had been a trick, then. A means of luring me to my ultimate fate. A fate, I now realised, which lay not in my own death by flame, but in the death of my daughter, Gwendolen.

As the doll sprinted towards the door of the house, I plunged after it, realising I had no way of catching it in time.

It collided with the wooden boards of the porch, recently soaked with the ink exploding from my own body . . .

And the whole house erupted.

A rising wall of fire licked upward around the front door, blocking my way in. Within seconds, the entire front was aflame, and there was no longer any way at all that I could enter.

Then I heard Gwendolen's cries from the attic high above. 'Daddy! Help me! Please! Daddy! Help me!'

But there was no way I could help. Nothing I could do to save her. As I fumbled against the door, my arms burning in a vain attempt to break through, I collapsed to the ground, despairing. Then, as the flaming heat licked ever higher, I crawled back over to the trees, seeking shelter, weeping as the cries from the attic above me finally fell silent.

Then I pulled the paper bag from my head, realising it was simply a covering now, and unfolded the ragged strip of leathery parchment in my hands. Staring up at me, sneering, was the crumpled portrait of Anton Mathers.

Then only the laughter of Arabella remained.

★

Most of the house had gone, taking the basement with it too, this time. As I looked down those scorched steps, I saw only a twisted mass of molten iron below; the remains of Anton Mathers' letterpress.

I moved through the ruins slowly, stepping over the rubble where the front door had stood, and made my way up the blackened remains of the burned stairwell.

Was it possible? I wondered. Could Gwendolen have survived? If the door I could now sense above me, the door leading to that dark and lonely attic room . . . If *that* had survived, could not Gwendolen have also been spared?

Carefully, not wanting to make any sudden movement that might cause what remained of the house to come crashing down about me, I made my way slowly up the damaged staircase.

Maybe it was an act of mad desperation. A forlorn hope. Maybe any second now, I would be plunging to my death as the ruins gave way, taking me and whatever remained of Gwendolen along with it. But at least we would die together. Father and daughter. And if there was any chance at all, any remote possibility that I might still rescue Gwendolen from these ghastly ruins, I *had* to take it.

As her father, I had to risk all. Prove to my daughter I cared.

249

Show Gwendolen that I truly loved her.

I was outside the door. The locks were gone, melted in the intense heat of the flames. I leaned my head inward, resting it against the charred wooden panelling, and listened.

Something was inside the room.

The room I'd locked her in.

A voice . . .

Faint it was; hardly a sound at all against the wild wind blowing in from the coast beyond.

But definitely a voice.

Gwendolen's voice.

I pushed gently at the door, not wishing to upset the delicate balance keeping what remained of these floundering ruins standing.

And there I saw her. Sitting in her small wooden baby chair.

My Gwendolen.

My precious, darling daughter. Untouched. Undamaged by the flames.

My dearest, beautiful daughter.

A *doll*.

Tenderly, I picked up the toy. It was the exact likeness of our girl, right down to the first beautiful dress we'd picked for her together, before everything in our lives began to go wrong.

'Gwendolen,' I said, starting to cry.

'Daddy,' said the doll, its arms and legs moving uncomfortably in my hands, wanting to be set free from my grasp.

'Daddy, help me. Please, Daddy, help me . . .'

It was my daughter's voice, I knew. But I couldn't help her now.

I could never help her again.

I set the doll back gently on its chair, then made my way back slowly down the stairs.

Hoping the house would fall with me.

The End

EPILOGUE

'He's crying again,' said Nullman, consulting a fresh ream of medical readouts.

Roz peered closely at the glass. She couldn't tell with all that fluid surrounding her former author.*

'Well?' she asked, glancing up at Nullman. 'Was it worth it? Did you find the leak?'

'We did,' said Nullman. 'As soon as Valesco gets back from B&Q, we'll start blocking up the hole.'

'And Nick?' asked Roz, reaching out with one hand to caress the tank he was encased within. 'What about him?'

'What *about* him?'

Roz turned aside, stifling her own tears. Aye, she guessed. That, ultimately, was the rub. What *was* Nick Steen about, deep down?

She looked in at him, adrift somewhere amid the swirling, unknowable turmoil of his own mind.

Alone. Stranded, in the dark endless space of his own internal cosmos.

Then she went and had lunch.

---

* They'd moved him back into the water tank again. GM

THE RANDYMAN

PROLOGUE

Have you seen the Randyman, streaking through the night?
Have you seen the Randyman, flashing them a fright?
Wrapped up in his mackintosh, with his grubby trilby?
If you aren't now dead in bed, then pretty soon you will be.
Watch out for the Randyman, who's living in your pillow,
Beware his grubby mackintosh, when both flaps start to billow . . .

Seventeen times, Nick remembered. Say his name seventeen times and he'll appear. And, if the legend was true, and you happened to catch sight of whatever the flashing dream-demon kept inside that billowing rain mac of his, then blood would rush instantly to your extremities; the body's internal temperature would rise suddenly under the collar area, and before you knew it, you were dead.

From *exposure.**

If Nick's memory wasn't playing tricks on him, and it still might be, given he'd lain slumbering for months in the unreal oblivion of a comatic state, then the legend also had it that even if you woke up

---

* Not the weather-related kind. GM

from your bad dream, the terrifying Randyman could follow you into the real world, and trap you in a waking nightmare.

If that happened, all you could do was run. Because if you ever caught sight of the Randyman's terrifying particulars, even for one fraction of a nanosecond, it was lights out for you, and no chance in hell of your relatives ever catching a final glimpse of your face in the casket. Not with that red-skinned, wide-eyed grimace of horrified shock frozen on your bloated visage. The frigid, tell-tale rictus of the fatally *exposed* . . .

Nick shuddered, forcing his mind elsewhere. Why was he even thinking about the Randyman when he had a much more pressing issue to contend with? Pressing being the operative word.

Nick stared down at his stonk-on.

It was hard to tell if he was seeing it for real or not. For even in the perpetual dream state in which Nick now found himself, the thing was covered by the same white sheets of the mobile hospital bed he vaguely recalled lying in when first he sank into a state of prolonged unconsciousness.

He glanced outward, into the inner space of his own mind, but there was very little he could see beyond the immediate area of his confinement. The far edges of his vision blurred into darkening shadow, but as he gazed down at the floor beneath the bed, he caught sight of grass, and thick brown mud clogging the gurney's wheels. He was in the middle of what looked to him like a rain-bogged field.

Evidently, then, he was still dreaming. And quite unable to hide the embarrassing tumescence he was no doubt wielding for real somewhere, and in full public view.

Not that Nick really knew where that was anymore. He'd been trapped in this dream state for so long that he could hardly recall events leading up to his physical incarceration in the real world. He felt sure he'd been imprisoned by some shadowy technical research facility, but who they were, and why they were keeping him here, was no longer clear in his mind.

All Nick knew was that he was backed up. Seriously backed up. And with no chance of self-administering some much-needed relief in this comatose state, he was bound to endure his towering obelisk of shame for the foreseeable, with no control over who, or what, bore witness to its ascent. He could be arrested for public indecency for all he knew, without even being remotely conscious of his crime. And then when, and if, he ever woke up, he might be facing an immediate, and lengthy, jail sentence. Surely there was *some* way to lower his muscular mast; commence countdown on his own long-delayed flesh-rocket.

He could try reaching down with his dream-hands, but could he genuinely wrestle himself into a less incriminating position? Wouldn't the gossamer touch of his fingers simply stoke his flames of pent-up passion even further, proudly and loudly announcing his shame to some long-suffering orderly?

Dammit, Nick Steen was no public park pervert. Even if his prolonged sexual dalliances with a sado-masochistic typewriter had frequently given his nearest and dearest regular food for thought, he was just an ordinary, red-blooded male. That was all. *Really*, that was all.

Yet here he was, trapped inside his own mind, with all the loosened inhibitions and rampaging primal urges of his unconscious id spilling outward, threatening to destroy his own admittedly liberal interpretation of what constituted public decency. Turning him into a depraved, primal, Pan-like sexual pariah.

What the hell could he do about it?

And then it hit him. *That's* why he'd been thinking of the Randyman, wasn't it? For although the terrifying dream-demon of Nick's imagination had been one of the most sinister creations he'd ever concocted, the truth was that the Randyman himself was simply a wronged innocent. A lowly toilet attendant by the name of Randy Streak, who'd been murdered by a group of pitiless teenagers convinced he was the local flasher who'd been terrorising Dankton Public Park.

In Nick's original novel, Randy had subsequently come back from the dead as a vengeful dream-demon, eviscerating the gang who'd murdered him by killing them in their sleep, deliberately embodying the cruel rumours they'd circulated about him and exposing them to whatever it was he kept in that billowing rain mac of his . . .

That's what was troubling Nick. If he couldn't deal with his own towering monument of mortification, he'd soon go the way of his literary demon, condemned by society for a crime he hadn't committed.

Nick Steen would become the real–life Randyman.

Randyman. Randyman. Randyman. Randyman. Randyman. Randyman. Randyman, Randyman. Randyman. Randyman. Randyman. Randyman. Randyman. Randyman. Randyman. Randyman. Randy—

No! Stop it, thought Nick. Don't say that name seventeen times.

Don't summon the Randyman, whatever you do. Because Randy Streak is the last person you want making an appearance right now.

But already Nick could feel a subtle change in his perception, and he realised with mounting horror that he had indeed already spoken the word 'Randyman' seventeen times, albeit internally, having mentioned that very word in a previous internalised brain sentence; if he added that mention to the sixteen instances of 'Randyman' he had uttered just after it, then it constituted a grand total of seventeen spoken 'Randymans'. Or Randymen.[*]

Without warning, an arm reached out from under Nick's bed. It was long – too long, Nick decided, as he watched the distorted limb snake slowly upward from below, a ragged brown trilby hat clutched in its glistening, sweaty hand. The lengthening appendage, which Nick now saw was enclosed by the stained, beige material of a

---

[*] No, it's seventeen 'Randymans'. GM

grubby rain mac, moved closer to the risen tower of Nick's private shame, and casually popped the trilby over his sky-bound appendage. Then, just as slowly, the arm withdrew again, sliding back under the bed as Nick's ears took in the rasping, wheezing snicker of a lecher's cackle.

It was an unnerving sound, as if the babbling guffaws of Sid James and Wilfrid Brambell had been combined aurally with those of Stacey Solomon, then blasted through the faltering loudspeakers of some deconsecrated church with gain and reverb levels set to max.

Before Nick could begin to wonder where the unholy limb had sprouted from, the brown hat mounted uncannily on the end of his rod cocked wildly to one side and the contours of a face appeared in the folds of the white sheet masking Nick's totem.

The face of Randy Streak.

'Hey Nick,' the face said. 'Who's a dirty boy?'

'Get lost,' growled Nick, realising he had no real voice left to speak with after such a long time spent in the comatic realm.

The Randyman rattled out a cruel laugh, reaching again from under the bed with its long arm to grab Nick's totem with its mitt.

'You can't wilt *me*!' it hissed, wrenching Nick's truncheon backward, in the direction of his feet.

Nick shrieked in pain as the Randyman cackled again. 'What say we give them a show, Nick? You and me, buddy boy. Let's go streaking!'

'No!' wailed Nick, feeling blood rush back instantly into his nether regions. 'Never!'

A second arm sprang up from the opposite side of Nick's bed. Nick watched as it reached over his midriff and grabbed the edge of the cotton sheet covering his body.

'It's *showtime*,' cackled the Randyman, yanking the sheet backwards, exposing Nick's naked flesh.

The demon's face was still there, Nick observed, only for real now.

No longer enmeshed in folds of cotton, the face was a mass of swollen, grime-streaked skin with red pimples. A terrifying visage that was somehow speaking, cackling, leering from the living flesh of Nick's own perpetually defiant punt-pole.

'Wake me up!' Nick yelled, unheard by anyone but himself. 'Somebody wake me up!'

But there was no chance of that happening, he knew. You didn't just conveniently wake up from a permanent coma. There had to be a significant, emotionally compelling reason.*

With a burst of raucous laughter, the Randyman was suddenly above Nick, its beige mackintosh billowing outward on both sides.

No, thought Nick. Not that. He had to look away. Had to avoid seeing whatever it was that the Randyman kept inside its raincoat. Had to prevent this literally nightmarish dream-demon from exposing itself.

But it was too late. The Randyman had already reached inward with both hands and torn open its raincoat. There, in the one area all humanity feared to glimpse, it lay.

The Randyman's very own shaft of death.

Its *toilet plunger*.

'No!' screamed Nick, all too aware of what came next.

At least, he thought, preparing for the worst, his comatose state meant there was no way Randy Streak could be unleashed into the *real* world. No way its demonic presence could follow him back into reality, like he'd done in Nick's novel series. At least the dream-demon was trapped here with Nick, inside the author's mind.

'Not for long,' hissed the Randyman, grinning down at him.

Yanking the plunger from its groin, the Randyman held it outward, toward the area of Nick's heart.

---

* Not strictly true from a medical standpoint, but works in this case as a subtle case of foreshadowing. GM

'No, wait! I know you're innocent!' screamed Nick. 'I didn't do that terrible thing to you!'

'Oh, but you did . . . *writer*!' snarled the Randyman, and then it rammed the plunger into Nick's chest.

And sucked up his soul.

CHAPTER ONE

'The Phantascape'

'Cigarette?' asked Dr Nullman, Chief Head of the Nulltec Corporation. Again, she offered the pack to Roz. And, again, Roz refused.

'Thanks, but I only smoke cigars,' said Roz. 'Or pipes, if I'm in a restaurant.'

And that hadn't been for some time, Roz reflected sourly. Ever since she'd accepted Nullman's invitation to remain locked in the medical research facility indefinitely as Nulltec's 'guest', Roz had found herself entirely relieved of her professional duties as editor of Clackett Publishing, and similarly deprived of any kind of social life. And though the luxury 'cell'-themed suite Nulltec had provided her with had finally been kitted out with a functioning light bulb and toilet, Roz still wasn't allowed her usual shopping trips into Stalkford, meaning she was currently clean out of pumice stones and marshmallow shag.

The only place Nullman *had* allowed her to visit, accompanied on each occasion by two members of Nulltec's security team, was Nick's own apartment, still uninhabited since the day he'd left on that last, fateful flight.* Having discovered Roz was in fact Nick

---

* See *Portentum* i.e. Tome 1 of this very anthology. I shouldn't have to do this. GM

Steen's former editor, Nullman had enlisted her services as a technical 'advisor' to Nick's rehabilitation programme, assigning Roz the task of locating any potent information she could uncover concerning Nick's private life, which might help in sealing up the huge dimensional mind-leak currently housed inside the writer's brain.

And, initially at least, Roz had been only too eager to help. After all, the hole to another plane of reality inside Nick's mind, through which the macabre denizens of his authorial imagination were currently pouring, had been threatening not just the security of Stalkford, but also the existence of its central shopping mall. Meaning that if someone didn't soon start sorting a solution to these recurrent supernatural eruptions, Roz's preferred tobacconist would soon be out of business and/or dead.

But events of late were giving her cause for concern. Nullman herself had recently force-fed Nick's subconscious a devastating tale that his conscious mind had long been attempting to suppress.* Not only that, but Dr Valesco and his team of scientists had recently enrolled the unconscious Nick in Nulltec's experimental dream-therapy programme, rigging up the author's mind, along with those of several other patients, to a scientifically engineered 'mind-plane' in the hope of creating an alternative shared dream-reality known – and soon to be trademarked – as the 'Phantascape'.

Roz had advised against it, but been completely ignored. Which, fortunately, she was used to.

'You are our last hope, Miss Bloom,' said Dr Nullman, lighting another cigarette. 'The situation is grave, as you can see.' She handed Roz a technical readout that Roz didn't understand and which she immediately handed back. 'Mr Steen's mind appears to have

---

* See *Arabella Mathers*, Tome 2 of this very anthology – I'm not doing this again. GM

disappeared from the Phantascape entirely. He is no longer respond-ing to our sensors.'

Nullman tapped cigarette ash into a bin beside her, then motioned for Roz to sit. She, Valesco and several other scientists were gathered around a large conference table in Nulltec's main administrative boardroom. Roz, who'd only just been summoned from her cell on the basement level, calmly took a seat at the table, lit up a cheroot* and helped herself to coffee.

'As you may know, Miss Bloom,' said Dr Valesco, who was sitting on Nullman's right, 'we recently enrolled Mr Steen's mind in Nulltec's experimental dream-therapy programme, along with those of several other volunteers. The whole thing's aimed at creating an alternative shared dream-reality, or scientifically engineered "mind-plane", if you will. We call it the Phantascape.'

'Except that Nick wasn't exactly a volunteer, was he?' said Roz, sucking down a deep lungful of Myanmar's less-than-finest before breaking into a violent coughing fit.

'Unfortunately,' said Nullman, trying her best to ignore Roz's wheezed rasping, 'ever since we first wired in Mr Steen's brain, he's proved fiercely resistant to the entire programme. We had hoped our other volunteers might somehow persuade him to brick up that mind-leak in his head without any undue fuss.'

'You don't know Nick,' said Roz, at last able to breathe again. 'He loathes builders.' She laughed, proud of her spontaneously pithy quip. Even Nick would have been impressed. 'In fact, *all* labourers.'

'So we've discovered,' replied Nullman, unamused. 'He point-blank refuses to pay them.'

Roz sucked in another lungful of smoke, her face immediately quizzical. 'I don't follow.'

'It's best to think of the Phantascape metaphorically, Miss

---

* *Not* the drug-addled kind. Say no to drugs. Never, ever take drugs. GM

Bloom,' Valesco explained. 'Though the dream-world is a shared psychic reality, its scientific workings are nevertheless best interpreted in fantastical terms. Your "rogue trader" analogy is, in fact, quite apt. Having charged several of our volunteers with the unenviable task of convincing Mr Steen to block up the hole in his brain, they appeared to him within the Phantascape in precisely that form. A group of door-stepping bricklayers hoping to make a quick buck via the offer of a cheap half-day's labour on Mr Steen's psychic fissure. Unfortunately, the author's inherent distrust of the working class meant that instead of effecting a quick and efficient fix, which would have effectively sealed up the leak in Mr Steen's mind with metaphorical cement, there otherwise ensued a violent dispute over alleged requests for cash-in-hand payments and unauthorised use of Mr Steen's upstairs toilet. Not only has the proposed work on Mr Steen's mind-hole therefore failed to begin, but he himself took a private shine to the bawdy wife of one of our metaphorical builders, and has been subsequently concentrating his vital mental energies on idle, unrequited erotic musings. The bottom line is that the hole in his mind still exists, but he's now refusing to co-operate. I suspect the main problem may be that he's severely "backed up".'

Roz smiled to herself. That old chestnut. She often wondered whether all the military confrontations throughout history might have been prevented if only certain political leaders hadn't been quite so 'backed up'.

'We need you to go in there, Miss Bloom.'

'I'm sorry?' said Roz, through another thick cloud of cheroot smoke. Nullman wafted it away as best she could in order to restore eye contact.

'We want you to join the Phantascape. Journey inside Nick Steen's dream-world and convince him to block up that wall. Who knows, perhaps you might even . . .'

'Perhaps I might even what?' said Roz, suddenly suspicious. She sensed something in Nullman's tone. Something ugly.

'Perhaps you might even . . . oh, I don't know . . .'

Roz held Nullman's eye, forcing her to come clean.

'Perhaps you might even grant Mr Steen some . . . shall we say . . . executive relief?'

'Absolutely not,' said Roz. Within, however, she felt oddly elated. Not by the prospect of relieving Nick physically, which Roz currently had little interest in (it was a Tuesday), but because she now had a chance to meet with Nick again personally. Finally, she had an opportunity to talk to him directly. Liaise with him. Convince him to somehow escape Nulltec's walls, which in Nick's case, she strongly suspected, were tantamount to being inside a prison. Finally, she had a chance to give Nick the letter.

She felt it there still, deep inside her pocket. No one in Nulltec had bothered to check her on the way in, so flustered had she acted concerning yet another missed opportunity to fill up on her precious stoved, flue-cured Virginia.

It was from Georgina, Nick's daughter. After years of silence, she'd finally written back to him, telling him she missed her daddy terribly, and wanted him to come and visit her. To see if they could get to know each other again, after Nick's divorce from her mother, Jacinta. And to see if he'd lend her some money.

If anything could wake Nick from his comatose state, it was this letter. Roz intended to read it to him right there in the Phantascape and, having woken him for real in the corridors of Nulltec, effect their escape together.

For Roz suspected deep down that Nulltec had no intention of freeing Nick, even if they *could* block up his mind-hole. His knowledge of other mortal planes, other cosmic dimensions, was too valuable to let him walk away a free man.

Without Roz's help, Nick was destined to remain a prisoner in

Nulltec: an Incarcerat, to use Nick's own term, for all eternity (or until he died, at any rate).

No way, vowed Roz. Nick Steen was coming home. Together, they'd report Nulltec, Valesco and Nullman herself to the authorities. Then they'd have this shadowy medical research facility closed down once and for all.

'I'll do it,' said Roz. 'No problem.'

'Good,' replied Nullman, handing her a printed form. 'Here's all the information you'll need to enrol. Our technical expert in charge of the Phantascape project is Dr Mike Crisis.'

There was a murmur of laughter from Valesco and the other scientists gathered around the table.

'The big joke being,' continued Nullman through a somewhat cruel smile, 'that he's technically not very good in a crisis. In fact . . .' – she looked around the table, preparing her moment – '. . .you *might* say that he was, ironically, *terrible* in a crisis!'

The gathered scientists erupted with laughter; Roz forced out a laugh, too. She had to keep up appearances if she had any hope at all of reading Nick the letter concealed in her pocket. And perhaps, as these gathered experts were evidently implying, Mike Crisis *was* a hopeless bastard.

'You'll find the Phantascape laboratory in the neighbouring building across our impressive glass bridge. Dr Valesco will show you the way.'

'Come with me,' said Valesco, rising from the table and leading Roz over toward the door. As she passed before him into the corridor beyond, Valesco turned back to face Nullman and winked.

'And that's the last we'll see of her,' whispered Nullman to herself, still smiling.

★

'Welcome to the Dream Team,' said Dr Mike Crisis, reaching out eagerly to shake Roz's hand while inadvertently knocking her chin. 'So sorry,' he said, reaching out abruptly with his other hand to steady her from falling, and accidentally striking her chin again.

'It's fine,' said Roz, pushing his hands away. 'I'm quite alright.' When her eyes had finally stopped watering, she took a good look at him.

Mike Crisis was tall, slim and on the youthful side of thirty, Roz guessed. And he was handsome, she decided. Strikingly so, in fact, but there was also an air of awkwardness about the man that belied his smooth and professional appearance. An invisible cloud of potential chaos lay dormant somewhere, Roz sensed. An unseen presence, almost. Like a firework wrongly angled towards a crowd of waiting spectators.

'I'm Dr Crisis,' he said, standing well back so Roz could enter the room without harm. 'The irony being that I'm apparently bad in a crisis,' he added, smiling. 'Not good in a crisis, which would, of course, be preferred.'

'I'm Roz Bloom,' said Roz, extending her own hand towards his.

Nervous, he grabbed it far too tightly.

'Ouch!' Roz yelped.

'S–sorry,' he stammered, panicking. 'You see, I've been twisting wire components. Don't know my own strength at the moment. Here – try this one.'

He grabbed Roz's hand again, this time with his other hand. A hand sporting a glove he'd completely forgotten to take off.

'Urgh,' said Roz, drawing back her own palm. The rubber was wet.

'God, sorry,' said Crisis, panicking again. 'I forgot to remove that.'

'What's on it?' Roz asked, watching warily as Mike stretched the dampened latex over his fingers.

'You don't want to know,' he said, laughing nervously. 'Really. Can I get you a cup of tea?'

THE RANDYMAN

'No, thank you,' said Roz. 'But do you have any marshmallow shag?'

'Loads,' said Mike, opening up a nearby cupboard. 'My mother once asked to me to buy her some cigarettes and before I knew it, I'd bought thirteen hundred packets of pipe tobacco.'

He handed a pouch to Roz, then walked over to a kettle on the far side of the room. 'I'll make one for me, at any rate.'

As Roz filled her pipe, she watched Mike from behind. So it was 'Mike' already, was it? she thought wryly to herself. Well, there *was* something faintly endearing about the guy. She smirked to herself as he dropped not one but two china mugs, shattering them into pieces on the laboratory floor. Then gasped instinctively as Mike bent over, his rear end facing her, to mop up the scattered shards.

Even though it was largely obscured by his lab coat, Roz could tell he had one hell of an arse.

What on earth was she thinking? Why, she'd only just met the guy a minute or so ago, and already she was obsessing about his rear cheeks, like some panting female baboon on heat. She hadn't even stopped to take in her immediate whereabouts.

Forcing her eyes away from Mike's buttocks, which he'd accidentally fallen back on anyway while losing his balance in pursuit of an outlying shard, she examined instead the interior of his laboratory.

The enclosure was large and light green in hue, surrounded on all sides by the familiar-looking banks of medical monitors and computer terminals. But in the centre of this particular room, arranged in a wide circle, were several slumbering patients lying upon static gurneys. Their feet met in the middle, while their heads pointed outwards, separated from the next in line by a distance of about a couple of feet. There were eleven patients in total, Roz counted, and like Nick, their scalps had been shaved and fitted with small sensor pads, each transferring minute electrical signals via connecting wires to a large processing unit on the far side of the room.

'You might think I'm conducting ordinary electroencephalo-grams,' said Mike, rising from the floor and abandoning his plans for a cup of tea. 'But you'd be partly wrong. Yet also partly right. This is, to all intents and purposes,' he said, tapping one hand on the main processing unit, 'an electroencephalogram.' As he tapped it, the unit immediately let out a large spark somewhere around the back. With a look of concern, Mike quickly checked behind the apparatus, sniffed the air several times, then turned back to Roz. 'But instead of monitoring certain conditions in the brain, it monitors one's dreams. Allowing us, via an elaborate computer network we've been devel-oping here at Nulltec for several years, to home in on a patient's subconscious imaginings and *combine* several dreams together at the same time. The Phantascape, we call it.'

'Fascinating,' said Roz, wishing she could see his arse again.

'You see, these people,' he continued, indicating the sleeping patients before them, 'are all sharing each other's dreams. Bar this individual,' he added, looking down worriedly at one of the uncon-scious volunteers. He briefly checked the patient's vitals. 'Yes, for some reason,' he said, talking to himself now, 'this particular volun-teer is dead.'

'Dead?' repeated Roz.

'I think because I may have forgotten to feed him,' Mike added, running over previous events in his mind. 'In fact, yes, I remember now. Patient . . .' He quickly checked the sleeper's identity label. 'Patient K . . . was at the very end of the line last Tuesday . . . when I was filling up everyone's drip.' He nodded to himself, certain now. 'And this one ran out, if I rightly recall . . .'

A look of sudden confusion, then one of mounting concern, crossed the doctor's face for a brief second, before the expression changed yet again to another emotion entirely. That's it, thought Roz, recognising the mood as it materialised before her. *Shame.* That's the new look on Dr Mike Crisis's face. A look of *shame.*

'You see?' Mike said to Roz, his eyes welling up suddenly. 'This is what I'm talking about. This is the kind of crisis I cause, not avert. Just once, Roz, I'd like to *solve* a crisis, instead of turning a bad crisis into an even badder crisis.'

'Or "bigger" crisis?'

'That, too.'

'But surely this particular crisis wasn't a previous crisis that you then escalated into a bigger crisis, Mike,' said Roz, trying to comfort him. 'Surely this crisis is simply a one-off crisis?'

'You don't know the half of it,' said Mike Crisis. 'There's a crisis with one of our patients. An ongoing crisis. He's no longer respond-ing to our sensors. In fact, he may even have gone missing, some-where in the Phantascape.'

Nick! thought Roz, suddenly.

'That's why they assigned me to the Phantascape project in the first place, Roz,' Mike continued. '"You're always one for dreaming on the job, Mike Crisis," they told me. "So we're making you head of Nulltec's new dream-therapy programme."' He looked grimly at her. 'They knew what they were doing, Roz. Because the Phantascape project is a dangerous one. And when something goes wrong, when there's a crisis, Roz . . . like this crisis . . . a disappearing patient . . . they know they can always blame Mike "He's Appalling in a Crisis" Crisis for it. When all along, I simply want to be known as Mike "Solved a Crisis Like the Missing Patient Crisis" Crisis.' He sat back moodily in his chair, which immediately tipped sideways as one of its wheel-bearings snapped loose.

'Nick Steen,' said Roz, catching the doctor's attention. Mike looked up at her. 'The patient's name is Nick Steen, right?'

'How do you know?' said Mike, scrambling to his feet again.

'Because I've been asked to find him, Mike. I've been told to enter the Phantascape.'

'No, Roz,' said Mike, shaking his head. 'It's too dangerous for a girl like you. This programme is still experimental. It's not safe for unauthorised persons.'

'I *am* an authorised person,' said Roz. 'It's on that sheet Dr Valesco handed you.'

'Oh, yes,' said Mike, reading the sheet of paper he'd singularly failed to take in first time round.

'And I'm not a girl, either. In fact, Mike, if you're lucky, you might well find I can be *all* woman.'

Mike failed to hear her, still assimilating the contents of Valesco's letter.

'Then I guess I, and you, have no choice,' he said, finally looking up at her.

'Where *is* Nick?' asked Roz. 'His body, I mean.'

'Over here,' said Mike, leading Roz across the room to the far wall, where a rectangular window looked out into an adjacent room.

At least Nick was no longer suspended in a tank of water, thought Roz. Then she blushed with sudden embarrassment. Even though she knew Nick had been 'backed up', she hadn't quite expected the sight now confronting her from his cosy-looking hospital bed. She hadn't expected *that*.

'Can't anyone do anything about . . . *that*?' she asked, somewhat embarrassed.

'We've tried everything in the book to deflate it. Bar one thing, of course,' he said, staring meaningfully at Roz, as if she alone held the key. 'Would you, Roz? Because I . . .' He gulped, sweat appearing on the top of his brow, then whispered, 'I just *can't*.'

'Nor can I,' Roz whispered back. 'And I mean that.'

'Fine,' said Mike, changing the subject. 'Then let's wire you in, shall we?'

CHAPTER TWO

'Dankton'

Roz awoke in what looked to her like a run-down city park. Except, of course, she hadn't awoken at all. She was dreaming now, and had only just this moment been put under by Dr Crisis, having pleaded with him for thirty minutes not to shave her head. He'd agreed eventually and had instead attached the sensors to a fake bald cap Roz always carried in her handbag and which had, at long last, come in useful.

She examined the bleak expanse of greenery she was standing in. The park was soggy underfoot, dampened by a downfall of recent autumnal rain. The sky overhead was grey and gloomy, still heavy with cloud. Above the far end of the park rose a number of neglected council flats, covered, even when viewed from this far distance, with ugly daubs of graffiti.

Despite it consisting entirely of dream, something about the place felt familiar to Roz. With a sudden spark of released memory, she recognised it as Dankton, a run-down town on the eastern edge of Stalkfordshire which she'd once visited with Nick on one of his less-salubrious research trips. She couldn't quite recall what specific horror novel Nick had been writing at the time, but she recalled she'd detested the place, while Nick himself had deemed it quite perfect for the book in question.

The park in front of her was large, but visibly empty at this early hour of the evening. Spatters of fresh rain could be seen passing through the beams of nearby street lamps, and further along the left-side edge, Roz could make out the drab contours of a grey, concrete dwelling. The unpleasant smell wafting from its direction suggested it was possibly a public convenience, so Roz turned the other way and examined the right-hand side of the park instead. There was no one here but her, it seemed. Where were all the other dreamers? Roz was under the impression that she'd entered a shared Phantascape, but currently it looked like she was the only one here. They might be further afield, of course, but she didn't much relish the thought of journeying into Dankton itself, past those imposing council flats overlooking the park's furthest edge.

But she had to find Nick, didn't she? Wasn't that the reason she was here?

So where was he?

'Nick?' she called out. Her voice echoed strangely, as if she'd been yelling inside an abandoned ballroom. There was no response.

'Nick Steen!'

Again, there was no response, except for a sudden lash of rain that fell upon her at once from above, then ceased just as swiftly, leaving in its wake only the foul, lingering stench of that far-off public convenience.

Roz shuddered, then stepped forward into the park itself.

And saw it.

A hospital bed, situated some distance ahead of her, standing alone in the middle of the grass. Except it wasn't completely alone, Roz realised. For she could see a patient in the bed. A patient covered entirely in a white sheet.

Roz paused for a moment, unnerved by the strange sight. She could feel her heels sinking into the wet mud under her feet.

She stepped forward again. This was a dream, after all, wasn't it?

Things were bound to be a little strange. Weird details like hospital beds in the middle of a grassy park might be completely normal here.

She decided she'd see who the patient was.

As Roz made her way forward through the grass, the smell of the public convenience once again wafted across from the left-hand side of the park. Dankton really could do with a clean-up, she decided. Even in its dream state.

As she moved closer to the hospital bed, stumbling across the soft, damp grass, she could see something rising from the surface of the bedcovers. Something completely still, yet positioned almost vertically, pointing upwards, toward the sky. Maybe it was the patient himself sitting up in bed, Roz wondered – but why would they be angled upright with a sheet over their own head? Maybe they were trying to shield themselves from the showering rain, she decided.

But surely a white cotton sheet wouldn't do much good against a heavy downpour? Then Roz saw what the shape *really* was. It wasn't a sitting patient, after all.

It was a stonk-on.

A *male* stonk-on.

'Nick!' yelled Roz, a smile breaking across her face as she suddenly quickened her pace toward the afflicted figure. 'Nick Steen, it's me! It's Roz Bloom!'

As Roz arrived at the bed, she could see that Nick's truncheon had practically set, like a concrete plinth, but there was little she could – or *would* – do about that. All she need do now was read Nick the letter from his daughter and then they could all get out of here. Out of Nulltec at last – and then Nick could go somewhere private and do what he needed to do, and everything would soon be back to normal. Even if 'normal' was still *abnormal* in Nick's case, what with all those escaping demons flying out of his imagination at all hours of the day and night.

Roz stopped dead in her tracks. The sheet *was* covering Nick's face, after all. Behind his jutting joystick, Roz could see that the sheet covered the rest of his body, including his real head. From here, she could see a small area of cotton over his mouth area, rising and falling with each intake of breath.

'Nick?' she said again, more warily now. Why wasn't he responding to her? Was he somehow asleep inside another sinister dream-world within his own sinister dream-world?*

'*Nick*,' Roz said again, more emphatically now, then reached out with her hand toward the sheet. She had to know. Had to know if Nick could hear her or not. Had to know if he was okay.

'It's *me*,' she whispered. 'It's *Roz*.' Swiftly, she tugged the sheet backward across the patient's face.

And uncovered Randy Streak.

'Hey Roz,' hissed the Randyman, leering up at her. 'It sure is a *relief* to see you!'

All at once, Randy's love-brush erupted like a lit rocket, shooting upwards through the sheet into the night sky, before exploding overhead in a huge burst of raining, coloured sparks.

'How's *that* for a performance?' laughed the Randyman.

Roz turned from the trolley and immediately ran back the way she'd come, stumbling in a wild, frightened frenzy over the wet grass. So it hadn't been Nick at all in that bed, she realised, staggering back blindly to . . . where? Where *could* she stagger back blindly to? There was nothing in front of her now but a green mist, from which, presumably, she'd first emerged when first entering the Phantascape.

'Mike!' she yelled aloud at the billowing cloud. 'Mike, get me out of here!'

'Not Mike, Roz. Randy! My name's *Randy*!' said that same cruel

---

* No, but that plot will be covered in a later book, so consider the idea copyrighted. GM

voice, as suddenly the face she'd last seen winking at her from the hospital bed loomed out of the green bank of cloud, stretching itself toward her on a long, protracted neck which Roz realised was interrupted at regular intervals by riveted kinks, like a plumber's U-bend.

Randy, Roz thought, trying to keep calm. I'm sure I know that name . . .

'Get away from me!' she yelled, unable to stop her feelings of panic, and turned back again in the direction of the park. The hospital bed was no longer before her, but from the left-hand side of the park came again that foul, stagnant odour . . .

Roz ducked to the right, making for the other side of the park, hoping to find another route into Dankton, where she presumed Nick and the other dreamers were currently idling. No doubt the latter were indeed the lazy labouring type after all, Roz figured. Probably knocking around some abandoned flat or fish-and-chip shop, dodging decent work when they ought to be out here, comparing notes with her about how to block up the hole in Nick's mind that had somehow released whatever foul dream-demon had suddenly pounced at her out of the shadows.

Then, suddenly, she had it. A dream-demon! Of course! That's where she knew the name 'Randy' from. For Nick had once written a series of novels about a dream-demon going by that very name, hadn't he? But what *was* the book? And even if Roz could remember its name, would that knowledge even help her at this precise moment in time, with the damned thing right behind her?

A horrifying thought struck her. Maybe there *weren't* any other dreamers here in the Phantascape, after all. Maybe they were all dead: not just the one Mike Crisis had accidentally starved, but every single sleeper in the laboratory. Perhaps this rampaging dream-demon had somehow destroyed them all without Mike or Nulltec's knowledge, and was now hell-bent on destroying Roz too.

All at once she could see it again, darting toward her from the right-hand side of the park this time, its brown mackintosh billowing in the chilling October breeze as the thing ran alongside her, daring to yank open its mac. Toying with her. *Taunting* her.

'Wanna see what I got, lady?' it yelled.

Oh God, thought Roz. It's going to flash at me. It's going to yank open that grubby mac and show me its roamin' candle again.

Or not, she thought suddenly – because some part of her mind was remembering something else now, recalling the details of that very novel Nick had written, which had been, even for him, one of the most odious tales of his career. A tale Roz had informed him, in no uncertain terms, needed a massive change if it was ever going to get past the editorial team at Clackett – or indeed a national censorship board, were the book ever to be adapted into a film one day (which it hadn't). For this terrifying, nauseating dream–demon currently pursuing her, she now knew, was none other than the demonic toilet attendant Randy Streak from Nick's novel *The Randyman*.

'Get a load of my rod!' the demon yelled, tugging open its mac to reveal, in the lower region of its groin, a protruding length of rubber-ended toilet plunger.

There was no mistaking it now, Roz knew. This was Randy Streak, alright. The forever-streaking, perennially flashing toilet attendant from beyond the grave, whom Nick had, in his naivety, assumed a reading public would return to in droves. And that plunger in its downstairs area was the terrifying weapon it used to suck out the souls of its victims before plunging them down into hell.

And the *smell*.

Roz suddenly realised, as she turned her head away from the demon's terrifying weapon toward that squat building on the far side of the green, that the rancid reek factory was none other than Randy's *home*. A disgusting public convenience. For the local gents' in Dankton Park was where Randy had been drowned by a local gang of youths, before emerging later as a hideous dream-demon, hell-bent on supernatural revenge.

And, she thought desperately as she sought to evade the pursuing demon, there would have been no *Randyman* novels at all if Roz hadn't advised Nick to add one crucial element. No run of ever-popular sequels. No *Randyman 2: Nightmare in Dank Town*; no *Randyman 3: Mirror Streaker*; no *Randyman IV: Nightstench*; no *Randyman V: U-benders (aka U-Bend or U-Break)*; nor all those other terrifying toilet-attendant-based horror novels leading up to the final instalment, *Randyman 17: Death Plunge Sally*. None of these would have existed if Roz hadn't advised Nick to make one small change. One tiny alteration that turned the entire series into a prolonged near-masterwork of supernatural terror.

Make Randy a *victim*, she'd said. A badly wronged, pitiful soul who'd never once been the disgusting and dirty old sod the local youths who'd murdered him had called him, day after day, night after night. It had been Roz's idea to make Randy the beleaguered, victimised scapegoat of a sick society. It had been her suggestion that Nick should develop Randy's back story and prevent him being labelled as a genuine sex pest. With Roz's help, Randy's character had assumed a depth and grace Nick Steen would never have thought up himself.

Why, Randy Streak had simply been unable to fix all the blocked pipes in that neglected public convenience he'd been assigned to. Which is why he spent so long in the block alone, with no one outside knowing who he was or why he was hanging around in the gents' toilet for such lengthy periods of time. And his clothes, too. Roz had even justified those. For that grubby rain mac and flasher's trilby Nick had come up with also had their own back story. Why, was it Randy Streak's fault that Dankton Council had failed to provide him with any more official donkey jackets or rubber waders, owing to the endless drainage and wear caused by ever-exploding pipes and flooding U-bends? Was it Randy Streak's fault that he'd been forced to purchase a cheap raincoat and hat instead, in order to keep himself dry and dapper in such a moist environment?

And then the ultimate detail. The *coup de grace* Roz had insisted Nick add to his sordid little horror tale, which had turned Randy Streak's demonic and morally questionable hauntings on its head, transforming his actions into an empathetic war of supernatural vengeance against his former killers.

For Roz had told Nick to turn Randy's unfortunate home – that miserable public convenience in Dankton Park he permanently frequented – into the very source of his own violent death.

Thus then, the story went, that late one night, the local gang of youths who'd mercilessly bullied poor Randy Streak, spreading rumours that the innocent bog attendant was nothing less than a dirty old man in a mac – a miserable toilet-trader-come-flashing-flesh-dangler – crept up as one on that lonely toilet block in Dankton Park where Randy was at work within, and disconnected the sewage pipe outlets. Then the murderous gang, doubling down on their evil act, carefully re-piped the toilets' outlet flow back into Randy's block, meaning the pipes and U-bends Randy Streak was attending to began to rapidly refill, pumping raw sewage from the neighbouring tower blocks back into the park's only public convenience, with Randy Streak trapped inside . . .

Then, stealing Randy's spare plunger supply from the toilet's adjacent stock cupboard, the gang had gone to work on every nook and cranny, plunging the town's escaping effluence back into the small toilet block, until the water pressure inside built to catastrophic levels, and what little remained of Randy's half-drowned body exploded amid a geyser of Dankton's not-yet-fully-degraded sewage . . .

It had been a genuinely messy end, but with Roz's help, Randy had, as a result of his cruel and pointless murder, become halfway palatable to Nick's readers, and his success as a pulp-paperback horror villain partly assured.

But why was Randy Streak running around here, inside the Phantascape?

'I'm going to plunge your soul, Roz Bloom. Plunge it down to hell!'

The Randy demon yanked the plunger from its groin and held it aloft, laughing wildly at her.

There was nothing else Roz could do. She turned yet again, and ran in the opposite direction.

Toward the gents' on the far side of the park . . .

She knew it was a madness; knew that this was where Randy Streak had lived and died, but there was no other place to run.

'Mike!' she screamed again, loudly. 'Mike Crisis, wake me up, damn it! Wake me up!'

'How are your pipes, lady?' laughed the Randyman, suddenly rising upward from a patch of grass in front of her, its neck once more an extended length of plastic piping, interrupted at regular intervals by twisting U-bends, branch vents and rusting ball check valves. 'Need a new closet flange?' cackled the dream-demon.

Roz lunged her body to one side in an attempt to dodge the Randyman's leering features, only to find its neck pipe extending with her, so that the head of Randy Streak became a steady companion as she ran.

'Nice drip leg,' said the demon. 'Quite a tailpiece! Wanna see my *float ball?*'

'Go away!' cried Roz, running left again. Randy's head went with her.

'Fancy aerating my faucet, lady?'

Roz realised she was still heading in the direction of Randy's toilet block.

She stopped suddenly, turning around yet again. Far behind was that same bank of green mist through which she'd entered the Phantascape, but in front of it now lay a complex network of detailed plumbing work, a vast maze of tubes and piping that had somehow formed itself from Randy Streak's extending neck.

Becoming increasingly dizzy, Roz turned back to face the right-hand half of the field, hoping that at least the path leading toward the distant flats was now clear. But instead she was met with the same sight. A mass of seemingly endless pipework, with jets of steam bursting from intermittent valves.

She was trapped.

'Come to my cubicle, Roz Bloom,' hissed Randy, its head snaking round her body to face her own once again. 'And I'll show you my sump pump.'

'Never!' Roz shouted.

'Then get sucked!' screamed the Randyman, its long, mackintoshed arms suddenly appearing from two pungent vent stacks fixed either side of its neck. One of them clutched in its hand the demon's terrifying signature toilet plunger, a Stonky 79-6C MasterClogger with detachable drip tray. Roz prayed in silence as the demon levelled the weapon in the direction of her heart.

'Wait!' she cried, eyes pleading with the dream-demon. 'I know you're innocent! I know you were murdered by a gang of local youths! I know you're not really a stereotypical seventies sex pest!'

The plunger stopped stock-still in mid-air, inches from Roz's chest. The Randyman's smile dropped as a look of sadness entered its eyes.

'You see,' continued Roz. 'I told Nick to add that bit in. So that there'd be a sympathetic angle to your character. So that readers wouldn't immediately throw Nick's books – and you – into the nearest rubbish bin. *I* gave you life.'

The Randyman's arms and neck somehow retracted without Roz really seeing anything, until he was standing before her in his mackintosh again, looking like a normal man (although one you'd still avoid if you saw him in the street).

'Then join me,' said the Randyman, its voice softer, mellower and less Sid James-like than before. 'Come live with me, Roz Bloom. Come stay with me in my toilet block. A house made for two, seeing as cubicle three's currently blocked again. Together, you and I can fix that cracked urinal and erase, at long last, the big brown smear over the hand-sink mirror. Come with me, Roz Bloom . . .'

The Randyman lowered its plunger, and held out its other hand.

No, thought Roz. I can't. I can't! Despite knowing that Randy Streak was really a poor innocent, Roz couldn't quite bear to be near someone who drank their morning tea from a disused backflow prevention device.

'Mike!' she screamed again. 'Wake me up! Please! Wake me up!'

'No!' roared the Randyman, raising its plunger once again. 'Join me, Roz Bloom, or be ex-plunged!'

Roz sensed she had about a second or two left before Randy Streak's plunger sucked out her soul. As her hand travelled instinct-ively to the region of her heart, preparing itself for a final, desperate defence, she felt something solid under her hands, perched there in the breast pocket of her coat.

Her fountain pen.

As the Randyman commenced its deathly plunge, Roz whipped the fountain pen from her pocket and, moving as fast as she could, stabbed the pointed nib hard into her leg . . .

CHAPTER THREE

'The Randyman'

. . . and woke suddenly, back in the laboratory. She lurched immediately from the bed she'd been lying on and rose into a sitting position, yanking the wires from her sweating bald cap.

'Help!' she cried. 'Someone help me!'

At the sound of her yelling, a figure snorted from a nearby chair. As Dr Mike Crisis woke from sleep, the book he'd been reading dropped to the floor.

'Mike!' yelled Roz, hurling the clump of wires in his direction. 'Where the hell *were* you?'

'Huh?' he muttered, still drowsy from sleep.

'I was trapped in the Phantascape, with that . . . that *thing* chasing me!'

'Trapped?' said Mike, still groggy. 'Thing? . . . Chasing you?'

'That demon thing. That's not a dream you have operating inside the Phantascape, Mike Crisis. It's a *nightmare!*'

Roz felt good letting off a little steam. She so rarely got the chance to do that with Nick, who always immediately threatened to call the head bods at Clackett and have her fired for any signs, faint or otherwise, of insubordination towards their much-valued author. Not that they'd said anything to Roz when he'd actually called on that one

284

occasion. In fact, she'd heard they'd simply laughed at him. But still, it wasn't worth getting on Nick's bad side, given how prolific he was as an author. He kept Roz in work, after all, even if by and large the editing notes she typed up for him were immediately rebuffed, rejected and posted back to her with insufficient postage attached.

'What demon thing?' said Mike, slowly coming round.

'That damned dream-demon in a flasher's mac. Randy Streak.'

Mike still looked confused.

'The Randyman!' snapped Roz.

That woke him up.

'You . . . You mean *this* guy?' He picked up the book he'd been reading from the floor and showed Roz the cover. It was a paperback copy of the original *Randyman* by Nick Steen. The one book of Nick's that Roz had successfully slightly edited.

'Why the hell are you reading that thing?' asked Roz, starting to feel reality crashing down around her all over again.

'I'm sorry,' said Mike. 'I must have fallen asleep reading it. Typical me, I'm afraid. I always set out to stay alert and monitor my patients in a thorough and professional manner, but then end up falling asleep while I'm supposed to be staying awake. I swear it's all to do with that damned name of mine, Roz. I tell you, having a moniker like Mike Crisis when you're trying to iron out a veritable litany of professional errors and innate human weaknesses is pretty draining. I sincerely believe it's why I keep falling asleep on the job.'

'I asked you a question, Mike,' said Roz. 'Why are you reading that book?'

Mike turned the novel over so that he could get a good look at the cover illustration. 'It's a pretty good read, this, Roz. And Mr Steen himself wrote it, I understand?'

'Yes, he did,' said Roz. 'And right now that thing's in there, in the shared dream-world you're supposed to be overseeing. The Randyman's loose inside the Phantascape.'

'Impossible,' said Mike, getting up from his seat to check the monitoring equipment, before tripping on a wire and accidentally disconnecting everything. 'Damn it,' he said. 'I knew I shouldn't wear slippers on the job. Just lulls me into a false sense of comfort and I start slouching around.'

Roz rolled her eyes. Despite being initially attracted to Mike Crisis, she was fast going off the idea. 'Who gave that book to you?'

'Nobody,' he replied. 'I was just reading it for research. Someone left it in the locker room.'

'And you've been reading it on the job?'

'Yes,' said Mike. 'Should I not be? I'm only trying to get acquainted with Mr Steen's oeuvre, so that I can better control his input inside the Phantascape.'

Something wasn't adding up, Roz decided. Why, of all the hellish creatures in all the hundreds of books Nick Steen had written, would this particular murderous dream-demon be suddenly set loose inside a real-life dream-therapy experiment, just as the overseer of that very same experiment was reading the book featuring said dream-demon while on the job?

It was too great a coincidence to be put down to mere bad fortune. This was Mike Crisis, after all, thought Roz. And when you considered the doctor's chequered career and propensity for escalating a crisis instead of easing it, it all suddenly became a damn sight clearer. Of course Mike Crisis had inadvertently caused the demon's accidental escape. It didn't need looking at any further.

'So were you reading that particular book while I was in there?' asked Roz, accepting the bandage Mike handed her to help seal the gaping fountain-pen-shaped hole in her leg.

'I was,' admitted Mike, 'but that shouldn't affect the programme itself. You can only gain access to the Phantascape by being wired in via your brain and knocked out with industrial-strength sleeping pills.'

Roz thought for a moment, wondering whether she should word her next question carefully or not. Then she decided her leg was in a lot of pain and came straight out with it.

'Do you read your books aloud?'

'Aloud?' said Mike, a sudden look of embarrassment spreading across his face. 'Of course not, Roz. I'm not a child. Only children read books aloud.'

'Or people with reading difficulties,' said Roz. 'That's nothing to be ashamed about, Mike. Nick himself reads with his face mere millimetres from each page. Luckily he rarely has time to read, because he's so busy writing.'

'I don't read aloud,' growled Mike, scowling.

Roz sighed. She had to go in hard. 'Look, don't turn another major crisis into a catastrophic crisis, Mike. We currently have a huge problem with the Phantascape. There's a dream-demon running loose inside which may soon suck up the souls of these slumbering volunteers. Now tell me the truth. Do you read stories to yourself aloud?'

'Okay,' said Mike grumpily, striding over to the far side of the room, his head turned away from Roz's own. 'I *do* read aloud. I can't help it. It helps me picture the scene and I like doing the voices. There,' he said, turning to face Roz again. 'Are you satisfied?'

'Not really, Mike,' said Roz. 'Because that means that you've inadvertently awoken memories of Nick's terrifying dream-demon, the Randyman, inside his conscious psyche, which has since been released into the Phantascape. The project's a potential disaster waiting to happen, Mike. Because whoever dares set foot inside the Phantascape now is taking their life into their own hands. In fact, it's worse than that,' said Roz. 'They're putting their lives into *your* hands. You alone control their safety inside the Phantascape, Mike Crisis. But you now have a rival, threatening the lives of every single person you wire in. A dream-demon. A terrifying monster of the mind, hell-bent on plunging everyone's souls into Hell.'

'Then I guess I ought to abort the project,' said Mike.

'You think?'

'Look, you don't understand, Roz. It's not as easy as all that. Nullman gave me this job as a way of proving myself. If I don't measure up for once in my professional life, all my hopes of becoming a brain surgeon will be dashed. I need to prove that, just once, Roz, I can turn a diabolical crisis into only a minor crisis. Or ideally not remotely a crisis at all. If I don't turn the Phantascape project into a success, I'll never get a chance to have a scalpel in my hand, hovering over the exposed brain of some quivering innocent. I'll never get the opportunity to get stuck in to that troublesome lobe and remove all the bad bits of brain.'

'I think that's probably a good thing,' said Roz.

Mike sighed, his shoulders slumping with sudden dejection. 'You're just like all the rest.'

'Look, there won't *be* any "all the rest" if you don't measure up in this particular crisis, Mike Crisis,' snapped Roz. 'Haven't you read that book fully? From page to page?'

'I skipped a few bits,' said Mike, forlornly.

'Well, I suggest you read it in *full*,' said Roz. 'Plus all the sequels. Away from this laboratory, I might add. Because then you might realise that Randy Streak, the dream-demon known as the Randyman, also has the ability to follow its victims into the real world when they wake up. *Our* world, Mike! The Randyman can escape into *our* reality, turning the very world around us into a living, breathing, *waking nightmare!*'

'No, Roz . . .' whispered Mike, a look of fear in his eyes. 'Surely not?'

'Yes, Mike,' said Roz, correcting him. 'A waking nightmare inside this very building. Not even the walls of Nulltec would be able to contain it!'

'So I really *should* go and report all this to Dr Nullman, then?'

'Yes, Mike,' said Roz, exasperated. 'You should.'

Mike nodded, solemnly. 'And cancel the programme outright, I guess.'

'Yes, Mike,' sighed Roz. 'And cancel the programme outright. No ifs. No buts.'

Mike nodded again, thinking deeply, then finally looked up, a fresh and hitherto unseen determined expression on his face. An expression that immediately faded as he looked earnestly at Roz. 'Can you come with me?'

★

They got lost three times crossing the impressive glass bridge back into the main building when Mike stopped to take in the view below (mainly grass), then forgot which direction he'd been walking in. Eventually, Roz steered him the right way again and they reached Nullman's office without further incident, apart from Mike tripping on a flat floor-tile, which necessitated a brief detour via the first aid room. An hour later, they were finally outside.

Three hours later, they were allowed in.

'And you're saying that the entire Phantascape project has to be aborted?' said Nullman, steelily.

'I don't know,' said Mike Crisis.

'You *do* know,' said Roz, nudging him.

'Do I?'

'Yes.'

'Okay.'

'Tell her, then.'

'Who, Dr Nullman?'

'Yes, that's why we're both standing here.'

'Right . . .' He looked up nervously at the Chief Head of the

Nulltec Corporation, gulped, then finally spoke. 'That's not what I'm saying to you,' he said.

Nullman's glare softened a little. Then Roz nudged him again.

'That's what I'm *telling* you, Nullman,' he added.

Nullman's glare returned, harsher now. 'And who are you to tell *me* that?'

'I'm . . . I'm . . .'

Roz nudged Mike a third time.

'I'm Dr Mike Crisis, that's who. And you'd best remember that name, Nullman, and remember it well. Sorry, I meant Dr Nullman. You have a major crisis unfolding in the Phantascape project. A major crisis that could soon escalate into an even more major crisis.'

'A catastrophic crisis,' whispered Roz.

'A *catastrophic* crisis,' added Mike Crisis. 'A catastrophic crisis, that if left unchecked, could itself escalate before you know it into an even more catastrophic crisis.'

'An apocalyptic crisis,' whispered Roz.

'An *apocalyptic* crisis,' Mike added. 'And then, if *that* in turn is left unchecked, you might even be facing a post-apocalyptic crisis.'

He glanced at Roz, who nodded back at him approvingly.

'Oh come now, Dr Crisis,' said Nullman. 'We're hardly going to be operating anywhere near that small nuclear reactor we maintain in the darkest bowels of the building, are we?'

'I don't know,' said Mike, genuinely confused. He looked at Roz. 'Are we?'

Roz decided to take over. 'Look, Dr Nullman, a terrifying dream-demon has escaped from Nick's mind,' she said. 'And it's currently capable of infecting the minds of everyone else wired into the Phantascape.'

'I see,' said Nullman, finally looking mildly concerned.

'That means everyone involved in the project is potentially going to have their souls sucked out and thrust into Hell by a demonic toilet plunger.'

'Run that past me again,' said Dr Valesco, interrupting. Roz had almost forgotten he was there, so quietly had he been waiting at the table, pulling tiny hats down over the heads of small mice in a plastic tray, covering their eyes. Roz shuddered. These Nulltec 'experiments' were starting to grate on her. She'd be reporting *that* to the authorities, too, as soon as she was able. No one should have to witness the heads of small mice being artificially blinded in a plastic tray, even if the experiment was essential to Mankind's wellbeing.

'Nick once wrote a story called *The Randyman*, about a dream-demon called Randy Streak,' Roz explained. 'He was a toilet attendant accused of being a flasher by a group of local youths who one night murdered him inside the rancid local gents' he was perennially servicing. Randy then came back from the grave, haunting the dreams of the killer youths in the form of the terrifying Randyman; a dream-demon wielding a Satanic toilet plunger intent on sucking out the souls of the gang before flushing them down to Hell. But here's the catch,' said Roz, looking round to ensure she had everyone's undivided attention.

Valesco was looking elsewhere at that moment, though, so she waited until he looked back in her direction again. Then resumed.

'The Randyman can follow people back from their dreams into the real world – the demon's plunger essentially enables it to pump itself through the U-bend of dream into another reality. Meaning that if something isn't done immediately to check the Randyman's influence over the Phantascape project, pretty soon we'll be dealing with a real-life dream-demon here on the ward. A ghost in the form of a pervert in a mac at loose inside the facility.'

There was a moment of stunned silence as Roz's words slowly sank in. Finally, Nullman spoke.

'And how did this particular book get *into* the Phantascape, exactly? We're monitoring every thought rising from Mr Steen's unconscious mind. Anything potentially dangerous – like the novel in question, or its numerous tired sequels – could never have seeped through into his subconscious mind without *our* knowledge and immediate intervention.'

Mike grew suddenly sheepish. Roz felt a momentary wave of sympathy for him, then decided that she didn't fancy him after all and elected to land him in it. After all, it was the only thing that might lead towards Mike Crisis mastering a potential crisis rather than the crisis itself mastering Mike Crisis.

'He read the book aloud,' said Roz, turning to face the former brief object of her affections. 'I'm sorry, Mike.'

'Don't be,' he said. 'I deserve all I get.'

'*Why* were you reading that book?' demanded Nullman.

'I found it in the locker room,' Mike said, weakly.

'Rubbish,' said Valesco, pulling a miniscule sou'wester over the eyes of another confused mouse. 'We sent that book to you directly with the specific instruction to destroy it. The letter we sent to you said on no account must you read that book aloud anywhere in the vicinity of Mr Steen while his comatose body was engaged inside the Phantascape project.'

'I didn't receive any letter,' said Mike.

'Enough lies, Dr Crisis!' snapped Nullman. 'You've already made a complete hash of the Phantascape project, and now you're making your position infinitely worse by attempting to weasel your way out of any form of personal responsibility.'

'Or culpability,' added Valesco, temporarily blinding two more mice with miniature baseball caps.

'We are holding you entirely responsible for what has happened to the Phantascape project, Dr Crisis,' said Nullman sternly. 'But it will not be cancelled, terminated or aborted. Unless you take immediate steps to rectify the situation, you will be dismissed from our institution permanently and your scientific career will be over.'

'But how?' said Mike, his voice wavering. 'How do I do that?'

'God, you're quite pathetic, aren't you?' snapped Nullman, lighting a cigarette and blowing the smoke directly in Mike's eyes so that, at long last, he began to cry.

'By solving this crisis before this particular crisis solves you. Capture that dream-demon in the Phantascape and send it *back* through the mind-gap in Nick Steen's brain. Then seal the metaphorical wall up once and for all.'

'But what if the Randyman finds a way into our own reality first?' interrupted Roz, having realised Mike was currently in no position to engage intelligently with the conversation. 'Before we get a chance to send him back through that hole to another dimension in Nick's mind, I mean? What if he beats us to it?'

'Then use bait to trap him,' said Valesco, looking up again from his tray of fully blinded yet brightly dressed mice.

'An excellent idea, Dr Valesco,' said Nullman coldly, the trace of a faint smile visible on her lips. She glared meaningfully at Roz. 'I'm sure Miss Bloom will oblige . . .'

CHAPTER FOUR

'Crises'

Halfway across the glass bridge, Mike drew to a halt.

'Please keep walking, Mike,' said Roz. 'Otherwise we're liable to get lost again.'

'Why not stand directly in front of me, Roz? Then I'll know which direction we're headed in.'

Roz rolled her eyes again and stood in front of Mike.

'Look, Roz, you don't work here full-time. I do. I'm forever getting lost in these seemingly endless Nulltec corridors. That's why I always get distracted when walking across this glass bridge. It's the only time I get to see *out*. And sometimes, when that pain of being terrible in a crisis really gets to me, all I want to do is just stand right here in this spot and look out on to that area of grass below me and imagine myself lying in it, feeling the brush of natural vegetation against my skin, watching those glorious white clouds roll by over-head. Believing that somewhere, somewhere out there, lies a world in which Mike Crisis is an asset in a major crisis and not a liability. A world where people actively seek out Mike Crisis for solutions to their crises, rather than running sniggering from him in an effort to escape an ever-worsening crisis. *That's* why I get lost here, Roz. Because this glass bridge is the only place I can see clearly.'

THE RANDYMAN

'This is entirely the wrong time for self-reflection, Mike,' snapped Roz sternly. 'The terrifying scenario we now find ourselves caught up in has barely even begun, and you're already indulging in a point-less, ruminatory bout of internal self-pitifance. I wouldn't object if we were near a point of ultimate crisis, some way further into this macabre series of events we sense unfolding frighteningly about us, but we've barely even begun our journey into darkness. And frankly?'

'Yes?' replied Mike, looking suitably chastised.

'Frankly, Mike Crisis, *I* should be the one feeling sorry for myself. *I'm* the one who's been chased by a dream-demon. *I'm* the one who's nearly had my soul sucked out by a cursed plunger and who's now been told to return to the Phantascape in order to entice the Randyman back into a hole in Nick's head, currently located some-where inside a dream-version of Dankton, probably in one of those disgusting-looking distant tower blocks I glimpsed on the horizon. *I'm* the one the Randyman has asked to move in with it, Mike, which will no doubt mean having to pretend I'm interested in the contents of its grubby mackintosh for the foreseeable. And yet despite all that, I wouldn't dare to start feeling sorry for myself until I was at the *ultimate* crisis point – say, around three-quarters of the way into whatever eerie events may yet transpire. So buck up and stop feeling sorry for yourself, because we have work to do.'

Mike looked at her, nodding firmly. 'I'm sorry, Roz.'

'And stop *apologising*, dammit. Just start thinking, will you?'

Mike placed both hands on Roz's shoulders, commanding her attention. 'Listen Roz, I meant every word of what I said back there. Neither Nullman nor Valesco gave me a letter instructing me to destroy that book. Like I said before, I found Nick's novel in my locker room. Inside my *own* locker, if you really want to know.'

'Are you lying to me, Mike?' asked Roz, staring deeply into the doctor's eyes. She wanted to believe him, but knew that he was essentially a pathetic individual.

Mike's orbs darted immediately to the left.

'I knew it,' Roz said, coldly. 'I *knew* you were lying to me.'

'No, Roz,' said Mike, releasing her shoulders. 'I meant it. My eyes darting left just then was merely another example of my own brain's innate crisis-escalating tendencies. It's as if my own mind wants to condemn me for something I haven't yet done! Sometimes,' he said, grasping his head tightly by the temples, 'sometimes I'd like to sit down and perform some damned brain surgery on my own head! Just sit down at a mirror somewhere and slice my own skull apart. Root around inside it for a bit and pull out those damned synapses which are always telling me I can't do anything right!'

He burst into tears.

'Stop, Mike, stop!' said Roz, hugging him close. She couldn't help it. Part of her still felt for Mike physically, and this seemed the best possible way to get a good feel of his arse. Wondering whether she might get away with moving one hand surreptitiously downwards in the direction of his butt, Roz eventually decided against it, suspecting the motion was technically illegal, despite her being a woman. She pushed Mike away.

'Listen, Mike. You don't have to lie to me, okay? I know you're bloody hopeless in a crisis. I know you read that book aloud to Nick because you're instinctively unable to conduct yourself in a competent and professional manner. But the bottom line is that we have to sort out this particular crisis as a matter of urgency, and I have to tell you now . . .' She paused for a moment, unsure whether she should say what she was about to say.

'What, Roz?' said Mike, pleading with her. 'What do you have to tell me?'

'That I'm not going back in there, Mike. The Phantascape, I mean. I'm not letting you wire me in again.'

'But you *have* to go in, Roz,' said Mike. 'They've said you must. They've told me to use you as bait.'

'Then you'll have to find another way,' Roz insisted, turning away from him abruptly and walking across to the far side of the bridge.

Mike immediately began walking in the opposite direction, back towards the main facility, then realised Roz wasn't in front of him and turned back round, quickening his pace to catch up with her.

'You *must* go in there, Roz,' he said. 'Or I'll get in trouble again. They'll fire me. I'll never make it into the exciting world of experimental brain surgery.'

'I don't care,' said Roz, striding boldly ahead. 'I'm not going anywhere near the Randyman again. It's rank.'

'But Roz,' Mike shouted, tripping over some dust before rising again, then sprinting to catch up with her. 'If you don't go in, how can we possibly get rid of the dream-demon?'

'That's your problem, Mike, not mine. I'm willing to help you, but this is a task *you're* ultimately in charge of. You deal with it. I'm going back to my cell.'

'Fine,' Mike yelled. 'Then maybe I'll just kill Nick Steen.'

Roz whirled round, unable to believe what she'd just heard.

'Yeah, you heard me,' howled Mike Crisis. 'I've accidentally let one patient starve to death. Why not another one? And if Nick Steen dies, presumably the dream-demon inside him also dies. Given the damned thing's coming out of his own head. There. Problem solved. Crisis averted.'

'You can't do that!' Roz cried.

'I can, Roz, and I will,' he said. 'You said yourself, it's high time I took control of things. High time I turned this crisis into less of a crisis. Well, now I will. And once I've switched off Mr Steen's life-support system, then Mike Crisis will forever be known as a man who's great in a crisis, as opposed to being perpetually bloody appalling in a crisis.'

He stormed past Roz, off the glass bridge and into the waiting elevator that would soon take him up to the main laboratory floor.

'Wait!' Roz cried, running after him. 'Wait for me!'

Her body became trapped painfully in the closing door, owing to Mike not realising that basic elevator etiquette meant you were expected to attempt to hold the door in the event of any straggling ascenders or descenders trying to hitch a lift with you.

Mike dragged Roz's body through into the lift, scraping both her legs on the metal door-frame.

'You idiot!' she said, once she'd been pulled through.

'Not for much longer, Roz,' Mike huffed.

She could sense something different in him now. An anger, maybe. An anger borne of desperation and, more frighteningly, determination. The determination of a blind and reckless crisis-amplifier.

'If you dare touch a hair on Nick's head, I'll destroy the hair on *your* head,' said Roz, warning him. And in that moment, she caught another new emotion in Mike's expression. A trace of sadness, she thought. Evidence, uncertain though it might be, of emotional hurt. Was it possible that Mike Crisis fancied her, too?

She stared meaningfully at him, raising her eyebrow suggestively while hitching up her skirt over one knee. Mike gulped, then hit the elevator button. The lift began descending rapidly to the lower floors.

'Your laboratory's upstairs,' said Roz.

'Damn,' said Mike to himself, hammering the 'up' button frantically. The lift stopped at another floor, allowing two scientists holding a mutant baby in a pair of forceps to step in. By the time they'd got out again on floor thirteen, the sexual tension between Roz and Mike was proving completely unbearable.

'Are you and Nick Steen an item?' asked Mike, his casual tone at odds with his flushing cheeks.

'How do you mean?' said Roz.

'Well . . . Are you and he . . . *lovers*?'

Should she pretend, Roz wondered? Just for one blissful, golden moment? Did it really matter that she and Nick weren't? But then

Roz stopped herself, realising, as she always did in these situations, that these complex emotions regarding Nick's potential attractiveness were merely a lingering trace of her favourite author's imaginative influence on the world around her. A remnant of Nick's fictional mind, having a perpetual effect on those living – and generally suffering – in its wake.

'No,' she said. 'We're not lovers. And never have been. He's just a great writer, okay?'

'Really?'

'Really. A really, *really* great writer. The best. And for that reason alone, you can't kill him, Mike. You just can't.' It was her turn to cry. Her turn to reveal an emotional hurt, deep down within her. She reached into her pocket for a tissue, seeing that Mike wasn't going to offer her one, and dried her eyes.

Mike reached out, placing a hand on her shoulder again. 'I have to,' he said.

Before Roz could respond, the elevator door opened again and they were back out on the main corridor leading up to the laboratory currently housing the Phantascape project.

Mike had lost his identity card, so had to phone down for permission to enter his own room, but within three hours they were both back inside the laboratory.

Mike briefly checked the monitor screens, making sure the drips feeding the volunteers were still half-full, then crossed over towards the window of the adjacent room, overlooking Nick's bed.

Roz was already there, quivering with fright.

'He's gone,' she said.

'Gone? What do you mean "gone"?'

'What I said, dammit!' cried Roz. 'Nick Steen's body has gone!'

Mike looked into the room beyond. She was right. Nick Steen's body had vanished. Before them lay an empty gurney. Everything – the bedding, the monitoring equipment, the wiring – everything keeping Nick Steen connected to the Phantascape had been removed.

Mike rushed over to the main computer terminal again, looking frantically through the readouts.

'It doesn't make sense,' he said. 'I'm still getting life-signs.'

'Meaning?' said Roz.

'Meaning somehow, somewhere, he's still plugged in to the Phantascape.' Mike turned to face her. 'Nick's still part of the programme. Only we no longer have access to him. Someone, or something, has taken his body away.'

'Hopefully some*one*,' said Roz.

Suddenly there was an unholy laugh, coming from above her. Or below. Roz couldn't tell. It sounded like the cackling of Sid James mixed with Wilfrid Brambell's bad-breathed whining and the spirited guffawing of Stacey Solomon.

'Then again, maybe it's some*thing*, as you say,' Roz said, looking nervously at Mike. 'Did you hear it?'

'I heard something,' said Mike. 'But I think it was my stomach rumbling. I haven't had lunch yet.'

So only Roz had heard it. That terrifying, soul-threatening laugh of the Randyman. Was she going mad? Or had the dream-demon itself stolen Nick from this place? Was the Randyman already loose in Nulltec? Had it somehow escaped the Phantascape without Roz knowing and kidnapped its own creator? Had it, God forbid, already plunged Nick's soul into the depths of Hell?

Mike whooped in sudden realisation. 'Of course!' he yelled. He turned to face Roz. 'Don't you see?'

'See what?' Roz replied, still frightened.

'I was telling you the truth all along, dammit. *Nulltec* have taken Nick's body. No doubt Valesco's team came down here while we were having that dramatic emotional confrontation on the bridge and took Nick away from us. Because we were getting too close to the truth, Roz. We were rumbling their game. I said they were lying when they left me instructions to destroy that book, Roz, and I meant it. Don't you see? If they simply wanted to block up Nick's mind-leak, why didn't they just kill him, like I was considering doing? Why go to all the bother of keeping him alive if the simple answer to blocking up the hole in Nick's mind was to destroy that mind?'

Mike had something there, Roz realised. Why *hadn't* they killed Nick already?

'Maybe that's what they're doing now,' said Roz, unable to quell her fears. 'Maybe that's *why* they've taken him. Maybe they're about to murder him, literally as we speak.'

But no, she thought, forcing herself to think rationally. Why would they do that, she theorised, when Mike himself was becoming desperate enough to carry out that very job? Why deny their ultimate scapegoat the chance of wrecking his own career and leaving them entirely blameless for Nick's demise, unless they were instead intent upon keeping Nick *alive*? Maybe Nulltec were indeed up to something nefarious, like Mike was implying. Maybe they *wanted* the Randyman running loose inside Nick's brain . . .

Which brought her right back to square one. Had the Randyman *itself* taken Nick away?

'What do we do?' she asked, trying to calm her fears. Because all the options were crap.

'I guess I could phone Valesco's office and see where they're keeping him?'

'Don't be stupid, Mike. They've kidnapped Nick for a reason. They're hardly going to tell you or me where he is now, are they?' Roz straightened her skirt, which she realised was still hitched up over one knee.

'There's nothing else for it,' she said. 'I have to go in again. I have to go back inside the Phantascape. If I'm going to find Nick anywhere,

301

it'll be in there. I have to search for Nick inside that terrifying dream-world, even though it's the last thing I want to do.'

'I'll come with you this time,' said Mike.

She nodded, even though she knew that was potentially disastrous.

The truth was, she did need some help this time. Because the last thing Roz Bloom wanted in the whole world was to be trapped inside the Phantascape with Randy Streak, the dream-demon known as the Randyman, *alone* . . .

CHAPTER FIVE

'Plunging'

But Roz *was* alone. As she found herself standing once more on the fringes of the bleak and gloomy Dankton Park, she realised amid the wet, autumnal bleakness that Mike Crisis was no longer beside her as he'd said he would be, and that again she'd made the transition into the Phantascape unaccompanied.

Had she fallen asleep by accident as Mike was wiring her in? No, he'd wired himself in first, hadn't he? Then realised he required his own head to be unwired in order to be able to wire in Roz's head, so had disconnected himself again, before wiring her in first. Was that when she'd fallen asleep? No, she'd waited for him, hadn't she? Watched him as he wired in his own head again and lay down on the bed beside her, vowing to go into the dream-world together. And, now that she was able to brush off the initial drowsiness of dream, Roz remembered calmly accepting the sleeping drug he'd handed her; recalled them holding each other's hands, counting down to ten, then swallowing their pills together.

So where the hell was he?

The cold October breeze blew about her, chilling her vitals as heavy raindrops struck the shoulders of her overcoat. Roz stared intently across the park, keeping her eyes on the distant tower blocks she was headed for, instead of the grim concrete toilet block on her left, which she was nevertheless constantly aware of. She had to get across the park as quickly as possible, before the Randyman could make another unwanted appearance. But Roz knew that was easier said than done while she was wearing a pair of uncomfortable high-heeled slingbacks.

Her gaze fell suddenly upon a brand-new pair of trainers sitting directly beside her on the nearside edge of the park. They looked eerily incongruous, Roz thought. As though they'd been waiting here especially for her. Why, they were practically inviting her to try them on, weren't they? And they looked really cool, too. Factory-laced white pumps with pastel-yellow banding and air-cushioned ice soles. If Roz put these shoes on now, instead of her usual sling-backs, she might make it across the park to those tower blocks in record time.

Quickly, Roz swapped her shoes over, ditching the slingbacks, and strode forward across the park in her new trainers at a determined pace.

She paused frequently on the way to admire them, raising each shoe upward so that she could mentally absorb the customised tread pattern on each outsole, growing mildly chagrined that they were already stained with the sodden mud she'd been trudging through.

Then, realising she was wasting precious time, Roz turned her attention back to the park in front of her and immediately caught sight of a familiar form some distance ahead. A creepy-looking figure in a brown mackintosh and trilby, standing stock-still on the far side of the green.

The Randyman . . .

'Like my gift, Roz?' it said.

Damn it, thought Roz. That brand-new pair of trainers had been a trick. A trap designed to slow her progress, rather than speed it up. If only she'd ignored the shoes. If only she had kept her painful slingbacks on instead, rather than swapping them over for these replacement trainers and subsequently pausing at frequent intervals to take in their amazing look and feel. She should have resisted temptation and continued to march at a determined pace across Dankton Park. Then she might already be standing safely and soundly on the far side of the green.

After all, that had been her intention, hadn't it? To make her way across the green in record time in order to avoid any further encounters with that mischievous flashing dream-demon previously known as Randy Streak. Only now did Roz realise that by putting on this brand-new pair of trainers he'd gifted her, she'd actually *lost* whatever benefit in time she'd hoped to gain by setting forth across the park at an increased speed, and had instead only *added* to the time expended, crushing in one fell swoop all hope she'd once had of reducing her journey time in order to ensure her safe and snag-free migration across the park.

The damned irony of it . . .

Now where could she run? Behind her was that huge bank of green cloud again, through which she'd entered the Phantascape. She could try running back through it, but could she really risk losing her way inside a green mist with Randy Streak in hot pursuit? And there was no point trying to hide from the dream-demon in the whirling smoke, either. No doubt somewhere on that U-bended neck, there'd be a convenient gas cock that would effectively close off the supply of smoke, exposing her again in an instant.

And she couldn't run to her left, either. Not if she wished to avoid the toilet block that was Randy's home. So where the hell *could* she run?

Then it struck her. This was a dream, wasn't it? So why, then, couldn't she simply fly?

She looked up, preparing to launch herself into the heavens, and saw Randy Streak floating directly above her, mackintosh billowing, toilet plunger poised in one hand.

'I control the dream, Roz,' whispered the dream-demon, its voice sounding as if it were coming from inside her own head. Either that or being piped through a semi-blocked industrial vent stack. 'I've come for you . . . Come to take you back . . .'

'Back where?' said Roz, dreamily. Was she going mad, or was there something vaguely attractive about those bronze gate valves protruding from the Randyman's abs? Something mildly titillating, even, about that gleaming hose bib (also known as a common outdoor faucet) visible now in the area of Randy Streak's groin (which the demonic toilet plunger had otherwise been covering up)?

'Yes,' murmured Roz. 'I will come with you . . .'

'Then grab my nipples,' said the Randyman, revealing two short pipes on its chest that would ordinarily connect couplings and other fittings.

Roz did what the Randyman commanded, and found herself ascending into the air, enveloped in the stained folds of the dream-demon's grubby beige mac. It smelled of wastewater and pipe-cloggings, and part of Roz wanted to let go. Wanted to drop from the Randyman's pipes and fall to a blissful, sewage-free death. But then the dank smell of unwanted overflow began to lift, and Roz sensed that the fluid dripping from the Randyman's flesh pipes was grey water only, i.e. used water emerging from common non-toilet fixtures, as opposed to a typical bog-based leak.

It – he – was changing, Roz realised. The further Randy Streak got from the horrors of his past, from the grim circumstances of his toilet-based demise, and the closer he got to Roz, who'd convinced Nick to give the dream-demon a sympathetic back story, the less stinky he was becoming.

Could it be true, Roz wondered. Could the Randyman be seeking some form of spiritual salvation through her?

'Come with me, Roz,' he whispered, his voice sounding again like it was inside her own head, yet smoother this time, as if piped now through some modern industrial power flush system.

'Come to my house . . .'

They were descending, Roz realised, back to the ground below. As the sides of the dream-demon's mackintosh flew apart, Roz finally saw the building they were heading toward.

It was the lonely, run-down public toilet block, only now it was decorated with clumps of sodden dandelions and leftover bunting from the 1977 Queen's Jubilee.

'Come with me, Roz . . . Live with me . . .'

The Randyman took Roz by the hand and led her in the direction of his former maintenance cupboard.

'I'll get all this re-floored,' he added, 'and order an extra chair for you.'

'No . . .' murmured Roz. She knew she had to get out. Knew she had to find Nick, but something was stopping her. Something speaking to her from deep inside. Something she couldn't help but feel toward this poor, misunderstood council-employed toilet attendant. It was pity, she decided. Because all he'd ever wanted was to keep the pipes in this particular gents' facility clean and unblocked. Keep them flushed through so that he could get home for a well-earned steak-and-kidney pie for one in front of a flickering television set before the inevitable 1 a.m. emergency council call-out requiring him to go and disperse yet another nocturnal loiterer.

And they'd called *him* the sleazy one. Mistaken *him* for a crusty-clawed cubicle-clinger. Blamed Randy Streak *himself* for being a perennial urinal gland-shaker.

It wasn't fair!

But this . . . Roz thought, examining the interior of Randy Streak's maintenance cupboard. The buckets, the piping, the exact spare plunger supply the gang of youths had used to pump the alleged

307

bog-loiterer to death; the stagnant mops, the broken radio that now merely hissed, the nicotine-stained spot-the-ball collection plastering the entirety of one wall. She couldn't face this, could she? Was this to be Roz's lot? Married to a dream-demon in some nightmarish khazi that could never be pumped dry? Was this the happy future she'd planned when she first began her career in horror paperback publishing? Spending the rest of eternity as Randy Streak's undead lavatory-scrubber assistant? Maybe he'd expect her to service *his* pipes as well? Maybe he'd ask her to pump his float ball or even, God forbid, wrench his floor flange?

No! thought Roz. I can't. I don't want this life. As much as I feel pity for Randy Streak, I don't want to vent his rim hole.*

'No . . .' said Roz, woozily. 'I don't want to live in a public gents', Randy.'

'You don't, Roz?'

'No, Randy, I don't. I really don't.'

'But this is my home. My life. My *death* . . .'

'I know, Randy, but . . .'

'All this can be yours too, Roz Bloom. *Your* home. *Your* life. *Your* death . . .'

'Like I say, Randy, I really don't want . . .'

'Listen to it,' hissed Randy, holding his plunger aloft, over his head, as though searching for the sound. 'Listen to its vibration . . . Listen to the calling of the water hammer.'†

The Randyman looked down again at Roz, his nose, chin and lips dripping with overflowing grey water. 'Come, Roz . . . Come and *mop* with me . . .'

---

* A series of small holes around a conventional toilet bowl. Water flowing from each rim hole washes over the bowl's surface and in the process refills the toilet bowl itself. In Randy's case, this is located in the area of his anus. GM
† A loud noise or vibration caused by pipes being turned on or off, itself caused by the sudden surging or stopping of water within said pipes. GM

'No . . .' she whispered again, but knew that her will was slowly being sapped. Maybe it was that now strangely alluring scent of the dank spillages surrounding them, or perhaps it was the hypnotic drip of wastewater leaking through the perishing closet flange, threatening the structural integrity of the backwater valve (which should, in theory, prevent disposed sewage from re-entering a building), or maybe it was the dizzying pattern in that swirling, mildew-covered ceiling overhead, or the looming presence of the temporary septic tank housed beside Randy's makeshift lunch area, but Roz no longer felt she had any power to resist. She no longer felt she possessed sufficient energy to counter the Randyman's dreamlike gaze, nor the strength of will needed to oppose the terrible suck and pull of that horrendous industrial-strength plunger of his.

She was trapped – forever – in the Phantascape. A prisoner, for all time, of the dreaded Randyman.

The pen . . . It was her own mind whispering to her . . . *The fountain pen* . . . *To wake you up* . . .

Then she remembered she'd handed that very pen to Mike . . . and Mike, being Mike, had forgotten to hand it back.

It was useless to resist. As the dream-demon leered in toward her for a last embrace, Roz wondered which of the cubicles next door she should tackle first, and made a mental note to ask Randy if he had any small-size Marigolds . . . And then she felt a sudden pain in her leg.

'Ouch!' Roz yelled, looking down. A stream of blood was running over her right knee. Then she felt another stab. In her arm this time. She raised her elbow to examine the wound and felt a similar pain in her other arm.

'Ow!' she yelled again.

Suddenly, her surroundings started to fade. The Randyman, for a brief moment, appeared to disappear inside the folds of his mackintosh, becoming almost immaterial. Then, too, the stained wall-tiling of

Randy's own public convenience began to vanish as Roz fought to contain the pain she was feeling in all her limbs now. Here came another! And another! Hell, she was being stabbed, she realised. Stabbed numerous times in her arms and legs. 'Get off me!' Roz yelled.

'Hey, I'm not doing a damned thing, lady,' said Randy, an offended look on his face. 'I only plunge people's souls to Hell.'

'Then who the hell is stabbing me?' Roz cried.

'*Stabbing* you?' roared the Randyman, confused, as Roz finally understood what was happening . . .

★

. . . and woke suddenly in the laboratory again, to find Mike Crisis jabbing her own fountain pen repeatedly into her arms and legs.

'Bugger off!' screamed Roz.

'I'm sorry, Roz!' said Mike, still jabbing, before remembering he'd just been told specifically not to jab her. 'I didn't know how else to wake you.'

Roz snatched the pen from him and ripped the wires from her bald cap. 'Where the hell were you?' she snapped. 'I was all alone in there again, with Randy Streak coming after me with that fetid plunger of his.'

'I ran out of sleeping pills the second you went under, Roz,' Mike said. 'I tried looking around for more, but whoever stole Nick's body from the lab also stole the contents of my sleeping pill collection. I rang a local pharmacy but they weren't getting fresh deliveries until next Wednesday, by which time I imagined you'd be almost completely dead. So I knew I had to act fast. After grabbing lunch-on-the-go, I began thinking through all the possible ways I could go about waking you up. You see, whoever had taken Nick's body, and my sleeping pill collection, had also taken my sleep-suppressant pill collection. Then when you started screaming and moaning in your sleep, I knew I had no choice, so I started stabbing you with the pen. And thank God I did, right?'

'I guess,' said Roz, feeling her wounds. 'Hand me some antiseptic cream and some plasters, would you?'

Mike nodded, rising to oblige her, when suddenly Roz screamed.

'The others!' she yelled, looking at the dreaming sleepers who lay around them. 'Look, Mike! They're all dead!'

Mike looked, his eyes shifting from Roz's bed to those of her fellow experiment volunteers. Roz was right. All of them were in an advanced stage of decomposition. He grimaced in sudden embarrassment, and looked up again at Roz.

'I . . . I . . .'

'Didn't you even notice?' snapped Roz. 'Didn't you smell them starting to rot? And rotting pretty quickly by the look of things?'

'Of course I knew,' he said, grinning suddenly at her. 'After all, *I* killed them, didn't I?'

Mike tore aside his lab coat to reveal a brown mackintosh concealed below it, then calmly ripped off his own face. As the mask of waxy flesh fell away, through it appeared the dripping, bloodied visage of the Randyman.

'I'm here to flush you out!' the dream-demon snarled. 'Like I've flushed out all these others.' The Randyman pointed with its plunger at the various dead dreamers, then angled its weapon at Roz.

'So you won't marry Randy, after all, huh?' it snapped. 'When all along you're the one who's supposed to care for me. Unclog me. Twist my angle stop. You, who were meant to be the anode rod in my corroded water tank.'

'I can't, Randy! I just can't!'

'Then DIE!' screamed the Randyman, slamming its plunger into Roz's heart . . .

★

... which beat wildly as she woke suddenly from sleep again, to find Mike Crisis firing several bolts of electricity through her body from a pair of defibrillator pads.

'Thank God you're awake, Roz!' he screamed. 'Now stand well back!'

Mike slammed both pads on Roz's chest again.

'No, Mike!' she screamed, then felt her internal organs convulse wildly as two more harsh jolts of electricity shot through her nervous system. 'I'm the *patient!*' she yelled, when he'd finally stepped back again.

'Of course!' Mike said, slapping his own head with one of the defibrillator pads, giving himself an electric shock as well. When he'd finally recovered, he looked over at Roz again. 'I'm sorry.'

'Never mind,' Roz said, sitting herself up in bed, her heart pumping wildly like she'd been marinated in caffeine. 'What's happening to me, Mike?'

'You've been dreaming,' he said. 'I didn't know how else to wake you.'

'What about my fountain pen?' she said, still trying to recover from the electric shock.

'I lost it, I'm afraid, Roz. I must have dropped it in someone's colon when I was assisting with some rudimentary bowel surgery an hour ago.'

'How long have I been out?' she asked.

'Three days.'

'Three *days*? Why weren't you in there with me?' she snapped.

'I had to attend to these,' he said, indicating the circle of empty beds lying around the laboratory.

Roz couldn't believe she hadn't noticed yet. The other volunteers in the Phantascape project had completely vanished.

'What happened to them?' she asked, fearing that the dreamers previously surrounding her were now dead somewhere, just as they had been in the terrifying events of her recent nightmare.

'The second you went under, they began to scream, Roz. All of them went into sudden cardiac arrest. I had to forget following you in and try my best to save whoever I could. Unfortunately, my best wasn't good enough. Nowhere near good enough.'

'How many survived?' asked Roz.

Mike sighed, and held up four fingers. Then slowly lowered them, one by one. 'None.'

'None?'

'Everyone inside the Phantascape programme appears to have died of fright, Roz. And that's not all.'

'What else?'

'When they died, they were no longer the people they said they were.'

'What do you mean, Mike?'

'They'd changed, Roz. Their histories, their backgrounds; even the personal address details inside their wallets. They'd become completely different people.'

'What kind of completely different people?'

'The completely different people,' Mike said slowly, preparing Roz for the worst, *'who once murdered Randy Streak.'*

CHAPTER SIX

'Waking Nightmare'

Roz checked the identities of the deceased a third time. Whoever they'd been previously, there was no mistaking who they were now. Each of the names she and Mike found on their various driving licences and bank cards matched the fictional names of those youths who'd murdered Randy Streak in Nick's original novel.

'You know what this means?' said Roz.

'No idea whatsoever,' said Mike.

'It means that Randy Streak – the Randyman – has now escaped from the world of dream into *our* reality. He – or *it* – either followed me through, or followed one of these poor wretches. We're now living in a waking nightmare, Mike. A major catastrophe has turned into a calamitous catastrophe.'

'All on my watch . . .' Mike mumbled.

'All on your watch. Except you weren't really watching, were you, Mike? You were more sort of blindly ignoring events spiralling downward into total disaster around you.'

'I guess that's true, Roz.'

'So what are you going to do?'

He bit his lip for a moment, pondering, then fixed her with a determined look. 'I don't know.'

'There's no way I'm going to be travelling back inside the Phantascape again,' said Roz, 'and there's no point, anyhow. The Phantascape has now come to us. In any case, I couldn't see hide nor hair of Nick in there. The Randyman must have either hidden him somewhere or, God forbid, sucked his soul out already and plunged Nick straight down into Hell.'

'I still say we should kill him,' said Mike.

Roz looked at him sharply. 'What do you mean?'

'Well,' Mike said, sensing this could be a chance, at long last, to prove himself. 'Nick's physical form must still exist in reality somewhere. His vital signs are still showing on the data readouts. Look.'

He handed Roz a sheet of paper with some squiggly lines on it that she didn't understand.

'These squiggly lines tell me that he's still wired into the Phantascape; it could mean his physical presence is crucial for the Randyman's ability to survive inside this realm. Otherwise, surely the Randyman would have destroyed him first, Nick being chief instigator of this entire Randy Streak tragedy. Nick's body must therefore be a link. A bridge, if you will, between worlds.'

'But for how long, Mike? Maybe Nick's body's here, but what if his soul's already gone?'

'Look, Roz,' said Mike, moving close to her. 'We're in the middle of a calamitous catastrophe, right?'

Roz nodded. 'I guess.'

'Meaning we're going to have to make some tough decisions in order to save Stalkford from the evil machinations of this terrifying Randyman. You've said yourself that we're now living in a waking nightmare, where the world of dream and reality are combined as one.'

'Correct, Mike.'

'Well, the way I see it, if Nick's body is still wired into the Phantascape, it must mean his physical existence is crucial to the

315

Randyman's ability to survive inside this realm. Nick's body is, there-fore, a link. A bridge, if you will, between worlds. I suspect that even if Nick's soul has been plunged and sent down to Hell, his body is still integral to the Randyman being able to remain in our world and haunt our own reality. Meaning that the mind-hole in Nick's brain, that gap to another dimension through which his imagination is leaking, is still vital to the Randyman's success. Otherwise Nick would be dead already, which he's not. According to this data.'

Mike showed Roz the printout again, which she still didn't understand.

'So,' she said, theorising herself, 'if we can somehow find out where Nick's body's been hidden, and are able to block up his mind-leak as originally intended, we may yet have a chance to save the world from the Randyman?'

'Exactly. Or we can simply shoot Nick in the head.'

'No!' Roz snapped.

'Yes!' Mike Crisis snapped back at her. 'If Nick's soul is gone, Roz, then his body's just a channel. If we blast his head into a million tiny fragments, the hole to another dimension will no longer exist, and neither will the Randyman. Then Stalkford can return to normality once again, and I'll have turned a calamitous – nay, disastrous – crisis into a barely manageable one. With your help, of course.'

Roz didn't like it one bit. She couldn't believe that Nick's soul had been sent to hell already, and his body left as an unwilling conduit. She *wouldn't* believe it! If they could somehow find Nick's body, wasn't there some way in which they could reverse the process? If the hole in Nick's mind opened up into other dimensions, couldn't it open up inside Hell as well? In which case, couldn't Roz travel into Hell and save Nick again, like she'd once saved him from the Prolix?*

---

* See *Type-Face (Dark Lord of the Prolix)* in Garth Marenghi's *Terror Tome*. In fact, buy it rather than see it. Then read it. GM

Again, Roz's mind returned to that other quandary she'd been pondering previously. If normality really could be restored through simply destroying Nick's physical frame, then why hadn't Nulltec killed him already in order to seal up Nick's mind-hole? Maybe Mike was right – maybe they *were* keeping it open deliberately. Maybe Nulltec *hadn't* ordered him to destroy that copy of *The Randyman* via letter, after all. Maybe it was *Nulltec* who'd been lying, not Mike. And maybe they'd sent Roz into the Phantascape not to seal up Nick's mind-hole, like they'd said, but to have her destroyed instead by a Randyman they already knew was running loose inside.

If that was true, then what were they really up to? What possible plan could they have which involved releasing a terrifying dream-demon into our own worldly reality? Especially when Nick himself might have easily done that for them for a small fee.

Something didn't add up, and if Roz was to stand any chance of saving Nick, and the world, from whatever evil plan Nulltec had up their sleeves, she had to locate Nick's body. But that was likely to be just as tough as it had been in the Phantascape, now that the Phantascape was itself appearing all around them.

'We've got to find him,' said Roz.

'And kill him,' added Mike.

'No, Mike. We're not killing Nick Steen. Because if what I think might be happening is indeed happening, then the only chance we have of restoring Stalkford to normal and ridding the world at large of both the Randyman and the Phantascape is to find Nick's body and somehow drag his soul back from Hell. Then together, all three of us can close that door in Nick's mind-gap, lock it up behind us and throw away the key.'

'Fine, Roz,' said Mike. 'We'll play things your way. For now . . .'

Roz sensed a new bearing to Mike Crisis. He was speaking with something like confidence, at last. But if it was confidence, Roz knew deep down it was misplaced confidence. Arrogance, even. Now she'd need to keep an even stronger eye on Mike Crisis, she realised, aware that at any point he could send them all spiralling down once more into disaster.

'You'll do as I say, Mike,' said Roz. 'Because if you don't, and you screw this whole thing up again, I'll make damned sure you're known henceforth under a *different* name. Not Mike Crisis anymore. No, I'll sort the entire thing by deed poll. If you dare screw this up, I'll be officially changing your name to Mike Catastrophe.'

The doctor gulped, sweat brimming immediately on his brow. 'Understood,' he said.

'I hope so, Mike. I really hope so.'

'So do I.'

★

The glass bridge leading into the main building was no longer a glass bridge. It was now thickly glazed and frosted in numerous areas, resembling the non-transparent glass-block windows of a run-down gents' toilets. Roz and Mike made their way carefully across it, Mike stopping once again at one small area of clear pane.

'It's nothing but a muddy field now,' he said gloomily, staring through the glass at the ground below. Then he looked upward. 'And look at those clouds in the sky,' he said. 'They've gone all grey and moody.' He stopped suddenly, catching sight of something else in the distance. 'And those tower blocks weren't there before.'

'It's Dankton,' said Roz. 'Well, a dream-version of Dankton. It's entered our real world, where admittedly the real-life Dankton actually exists. So I guess there are now two Danktons.'

Mike sighed in exasperation. 'This clash of reality and dream looks like it could become mightily confusing,' he said, scratching his head.

'And it's bound to get far worse,' Roz cautioned as she reached out for the door handle allowing access to Nulltec's central building. It was now the shape of a conventional toilet flush.

'You know, the longer the Randyman maintains its damp grip on our mortal plane, Mike, the more reality is going to start resembling the eternally-soiled, slippery interior of a run-down public convenience. We're in the Randyman's nightmare now, Mike. Don't forget that. Randy Streak drowned in a swelling block of pumped effluence and wants to turn our world into a septic tank, too.'

She pulled the flush handle and the door to the main building opened, accompanied by the sound of rushing water somewhere behind.

The corridor beyond was dank, with small damp patches overhead dripping with liquid from the floors above.

'And you think we should try Valesco's office first?' Roz asked.

'Well, his fiendish medical mind is behind every nefarious plan undertaken by Nulltec,' said Mike. 'So if Nick's comatose body is hidden somewhere in the building, he'll know where. It's going to be difficult, though. I've heard he double-locks the door to his office. And also slides over a security chain.'

Roz nodded, sombrely. It sounded like an impossible task. Doomed, even, but they had to try. If Valesco had information on Nick's whereabouts, and it sounded like he might, given he was in sole charge of Nulltec's secret and ethically unsound business practices, then they had to attempt breaking in. Even if that meant buying a wrench from B&Q.

Roz stopped her thoughts right there. Who was she fooling? Before long, there would hardly be a DIY convenience store left in the entire county that wasn't filled solely with parts dedicated to the plumbing industry. And the last thing one did with a network of plumbing inside an immersion cupboard was start bashing at it with a damned wrench. No, buying a wrench from B&Q was completely out of the question.

'Where is Valesco's office?' she asked.

'Up here,' Mike replied, pointing straight ahead. 'Then a lift down to floor thirteen.'

'Are you sure, Mike?' asked Roz, aware that Mike's sense of direction was scant at best.

'No,' replied Mike.

Roz sighed. Well, one direction was as good as any, she decided. Stepping forward, she could see that the world of Randy Streak's nightmare was changing the place permanently, turning the white, shining walls into a stained, damp shade of moody grey, thick with mulch and suspicious-looking flecks of green crust.

'Here's the lift,' said Mike, jabbing what had once been a button on the wall before them. The protuberance burst, sending a jet of oily, yellow-coloured ooze dripping downward on to the floor below.

'Remind me to call the maintenance department,' said Mike. 'I'll do it once we're inside Valesco's office. Just in case this minor lift-based crisis turns into a potential major one in the near future.'

'Don't tempt fate, Mike,' said Roz as the elevator door slid open. The interior of the lift stank of rotting river.

'After you,' said Mike, motioning Roz forward.

The floor below her feet squelched as she entered the elevator. She turned, glaring at Mike, who cautiously followed her inside.

Roz reached out and pressed the button for floor thirteen, which likewise burst like a yellow boil. She grabbed hold of Mike instinctively as the lift lurched into sudden motion.

'You can't call maintenance about the state of this lift, Mike,' she said, despairingly. 'You might as well call security while you're at it and handcuff ourselves in the meantime.'

'Of course,' said Mike, 'They'd be on to us straight away.'

'We'll just have to hope the condition of this lift improves, rather than deteriorates,' said Roz, 'if we're to have any hope of using it again.'

'Blimey, Roz. I hadn't thought of that.'

'Then start thinking, Mike,' snapped Roz. 'Nick's survival depends on us thinking before we act.'

Mike shrugged her away, forcing Roz to balance herself against the boil-infested wall. She couldn't blame him, she guessed. She *had* snapped at him. But now she'd probably lost her last ever chance of grabbing Mike's arse.

Oh well, she sighed inwardly. Perhaps it was never meant to be.

The lift stopped with a sudden jolt, sending them once again into each other's arms.

Roz dropped her hand immediately and seized Mike's arse.

'What the hell are you doing?' he said.

'Sorry,' said Roz, releasing it slowly. 'My mistake.'

You fool, Mike, she thought. You hapless fool.

'We're here,' said Mike, bursting another boil to open the lift, realising with bitter regret that he'd just blown his final chance of reciprocating Roz Bloom's unexpected-yet-not-particularly-displeasing arse-fondle. 'Floor thirteen.'

The door swung open to reveal an entire corridor filled from floor to ceiling with plumbing outlets.

'Valesco's office is at the far end,' said Mike.

As they walked along the corridor, Roz bent her head to avoid the hissing vents and steaming gas valves, knowing full well whose influence had put them there.

Grasping another flush handle in the far wall, Roz yanked downwards, hearing the distant sound of a busted flush. The door into Valesco's office wouldn't budge.

'Looks like you were right, Mike. Double-locked, security-chained and now a busted flush to boot.'

'Stand back,' said Mike, pulling out a Magnum .357 revolver.

'Where did you get hold of that?' Roz asked, amazed.

'My parents gave it to me for my sixteenth birthday, Roz. Apparently, it worked out cheaper than driving lessons.'

'They bought you a big gun?'

'I was always asking for a big gun, Roz. Maybe it's because I wanted to be a big gun, one day. Who knows? But whatever the real reason was, my parents bought me a big gun.'

'Lucky for us.'

'Exactly,' said Mike, aiming the barrel at Roz. 'Can you look into this thin end and see if there's a bullet inside?'

'I'll take the big gun, Mike,' said Roz, grabbing the big gun from Mike's hand. He was about to protest, but at the touch of Roz's hand, which she deliberately kept in contact with his for longer than would normally seem appropriate for such a big gun-snatching movement, Mike acquiesced.

'Sure, Roz,' he said. 'Perhaps I'm not the one best suited to handling a big gun, after all.'

'I'm sure you're best suited to handling other big things, Mike,' Roz said, fruitily.

Mike looked confused.

'Like big *buns*, say?' Roz arched her eyebrow upward once more.

Mike still looked confused.

'Or big *dumplings*?'

He shook his head, now looking vaguely panicked.

'Oh, forget it, Mike,' said Roz, turning her attention back to the door. That was the very last time she was going to bother.

Mike slapped his head, finally understanding, as Roz levelled Mike's big gun and opened fire at the flush handle. The mechanism exploded, blasting open the door in a shower of grey water. A second shot destroyed the security chain, which croaked and bubbled like a sucking plug, and then she and Mike were inside Valesco's office.

'Here,' she said, tossing the big gun to Mike. It was completely rusted now, as though it had been sitting under a dripping tap for decades.

'What the heck?' cried Mike. 'My parents bought me that big gun for my sixteenth birthday.'

'Remember, the Randyman's in control of the Phantascape, Mike,' Roz said. 'It must have heard those shots and tried to stop us using the big gun again. It's bound to be on its way here, even as we speak. We need to move quickly.'

Roz rummaged through the filing cabinets while a subdued Mike searched Valesco's desk.

'Ward Nine,' said Mike, flicking through some internal memo sheets. 'In the basement level.' He paused, a look of disbelief and hurt upon his face. 'They've moved him to another dream ward.'

'A dream ward?' said Roz, looking up from the filing cabinet.

'That's what it says here. I thought my dream ward was the only one Nulltec had. But according to this, they've been running another one at the same time, without my knowledge.' He looked at Roz. 'I thought they'd given the job of overseeing the Phantascape project to me alone, Roz. Yet all along there's been another dream ward operating at the same time. Why?'

'Something strange is going on, Mike. Read this.'

Roz handed him a letter she'd found filed in a folder of recent correspondence between Nullman and Valesco.

'"*A reminder, Dr Nullman*,"' Mike read. '"*To leave a copy of* The Randyman *inside the locker of Mike Crisis. As I'm sure you're aware, he's bound to screw up this final job like all his other failed tasks. With luck, he'll read the book aloud like the sissy he is and fill Nick Steen's subconscious mind with thoughts of the Randyman, thus easing the dream-demon's escape into the Phantascape.*" Why, Roz? What does all this mean?'

'They set you up, Mike,' Roz replied, as tenderly as she could. 'They knew all along you'd turn a potential crisis into a major crisis. They wanted you to fail. They wanted you to release the dreaded Randyman into our own reality.'

'But why, Roz? Why?'

Roz's brow furrowed as she fought to work it all out. There had to be a reason. Some dastardly purpose or plan they weren't yet party to. But whatever the thing was, it would have to wait. Because at that precise moment in time, Randy Streak burst through the wall.

CHAPTER SEVEN

'Dream Demon'

Or at least, Randy Streak's *head* burst through the wall. A head swollen to such monstrous size that there was little room for any other part of Randy Streak's anatomy. Which Roz, at least, was grateful for.

'I've come for you, Roz,' leered the dream-demon.

'Greetings, I'm Mike,' said Dr Crisis, proffering one hand in the direction of the apparition's monstrous mouth.

'You fool, Mike!' screamed Roz from across the room. 'That's Randy Streak!'

'Who?' said Mike, confused.

'The dream-demon!'

'Nick Steen's dream-demon?'

'Yes!' bellowed Roz. 'The Randyman!'

'Jeez!' yelled Mike, taking evasive action at last. 'I really should have put two and two together!'

As Mike hurled himself behind a nearby desk, the jaws of the Randyman bit down, tearing a large gap in the wall its head was jammed through, a bit like a great white shark eating through the bottom of a boat, if the boat were standing vertically on its head and the shark had the head of a dream-demon instead.

'If you don't come to me, Roz,' hissed Randy Streak, between mouthfuls of brick, 'I'll come to you.' Its voice was watery now, as though it were being piped back through a broken backwater valve. Jets of fluid burst through sudden holes in the wall as it bit down again. Then the entire room began to disintegrate around them, fountains of liquid shooting up violently through the floor.

'Grab hold of something, Mike!' shouted Roz, from her position behind Dr Valesco's filing cabinet.

'Do you mind if I grab *you*, Roz, like you grabbed me in the lift?' Mike yelled back.

'That doesn't look achievable in our current situation, Mike, and even if we were able to grab hold of each other, now's not really the time for potentially feeling each other up. So I recommend you grab hold of something close by, instead.'

'But what if I can never grab you again, Roz?' Mike cried out.

'If you don't grab something pronto, Mike Crisis,' yelled Roz, 'you'll not grab anything at all in the world ever again, least of all me!'

Suddenly a jet of grey water shot through the nearby wall, striking the side of Mike's head.

'Mike!' cried Roz as she watched his body fly across the room like a speeding jet plane. Then the helpless doctor slammed against an opposing torrent of grey water and was flung backwards at an angle toward a towering geyser of brownish backflow. Mike's body struck this third fountain hard and was immediately catapulted upwards again, eventually coming to a precarious halt at the frothing head of this unholy spring.

'Mike!' Roz yelled up. 'Are you alright?'

'I think so,' said Mike, 'but I'm going to need a change of lab wear, that much is for sure.'

God, he was brave, thought Roz. And funny, too, in a way. If only he wasn't such a hapless loser.

'We're a bit closer to each other now, Roz,' cried Mike from his position high above her. 'Maybe I can leap down from up here, right into your arms!'

'We're not remotely closer to each other, Mike!' yelled Roz. 'Now for Pete's sake, keep your mind on getting out of here in one piece, rather than engineering ways in which we can somehow get physically close enough to each other for a surreptitious fondle.'

The Randyman burst forward again, forcing its head further through the hole in the wall.

Roz turned in horror to find the dream-demon chomping its way across the floor of Valesco's office, making its way toward them. Now the room itself was starting to fill with murky-looking unidentifiable fluids.

This is the way Randy Streak died, thought Roz, grimly. Now it's doing it to us. The Randyman is taking its revenge ...

'Come with me, Roz,' said the Randyman, its words clear again, as if its pipes had suddenly cleared, even though its literal mouth, Roz saw, was still crammed to the gills with floor tiles. 'Come with me to my cubicle and we can de-clog the facilities together!'

'No!' screamed Roz. 'Never!' She looked up at Mike, still balanced on the top of the massive spray of water. 'Jump, Mike!' she yelled to him. 'Jump into my arms!'

But before the feckless doctor could launch himself downwards from the towering geyser, the Randyman clamped its jaws down on another mouthful of flooring, thrusting its powerful head forwards with each fresh bite.

Then the room broke in two.

Roz fell backwards as her half of Valesco's office tipped away from the other side. She glimpsed Mike falling from his fountain of water to the ground on his teetering section as the pressure below the geyser finally gave way.

When the severed halves of Valesco's office finally settled, Roz crawled forward on all fours, peering over the edge of the severed floorboards before her. Below she could see nothing but stars. Millions of stars in a vast sky of impenetrable black. Yet stars that, from this distance, looked a sickly yellow in hue. Surely stars should gleam and sparkle? Yet these were dull and greasy in appearance. Then the black seemed to lighten slightly, until it became a dull brown and, in horror, Roz realised that she wasn't looking down upon some cosmic vision of black infinity after all, but instead the slimy, ordure-spattered stains of Randy Streak's mackintosh.

A creature, Roz realised. The Randyman was now a gigantic *creature* moving below them. One swollen to monstrous, terrifying proportions. As she watched, the demon below began to move, and she realised its vast body was slithering forward. Then she glimpsed something else. A gigantic wooden rod, moving alongside the brown slick of its vast, greasy coat, ending in the gigantic circular rim of a vast rubber attachment.

The Randyman's plunger. Its colossal, swollen, soul-destroying plunger!

'We have to get out of here, Mike!' cried Roz, scrabbling over the slowly cracking floor of the suspended half-room that had once formed Dr Valesco's private office. 'I don't know what's going on down there, and perhaps it's still all a dream, but the Randyman seems to be mutating into something even worse than the basic dream-demon it first appeared to me as. It's now some form of bloated water-grub that thinks absolutely nothing of eating up an entire medical facility in an effort to get its teeth into us. I suggest we find a way out of our respective part-suspended half-rooms asap.'

She watched as a pair of human hands clawed over the precipice on the other side.

Then Mike's head popped into view. 'We seem to be suspended in mid-air, Roz, each in a teetering half-room over a vast cosmic abyss, with the giant head of a dream-demon known as the Randyman eating what's left of the connecting floorboards between us.'

'I just said all that, Mike. You don't need to explain it all again to me as though I somehow haven't yet fully processed such a complex and logic-challenging visual image. I'm right here and can see it, too. But that's not a vast cosmic blackness below us. It's the dirty, water-stained rain mac of Randy Streak, which is connected to the vast head of the demonic Randyman slowly making its way back towards us.'

'Come with me, Roz!' cried the Randyman, its huge eye staring at her through the vast gap in the floor. Then the dream-demon expelled a burst of raw sewage from its open throat, soaking the entire room.

'You won't go with it, will you, Roz?' yelled Mike, his face suddenly sad. 'You won't leave me for the *Randyman?*'

Another burst of sewage exploded from the Randyman's mouth as it belched up a couple of undigested floorboards.

'No, Mike,' cried Roz. 'Though technically we're not even going out with each other yet. But just in case we do decide to become better acquainted at some point, I'm coming with you. Not Randy Streak.'

'Then leap over to my side, Roz,' Mike yelled back. 'Because on my half of the former office of the sinister Dr Valesco, I can see a stretch of corridor running along the floor through the open door behind me, which, if memory serves, leads directly back to that elevator system which can take us straight down to Ward Nine in the basement level, where Nick Steen is currently being held – remember?'

The leap was dangerous, Roz knew, but it was her only chance. Unless she wanted to spend an eternity with a gargantuan-sized Randy Streak dream-demon.

'I'll take a good run-up,' Roz said, rolling backwards against the slanted wall behind her in order to give herself a decent charge forward.

Then, having gathered her remaining strength, Roz bounded forward from the wall in the direction of the broken edge of flooring immediately ahead.

But as she did so, Roz's half of the room began to tip upwards even more steeply, and as the row of filing cabinets she'd been rifling through moments before came crashing back towards her, Roz realised something large and heavy had struck her half of the room from below.

She felt her strength wane as the floor she was running across continued to angle upwards like the sudden, steep rise of a hill. Then she realised there was no chance at all of her scaling its peak.

'Roz!' Mike shouted down at her, staring over the precipice from his side. He watched her slide backward again in the half-room below him, toward the rear wall, as what little office equipment remained there tumbled back with her, collecting in a jumbled heap around her as she fought in vain to thrust herself upwards.

'It's no good, Mike!' cried Roz. 'Something's pushing against my side of the room from below.'

And then that something appeared in the crevice between them.

'I can see it!' yelled Mike from his side of the chasm. She could hear him now, and his words chilled her to the bone.

'It's the plunger, Roz! The Randyman's giant, oversized demonic plunger! The massive rubberised rim is pressed hard against the floor of your half of the room. You *must* leap to me now, Roz, or you're going to get sucked downward into the bowels of Hell when the dream-demon decides to yank it back again the other way. Which it's literally just about to do!'

Roz tried thrusting her body forward again, but it was no good. The forces of gravity were working against her, and there was no way she could make it up the sloping floor to the edge of the precipice now.

'It's no good, Mike. You'll have to go on alone. Without me!'

'No, Roz! I can't.'

'You must, Mike! And you will! You alone can save Nick Steen and Stalkford now. You alone can drop down into that corridor below you on your side of the half-room of Dr Valesco's former office and head towards the elevator shaft we used earlier, press the button for the basement floor and then make your way on to Ward Nine. You alone can find Nick, and bring him back from the jaws of Hell. If that's where he currently is!'

'Thinking about it, Roz, if you do get sucked down into Hell on your side, then we might still be able to hook up again when I get there, too.'

'I don't think so, Mike. Because if I get sucked down into Hell via this latest incarnation of the Randyman, I very much doubt it'll allow you and I to hook up in any way at all. In fact, I think it'd destroy us both before it would let any kind of hooking up happen!'

'Then this is the end, Roz,' Mike cried from above. 'The end of everything!'

'Yes, Mike!' Roz was fighting back tears. 'Unless you can think of anything else? But as far as I'm concerned, I must confess I'm pretty much stumped for an alternative!'

There was a sudden pause as the giant tilting motion of the room appeared to reach its apex, then a terrifying industrial squelching sound erupted as Roz felt the floor below her slowly contract, as if tugged from below amid the maelstrom of some giant cosmic vacuum. Death was nigh then, Roz figured. The Randyman was about to yank Roz's world to Hell with that mountainous plunger.

'I can't let it happen, Roz,' cried Mike, from somewhere above her. 'Not on my watch. And with you dead, what's the difference anyway?'

'What the hell are you drivelling about, Mike?' Roz bellowed, preparing herself for the final, dizzying descent.

'I'm saying that I'm going to rid us of this darned dream–demon once and for all, Roz. I'm going to find Nick Steen in Ward Nine on the basement level below me . . .'

'Yes, Mike?' answered Roz, feeling her stomach suddenly start to lurch as the ground below her began to shift. 'And what then?'

'Then, Roz, I'm going to kill him!'

'No!' shrieked Roz as the floor under her shot downward with one final tug of the Randyman's plunger. For a moment she was airborne, entirely weightless against the sheer force of her half-room's downward trajectory. Then she was shooting down again, so fast that the glimpse of Mike she caught as she descended began almost immediately to recede, one hand clutched uselessly over the edge of the precipice as Roz flew immeasurable distances below him.

'Don't . . . kill . . . Nick!' she yelled as she descended at speed into the depths of an unknown abyss, but if Mike Crisis heard a single word of Roz's frantic plea, she would never know.

For she was plunging ever downward, now consumed by the pull of the Randyman's contracting plunger. She heard the burst of exploding masonry as the floor she was crouched upon plummeted downward through multiple levels of concrete flooring.

In desperation, realising that in mere seconds she might be obliterated as the falling half-office slammed into whatever lay below it, Roz yanked open the drawer of the open filing cabinet she'd previously been rifling through, and frantically climbed inside. Luckily, once she was ensconced within it, the sliding drawer held fast against the side of the wall it was rammed against, cushioning Roz within like a mouse in a matchbox, until, finally, but inevitably, the collapsing half-room struck its final obstacle.

There was an almighty splash, and Roz sensed the cabinet she was cocooned within sink suddenly into a soft and pliant surface. Then the drawer eased forward on its sliders, released by the sudden disappearance of a neighbouring wall. As the filing cabinet opened, letting in a flood of water, Roz suddenly panicked, more from seeing a

332

floating wad of tissue paper entering the interior of her protective space than any fear of imminent drowning. Realising it was time to move, Roz kicked herself outwards, freeing her body from the protective metal life-buoy.

Then she was swimming upward, through a pool of what she hoped wasn't wastewater, but suspected probably was, kicking her legs desperately against the soft, vaguely nauseating touch of unidentified matter, until at last she broke through the surface.

And found herself inside a long, dark tunnel.

Oh, God, she thought. Am I in stuck in a sewer? Have I somehow found myself falling into Nulltec's wastewater system by mistake? Will I ever get clean now?

She looked around. As far as she could see, there was no trace of the remains of Dr Valesco's office, unless what was left of it had sunk far below her, into those murky depths from which she'd just emerged. Glancing above her head, Roz was shocked to see that there was no evidence at all of any gap or hole in the ceiling. No evidence that she'd recently plunged through it from somewhere far above. Then how had she got here? And the tunnel floor below her. That ocean of overfill. Why, it was nothing now but a small stream. Roz could even stand up in it now, the water level barely covering her two feet.

She looked ahead and saw that the tunnel led toward what seemed to her to be a distant room, lit from within by a row of cold overhead strip lights. The constant echoes of dripping water from the tunnel ceiling masked the sound at first, but soon Roz's ears managed to pick out a noise coming from inside it.

As Roz strained to hear against a sudden cacophony of flushing pipes, she finally distinguished what sounded to her like a low, Sid James-style cackle, echoing along the tunnel in front of her.

'Hey, Roz,' said the voice of the Randyman, piping through the tunnel from the room ahead. 'So you found my place, after all?'

Before she could turn and run the other way, a sudden flood of rushing water below Roz's feet swept her up in its current and sent her sailing helplessly along the tunnel floor towards the Randyman's house.

And whatever was waiting for her inside.*

---

* I.e., the Randyman. GM

CHAPTER EIGHT

'Flushed'

Roz tried in vain to brace herself as she rushed at speed along the tunnel. She suspected from the occasional glimpse of mismatched check and backwater valves that it was in fact a water pipe she was being funnelled along, one that had recently been re-plumbed from an outlet into an inlet duct; an uncanny mirroring of the way in which Randy Streak had died, she considered grimly, as she rushed headlong within the heavy torrent.

God alone knew what awaited her in the room she was currently speeding toward, but one thing was certain. Roz was now part of that murderous septic flow that had once blasted backward into Randy Streak's workplace, filling the entirety of his lonely khazi block with back-borne spew, drowning the doomed maintenance man in an unholy silt before the sheer pressure of his overflowing cubicle-house caused the roof of the entire toilet block to explode upwards into the air, showering Dankton in a towering torrent of recirculated wastewater.

Before Roz could take in the sheer enormity of that terrifying thought, she was at the mouth of the pipe and bursting into the room amid a flood of frothing chemical spume.

As she came to a halt on the tiled floor, Roz looked around her, half-expecting the Randyman to be waiting right there. But she was alone inside a room that looked very much to her like a ladies' toilet, only one that was hideously befouled.

Myriad unknown stains marked each wall, and graffiti was scrawled across every available space. Roz didn't have to read the words to know what messages these contained. The illustrations themselves did that. She nudged open one of the cubicles and reeled backwards from the sight within. An unflushed toilet, full to the brim, and alongside it, something far, far worse. What had once, many years ago, started its life as a toilet brush, now resembled something closer to a medieval mace, spiked with poisons so foul it might have been employed as a rudimentary siege weapon.

Roz stood up and made her way over to one of the hand-blowers in an attempt to dry herself off. She punched the button but nothing happened. She tried the next blower along. It appeared to work at first, until Roz realised in horror that the air was perpetually cold, and would be almost entirely useless as a drying device.

She then turned toward what she assumed were some adjacent sinks, fear mounting within as she moved ever closer to the three oval white basins hanging vertically against one wall. Inside each was a small plughole, yet all three were clogged with what looked to Roz like an unholy thatch of unidentifiable matter. A mixture of human hair and Wrigley's gum, alongside what claimed on its brightly coloured plastic surface to be some sort of device for preventing congestion, but which had somehow slid vertically to one side of the pan, so that it was singularly failing to come into any contact at all with the plughole it was meant to be covering.

God, thought Roz, in sudden recognition. So *this* was a urinal. And from the foul state of the floors and walls, and the sharp, acrid stench of urine that seemed to be emanating from almost every conceivable space (bar the toilets specifically installed to contain it), Roz knew that the place she'd been thrust into against her will was not a ladies' toilet at all, but a *public gents'*.

She'd known they existed, of course. But she'd never known, nor once suspected, that they'd be *this* bad.

And the situation, she realised as she shrank back from the soapless dispensers and foully flecked mirrors, was only getting worse. Because the very water upon which Roz had shot into the room was still flowing inward from that hole in the wall, covering the floor now in several inches of fluid. And rapidly *rising* . . .

I'm going to drown in here, thought Roz. I'm going to drown like Randy Streak drowned. In an ocean of re-flushed waste.

Suddenly a cruel Sid James, Wilfrid Brambell and Stacey Solomon-like laugh sounded through the room. It was coming from another pipe, up by the ceiling – from which, Roz now saw, yet more waste-water was flooding in!

Or had it come from this other one? Roz wondered, noticing there was now a third pipe jutting from the wall. And now a fourth . . . And a fifth!

'Jesus!' cried Roz, aloud. 'There are loads of pipes!'

'Say hi to my pipe organ, Roz!' snarled the voice of the Randyman, its large eye staring in again at Roz through one of the holes. 'Wanna play?'

'Let me out of here, Randy,' said Roz, affecting anger, though in reality she felt like she might need to make an emergency trip to one of the cubicles as a matter of urgency, if there was a single one left that wasn't overflowing. 'I've been good to you,' she continued. 'I gave you a sympathetic back story when no one else at Clackett cared one way or the other, least of all Nick himself.'

'Then *you* killed me, Roz,' roared the Randyman. '*You* drowned me in wastewater.'

'That's technically true, but I'm also the reason the reading public lapped you up, Randy, pardon the pun. I'm the reason you went on to star in a further sixteen sequels.'

Suddenly the rushing water pumping through the numerous wall pipes stopped. There was a strange silence, interrupted only by the echo of constant dripping.

'I'm your best friend, you see?' said Roz, her voice bouncing off the befouled floor tiles. 'In fact, I'm your only friend. My editorial recommendations alone gave you life.'

She waited for a reply, but received no answer. She looked up and saw that the Randyman's eye had vanished from the hole above her through which the dream-demon had been staring at her. Unsure what was happening, Roz waded across the floor toward one of the other holes, wondering if the Randyman had changed position.

But this hole, like the other hole, was completely black.

'Hello?' she called through the dark, festering pipe. 'Randy Streak?'

Again, nothing but silence and the slow, persistent drip of various pipe inlets.

Then a deep reverberation pounded Roz's ears as the walls and floor under her shook like the initial tremors of some devastating earthquake headed her way.

The water under her feet began to lap to and fro, then Roz lurched sideways, her body upended by some invisible force she could sense but not yet define. A row of bricks in the wall behind her crumbled backward in a sudden spray of dust. Concrete crumbled from the collapsing partitions as Roz suddenly realised what was happening. Randy Streak's eye had vanished from the hole, alright, but the blackness in its place was anything but the darkness of an internal pipe wall.

No, the blackness was that vast, sucking wall of vulcanised rubber again.

'Not more!' shouted Roz. The retreating bricks bulged suddenly forwards from the wall in a shower of exploding dust as the immense vacuumed pressure of the Randyman's giant plunger gave way to the dream-demon's powerful forward thrust.

Roz flew across the room as the side of the toilet block caved in beneath a tidal wave of unholy wastewater.

For one terrifying moment, Roz was completely submerged. Grimly, she held her breath, terrified that she might never rise to the surface again; that, as a result of that foolish slice of editorial advice she was now living, nay dying, to regret, she was about to die the same hideously cruel death as Randy Streak, drowning in an unholy tide of regurgitated waste . . .

As Roz flailed wildly in the murky depths of whatever the collective residents of Dankton had last physically expelled, she prepared to meet her maker. Ironically, this was precisely what the Randyman was doing too, in that Roz was technically *its* maker, but she didn't think it would get the joke, so elected to let it pass.

Unable to hold her breath for a second more, Roz struck for a surface she knew could not be there, and did her level best to die before her brain's survival instincts finally forced her mouth open.

But her brain refused to play ball.

As her jaws finally parted and a surge of unholy water prepared to flush itself through her system, Roz's mouth instead took in a lungful of air.

She gasped, sucking in glorious oxygen as the water level subsided rapidly about her.

She opened her eyes and saw that the wall against which the Randyman had forced its plunger had now completely collapsed inward.

The escaping waste, Roz noticed, was flowing away in small streams through the broken bricks, passing in muddy rivulets toward a distant field of sodden grass.

Roz looked up at the tower blocks looming over the area of neglected parkland she was now facing. A red, moody sun hung low on the horizon, slowly giving way to a heavy bank of grey clouds moving in from the east.

She was in Dankton again.

The Phantascape had almost swamped reality entirely, then. And now it looked like she was going to be trapped in this place forever. But as she rose groggily to her feet, a hand clasped her shoulder gently from behind.

'Live with me, Roz,' whispered the Randyman in her ear. 'Together, we can plunge our way down to Hell . . .'

She sensed the Randyman's plunger at her shoulder, pointing forward at the field before them, where a great fissure had opened up suddenly in the ground.

Into it, slowly at first, yet gradually gathering pace, fell everything around her: the bricks of the toilet block, the park benches, the trees. Even the tower blocks began to topple and sway in the distance, bending toward her, all of it flowing with the released water down into that deep chasm before Roz's eyes, rushing downward in a cascading waterfall of gathered shit, right down into the very bowels of Hell.

'Is that where Nick is?' Roz asked, thinking aloud. She didn't really expect an answer, but if Nick *was* in Hell, she might yet stand a chance of saving him – or failing that, at least she'd have some company while flailing for eternity inside a flushed torrent of backed-up waste-matter.

'Nick Steen is dead,' whispered the Randyman. 'Mike Crisis just shot him.'

'No!' said Roz. 'He can't be. I mean, if Nick's dead, surely you'll be dead, too?'

'Is that what Mike Crisis told you?'

Roz thought for a moment. It was indeed what Mike Crisis had told her.

'That guy's full of shit. I don't need Nick Steen to survive, lady. I've already sucked up his soul. I'm your world now, Roz. The Phantascape is here for ever. This is reality. Nick Steen is dead, and it's just you and me, baby.' The Randyman clasped her shoulders with both hands. 'You and me, Roz, old girl. Forever . . .'

She felt herself gliding forward, toward the great crack in the surface of the earth, which would plunge her down, down, ever downward, into the kingdom of eternal damnation. She'd failed. Nick was dead. Mike Crisis had killed him, after all. Whom should she blame now? Mike, for turning a colossal crisis into a gargantuan crisis? Nick, for creating this entire disaster by sleeping with a cursed typewriter and dreaming up something as foul and morally objectionable as the Randyman? Nulltec, perhaps, for continually operating without a moral or ethical code? Or maybe herself, for being so preoccupied with slingbacks and sales reports that she hadn't seen this particular dilemma coming? For giving this most odious of dream-demons a reason to seek out supernatural vengeance against a cruel and unforgiving world?

Maybe all of us are to blame, Roz figured. Maybe there had never been any path open to Mankind other than slipping down to Hell in a flood of its own piss and shit. Then, without warning, she felt the pressure on her shoulders suddenly lift.

At the same time, she heard an unholy shrieking close behind her. Then that shriek was itself joined by another shriek, and Roz realised she would have to turn round fully in order to discover what the hell was going on.

And something was definitely happening, because she was no longer heading toward that sprawling fissure in the ground.

Bracing herself, Roz turned round.

And found herself staring into the face of Barbara Nullman. But not the Barbara Nullman Roz knew. For this Barbara Nullman had the lower body of a giant salamander, its reptilian skin entirely black, save for a generous peppering of foul, yellow spots.

Somehow, Nullman, and her dreaded Nobel Prize-winning

extracted R-Complex,* had entered the nightmare world of Randy Streak.

And whatever this foul thing that Nullman had turned into was, it was currently battling with a network of extending pipework that was slowly wrapping itself around her newly-metamorphosed body.

Roz caught sight of a brown trilby and the hint of a stained mackintosh among the web of plumbing surrounding her, and realised that the Randyman and the Nullman salamander demon were in the thick of some terrible fight to the death.

'It's time for you to die, Randy Streak,' hissed Nullman, confirming Roz's previous suspicion.

'Who let *you* into my domain?' countered the Randyman, doing its best to encase the Chief Head of the Nulltec Corporation in an intricate network of sprawling dip tubes and self-connecting branch vents.

Behind the warring beasts, Roz caught sight of the public convenience once serviced by Randy Streak that she'd so recently burst out of. To her surprise, it no longer resembled the public convenience once serviced by Randy Streak at all. Instead, it now looked like a medical laboratory of some kind, and Roz had the uncanny feeling that she was caught between two opposing dream-worlds, one ruled by the terrifying dream-demon Randy Streak, and the other ruled by yet another terrifying dream-demon formed from the body of Barbara Nullman and that of the human brain's dreaded R-Complex, Mankind's deep-rooted reptilian instinct also known as the basal ganglia or basal nuclei, containing the brain stem, limbic region and the amygdala, housed deep inside the human brain – which Roz knew from her studies of Nick's previous visions assumed the form of the arse-end of a salamander.

---

* Which took the form of a black and yellow-spotted salamander's tail. Again, see *Portentum* in this very book. The first one. *The first story.* GM

But how was all this possible? Was the world now formed entirely from an overflowing Phantascape? Did reality no longer exist at all? Had Nulltec's dangerous dream experiment resulted in a complete and total breakdown of rationality and logic, engulfing the entire globe in a terrifying storm of imaginary monsters culled from the world of ultimate nightmare? One far worse than those denizens of the unconscious mind previously unleashed into reality by the hole to another dimension currently housed inside Nick Steen's own brain?

It certainly looked that way, thought Roz.

But whatever the reality was right now – and who knew what it might be in another minute's time – Roz knew she had to escape the violent clashing of these horrifying demons in front of her. Behind her lay Dankton and that hole into Hell, which she knew would be her permanent home if the Nullman Demon lost this titanic struggle.

Yet if somehow the Randyman were to fail instead, then Nullman would no doubt move on to Roz next. Roz had to run while she still could, and find some way back into the corridors of Nulltec – if those corridors were even real anymore. She had to find out what Nullman's plans really were regarding the Phantascape project, and the terrible grip it now held on what had formerly been known as reality.

As the beasts before her thrashed and roared, Roz got down on her knees, preparing to crawl past them if possible, hoping to reach a door she could see had appeared in the wall opposite, from the part of reality now controlled by the Nullman Demon.

But it was impossible, she realised. No way could she get past those roaring Hell-beasts without being crushed, stomped or eaten. No way could she flee through the contested ground of these warring colossi.

Then she heard the voice of the Randyman, whispering, deep inside her head.

'A gift, Roz. Another gift, for you . . .'

And suddenly the door in question was beside her.

The Randyman had saved her, Roz realised. Gifted her a convenient door. Perhaps this was merely an ostentatious demonstration of its power; an audacious display of the control it was determined to wield over this newly contested Phantascape, but the Randyman had granted Roz the path to freedom. Calmly, she waited for both demons to lunge at each other again; then, satisfied that they were sufficiently distracted, she yanked open the door and ran through.

Forgetting to close it behind her . . .

CHAPTER NINE

'Lucidrix'

Roz turned back, remembering that she'd forgotten to close the door behind her, and rectified her mistake.*

Ahead of her lay a long corridor, which once more resembled the interior halls of Nulltec. Roz knew her immediate surroundings might change form again at any moment, however, depending on which of the demons behind her eventually emerged triumphant.

Deciding she must find the elevator shaft again as quickly as possible, Roz sprinted along the path ahead, reached a crossroads, then turned right down another corridor. She followed a sign marked 'Lift' and located the elevator shaft at the far end. She began to feel calmer again, seeing that the door of the lift was metallic in structure, like those she'd been used to before they'd started becoming slimy and grease-slicked in appearance.

She slipped inside, waiting for the elevator doors to shut behind her, then froze in sudden terror. Instead of the button panel on the wall beside her, the lift's mechanism seemed to be controlled by a chain-flush dangling at shoulder-height. Roz felt a splash of water

---

* This may seem anti-climactic given the ominous tone of the previous chapter ending, but it is essential that you, the reader, keep turning the page. GM

on her head and realised fluid was dripping from the elevator's ceiling above her.

So Randy Streak's influence was still at large, then. His nightmarish world was still affecting reality on Nullman's side of the Phantascape. Evidently the two were still fighting it out.

Roz looked up and noticed that the maintenance panel in the top of the lift was open, through which water was leaking. Beyond the gap, she could see the interior of the main elevator shaft. It stretched upward for what looked like miles, and what she'd assumed might resemble a hollow cuboid leading up and down toward consecutive floors instead looked like the internal fittings of an industrial water pipe. She heard a noise directly above her, and caught sight of someone's leg moving on the roof of the lift.

There was a person up there.

Probably a maintenance operator, Roz guessed, hearing the sound of clanking tools and someone doing repairs. She was about to call out for them to hurry things up so that she could descend urgently to the basement level, when she glimpsed the foot in the gap again and realised it wasn't a foot at all.

Those small circles of light she'd glimpsed in the darkness above her weren't the studded glint of hobnails on a worker's boot. She could see, as they slowly descended into the lift itself via the open hatch, that they were instead yellow spots. Yellow spots on a smooth, black surface. As the thing lowered itself further into the shaft, dangling in front of her like a baited worm, Roz realised they were the markings of a salamander's tail.

She screamed as the thing darted right, angling itself toward the hanging flush handle. She watched as the tail curled round the chain like a snake, and yanked downward.

All of a sudden, Roz heard the loud whooshing of a triggered flush as a wave of water plunged down from above, straight through the gap in the roof above and into the lift.

So the dream-demons were ganging up on her, were they? Taking a wee break from hostilities to join forces against her? Maybe that meant they both knew Roz was a potential threat.

That gave her renewed courage, at least. And she'd need it, as all at once the elevator began to drop with the downward torrent of water, falling for what felt like an eternity. Roz's stomach turned as she bore the full brunt of the deadly plunge, realising this is what it must be like to be flung, against one's will, over the top of Niagara Falls or a similar massive waterfall,* until finally the lift juddered to a sudden, violent halt.

But water was still pumping in through the hole in the hatch above her, and as Roz struggled for breath amid the never-ending torrent of water, she caught sight of the salamander's tail still reaching in from the roof above, moving now from the pulled flush chain towards the interior of the lift itself, curling downward towards where Roz now floated, submerged and struggling for air.

She was in what now to all intents and purposes resembled a cramped shark cage, yet the beast itself was inside the cage with Roz (said beast being in this case a giant salamander's tail, as opposed to a murderous great white). As she fought to avoid the demon's darting tail, Roz could have kicked herself. Why hadn't she remembered to bring her lady's handbag with her during her search for Nick? For as long as she could remember, she'd always carried a snorkel and diving mask with her in case of an emergency just like this one. And yet like a fool, today of all days, she'd left everything in the lab beside her bed when she'd entered the Phantascape.

Perhaps the Randyman might will it into being, like it had willed that convenient door through which Roz had escaped. But she couldn't afford to wait and find out. The Randyman might have

---

* She'd actually felt this before, during her previous deadly plunge, but the effect was heightened now. GM

ceased granting any more gifts. Might even have lost its titanic struggle with the Nullman Demon. No, Roz had to think on her feet (technically off her feet, as she was floating), and she had to do it fast. She whirled around in the submerged elevator car, kicking outward with her heels, trying her best to avoid the slithering tail as it curled and slid from one side of the lift to the other. Seeking her, sensing her, hunting her. *Attempting to locate her.*

How long could Roz last, she wondered. Fortunately, she'd grown up in a Cornish pearl-diving community, so could hold her breath for almost sixty seconds,[*] yet thirty-seven seconds of those had already passed, meaning she had only twenty-three seconds' worth of withheld oxygen left to spare. Twenty-two if she counted down from now. Or twenty-one from now. Horrified that she only had twenty seconds' worth of withheld oxygen left – nineteen now, and now eighteen, in fact sixteen by the time she'd finished thinking this part of the imagined sentence in her head (possibly fifteen or even fourteen by now) – Roz realised that time was fast running out.

Then she felt herself being squeezed. In horror, she sensed something wrapping itself around her body, cutting off her vitals and reducing her ability to withhold her breath even further, meaning that she probably now only had around five seconds of withheld oxygen left before she absolutely needed to breathe in air again.

But there was little chance of that happening. Even if she no longer had the problem of water to contend with,[†] the sheer weight of the salamander's tail crushing her, dragging her across the floor of the elevator car and bashing her against the walls in an effort to stun

---

[*] This ability had helped her before when she'd almost drowned while being submerged in a previous chapter. I didn't bother to say that then, because the chapter in question was working perfectly without it. GM

[†] Admittedly, it's not fetid water like the liquid she'd been drowning in in that previous chapter, but there is additional risk to her safety in the current scene, which distinguishes it sufficiently from the first. Both scenes, I will add, are overflowing with intrinsic literary merit. GM

her into unconsciousness, would mean that she couldn't take in a breath of oxygen anyway.

Again, she kicked herself for forgetting her lady's handbag, from which she might have drawn something sharp like a spare stiletto heel with which to cut feverishly away at the demon's tough, reptilian skin. But, like I say, she'd left that in the lab of Mike Crisis.

As Roz looked up at the surface of the water overhead, gaining one last tantalising glimpse of the open vent in the roof above, where precious air might yet exist, she knew that her time was up, and prepared herself to die. With that knowledge came a strange, eerie sense of déjà vu, as if she had somehow been here before.[*] Then, she recalled that she had indeed been in a similar situation to this before, and decided to stop worrying so much about the déjà vu element.

All at once, the pressure on Roz's body lifted and she felt the salamander tail loosening around her. At that exact moment, the level of the water inside the lift also began to drop. As the fluid sank lower, past Roz's face, she gasped loudly, drawing in a deep lungful of oxygen. She could see now that the lift door had opened up on the basement level, releasing the water out on to the floor beyond.

Roz glanced up at the ceiling of the lift and saw the dangling tail of the salamander reaching over once again for the chain pull. Realising she had mere seconds left before the lift once again began to fall, Roz forced herself up from the lift floor and lunged through the open door into the corridor outside, just as the salamander's tail yanked the chain a second time. Roz listened for a moment to the lift plunging even further downward amid a rush of cascading water, down into the undiscovered depths of some unknown subterranean dream-world.

Well, Roz reflected. The minor lift-based crisis she and Mike had

---

[*] See previous note. This detail is wholly intentional and not a 'quick fix'. GM

encountered earlier had certainly turned into a major one in that near future they'd both feared.

As if in answer to her thoughts, she heard a familiar-sounding voice call out from behind.

'Roz!'

She whipped round to see Mike Crisis emerging from a nearby room. 'Mike!'

'Thank goodness you're here, Roz. I've found Nick.'

'I know,' said Roz, immediately becoming moody. 'And I know exactly what you've done to him, too.'

'Do you, Roz?'

'Yes, Mike. You've killed him, haven't you? The Randyman told me all about it. You've killed Nick Steen and now we don't stand a chance in hell of reversing the flow of the Phantascape.'

'I didn't kill Nick, Roz. Well, okay, I tried, I'll admit, but my gun kept jamming.'

'You tried to shoot him with that rusty gun?'

'So what if I did? It doesn't matter, anyway, because it seems that even in my own dreams I'm unable to avert a crisis. There I was, with all the means at my disposal for solving a major crisis once and for all, and instead I've simply gone and prolonged the crisis. Nick Steen's still alive and so is the Randyman, and the dream-demon's getting stronger all the time.'

'Except that it's not, Mike,' said Roz, getting to her feet at last without Mike offering any help. 'I've just left Randy Streak battling with a similarly terrifying dream-demon partly formed from the body of Barbara Nullman. And when I last looked, it looked like she was holding the upper hand.'

'Nullman? In the Phantascape?' Mike was having difficulty processing Roz's words. 'Then that explains it.'

'Explains what?' asked Roz.

Mike's features set into what one could have described as a

'determined' look, but which Roz instead chose to interpret as a 'misguided' one.

'Come with me, Roz,' he said, 'and I'll show you.'

He led her along the basement corridor, which was green in colour, unlike the sterile white environment of Nulltec's upper corridors, and through a door marked 'Ward 9'.

'Through here is Valesco's second office,' whispered Mike as he and Roz moved into a lengthy-looking outer laboratory. Various specimen jars lined each wall, some containing items Roz chose to look away from, then looked back at because she couldn't contain her own twisted curiosity. Things like five-tailed gerbils, bat-babies, floating eyes on stalks (some wearing spectacles), nerve-people (mainly eyes again, but attached to a 'body' consisting only of float-ing nerves) and the customary tank of mutated offspring labelled 'Potential Circus Act'.

Mike led her round these, through a door on the far wall and into a second laboratory. Here he turned to face her, placing one finger over his lips.

'You need to be really quiet now,' he said, loudly.

'*Shhh*!' said Roz, hushing him.

Mike screwed both eyes shut in embarrassment and slapped his own forehead. 'God, so sorry,' he whispered.

'Where are we?' Roz mouthed.

'We're outside Dr Valesco's second office.' Mike pointed to another door in the wall behind them. Adjacent to it was a horizontal pane of glass, lit from within by a pink tinge, clashing eerily with the sickly pale green of the laboratory's intended colour scheme.

'That's another observation room,' Mike said, pointing to the distant glass. 'Valesco's second office opens into it from within. He's at work in that second office at the moment, but have a look at what's in there.'

Mike got down on his knees and ushered Roz to follow him.

Together, they crawled over to the glass pane and raised their heads over the edge of the ledge. In the room beyond, with their heads wired up to the usual banks of monitoring equipment, lay the sleeping bodies of Nick Steen (still fully erect) and Barbara Nullman.

'Nullman's wired into the Phantascape, too?' asked Roz.

'You said so yourself, Roz. Dr Valesco's wired her in. This is where they moved Nick to. I guess so that we wouldn't be able to find him and wake him up before Nullman had a chance to put her own nefarious plan into action.'

'Her own nefarious plan?'

Mike ducked his head downward, indicating to Roz that she should do the same. He shuffled himself along the wall toward the door leading directly into Valesco's second office. Roz followed. Drawing up outside the door of Valesco's second office, Mike turned back to face her.

'I snooped in there earlier while Valesco was attending to Nullman,' he said. 'And saw these on his desk.'

He extracted a small object from his lab coat pocket and handed it to Roz. It was a bottle of tablets.

'Sleeping pills,' Roz said, sighing. 'Presumably so that both Nullman and Nick will sleep when required to. Hardly a great revelation, Mike.'

He shook his head, smiling at her, then turned the bottle round. 'You didn't read the label, Roz.'

She scrutinised the medical name but didn't recognise it. Maybe they were stronger tablets than the ones she'd been taking.

'What are they?' she asked.

'You won't find them in any conventional medicine catalogue, Roz. Let's just say that.'

'Why?'

'Because these are new pills, Roz. Secret pills. Invented by Dr Valesco, here in his lab. These are Lucidrix pills.'

352

'Lucidrix?'

'Pills which allow you to dream lucidly. Lucid dreaming, Roz, is the ability to control your dreams while you're dreaming.'

'I know what lucid dreaming is, Mike. That feeling when you're suddenly aware you're inside a dream and, in that very moment of revelation, are able to control the dream. But surely that's a myth?'

'Not anymore, Roz. Nulltec have developed a pill that will allow you to control any dream you have. Right now, I imagine Nullman is controlling hers.'

'Of course,' said Roz. 'That's why she's appearing inside the Phantascape.' Then a terrifying thought struck her. 'Oh, God,' she said, clutching Mike's arm. 'It's even worse than we feared, Mike.'

'Even worse than we feared? I don't know, Roz. I'm pretty fearful, to be honest.'

'Worse than you could ever imagine, Mike. Because if what I think is on Nullman's mind is, in fact, on Nullman's mind, we could now be facing a danger far more evil and destructive than even the Randyman itself.'

But before she could explain what that was, the lock to Dr Valesco's office snapped loudly in their ears and the door behind them flew open.

CHAPTER TEN

'The Pink Death'

'I'll take those, young lady,' said Valesco, holding out his hand for the bottle of pills. In his other hand, the doctor held a strange-looking gun. The barrel, aimed at Roz's chest, consisted of a medical syringe, the interior of which glowed with an unspecified pink liquid.

Roz maintained her grip on the bottle.

'Hand them back to him, Roz,' said Mike. 'I don't know what that pink liquid is inside that syringe pistol he's holding, but I doubt it's raspberry flavoured.'

Roz nodded, sensing that for once in his life, Mike had spoken a degree of sense. She handed the bottle of Lucidrix back to Dr Valesco.

'It's my fault,' said Mike, bitterly. 'I should never have made us stop directly outside the door of Dr Valesco's second office for a strategic chat. We should have discussed things by the neighbouring observation window instead, where he would have been slightly less likely to hear us. Good old Mike Crisis does it again.'

'It was indeed a stupid idea, Dr Crisis,' said Valesco, ushering Mike and Roz through the open door, into his own lab. 'Nevertheless, I've been watching you for some time. I deliberately let you steal these pills, knowing full well you'd only return here once you'd located Miss Bloom, so desperate were you to impress her with anything remotely approaching an act of competence. But you were captured on my closed-circuit television monitors the moment you broke into my first office upstairs. Of all the stupid ideas.' He grinned, ushering Mike and Roz further into his private laboratory.

'But then you're full of stupid ideas, Dr Crisis,' he continued. 'Like reading a novel about a dream-demon aloud to an author whose mind currently houses a portal to another dimension, and who was at that very moment simultaneously wired into an experimental dreamscape project connecting the minds of others inside a shared psychic reality. That was particularly stupid.'

He ushered Roz and Mike at syringe point still further into his second office, which, like every other room in Nulltec, was adorned with complex scientific equipment and an endless array of technical gadgetry. They moved past the door, which Roz realised must lead to the observation area where both Nullman and Nick were sleeping, and found themselves standing at last against the far wall.

'You let him do it, though, didn't you, Dr Valesco?' said Roz. 'If you and Nullman knew the Phantascape project was so dangerous, why didn't you terminate the entire programme when we spoke to you about the Randyman's escape? No, you had other plans, didn't you? Other plans which involved Dr Nullman entering the Phantascape herself under the influence of those experimental lucid-dreaming pills we stole and then handed back to you. Pills that allow the swallower to control their dreams, and, now that the Phantascape has entered reality itself, reality itself.'

'Those pills,' said Valesco, 'are going to win Dr Nullman another Nobel Prize.'

'Nullman, or you?' asked Roz, hoping she might be able to stir up some competition between the two scientists, as Nick had done previously in an imaginary confrontation between the two.*

'On the contrary, Miss Bloom. Dr Nullman and I will be presenting Lucidrix to the world scientific conference together. So there's no hope of you dividing and conquering us on that front. I supervise the experiment here at Nulltec, while Dr Nullman operates her side of the project "from the beyond". One day soon, with proper funding in place, we will establish an overseas facility in the beyond the beyond. But for now we are operating in perfect sync, largely via walkie-talkie.'

'That's not the plan and you know it,' said Roz, fighting to pin down the slippery scientist. 'Nullman's making changes to the Phantascape already, thanks to these ruddy Lucidrix pills of yours.'

'She's in the process of killing the Randyman,' said Valesco. 'Ridding the world of a terrible supernatural threat. Something which neither you, nor Dr Crisis, have been able to do, I might add.'

'Is she?' Roz countered. 'I can't help but recall you and her deliberately intending to free the Randyman from Nick's unconscious mind by leaving that copy of Nick's novel in the locker of Mike Crisis.'

'There is that,' said Valesco.

'Because she *wanted* the Randyman to escape, didn't she? That's why she enlisted me for the Phantascape project in the first place. It wasn't to block up a hole in Nick's mind by negotiating with some damned labourers he was refusing to pay. That was a blatant lie. No, she needed the Randyman to follow someone from the world of dream *back into reality*. Needed the dream-world of the Phantascape to bleed out into reality itself. And Nullman knew all along that the best way to make that happen was by putting me in there. Sending

---

* Again, see Tome 1 of this book if you really can't remember crucial details that other ordinary readers have no trouble whatsoever in recalling. Go sort your attention span. I bet you're in your twenties, right? Then buck up. GM

in Roz Bloom, the person who'd given Randy Streak a sympathetic back story, and so the victim he'd be most likely to follow back into the real world.

'And it worked, dammit. Now the Randyman's at loose in a waking nightmare which Nullman's now in full control of, owing to those darned Lucidrix pills. And once she's destroyed the Randyman, whom she no longer has any need of, she'll be in full charge of reality. She'll be unstoppable, Valesco. The worst dictator this world's ever seen. Able to bend reality itself to her will. And that's bang out of order. Plus, if you'll permit me speaking out of turn here, borderline unethical.'

'Since when has Nulltec cared about ethics?' said Valesco, raising the syringe gun toward Roz's head.

Then he opened fire.

As the pink tube shot forth from the doctor's barrel, the entire world slowed in Roz's mind.

Then she realised this wasn't because she was so close to death, but because everything was indeed now operating in slow motion. As she waited anxiously for the harsh, penetrating jab of whatever lay inside that deadly flying needle, something began to cross the gap between her and the propelled syringe. Something large in shape, and bright white in hue.

A flapping lab coat.

Roz could hardly believe it, but Mike Crisis was propelling himself at a snail's pace between her and the approaching needle, moving at an uncannily slow speed. She watched Mike's jaws slowly parting, releasing as they did so a spray of expelled saliva, while his front teeth clamped down by degrees on slowly quivering lips as he screamed to her in long, protracted syllables:

'RRRUUUNNNN RRRROOOOZZZZ, RRRUUUUUNNNN!!!'

Roz watched, helplessly, as the propelled needle embedded itself into Mike's arm instead, his body continuing to pass through the air at the speed of a yawning sloth, before finally crashing, almost an hour later, into a nearby desk crammed with steaming potion bottles.

These phials then exploded glacially in an arc of slowly shattering glass as Mike's body eventually slammed against the laboratory furniture and rebounded by degrees off the wall, gliding back in the opposite direction, toward Roz.

'OOOOUUUCCCHHHH!' Mike cried in a distorted, low-pitched howl as he passed Roz again about three minutes later, spiralling between her and the flabbergast-faced Valesco at the speed of a juddering mobility scooter, arms flailing around him like someone's hair in a shampoo advert.

Then, as suddenly as it had commenced, normal motion resumed. Roz screamed as Mike hit the deck with a crumpling thud, grabbing immediately at his injured arm, from which Valesco's syringe was still protruding. The whole of Mike's arm was glowing a bright pink, Roz saw. Whatever he'd absorbed in Roz's stead had somehow caused his entire right half to shine with a phosphorescent neon-pink glow.

'You saved my life, Mike!' Roz cried, trying to make him feel better about his pink arm. 'How did you do that?'

'I just imagined myself flying forward in slow motion, Roz,' yelled Mike between gritted teeth. 'I guess because when I first picked up those pills, I thought they were sweets, and I must confess I licked the side of one of them to test its flavour, although I then rejected it as it was largely aniseed, which I hate. But that slight element of control I just had over the world of the Phantascape is no doubt a result of that tiny lick. But I imagine I've now used up almost all the control of the Phantascape I gained by licking the pill, hence the abrupt end of that slow-motion sequence just now – meaning, I presume, that there won't be any more. If only I could have stomached the taste of aniseed and swallowed the entire pill, I might even now be in control of events like Nullman, and effecting a solution to this ongoing crisis. But, in true Mike Crisis fashion, I've blown it again, somehow managing to absorb whatever poisonous material Valesco was keeping inside that syringe gun of his with no hope of controlling its effect. The only light in this particular tunnel, Roz, is that for once I'm happy to endure a spiralling personal crisis, if it means I've been able to reduce to some degree your own particular ongoing crisis.'

'Stop talking, Mike!' yelled Roz. 'Valesco's already reloading his syringe gun with that unspecified pink liquid, even as we speak!'

But she was too late. As Dr Valesco took aim at her again, Roz readied herself to receive the imminent jab of a second propelled pink syringe. Then Mike leapt suddenly from the floor, ignoring his pain, wielding his injured arm like a wooden club.

Which it now resembled. For the limb had grown exponentially in the last five seconds, swelling to gigantic proportions. As Mike's swollen elbow connected hard against Valesco's face, the thing exploded like a propelled water balloon, showering the front of Valesco's head and body in a wide burst of pink, glowing liquid. Rivulets of the scorching chemical smoked and hissed as they ran across Valesco's face, burning his cheeks like tossed acid.

'No!' screamed Valesco, clawing at his smoking skin. 'This stuff's absolutely lethal, you know!'

'What is it?' Mike yelled back, curiosity temporarily overcoming his raging bloodlust.

'It's an explosive acid,' cried Valesco, clutching at his disintegrating face. 'At first it burns through layers of the skin. Then, when it's penetrated down far enough, it reacts with the calcium in your bone marrow and explodes like a stick of dynamite.'

'Fascinating,' said Mike, throwing himself at Valesco again. They grappled desperately with each other, Mike somehow blind to the burning of the pink syringe fluid flowing through and from his own blasted stump. Meanwhile, Roz hovered uselessly, unsure what to do.

'Go and wake Nick, Roz!' cried Mike Crisis, pointing uselessly with his stump in the direction of the observation room opposite. 'We need all the help we can get if I'm to sort this particular crisis,' he said. 'In the meantime, I'll do my best to yank this bottle of pills from Dr Valesco's lab coat pocket before the pink exploding acid penetrates his bone matter and blasts both him, me, and the pills it is *essential we keep intact*, into kingdom come. Because without these pills, Roz, we have no hope of controlling the Phantascape and getting reality back to normal again.'

Yes! thought Roz, snapping out of her glazed stupor. I must indeed wake Nick! Nick Steen will know what to do. She ran through the laboratory toward the observation room door and pushed it open.

There he is, Roz thought, sighing deeply within. There he is, at long last. The man who'd been incarcerated here for months against his will. The man she could now hopefully free from his own living nightmare.

Nick Steen!

Then Roz glimpsed the other figure in repose directly beside him, and her body shuddered with an instinctive revulsion. For here lay the woman who'd consumed Steen's own mind, unleashed and then destroyed the dream–demon Randy Streak, all so that she alone could rule reality.

Dr Barbara Nullman.

Should Roz kill her first? It would be easy, after all. She could smother her right here with a pillow, and all would be well again, without the need for Mike to wrestle those Lucidrix pills back from the disintegrating Dr Valesco. The unimaginable horror of Nullman's plans for world domination, assuming she'd succeeded in destroying the Randyman, would be over in an instant.

But what guarantee did Roz have that Randy Streak had been defeated yet? The last she'd seen of her pursuing dream–demon, it had been involved in a titanic death struggle with the monstrous demonic form of a dream-altered Nullman. If Roz killed the real-life version of Nullman sleeping before her, and Randy Streak was still haunting reality, then Roz might be back to square one, with the Randyman once again in full control of the bleeding Phantascape and fully intent on taking Roz back with it into Hell.

No, it made sense to be cautious, she decided, as much as she'd like to rid the world straight away of this malicious medical missy. She should wake Nick first, and then together, they might have enough collective strength of will left to combat whatever beast won that ongoing battle of the dream-demons.

Yes, she decided. I must wake Nick first.

Roz reached inside her coat for the letter which contained the message from Nick's daughter, knowing full well that the words from his darling Georgina would immediately shake him from his near-permanent coma, and proceeded to withdraw it from her pocket.

But the letter never emerged.

'Hi, Roz,' snarled Nick, his eyes darting open.

Except those weren't Nick's eyes, Roz realised. Nick's eyes were cobalt blue. These were amber in hue.

The eyes of Dr Nullman!

'That's right, my pretty!' the doctor screamed as her head burst suddenly through Nick's own, squeezing itself through the author's torn and parted skin. Roz watched as razor-like teeth chomped down on shards of Nick's collapsing skull and the monster hiding within her favourite author slowly climbed out.

Gasping with revulsion, Roz laid eyes on the other sleeping form – the figure she'd previously assumed to be Nullman. It, too, had changed form. Now she saw that *this* was Nick. She realised in horror that if she'd gone along with her initial instinct to destroy what she'd believed to be Nullman's sleeping form, she'd have ended up smothering Nick himself, believing him to be the malicious Chief Head of the Nulltec Corporation!

'Exactly, baby doll!' cried the thing that was Nullman, now almost fully emerged from the carcass that had previously resembled Nick. The demon was fat and oily, consisting of a bloated, amorphous mound of boneless flesh vaguely human in shape, yet flecked with random clumps of toilet piping that seemed to emerge, boil-like, from the surface of its flesh, along with irregular clusters of puffing cigarettes protruding from various unspecified orifices. They looked like miniature pipe organs. Much of the Nullman Demon's body was yellowed with nicotine, while other areas looked like they'd been formed from a cluster of superglued fingernails, all daubed in Nullman's signature shade of burgundy red.

But they no longer looked alluring.

They were just rank.

'You puffed up, toilet-piped bitch!'* yelled Roz. 'I could have killed Nick straight away and been none the wiser!'

'Too bad, my pretty,' hissed the Nullman Demon, spitting out a thick globule of dampened ash. 'But if I can change the subject just for a moment,' it added, 'there's a problem with absorbing a dream-demon consisting largely of sewage waste.' It paused, examining the globule it had just expelled. 'When mixed with cigarette ash, every-thing just goes clumpy. Please inform Dr Valesco as I can't get him on the walkie-talkie.'

Valesco! Roz suddenly remembered. What the hell was happening in his office? How the hell was Mike Crisis getting on trying to wrestle those Lucidrix pills from the doctor's melting chest? Before she could shout through for a progress update, the Nullman Demon spat again, hawking a great wad of wet ash in Roz's direction.

Roz ducked just in time, the globule slamming against the obser-vation room window, cracking it in two.

---

* The employment of the word for 'female canine' here is fine and socially acceptable, the word in question being spoken by a decent lady character and directed at a former indecent lady character. GM

'So you've defeated the Randyman, have you?' Roz asked, stalling for time. She realised that she didn't really have a plan of action, now that she was wholly unable to read Nick the letter from his daughter undisturbed. And from the sound of the crazed thrashing in Valesco's second office next door, Mike Crisis had his own problems to contend with.

'Yeah, I ate him up,' roared the Nullman Demon. 'Swallowed him whole. Wanna see?'

The demon whipped its vast salamander-like tail around and pointed to a particularly large yellow blister on its behind. From within the pale oval boil screamed what looked like a small head, which, Roz saw, amid the grue within, wore a distinctive brown trilby.

'Randy . . .' Roz whispered, clamping one hand over her mouth for fear of puking. 'What have you done to him?'

'Help me!' squealed the absorbed Randy Streak, appealing directly to Roz. 'Help me!'

'I can't, Randy!' Roz felt horrified, yet strangely moved by the pathetic sight. For though she loathed the Randyman, knew that the terrifying dream-demon was the cause of this entire catastrophe, she still felt a pang of sympathy for the toilet attendant it had once been. After all, Randy Streak had never hurt anyone, had he? That poor, lonely clog-shifter had never asked to end up as a particularly noxious pustule on the arse of a usurping female dream-demon, had he?

'*I'm* in control now,' snarled the Nullman Demon. 'I control reality!'

Roz shuddered. Presumably that also meant Nullman now controlled the enforcement regulations for Nulltec's much-feted conference parking facilities. She recalled that her own car was still parked in Nulltec's appointed visitors' section, and she had so far successfully challenged an ongoing fine as she was technically Nulltec's 'patient'. Yet that could all change if Nullman finally gained access to her own clamps and could legally designate the area as 'private land'. In *that* case, Roz would not only be facing a reality warped by the terrifying Nullman Demon, but also fresh negotiations with court-appointed bailiffs, from which resultant legal fees might rapidly escalate.

'You monster!' screamed Roz.

'Die!' screamed the Nullman Demon back at her, lunging itself toward Roz for the final kill.

Then Valesco exploded.

CHAPTER ELEVEN

'Hell on Earth'

The floor gave way beneath her and Roz found herself plunging downward yet again. With her fell the sleeping Nick – still in his bed and fully erect – along with the surrounding laboratory equipment and all that remained of the sleeping chamber itself. Behind her dropped the exploded remains of Valesco's blasted second office, the remains of the evil doctor himself, and presumably Mike Crisis, too, who'd been in the process of grappling with him when he'd erupted.

A series of weakened floors gave way beneath the falling detritus of Ward Nine, slowing Roz's descent. Jeez, she thought as she continued to plummet through them. Just how far down below the earth's crust does Nulltec go exactly? But before she could even begin to hazard a guess, Roz felt herself slam into a patch of soft, damp ground.

When the dust eventually settled, Roz saw she was lying inside a vast, cavernous factory. Jets of steam hissed around her from all directions, emitting themselves from numerous pipe outlets running along every visible surface. Innumerable metallic gantries created a grill-like mesh everywhere she looked. No doubt this subterranean industrial plant was where Nulltec powered the near-limitless technical demands required for their facility above.

Amid the mounds of rubble created by the destroyed floors, Roz could see what looked like a gigantic boiler ahead of her, hundreds of feet high, its metallic surface miraculously untouched by the collapsing floors. Brightly coloured lights flashed from various consoles attached to the vast structure, which Roz assumed to be a big battery of some kind. Between her and it lay Nick, still sleeping away in his largely intact hospital bed.

Though the size of the underground cavern was vast, Roz felt more trapped here than anywhere else she'd been, so claustrophobic was the effect of knowing how far below the earth's surface she now lay.

And then she heard the rumbling.

It was coming from in front of her, she thought. But before she had a chance to crawl forward to Nick's sleeping frame and read him the letter from his daughter in order to engage his help in getting out of here, a mound of refuse in front of her rose with a violent burst and the Nullman Demon emerged from within.

'Now where were we, my pretty?' the thing snarled, resting its gaze upon Roz.

Oh, God, its hopeless, thought Roz. She couldn't wake Nick, and there was no chance at all of Mike helping her out, the feckless doctor having been in the immediate vicinity of Dr Valesco when he'd exploded in a burst of pink flame. All was lost.

Then she heard it. A vague slapping sound coming from some-where behind. With the only light coming from those flaming gas jets high up on the distant gantries, Roz couldn't yet see what she was hearing.

Trapped as she was inside this underground no-man's land, Roz forced her body backwards into a small crater of refuse in order to avoid the slithering Nullman Demon's advancing form. Then, poking her head upward above the rear-side rim of the crater, she saw, just a few yards away, a miraculous sight.

It was Mike, still clutching the exploded Valesco, who was now essentially little but a spine with half a head on top. Both men lay sprawled on the ground, still wrestling with each other by instinct in a pool of blood, bone and steaming pink chemical. Both doctors were largely obliterated, though what remained of Mike was doing his very best to pound Valesco's exposed skull into the ground with his phosphorescent arm-stump. As Roz watched in horror, she saw Mike's other arm was horribly withered, then realised it was turned inward, clutching something close to his chest, as if to protect what-ever was concealed there from the violent forces it, and he, had recently been subjected to.

'Mike!' Roz yelled.

He turned to face her with his glowing pink head. Then pushed himself up from the floor he was partly sticking to and held up the intact bottle of Lucidrix pills.

'I got them!' he cried.

'You genius!' Roz yelled back at him. 'You did it!'

'I did it!' Mike cried, coughing up half a lung.

'Now swallow one!' Roz said, aware that the Nullman Demon was still advancing upon her from behind. She could hear – and, more importantly, smell – the damned thing getting closer all the time.

'I can't, Roz,' Mike replied.

'You must, Mike!' Roz sensed the desperation in her own voice. 'That way you can be in control of the Phantascape, too. You'll be able to dream yourself well again and be strong enough to rescue us all!'

'No, Roz,' gasped Mike, shaking his head. 'I can't risk that. Sure, I'm doing okay at the moment. Whatever small amount of Lucidrix I managed to lick off the side of that tablet has stood me in good stead, but my luck can't last. If I try and open this bottle now and neck its contents, it'll no doubt slip straight from my fingers and roll off into some distant corner. Or the sheer nervous tension will cause me to suffer a catastrophic cardiac arrest at this most crucial of moments. I can't risk causing that kind of crisis, Roz. Here. You take them.'

He flung back his arm suddenly and threw the bottle of pills toward Roz.

They sailed right over her head.

'No!' Roz cried, the desperation she'd heard in her voice now sounding like outright devastation. This had been their only hope of defeating the Nullman Demon, she knew. If, as Mike had no doubt intended, Roz had been able to catch the bottle in her hand and neck those pills herself, then she'd have been able to control the Phantascape, too. She, like Nullman, would have been a ruler of dreams. But Mike had blown it big time again, fumbling the most important throw of his entire life by pitching their final hope straight over the head of the intended recipient, directly into the path of the enemy.

'You fool, Mike!' screamed Roz, no longer able to contain her frustration. 'That was our only hope, dammit! Our only chance to beat Nullman! Our only chance of regaining control of the Phantascape, and by extension reality, and you've sent it spiralling way over my head and into Nullman's grasp!'

Roz watched the arcing bottle of Lucidrix pass over her, landing directly in front of the slithering Nullman Demon.

The monster smiled, licking its lips, then scooped up the bottle of pills in its tongue, preparing to swallow it whole.

It's the end, Roz thought. The end of the world.

Or is it? she wondered, suddenly. What about the Randyman? What about that vanquished spirit of Randy Streak, trapped inside the spot on Nullman's behind? Surely he hadn't been completely destroyed if he was still able to see out from the back of her arse. He was only trapped in there, wasn't he? A prisoner, like Roz had been, and Nick too. Randy Streak was just as much Nullman's victim as they were. So why wouldn't it leap at any chance it might have to escape?

Roz shuddered inside. *I* am that chance, she realised. If anything was going to give the Randyman strength enough to fight its way out of the Nullman Demon's arse, it was Roz Bloom. She'd have to offer herself. She'd have to join it.

For it was the only way. If she finally did as the Randyman asked – if she agreed at long last to be its wife and live with it for all eternity in that public toilet it had decorated so lovingly with those leftover condom balloons, then maybe, just maybe, the Randyman would be able to escape and prevent the Nullman Demon from swallowing all the remaining Lucidrix pills and ruling the Phantascape until the end of time.

Sure, she'd lose her soul, Roz realised, but Nick, and Mike, and Stalkford, and Clackett Publishing, would still live.

And the Randyman *had* gifted her those trainers, hadn't it? And that convenient door.

She had to do it.

'*Randyman, Randyman, Randyman, Randyman, Randyman . . .*' she began to intone. Nullman's tongue ceased rolling upward in the direction of its mouth, not quite cognisant of Roz's plan.

'*Randyman, Randyman, Randyman, Randyman, Randyman,*' Roz continued, and then the Nullman Demon realised precisely what Roz was up to. Panicked, the monster slurped its tongue upward at full speed in an attempt to swallow the bottle of Lucidrix pills whole.

Roz tried to ignore the slimy folds of the thing's lolling mouth organ as she continued her incantation.

'*Randyman, Randyman, Randyman, Randyman, Randyman . . .*' Roz tried to speed up the words. Why had Nick insisted on people muttering the dream-demon's name seventeen times? She'd told him that five was sufficient, hadn't she? But alas, Nick had insisted on seventeen, one for every book he had planned, and now that number, like the series itself, was proving far too many. The Nullman Demon had the bottle in its mouth and was starting to swallow it. Roz, once again, was out of time.

Then the Nullman Demon's eyes widened abruptly as the contractions in its throat suddenly ceased. There was a loud release of air from somewhere behind and the motions in the monster's neck resumed, only in the opposite direction now, with the pills it had been in the process of swallowing sliding back upward, into its mouth.

There was a violent tremor from the Nullman Demon's rear end as the creature's body went into spasm. It began whirling around in circles, attempting in vain to ascertain what was currently happening to its arse like a dog chasing its own tail. Then Roz caught sight of the swelling yellow pustule on the demon's rear. It was pulsing outward, as if about to burst. Roz caught sight of an old trilby pressing upward against the taut, milky skin.

'*Randyman, Randyman!*' Roz yelled, completing her supernatural intonation. All at once, the head of Randy Streak burst through the Nullman Demon's salamander arse and bit it on the opposite cheek.

The Nullman Demon roared in agony, the force of the Randyman's clamped teeth forcing its throat muscles into spasm as the jar of Lucidrix shot out of its mouth and into the air again, loop-de-looping in giddy circles above them, before finally falling downward, toward the ground . . .

. . . straight into Roz's hands!

She could hardly believe her eyes, then, as the Randyman proceeded to consume the Nullman Demon's body from the arse-cheeks up. Roz saw there was nothing the Chief Head of the Nulltec Corporation could do about it, as while scratching one's behind was a relatively easy task to achieve for the layperson, anyone with severe weight difficulties, which the Nullman Demon suffered from in abundance, had the devil's own job of wiping, let alone scratching, their behind without professional assistance and/or a dishwasher-friendly medical scoop.

The Nullman Demon had neither, and there was nothing it could do to prevent the Randyman's assault. Once it had swallowed the Nullman Demon right up to the neck, the Randyman paused momentarily, as though to savour a final dish, then yanked out the plunger from inside its grubby mackintosh.

'Plunge this!' the Randyman shrieked, ramming the device against the Nullman Demon's head before sucking it inside out and expelling it violently through a hole that had just appeared in the ground, all the way down to Hell.

Roz applauded. 'Well done, Randy,' she said. 'You did it!'

Then, yanking the top off the pill bottle as quickly as she could, Roz prepared to neck the remaining Lucidrix. With the pills finally inside her, she could easily send the Randyman on its way without having to marry it after all.

The pills never got there. With a swift swipe of its deadly plunger, the Randyman smashed the bottle from Roz's hands. She watched it fly away, off into the distance behind her.

'Not so fast, Roz,' hissed the Randyman. 'You made a promise, remember?'

'Did I?' she replied, feigning innocence. Then the wall on one side of the room suddenly parted and Roz saw, in the dream-world appearing beyond, the grim, grey tower blocks of Dankton Park.

'You sure did, doll. You and me are getting hitched. We're going to live in a toilet till the end of time, Roz. We're gonna paint the town green!'

Then the dream-demon lunged toward her, cackling insanely like Sid James, Wilfrid Brambell and Stacey Solomon again. As it spread wide the folds of its grubby mackintosh, like a giant bat, the thing pounced at Roz with its demon plunger.

'Here comes my bride!' it screamed.

And finally, it *was* all over.

CHAPTER TWELVE

'Apocalypticum'

For at that very moment, Mike Crisis flew through the air between them and landed a powerful kick in the Randyman's plunger.

The dream-demon howled, scrabbling frantically at its rubberised rod.

'Kick 'em where they hurt, Roz,' Mike said, munching on a Lucidrix pill. 'By the way, those Lucidrix pills are all over the ground back there. The bottle Randy Streak knocked from your hands landed right in front of me.'

Mike adopted a karate stance, then flew at the Randyman with a mixture of exploding fists and roundhouse kicks.

He was almost completely healed now, Roz noticed. Those pills, in this half-dream, half-reality environment, were nothing short of a miracle!

'Where did you learn to fight like that?' said Roz, shocked at the sheer severity of Mike's assault.

'I dreamed it,' he said. 'After all, I'm in control of the Phantascape now. With Nullman out of the way, I'm the most powerful person present. Not even the damned Randyman can stop me!'

He sucker-punched Randy Streak, sending the dream-demon flying backward over the ground in the direction of the massive boiler-like structure Roz had noticed earlier.

'I'm not sure that's wise, Mike,' said Roz. Even though she was pleased to have escaped the clutches of Randy Streak, something told her that a world ruled by Mike Crisis was potentially a world more dangerous than one ruled by a dream-demon.

Mike grabbed the Randyman's head in his hands and slammed it against the ground.

'Take that, you grimy little pervert!' he yelled. 'You miserable toilet-trader! How would you like to be kicked inside a septic tank for a few hours? Or *days*? Or *weeks*? Or *months*?'

Mike punctuated each of these time-related words with a separate roundhouse kick, propelling the Randyman backward with each successive blow.

'Or maybe *years*?'

Mike picked up Randy Streak in his arms and hurled the dream-demon across the ground, propelling it closer to the vast metallic structure ahead of them.

Was that what the thing was, Roz wondered? A giant septic tank? Surely not? Surely Nulltec was connected to Stalkford's main sewage network? Even though the facility was located between two vast areas of natural woodland in the middle of nowhere, surely Stalkford Council had plumbed Nulltec into a central drainage system? But maybe not. Maybe the technical facility was situated so far away from the rest of society that they needed their own internal tank through which they could process all manner of human and industrial waste. They were a *secret* facility, after all, Roz recalled. If anyone was in need of a private industrial-sized septic tank, it was Nulltec. And yet this gleaming metallic structure looked little like a conventional septic tank. And surely if it was, she'd be able to smell it from this distance?

'You're gonna drown in your own filth, Randy Streak,' yelled Mike at the flailing, wailing dream-demon. 'You're going to choke on your own mess. And there's nothing you can do about it! Because

I'm Mike Crisis, damn it! Mike "he's damned good in a crisis" Crisis! And for once in my life I'm gonna make damn sure I do the right thing. And that means throwing your streaking, toilet-lurking ass into a mound of raw, toxic sewage. You're going back to Hell, Randy Streak!'

'No, Mike!' Roz had to stop him. This wasn't right. Randy Streak was *innocent*. Surely Mike knew that from reading the damned book? But then he'd admitted he'd skipped bits, and fallen asleep while reading it, she recalled.

In any case, Mike's judgement was impaired because he was in the middle of his own foolhardy rescue attempt, too bound up in his own mission to think about what the hell he was actually doing. All he wanted now was to impress Roz by showing her he could defeat the Randyman and bring her back from the jaws of Hell. He probably thought that by doing that, she'd once again be interested in copping a feel of his scrawny arse. But Roz was so over that.

Fair enough, he was getting results, and had saved her life, admittedly, but he'd overshot his load by a country mile. Now he was beating the poor Randyman to a pulp and threatening to murder it, just like those nasty youths in Nick's book. That was bound to end in disaster, Roz knew. Either the dream-demon would develop some new-found strength of will and fight back even harder against his oppressor, or Mike was going to live up to his name and do something so stupid he'd turn a devastating crisis into an apocalyptic crisis.

Roz froze. That word. That word told her everything she needed to know. That was no septic tank Mike was currently kicking the Randyman's flailing body toward. If only! No, that vast metallic structure before them was nothing less than the nuclear-powered reactor Nulltec had installed deep under the facility grounds. The nuclear reactor Nullman had casually tossed into conversation in that first meeting, and which both Roz and Mike had chosen to ignore.

Now those pre-nuclear chickens would be coming home to roost in a post-apocalyptic pecking shed if Roz didn't do something about it – and swiftly.

But what *could* she do?

The pills, of course! Whipping herself round, Roz crawled from the crater she'd fallen into and scrambled back in the direction of the exploded Valesco. There she saw them, scattered all across the ground. Small caplets of black and yellow, like segments of wasp. Carefully, and with a sense of awe, she picked one up in her hands.

Should she swallow it? Should Roz swallow a Lucidrix pill and assume control of reality? Look at how the experience was affecting Mike, massaging his bruised ego into an all-powerful force of primal destruction? What if she, too, ended up losing control, instead of gaining it? Becoming as manipulative and power-crazed as Nullman? Could Roz maintain control of her own moral compass were she to suddenly find herself so powerful that she was able to beat the Randyman single-handed, like Mike was doing right now? Wouldn't she potentially become an all-powerful dream-demon herself?

Then, through the hazy chaos of her thoughts, Roz remembered Nick, and knew she *had* to do it. She had to swallow this pill for Nick and his daughter, if nothing else. And as long as she held on to that thought alone, she knew she'd be okay.

For she could never destroy if she kept a goal like that in mind. Could never harm or maim. Why, she hadn't even been able to hate Randy Streak, had she? Instead, she'd been the one who'd urged Nick to give the villain a sympathetic back story. Had seen the good in him. And she couldn't destroy Mike Crisis now, either. No matter what sick journey of violent revenge he was currently wrongfully engaged in. Why, deep down, Roz loved men, however challenging, difficult and potentially dodgy they invariably came across as. For, deep down, men were what made the world go round, especially, say, those who were ground-breaking, innovative and influential story-makers specialising in the horror genre. And all at once, Roz knew she could enter the Phantascape with Nick and Mike, and control it after all. She could go in there herself and defeat Randy Streak in a humane way. Then rescue Nick, locate his daughter with him and all go home for a take-away curry.

With a smile, Roz swallowed the pill in her hand, mouthed 'I love you' to the world, and turned back toward Mike.

The pill took effect immediately. She didn't feel remotely drowsy, but she sensed her power instantly. It surged within her. She was no longer scared, she realised. No longer frightened of anything that the Randyman might do to her.

She was in control.

Roz only had to think and she was already there, beside Mike, as he prepared to launch yet another frenzied assault on Randy Streak's personal plumbing area.

'No, Mike,' she whispered softly. 'Release him.'

'Don't be an idiot, Roz,' said Mike, landing a giant boot in the area of the Randyman's groinal closet flange.

'Help me, Roz!' squealed the dying Randyman. 'Tell him to leave me alone!'

'I mean it, Mike!' Roz yelled. 'Leave Randy alone!'

'You're acting like a silly female, Roz,' Mike snarled at her. 'You stay out of this, okay? Leave this crisis to me, Mike "he roundhouse-kicks a crisis" Crisis.'

Mike grabbed the Randyman in his hands and hurled him forward again. The dream-demon's body slammed hard into the metallic wall of the nuclear reactor.

A devastating tremor reverberated from deep within the structure itself. The lights up on the distant gantries overhead began to flicker and fade as the power source fuelling them temporarily went offline.

'Mike, you fool!' Roz said. 'That's not a septic tank!'

'Of course it is! And it's where this slimy little Flash Harry's headed.'

She had no other option. Roz had to intervene. Concentrating her mind, she willed Mike away from the injured body of Randy Streak.

And as soon as she'd thought it, Mike was gone.

'Thank you, Roz,' croaked the Randyman, staring up at her with sad, wounded eyes. Then he vanished too.

And appeared several feet away, in exactly the spot to which she'd just transported Mike Crisis.

'I said leave it to me, Roz,' said the doctor, and recommenced pummelling his prey.

This was useless, Roz realised. They'd both swallowed Lucidrix pills so technically were now evenly matched. She was caught in a tit-for-tat battle with a rival dream-master. She needed extra help. Needed another person to back her up and weight the odds in her favour.

She needed *Nick*.

Roz only had to wish it and there she was, standing beside his gurney, leaning tenderly over his slumbering, balded frame.

She drew the letter from her pocket and began to read.

'Daddy,' she said. 'My dearest, darling, Daddy . . . It's Georgina . . .'

She witnessed a mild tremor in Nick's body. A small shimmering of muscular movement. Something in those words Roz had just spoken were already rousing him, stirring an emotional reaction deep inside. Instinctively, responding to what was evidently a huge swelling of pent-up feelings, Nick's eyes blinked open.

'Roz?' he said, his voice croaking. 'You found me. You brought me back from Hell . . .'

'Shh,' whispered Roz. 'There's no time to explain. Swallow this.'

She slipped one of the Lucidrix pills between Nick's parted lips, and immediately he was wide awake.

'What the hell's happening?'

'No time to explain, Nick. We have to stop Mike Crisis from pounding the Randyman against the wall of that nuclear reactor.'

'What nuclear reactor?' said Nick, looking round.

'That nuclear reactor!' yelled Roz, pointing at the huge nuclear reactor standing behind them.

'That's a giant septic tank, surely?'

'God, Nick, will you just help me!'

'In a moment, Roz. Right now, I really need to go and . . . er . . . relieve myself.'

'Forget relieving yourself!' Roz yelled, running back in the direction of Mike. What was happening to her? She was losing control of the Phantascape! All because of bloody, pig-headed men!

'Stop it, Mike,' she yelled. 'Put the Randyman down! That's *not* a giant septic tank, it's a nuclear reactor!'

But it was too late. Mike lifted the dream-demon in his arms, preparing to hurl the Randyman into the metal wall for a final time.

Then he stopped.

'You,' he muttered, confused, as the figure of Nick stepped out directly in front of him, wielding a Magnum .44 revolver.

'You did it, Nick,' squealed Roz. 'You willed yourself between Mike Crisis, the ailing Randyman and that wall of the nuclear reactor.'

'Of course I did, Roz. I could see that you and the entire world was in imminent jeopardy due to this punk's lethally self-massaged ego. Drop the Streak, buddy.'

Mike did as Nick commanded, dropping the Randyman to the ground, where he immediately curled into a foetal ball and started whimpering. Roz yearned to reach out and comfort the ailing dream-demon, but realised Nick wasn't yet finished with Mike.

'So you're a tough guy, huh? Well listen up, buddy. Sure, we all wanna be heroes. But we have to earn that right. And it takes a lifetime of small-scale heroics before you even get close to the medal-earning feats of bravery I'm able to provide. You very nearly escalated a devastating crisis into what I'd term an apocalyptic crisis.'

'Hey Nick, that's *my* phrase . . .' said Roz.

'Quiet, Roz.' Nick turned back to Mike Crisis. 'Thank God I was here to prevent that happening. At the precise moment I needed to relieve myself as well. That's true heroism, pal. You watch and learn. Because you've got a long way to go yet, sugar balls.'

'I'm sorry, Nick,' gasped Mike, his head dropping downward in shame.

'Now clean up this mess,' said Nick.

As he passed Roz, she dared herself to speak. 'Nick, I just want to say thanks. For everything. I couldn't have done it without you.'

'No need to thank me, Roz,' said Nick. 'Just live a good life. That's all I ask.'

'I will.'

'Now let's get out of here.'

He stepped past her. Roz watched him go, awestruck by Nick's selfless act of self-sacrifice, which had brought things to a happy conclusion in the nick of time. Tenderly, she reached down and helped the beaten Randyman to his feet. She'd get the dream–demon cleaned up and housed somewhere, and then, if he still insisted on marrying her, phone the authorities and get him taken away. Leading the beleaguered toilet attendant by the hand, Roz followed Nick, who was busy behind a distant boulder, no doubt relieving himself in one way or another, having bravely held things off when the moment called.

As Roz disappeared from sight, Mike gazed after her, tears of bitterness welling in his eyes.

Then, as those heavy, hopeless tears began to fall, he placed both hands on the wall in front of him, and, with a howl of futility and sadness, butted his stupid head against the dented metal lining.

And exploded the entire world.

★

Roz survived because she was still on the Lucidrix. Nick, too. Their dreams had saved them, thereby ensuring their ultimate survival in a post-apocalyptic world. But the Phantascape was gone now, blown up in a devastating nuclear explosion that had destroyed most of Stalkford. Mike Crisis and Randy Streak, too (the pill's effect on Mike had prematurely worn off). And everyone else who'd once walked and stalked the corridors of Nulltec.

'I should have listened to you, Roz,' Nick said, as they stared up at the fuzzy television screen above them in the relative safety of their private nuclear bunker some months later. 'I should have listened when you told me to stop flying those damned planes. Now look what's happened. Stalkford's been completely destroyed. Nothing but a dead wasteland above us. Everything completely gone.' He looked across at her. 'Mind if I have the last Blue Riband?'

'Help yourself, Nick. You've had all the rest. But remember, Nick. That's the last Blue Riband. The last Blue Riband in the whole of what's left of Stalkfordshire. Savour it.'

'Not quite true, Roz. There's a shop in the Spinal Mountains that sells Blue Ribands, unless I'm very much mistaken. And that, as you know, is where I'm headed.'

They looked up at the screen again as an image flashed across it. A grainy photograph of a distant town in the mountains, rumoured to house a small pocket of survivors.

'Must you, Nick?' Roz asked, already knowing what his answer would be. 'Must you go?'

'Yes, Roz. As I've told you a thousand times, I must. I must go.'

'Do you think you'll find her?' Roz asked, after a few moments of lingering silence. She handed Nick his backpack and a full Thermos of Irish coffee.

'I have to, Roz. Her letter said so. I have to believe she's still up there in the Spinal Mountains, just lazing about. I have to believe she survived.'

'And if you find her, Nick? If you manage to cross that post-apocalyptic hell zone above us. Will you do what she asked? Will you lend her that fifty pounds?'

'Maybe,' Nick said. 'But probably not. After all,' he asked her, deeply and profoundly, 'what use is money now, in a nuclear wasteland?'

'True,' said Roz. 'So, so true. By the way, I'll stay here, if that's okay? I hear there are mutants and things like that above us.'

'There are now,' said Nick, sighing. 'Turns out Nulltec failed to close that hole in my mind, after all. Meaning all the post-apocalyptic horrors I've imagined in my novels over the years are out there for real now. Waiting for me alone.'

'Then good luck, Nick. Sounds like you'll need it!' Roz laughed.

'Thanks, Roz. I'll bring you back that Blue Riband.'

'Thanks, Nick.' She was crying now.

Nick stepped into the lift that would take him up into the Deadish Zone, and a world enclosed by the all-powerful Bowl.

'One final thing, Nick,' Roz said, her voice wavering as the doors of the transmat-lift began to close.

'Yes, Roz?' Nick said, refusing to smile for fear it might give his former editor a glimmer of hope. And there was little of that left now.

'Not dark orange-flavoured, okay?'

'Not dark orange-flavoured,' he replied softly, as the metal doors closed over his face, and Nick Steen finally went in search of his missing daughter.

While Roz cleaned up.

The End

GARTH MARENGHI'S ACKNOWLEDGEMENTS

Carl Sagan for his R–Complex, but *nothing else*. Myself, yet again, for all that I do and am yet to do. My wife Pam for restraining me when necessary (and oft when *un*necessary), and my daughters, I guess, though none of them did a thing to help me.

MATTHEW HOLNESS'
ACKNOWLEDGEMENTS

I'd like to thank my partner Sarah Dempster, who as always read Garth's initial outpourings and bravely challenged all that might (i.e. would) offend. Likewise my mum and dad for their faith in both Garth and myself, two equally irascible horror hacks. Perennial thanks to Clara, who named and drew Throttle and Bribes in Garth's 'other' book once her substantial fee had been secured (twice). I love you all.

My literary agent Matthew Turner for handling Garth's output throughout (no easy task when you're a decent human being) and for much-valued advice and support. Sophie Chapman, Rhonda and Kim too, for managing my live shows, and Joshua Boland-Burrell and all at Live Nation for their persistent hard work on the same.

My editor Harriet Poland for providing sage guidance and eternal patience as the latest deadline loomed. Likewise Tom, Dominic, Kate, Alice, Liam, Lewis and all the team at Hodder for seeing me through that difficult second trilogy of self-contained yet thematically integrated horror-based mini-tomes.

As ever, Joe Avery for balding Garth so beautifully on another glorious front cover, and Alisdair Wood for three sublime glimpses of Garth's fictional homes.

Thank you, everyone.